My Bloodline

BY

KC KEAN

My Bloodline
Featherstone Academy Series #1
Copyright © 2020 KC Kean

This book is licensed for your personal enjoyment only. This book may not be re-sold or given away to other people. If you would like to share this book with another person, please purchase an additional copy for each recipient. If you're reading this book and did not purchase it, or it wasn't purchased for your use only, then please return to your favourite book retailer and purchase your own copy. Thank you for respecting the hard work of this author.

All rights reserved.

This is a work of fiction. Names, characters, places, brands, media, and incidents are either the product of the authors imagination or are used fictitiously. The author acknowledges the trademark status and trademark owners of various products referred to in this work of fiction, which have been used without permission. The publication/use of these trademarks is not authorised, associated with, or sponsored by the trademark owners.

My Bloodline/KC Kean – 2nd ed.
ISBN-13 - 979-8-666531-15-0

To my Forever & Always,

You'll likely not see this, or even consider a dedication in your name.

Yet you support me no matter what. Giving me your strength when I need it most, and your embrace when my soul calls for yours.

Thank you for being you and allowing me to be me. Whilst coming together and making the most beautiful us.

I love you, it's no secret, I say it a hundred times a day.

But to have it written in a book ...

Well that's more than infinity war!

This world isn't flowers and rainbows sweetheart. This world is death, it is corrupt, cut-throat and complete darkness. If you want any chance at surviving then I suggest you learn to see in the dark.

- Maverick Miller, Featherstone Academy

KC KEAN

PROLOGUE

My soul aches.

Blood everywhere.

My small hands tremble as I look at what I'm holding.

"Meu Tesouro." I hear, but my eyes refuse to seek where it came from.

This is all too much.

Curling into a ball, I block the world out.

Blood seeping through my clothes, my body unwilling to acknowledge its touch.

My heart hurts.

The darkness surrounds me, and I welcome it's presence.

My mind is grateful for the respite.

There was no me before this, only after.

Yet I don't remember why.

My subconscious locking it all away.

MY BLOODLINE

ONE

Luna

Leg up on the pedestal with his client now eye level with his dick, we're gonna be here all night at this rate. We've all got plans and if he doesn't stop thrusting himself in that poor girl's face, it'll be just my luck for Rafe to pop his head in. He owns Inked, the tattoo shop where we are, and the MMA gym next door too. I can see his car parked out front from here, and I don't want our plans to be blown.

Well, mine will be. He couldn't give a shit what these guys are up to, but he thinks I'm corrupt enough as it is.

"You done Marcus? We need to get moving." I can't

keep the irritation out of my voice, which only makes him smirk and try to up his game with this girl, who's loving it.

"You can't rush perfection like this, Luna."

Perfection? Man, all he did was tattoo an infinity band on her wrist. I've been here a solid 12 hours, trying to get Rafe to officially take me on as an apprentice so I can skip college. He won't even have a conversation with me about it, but I think if I keep showing up he'll eventually relent.

Ready to get out of here, I give Jake the eyes and he starts shutting the lights off in the back. Code for everyone to get out, the unspoken rule to grab your stuff and go. Everyone starts following suit like he's the Pied Piper.

"Hey sweetie, you wanna come hang with us tonight?" Marcus murmurs, with his lips against her neck. She's hanging off his every word, but I can barely deal with him on a normal day. Nevermind when he's trying to get laid.

Thankfully, Jake pipes up, "Marcus, you know the rules. No girls tonight."

"Yeah, but Luna's coming, so I thought ... "

"Fuck off, Marcus, you know the rules, Luna doesn't count. Besides, she's got bigger balls than you anyways." Jake snickers. Great, nothing riles Marcus up more than being interrupted and compared to me.

I don't need to be around for this, so I grab my jacket from the back of the chair, and start heading for the door. West is already there observing everyone, aware this could escalate quickly.

"Listen, Marcus, you can call it a night now or head out with us, either way you're leaving," West says, turning and heading out the door. I quickly follow, not wanting to deal with his usual crap.

"You want a ride or are you taking Dot?" Jake asks, always the organizer.

"You can go with West in the car, I'm taking Dot." I sigh, bored with the same conversation as always.

"You sure you don't want someone to be your driver?"

"I'm sure. I prefer my space, you know that."

"I know, and you know I always gotta check." Lifting my shoulder to him, I leave it at that. Jake's always trying to care, but I don't entertain him. I show care for Rafe, that's my limit. I don't need to add to the worry and stress I already have.

Jake shutters up behind Marcus, who's strolled off with his piece for the night. At least there wasn't an argument, but I don't miss the dark look in his eyes as they turn the corner. I get the tough decision he had to make there, fight or sex. Usually I'd choose sex, but tonight is different.

"You ready?" West asks.

He doesn't need words, a nod will suffice. That's all he's getting when I'm trying to focus, now that we're finally heading out. He gives me a smirk and heads to the car. I walk over to my baby, Dot; my Ducati 916. Flame red, slick as hell, and a throttle so throaty my insides weep with joy while passers-by hate me.

She's my pride and joy, a complete fixer upper that Rafe helped me with. We completed her six months ago and I've refused to travel in a car ever since. I never miss the pride in Rafe's eyes over Dot, our masterpiece, but I also don't miss the sadness, probably because he's always talking about how I don't need him anymore.

I'm 18 in the morning, and still Rafe is the only person I let past the walls I've built around myself. He saved me from the darkness, taught me how to have control over everything I wanted, and made me feel safe even when I felt alone.

Shaking the darkness away I put my helmet on, give Dot a little rev and take off. They know I'll want to get my adrenaline pumping first and a quick run with this throttle beneath me will do just that.

We're heading to the outskirts of the city tonight, to an old abandoned warehouse with dodgy as hell bouncers, cheap beer, and queues a mile long. Full of people wanting a good time that involves money, blood, sweat, and tears. Men will be flashing money at all who will look, and women will wear as little as possible hoping to bag themselves a slick fucker.

Usual Friday Fight Night means two rings, eight fights, and sixteen fighters willing to risk their lives based on their skills and strength. Some do it for the money, but most do it for the high you get from the adrenaline pumping through your veins.

When the clock strikes a minute past midnight, I'll be on the cards.

Tonight, I fight.

Getting my head in the right mindset I consider my life, remembering why I love the fight. The control.

I refuse to remember any of my life before twelve years ago. I started my life at six, a shell of a girl who feared a hug as much as my own shadow, or the bogeyman. The nightmares that played over and over every night would ruin a grown man, let alone a small child.

Rafe didn't really know what to do with me, so he made me fierce. He's my whole family, he keeps a roof over my head and food on the table. He was apparently my father's best friend since high school.

Well, he drew the short straw since my mother dropped me at his front door at six years old. Like I meant nothing to her, like what we lived and experienced was nothing at all.

Instead, leaving me to deal with all this shit in my own head. Where I refuse to accept or acknowledge the mess that led me here. Only allowing it to haunt my nightmares.

In return, Rafe gets a dead best friend and a child. Like I said, short straw.

Rafe does everything you'd expect of a father. He is my biggest protector and supporter. Always putting me first and teaching me independence. Although, if Rafe knew my plans for the night, he wouldn't hesitate to put a stop to it, and I'm not about to be caught now.

He's ex-Armed Forces, specializing as a sniper, with crazy skills in Martial Arts. So, what does he do to help a six year old girl fight through the darkness? He teaches me MMA; Krav Maga, Brazilian Jiu-Jitsu, Muay Thai - you name it and I'll be shocked if I can't pull something out of the bag in that category.

I went from a scared little girl, to taking Rafe down at 12 years old, and I mean he's 6ft. 2" and built like he's competing for the world's strongest man.

I still train daily, I love the feeling of being in control of myself. The feeling of each move and seeing it through, feeling my center and the power I have. My senses allow me to feel my surroundings, there's nothing like it. Well, except sex. Give me a man that's gonna let me ride him as much as he wants to go all alpha on my ass, and it's a close call.

This is the life I want, let my art flow onto skin during the day and pound it when the sun goes down. As long as I've got my bike, I'm content.

Money isn't an issue. My other skill set, that Rafe definitely doesn't know about, pays big. My ability to steal shit that people are willing to pay big for, has me more comfortable than most teens.

West knows, but he wouldn't breathe a word to a soul. He's the one who named my thief persona 'Moon' as in Luna Moon, asshole, but it somehow stuck. It's even funnier that my last name is Steele; Luna 'Moon' Steele at your service.

People look at my 5ft. 7" height and seemingly small frame and stroll on by. I wear loose fitted clothing to hide my defined body underneath. There's nothing better than catching them off guard. My dark brown wavy hair is usually thrown up in a ponytail or braids, and it's a rare occasion for me to wear make-up. Leaving my bright green eyes bare and myself unnoticeable.

Tonight is the first night I'll be able to fight. I've seen hundreds of them, but the owner, Murphy, knows Rafe, and as much as he lets me in to watch, he won't go over Rafe's head because he knows he'll likely lose his.

Murphy's excuse has always been my age, but when I was here last Friday, I somehow convinced him that after midnight it's fair game. I don't know if I'll be up against a girl or a guy and I don't really care. I just want to feel it, the pumping in my veins, the buzz in the air and the sweat running down my back.

Fuck, I'm ready for that feeling. Glancing down at Dot, I see I've dropped my speed. My mind focused on the ring a little too much. I turn on to a quiet road and floor it. No one's out here at this time, and you can pick up some good speed heading towards the warehouse.

I focus, considering my emotions. I feel determined, excited, and confident, not even a single ounce of me feels nervous or afraid. I live for this. All my training and sparring with Rafe and the guys at the gym, on a daily basis, has me ready.

Rafe says I can get destructive sometimes, out of control. It's like certain words can be said and I lose my sight. All I see is red and my fight or flight response goes into overdrive. Rafe and West think it could be set words that are a trigger for me, but hell if I've been willing to figure it out. I know of one phrase but even thinking about it rattles me. All I know is I have no control in those moments and that scares me more than the nightmares.

Turning the last corner, the Warehouse comes into view. Pulling up, I park next to the car, Jake and West hovering around, not wanting me to enter on my own. It wouldn't make a difference to me but right now I appreciate the fact that they're a barrier between me and anyone wanting to hold a conversation. A simple nod from West and we're heading in, a familiar face on the door.

"Hey, doll face, how's my favorite girl tonight?"

I can't help but slightly smirk and roll my eyes at him. Which earns me a megawatt smile, all teeth, and he lets us through knowing I won't respond.

West and Jake fight here every Friday, they usually pull someone in to babysit me but not tonight. Tonight, we're all heading in the same direction and my anticipation kicks up a notch.

"Sorry, Luna, there's only one set of lockers here," says Jake with a quick look over his shoulder.

I don't say a word, I just continue to follow. It's irrelevant. West has my gym bag from the car, and I won't be intimidated once we get in there.

This place is already grinding, music blasting through the speakers everywhere. Bodies pressed together like their lives depend on it. I'm being overlooked right now, no make-up on and my ass isn't hanging out. No one's glancing at me in my all black outfit consisting of my skinny jeans, leather jacket, and combat boots, just how I like it.

Following Jake to the right, the volume lowers slightly, and I see the locker rooms up ahead. It's 11pm and the next set of fights start in fifteen minutes. Each match starts at fifteen past the hour. There are two rings, so they always run both at the same time. I can't tell how the last matches ended but they're all clean and ready to go again.

Murphy's rules are minimal to say the least. No weapons, tape your hands, and the referee will only step in if you're about to be knocked out. Anything else goes.

Jake is up next. West will fight in the other ring at quarter past midnight like me. I haven't checked who any of our opponents are, because it doesn't matter. Although Jake will read the board out loud in the locker room like always.

Jefferson and Holmes are also up next, they barely have any brain cells left between them. Based on the amount of times they've pounded the shit out of each other, and they're dirty as hell. All because back when they were teens they fell into a love triangle with some girl. Ten years later and they're still brawling, and the girl is nowhere to be seen. Boys should have learnt to share.

Stepping into the room, the light feels like it's burning my retina compared to the dim setting outside.

"Sweet cheeks, if it's dick you're after you'll have to wait outside till I've finished."

I've not seen this guy before, but West slams my gym bag down, breaking my eye contact with the guy, and easing some of the tension from the room. I keep my facial expression neutral and stare him down. Nothing riles a guy more than a silent woman. They expect us to be all catty and shit.

"Oh shit," calls Jefferson. "You're the Steele on the board for tonight huh, Luna? Does Rafe know about this?"

"Steele? Are you fucking me? I show up here tonight and y'all think I'm fighting a little girl? What kinda place is this?"

Who even is this guy?

I haven't moved a muscle, not even to respond. I just keep my poker face in place and stare him down. Refusing to rise to him baiting me.

"Man, Murphy wouldn't agree to let someone fight if he didn't think they could, and if it's Steele you've been brought in for, it's because it would be too personal for any of us."

Wow, since when did Jefferson ever talk sense.

"You're all serious?"

Taking in how nobody's moved and I'm still staring him down, he shrugs, "Your funeral sweet cheeks. I'm going to socialize."

Jake squeezes my shoulder, like I need the reassurance. I want to shrug him off and tell him to piss off, but I don't, wanting to remain calm and unaffected.

"So, you've had the pleasure of meeting my opponent tonight, who are you guys fighting?" I ask.

Jake glances at the board while West gets comfortable. "West has someone by the name Horton."

"And you?"

"Seems like Tommy's trying to join the big leagues."

What? Oh fuck, seems tonight couldn't get any crazier.

I finally get my match with some cocky asshole and now my ex is fighting too!

KC KEAN

TWO

Luna

"You sure you're good?"

"Quit asking Jake, I don't need you babying me, I'm going up top to watch with West."

He stares down at me, like he magically expects me to start acting like a girl and back out of my fight. I think that's what he wants me to do, and it's times like this that I wonder if he even knows me at all.

"I'll change when we get back, have fun."

That earns me a wink. I never say good luck, it's not luck we need, it's skill and a love for grappling.

I head out and towards the stairs. The ground floor

consists of the rings, a dance floor, limited seating, and two bars. Upstairs is barely held together with metal piping working as a barrier for the wrap around, holding perfect views over the rings below.

It helps that the bar is quieter up here too. I take up my usual spot, dead center with a perfect view of both rings. I should probably pay more attention to Jake's fight tonight, especially if Tommy's here, but my spot sees all angles and access points. I feel in control with my viewpoint and that's my priority. I grab some water from the bartender, and I manage a small smile to say thanks. It's busy tonight, even up here, and I can hear the group of men to my right discussing the rumors that there's a girl on the roster. They think it's easy money against Steele, I can't wait to prove them wrong.

I hear the bell sound and Murphy announces the next two fights.

"Ladies and gentlemen, it seems we've got ourselves a lovers' tiff spotlight tonight. Ring One's set for our classic Jefferson and Holmes, and an extra special tonight in Ring Two we have Jake Blois and Tommy Mack. Show them what you've got boys. Who knows, one of you might even end up with the girl eventually."

"Is he fucking serious?" I look to West for answers, who just gives me a knowing smirk and turns back to ring two.

Like it's obvious.

Maybe it is, I see how Jake looks my way, but he just likes the idea of me. Whenever I'm truly myself, like tonight, ready to fight, he wants to change me and I'm never going to do that.

Tommy on the other hand, I couldn't care less. We split a little over a month ago when I walked in on him with Tiffany, the town whore, fucking on the sofa. I didn't even feel saddened by it. I mean the sex was average and he was convenient, but I didn't have any feelings for him. I ended it and refused his apologies because nobody disrespects me like that.

I'm not taking that shit. Ever. Especially when his lame ass excuse was because I was always too busy for him. No thanks. He was useful for getting off, but I can do that myself all the same with no expectations.

I've decided I'm not a one-man kind of girl anyway. I want a variety of dick, like a chocolate selection box. No commitments, just fun.

The bell sounds and the first rounds start, Jefferson and

Holmes are dancing around each other. Naturally, I barely pay them any mind. They can predict each other's moves too much for there to be any actual entertainment.

Turning my eyes to Jake and Tommy the tension between them is palpable and I can't help but roll my eyes. This fight is more like a pissing contest and I don't have the energy to watch it unfold.

Bored with them already, I take in the rest of the warehouse below. My eyes catch on the main doors opening and a group of five men walk in together scanning the warehouse. Something seems off, like they're looking for someone.

It doesn't help that they're all dressed identically in black, matching shaved heads and sunglasses, all with a red emblem on their hoodies. I see Murphy approach them and they greet each other. I watch the scene before me for a few more moments when the first-round bell halts my attention.

Glancing back to the ring, I notice blood on the mat. Lifting my gaze higher I see it's coming from Tommy. Looks like Jake got him with a mean hook. His left eye is already swelling, and the blood is coming from his nose.

I look back towards the entrance but no one's there now.

I cut my eyes back to the ring keeping my face blank,

to see the second round has started and Jake already has Tommy backed up against the cage. Pounding him repeatedly. Unwilling to relent.

Tommy is barely on his feet, and it looks as though Jake is ready to end this. He pulls his right arm back and delivers the final blow, forcing Tommy to the mat. The referee has seen enough and is calling time.

Tommy doesn't move for a minute while Jake looks straight at me, seeking my approval. I mean, he thinks he's fighting for my honor, but I don't need his help. I can feel Tommy's eyes on me trying to gain my attention too, but I'm not wasting my time.

With their fight called, I make my way back to the locker room so I can prepare myself and get changed. I can feel the buzz inside me ramping up knowing it's closer to my turn. I'm beyond ready for this, I've been training since I was a child. The want for it is suffocating. I need to get in that ring now.

Back in the dressing room, I'm not alone, but I prepare myself like I am. West and Riggs are changing while Jake hits the showers.

Grabbing my gym bag that West threw down earlier, I keep to the corner opting for as much privacy as I can without being obvious. I'm not shy, I love my body, my piercings, and my tattoos. I'd just rather not make eye contact with anyone in this room while I'm trying to focus, and I can already feel their stares and the heat in their eyes.

Throwing on my black sports bra and shorts, I also take a minute to put thick band-aids over my nipple piercings. I don't want them to catch, but it's also too much effort to take them out. I braid my hair down my back and methodically tape my hands.

I'm ready.

Finally looking up into the room I see Jake staring first, the lust clear in his eyes, but I can't let him entertain that idea. So, I move my eyes around the room, catching West trying to dance his eyebrows at me with a smirk. I can't help but relax at his antics and feel the tension release that I didn't even realize I was holding. The only other person in the locker room seems to be Riggs, who is staring me down like he can't decide whether to eat me or beat me.

Before anyone can say anything, a knock comes from outside and we're given the nod that it's time. West holds his hand out for a high five like we're in second grade or something, but I still can't help but participate. Glancing, neither Jake or Riggs have moved and they're both still staring me down.

Fuck sake.

I give them the middle finger and head out, hearing West snicker. I can't help the slight lilt to my mouth that I have at least entertained someone tonight, seen as every fucker here will have bet against me, and they're going to be leaving mad as hell.

I stand in the ring facing Riggs. There's a lot of people talking all at once when they see that there is indeed a female in the ring tonight. Their slight frowns tell me they'd have preferred me in little booty shorts, heels on and my tits hanging out, classic ring girl style.

Then they think they see an easy opportunity to make some extra cash. I can see Murphy holding back a little longer than usual as he sees more bet's taking place around us, against me for sure.

I'm zoning them all out. I've taken some of their energy to bounce off and now my sole focus is in this ring. I catch Murphy looking in my direction with what appears to be a hint of guilt and doubt in his eyes, but he blinks and turns in an instant leaving me unsure whether

I just made it up.

Murphy's grin is wide as he finally deems it time to begin. "Have I got a treat for you all tonight. In ring one we have our local Morgan up against Holden, who's in from Philly. In ring two we also have an import from Philly; Riggs, who tonight has the pleasure of competing against Steele in her first fight here, seen as she only turned 18 fifteen minutes ago."

If he doesn't get on with it, he might be the one to meet the end of my fist at this rate.

All the men are now looking intently at me, be it because I'm a girl up in here or the fact that I'm just legal. I don't know but I'm not going to take my eyes off Riggs, who's smirking at me and rolling his shoulders like it's the most relaxed he's ever been.

"You all know the rules, let's fight."

With that the bell rings and I stand stoically still. Nothing unnerves a man more than not immediately getting into a circling dance with them. Riggs' arms have risen to a fighting stance and he's bouncing on his feet. He notices me not moving and ... yeah, there's the look in his eyes I was waiting for. He thinks I'm unskilled and out of my depth and he relaxes his shoulders down, stands tall, and starts to approach me like his height alone is intimidating me enough to submit already.

When he realizes I'm not backing down, I see the resignation that he's gonna have to come at me first. He tests his arm space out around me watching for my reaction and I don't give him one. He goes to come at me properly this time, a slight bend to his knees and his arms raised, fight mode.

He's not prepared for me to raise my arms so fast to block his fist towards my face. His reaction time is quick, and he bounces back a little, ready to come at me from a different angle.

He definitely has the power behind him, which surprises me a little, but I don't show it. Instead I smirk, showing him my pearly whites. Which just seems to piss him off, so I can't help it. I snap my teeth together, bite me bitch, taunting him and he's had enough.

As he swings with his left hand this time, I dip to the right taking my elbow to his thigh and swinging my leg round to knock him down from behind. He goes to grab me, anywhere, to capture me in a hold but I rise just out of reach, and this time I hold my fighting stance.

The look in his eye's shows me I've surprised him,

but he thinks I'm a one trick pony. This time I go at him first with a swift jab to his ribs which he counters with a hit straight to my face.

Fuck. I won't be able to cover up a black eye.

While my body has leaned to the left slightly with the impact, he goes to grab me around the waist, but he isn't prepared for me to drop quickly to my knees and wrap myself tightly around his leg. This is it, like muscle memory, as if in slow motion, he staggers forwards and I push his momentum through with my shoulder into the back of his thighs, forcing him into a roll.

Grabbing his arm mid roll, I drop to my ass and pull that arm like my life depends on it, leading me to wrap my legs like a vice under his arm and around his neck in an arm triangle choke. I hold on tight, ready for him to try and get out. I feel him try to shuffle on the floor, and I pull his arm even tighter and squeeze my thighs, applying more pressure around his neck.

He goes slack almost instantly, then I feel it. Frantic tapping to my left leg, has the bells being rung. I give him a little extra squeeze before I let go, knowing the rules, but he'll be remembering me.

Standing, I allow the world outside of this ring to

filter back in.

The noise is deafening, there are a lot of shouts around me as my focus returns. I see bewilderment and jaws on the floor, but mostly I hear sneers.

'Fucking bitch'. 'She just cost me'. 'This is a setup'. 'Whore'.

I just smile, basking in my glory. This is just what it sounds like to be a boss bitch in a man's world.

Glancing around I see the shock across everyone's faces, until I see Jake smiling wide at me with relief. As much as these guys know how Rafe trained me, it seems they forget when we aren't in the gym.

Looking over to Riggs, his eyes are already on me, seeing me in a different light. Still shocked and not likely impressed by the turn of events, he moves forward to shake my hand out of respect, as my other arm is raised above my head by the referee and I'm officially announced the winner.

There seems to be a lot more people surrounding the ring than when I first entered it. I try to see how West's match is going, but with the amount of bodies that suddenly seem to be filling the ring, I can barely see. At least he's still on his feet.

I'm done now, I've taken in my fill of the noise and the excitement. I'm ready to get my cut from the bets and head out. I need to burn off the rest of this adrenaline.

Heading straight to the locker room I'm hoping I can grab a quick shower while the other fight is still going, and there's less people to worry about. Catching sight of West still fighting, I think I've found how I can burn the rest of this adrenaline off.

Sex.

There's no way I could approach Jake, he'd want to get married in the morning, but West? Maybe he could be down for some no-strings passion. With only his shorts on, I can see his chiseled abs and muscular thighs from here, and I could get down with that. His light brown hair is cut short at the sides and gelled on the top, his brown eyes always observing.

Murphy stops me just as I enter the hallway and hands me an envelope. I don't question how much is in there and that information isn't divulged. Staring me dead in the eyes, he holds for a moment then nods, not at me, more like in agreement with himself. Without a backwards glance he's gone. Odd.

As I shut the door to the locker room a chill runs down

my spine and my senses go on high alert. I give myself the smallest moment to ready myself, fully aware that I'm not alone in here. I turn quickly to assess the room.

I first notice the five men that caught my attention earlier when they entered the warehouse with their sunglasses on. I knew something was off with them, but I let them disappear into the crowd, as I watched Jake and Tommy.

Continuing around the room I see a defeated Rafe looking at his shoes, sitting in the corner, unable to meet my eyes.

What the fuck is going on?

Before I can even bring myself to ask the question I hear heels clicking from the showers, not wanting to take my eyes off Rafe, I finally pull my gaze in that direction.

"Happy Birthday, Daughter! I must say you put on a fabulous show for me, just like your Daddy. You're going to fit right in at Featherstone Academy, chop chop, you leave tonight."

I'd know them pointed heels anywhere, it's funny how suited they are to the dirt on the tiled floor. My mother stands before me in a grey tailored suit, with her blonde hair slicked back in a chignon and a thick layer of make-up like she's more than she actually is.

Any chance of a little birthday sex to come down from this high is well and truly out of the window now.

MY BLOODLINE

THREE
Luna

I'm a little stunned.

She's caught me off guard if I'm honest, but I'm trying to not show it. Veronica has shown up a few times over the years, barely hung around for five minutes, then she's gone again. I'm trying to process what she just said and the scene in front of me. I move towards Rafe trying to gain his attention. As I do, one of the guys that seems to be here with my mother, steps behind me and locks the door.

"Rafe, what's going on?"

He looks at me with such anguish in his eyes, I'm halted. He looks broken, this can't be because of the fight.

I mean I knew he'd be angry when he eventually found out about it, but the look on his face is something else entirely. We're not hearts on our sleeve's kind of people, but I can see the emotion in his eyes, the devastation.

"Luna, don't be rude, aren't you going to greet your mother?"

"Last I checked, I don't have a mother, you can leave now," I blandly respond, keeping my eyes trained on Rafe.

This woman is bat shit crazy. Standing here like she's given me the world and sacrificed herself to do so. The only one here that has sacrificed is Rafe, so it's him I'm going to look towards… to try and understand what the hell is going on here.

She cackles like I just told a cheap joke, slowly trying to approach me, forcing me to sneer in her direction.

"Luna, don't be silly. We're here to assist your transition to Featherstone Academy. Rafe knew this day would come. We don't have time to waste, especially if you want to grab a few of your things before we leave."

"Leave? I'm not going anywhere, definitely not with you or to some random Academy. I'm happy where I am, and I'd be even better if you would actually just fuck off, and take your fucking muscle men with you."

These guys are just milling around, taking up space. Clearly here to back my mother.

Before she can respond there is pounding on the door and shouts from the other side. I recognize Jake's voice, and as I go to unlock the door, a rough callous hand wraps around my arm. It's the same guy who trapped us in here. Well I assume it is, these guys are like standard issue bad boys, I haven't been able to differentiate them yet.

"Get your fucking hands off of me," I growl, as I glare at him.

He loosens his hold only slightly. "I can't let you open that door, Miss Steele."

What does this fucker mean, he can't let me? I don't answer to this guy. I'm practically growling through my teeth at him. I go to step back, but his hand remains wrapped around my wrist.

The. Fuck.

The thunder in my eyes finally has this guy letting go.

Damn straight, asshole.

If looks could kill I'd have burnt him alive with the fire in my glare, but instead I'm gonna have to get physical.

"Luna," Rafe calls, gaining my attention. Distracting me from the pounding on the door and this dead man in front of me.

I move towards Rafe. His tattooed hands braced on his knees, his long brown hair is slicked back into a man bun, his brown eyes searching my face. I don't like how his olive skin seems pale. I've never seen his giant frame look so small.

"Rafe, you need to explain to me what's going on. Why are you here? Why is Cruella back? And what is with the D list boy band?"

"I'm sorry, Luna, so sorry. I'd hoped things had changed and we'd avoided all this. I thought I'd been able to keep you out of their hell hole, but I was naive enough to believe your mother's words."

He rubs the back of his neck, his sign for being stressed.

"I did everything she asked to make sure they stayed away from you. It wasn't enough, I'm truly sorry, Luna. I swear if I'd known I'd have got us the fuck out of here when she first found us."

My mother moves to the center of the room, clearly missing out on all the attention.

"Like they wouldn't have found her Rafe. This is bigger than all of us and you know it. Don't try and sugar coat it and make her think there's hope, that'll only make it worse. I haven't got time for this and I've been as nice as possible, but we need to get moving. We've wasted enough time having to come find her. I humored the girl, I allowed her the time to fight, now let's go," she says, waving her hands in the direction of the door.

"Honestly, what the fuck is going on? Stop talking like I'm not standing right here."

My brain can't process what is going on around me. I have so many questions right now, but I can't seem to figure out which one to start with.

"Luna, I'm sure you are excited and have plenty of questions. I'll answer them in the car, we need to get moving. Now," Veronica responds, irritation ruining her whole sweet act.

Is this woman delusional? What reaction gave my excitement away?

None. No movement at all because I'm so far from excited it's unreal.

"Why aren't you listening? I'm not going anywhere!"

I want to punch her in the face.

I'm getting beyond angry now. She can't show up, out of the blue, yet again, suddenly expecting me to go anywhere with her. It's official Veronica Hindman is a narcissistic sociopath.

Fuck it.

"I'll happily take one for the team and knock some sense into you mother," I say sweetly, mocking her previous tone.

I slap her across the face.

Pleased that I got to smack a bitch, even if it wasn't the one I had intended to go for.

She screams like a banshee, hand to her cheek. Stunned I would touch her. The motherly act is gone now, and she steps toward me in retaliation as Rafe stands between us, ruining all the fun.

The guys have stepped in close too. As the banging at the door gets louder, and more frantic at the sound of her scream.

"Raphael, you better get this little bitch in line, and for the last time, we need to leave," my mother screams at him, using his full name.

I look at him. Why the fuck is he going to listen to my mother?

He isn't going to agree with what she's saying.

I don't care what Rafe's sorry for, he can explain it more when we get out of here. Right now, I just want out of this locker room and as far away from these lunatics as possible. He looks at me with resignation written all over his face.

"I'm sorry, Luna, this is out of my hands. Go with them, it's the easiest option for now."

How can he say that so calmly?

"Go with them? What the hell, Rafe?" I yell. It's worse because he's being too calm and relaxed about all of this.

"Luna, look at me. I promise I won't give up, but we aren't prepared right now and we're outnumbered."

"Open the fucking door then. Jake and the others are right there, better yet don't underestimate me. Us," I yell.

Eyebrow raised, arms out to the side. He knows what we are capable of, and he's just giving into her.

"I'm sorry, Luna, but the guys have no idea what they'd be walking into here. Your mother is right, it is about more than any of us, and we aren't going to solve the situation here by fighting."

"And I do? Don't just repeat what she's saying! She's just getting in your head like every other time she shows up. Tell me you're joking Rafe because I'm not leaving!"

I push at his chest, repeatedly. I know it's not his fault deep down, but these fuckers are caging me in. Giving me no option and he's letting them.

"I'm sor..."

"Stop fucking apologizing! God dammit Rafe, have my back here!"

Before he can respond, my so-called mother interrupts. "As sweet as this all is, time really is up."

With that, one of the meat heads jab Rafe in the neck with a syringe and he goes down. I scream, trying to run toward him, but then I feel a sharp sting in my neck and my world enters complete darkness as I meet the same fate as Rafe. Funny how cozy the darkness can be compared to the company of my own mother.

Oh god.

What the hell is the pounding in my head?

Damn, what did I drink last night?

Whatever it was, I need to keep away from it in the future because I feel like death. Trying to get myself in a more comfortable position, I move my hand to scrub my face when it catches and I still. Not yet opening my eyes, I try to focus better and assess the situation more.

Why the hell am I handcuffed?

This definitely isn't sex related, I wouldn't trust anyone enough for this.

I try to open my eyes to see what's happening around me, but the banging in my head is unbearable, so I try to think. Forcing myself to remain as calm as possible. I do not need to freak out right now.

What the hell happened last night?

Retracing my steps in my head, while my arm hangs in the air and my body remains stiff, I backtrack to what I can remember.

I took Dot for a spin after work and headed towards the warehouse. Jake and Tommy had a pissing match then I finally got my first official fight. What was that guy called? Rr .. Rry .. Riggs! Riggs, man I got that little bitch submitting in no time, even though he hit me hard to the face. Fuck, that could be why my eye feels sore, but it doesn't explain why I'm handcuffed. I remember leaving the ring and Murphy stopping me with the cash and then ...

Fuck.

It all comes back to me like a freight train. Being overwhelmed with the mental assault of the memories, all at once, has me nauseous.

My mother, those guys, and Rafe in the locker room. My mother kept going on about leaving and Rafe, Rafe agreeing with her.

Oh God, as if it's playing out in my mind like a movie. I see Veronica's fucking minion sink that syringe into Rafe's neck, and then I followed him to the ground. Damn, is that what I'm fighting off right now?

Before I can assess myself in more detail, I hear a throat clear.

"Luna, you can enjoy my company more with your eyes open, no?"

Fuck, I try not to wince at the sudden sound. Sadly, it's my mother's voice. I don't want to open my eyes because she says so, but I also don't want to seem weak.

Prying my eyes open, I push through the burn and glance in the direction her voice came from.

We're moving. I'm travelling backwards in the back of a large SUV, with two of the guys from earlier relaxing to my left. My mother is sitting in the complete opposite corner, with Rafe sandwiched in between her and another one of her puppets.

I see Rafe's tense posture, and it seems he came around a while before I did. I also don't miss the gun resting against his skull that my mother is holding or the giant smile on her smug as shit face.

"How nice of you to join us, Luna."

I don't know what she wants me to say to her right now. My head is pounding, my eye hurts as I haven't been able to ice it, and there's a general throbbing throughout my bones as if they let me drop to the floor without softening the blow, no one concerned enough to catch my fall.

Assholes.

Both of my wrists are cuffed together and looped through the handle just above me. I'd just like a minute to freaking process tonight, rest my head in my hands, relax the ache in my shoulders, slaughter these motherfuckers for ruining my win.

"I thought we'd given you too much there for a minute, seeing as that was four hours ago and big ass Raphael came around within the hour!"

I roll my eyes at the shit coming out of her mouth. I wish she'd just call him Rafe, her formalities are really annoying the hell out of me.

"Well, I'm not the size of Rafe, am I?" I state the obvious.

It seems they didn't fully think the situation through

and gave us both the same amount of drugs. Seeing as though I'm 5ft 7" and slim in frame compared to Rafe, the gentle giant. It's no wonder I was out for longer.

"Lucky for you, Rafe picked up what he thought you may need."

Man, does she just like the sound of her own voice or something? I roll my head back looking at the roof of the car.

None of her men are fazed by any of this, just satisfied to stare into space. Not even a murmured conversation between themselves.

"I've ensured you have the best dorm possible, as your family name deserves nothing but the best. I've already gone ahead and had it filled with the required clothing and footwear you'll need, along with any other bits I felt were appropriate. Now say, thank you mother."

I glare at her, "You don't know me enough to know what I need. Otherwise you wouldn't be taking me against my will to a place I've never heard of, let alone want to attend. So, I think I'll hold the thanks for now."

She sighs at me. Veronica fucking sighs at me, like I'm the one talking nonsense.

"Featherstone is the Academy for the leaders of the

Underworld across the States, some even coming in from other countries under special agreements. It was agreed before any of our times that the descendants would attend Featherstone and learn the Underworld, to follow in their bloodlines footsteps, including learning about the family name specialties, and skill sets, ready to take over when the time is right."

How am I supposed to get out of this?

Featherstone? What sort of Academy is even called that? I'm 18. If I'm supposed to be going anywhere it's college, and I don't want that either. I already know what I want, so why is this being forced? I'm gonna have to give myself a minute here to prioritize what questions I need to ask first.

"This is bullshit." I glare.

"You'll watch your fucking tongue, young lady! There's only so much of your attitude I'm willing to take and I'm at my limit. Let me tell you, you'd be dragged to Featherstone whether it was me doing so or someone else. It is your legacy to attend Featherstone whether you like it or not. It'll be best for everyone if you know your place and do as you're told from the get-go."

"What does that even mean? My legacy? I've never

even heard of this place. I have a life I'm happy with and it doesn't involve you or some academy that I have no interest in."

"Oh, Luna, it means you are bound to attend Featherstone Academy out of oath and loyalty to your bloodlines, as well as the founders. No will not be accepted as an answer. You should be appreciating the fact that I didn't come for you sooner and force you to attend the High School, like I did."

My eyes bug out at her. I can't help it, she's talking to me like I should know what she's babbling on about and I have no clue.

"What oath and loyalty to my bloodlines? You abandoned me when I was six years old, Mother, after we'd just experienced a life shattering ordeal that no one should ever have to live through! The same ordeal that killed my father!" I yell.

I'm starting to shake a little, she's got my memories floating to the surface and I can't deal with that right now.

My mother sits taller, hands poised on her knee.

"Steele, that is your main bloodline when attending Featherstone, your father's bloodline. I met your father at Featherstone as my legacy led me there also."

She's talking so matter of fact about it all, but completely overlooking any emotion. What the hell happened to this woman to make her this way? Is this how I'm going to turn out too?

"So, let me get this straight. You show up out of the blue again, on my 18th birthday, forcing me to leave my life behind. To attend an academy named Featherstone because both you and my father attended when you were younger. Now, I have no choice with regards to the whole situation, because it falls down to an oath I didn't take and loyalty to a bloodline I no longer have a connection to?"

It's official, she definitely is a maniac. How was she ever allowed to have a child? She is the least maternal woman I have ever met, and that goes back as long as I can remember. I don't ever recall a loving moment between us.

"Yes, Luna, that is exactly it."

Looking around the car no one is surprised by what she is saying, not even Rafe.

Rafe is taking this all in, not liking the fact that I'm learning all of this information, especially because it's coming from my mother's mouth. It's clear he truly thought he had spared me from all this otherwise he'd have been the one to tell me. I'm trying to digest all this information, but I just want an escape plan. I want to get out of this car and go the fuck home.

Meeting Rafe's eyes he shakes his head lightly at me, he knows what I'm thinking and that's his way of telling me it's not possible. All the training, the constant practice, the time and dedication, and we find ourselves in a situation out of our control and he's telling me to back down, that we aren't enough to get out of this? Why?

He must see the question in my eyes, the confusion, "Featherstone is connected to every piece of the Underworld, Luna. Every drug dealer, everything on the black market, every assassin, you name it. If it's breaking the law, they know about it, and if you don't fall in line you're dead, simple as that."

My brain can't process it. So, any illegal enterprise in the US is run by one giant organization who apparently calls the shots that you follow, or you're done for? Mulling this all over it suddenly comes to mind.

"Rafe, how do you even know all this?"

It's instant, the shame. He can't even look at me. I can sense why, but I want to hear it.

"Luna, you know Rafe was a good friend of your fathers since high school so if he went to Featherstone High, then so did Rafe, silly." She giggles like it's just trivial details, but it's not and Rafe knows it.

I don't know whether I'm angry or upset but I want him to look at me and confirm it. I hate that all the information is coming from her mouth.

"Rafe..."

"Yeah, Luna, I attended Featherstone High and Academy when I was younger. I hoped it would never matter so I never discussed any of this with you, but I did attend, and I honored the Gibbs bloodline."

Honored? Why are we calling it that? Am I reacting so differently because I'm just finding out now? Would I feel differently if I'd always known, grown up with it? I can't imagine I would feel any different than I do now, but no one will ever know. Looking at Rafe again, I question him, seen as he has all the fucking answers anyways.

"How long am I expected to stay for?"

"It runs very differently from a normal college. It's literally twelve months, Luna, that's all. You'll still get a few holidays off campus too, like you would anywhere. The classes will be pre-selected for you based on what is suited to your family line."

Twelve months? They want me to stay a whole year?

I look around the SUV, for what I don't know. Back up? I'm not going to get it off these men, they don't even care for our interaction. Apart from the two upfront, two of the guys are on their mobile phones while one is asleep, and we're definitely not being quiet.

Are they joking? The resignation in Rafe's eyes tells me he's definitely not joking. How are they expecting me to attend somewhere I don't want to be for the next fucking year? What's to say, come Fall Break, I run?

The thought is barely a blip in my mind, when I see my mother is still holding her gun to Rafe's head. As though they weren't apparently connected through my father in some way, like she didn't pass her child over to him without a care.

Something tells me there is no running, based on what both Rafe and my mother have said. So, I'm stuck with this lifestyle, and I didn't even get to create it myself. Running my brain over the slithers of information being drip fed to me, I know what I need to ask next.

"If what you're saying is accurate, what is it I'm supposed to be learning while I'm there?" I instantly regret it the second I see my mother's face brighten with the information she holds.

"Well, seeing as both of your parents are descendants, I have been able to place you for both paths, with your father's being the most prominent of course. Featherstone is also aware of your living arrangements, so I was also able to add a few of Raphael's skill sets to your schedule."

She's almost clapping with glee, trying to create suspense with the details she holds. I don't look at Rafe, but I saw him stiffen the instant she mentioned his name. I won't rush her. I can show patience. She wants me to goad her into saying it, but I can sit here all day long maintaining eye contact. She rolls her eyes at me knowing I'm not rising to her antics.

"Fine, my skills as a Hindman are infiltration of legitimate businesses and corrupting law officials..." She pauses, expecting a round of applause or something. Who knows, but she isn't getting a reaction out of me, or her lackeys, so I'll take that as a win for me too.

She continues, not fazed by my blank expression. "Raphael's skillset is weapons and combat."

Well that makes quite a lot of sense. Although it has me wondering if he was actually in the armed forces, or if his so-called sniper skills were used for other purposes. The look on his face tells me I am right, do I even know him anymore?

"And finally, your father's bloodline specializes in robbery, more specifically looting high value, sought after items, and well, Featherstone would like to thank you for your assistance so far. You have made quite the impression. Like father, like daughter they said. Isn't that right Luna 'Moon' Steele?"

Oh shit.

MY BLOODLINE

FOUR
Luna

After that, the car is silent. It seems everyone in the car knows who I am, what I've done, and that includes Rafe. They must be able to tell from the look on my face that I'm a ticking time bomb, and I need to calm down before I can continue any further conversation or gain any new information. I'm trying to understand how this is all happening, how they know.

Staring out the window, I take in the darkness around us as we coast down some highway to fuck knows where.

I can't remember a time when I didn't have an eye for shiny objects, but have I been that obvious? As a child anything with a shine attracted me to it, like a moth to a flame. Over the years that evolved into what was wanted by paying customers, and how much they were willing to pay.

Now that I understand where this desire came from, the items don't seem as shiny anymore. Well, not in the shimmering eye-catching way like they were, but more for their price tags.

When in my life could I have found myself under their spotlight?

The whole thing could have been a test from the beginning. Veronica mentioned 'like father like daughter'. Was it because of my father? Rafe?

I try to think back as far as I possibly can to my first memory of taking something that wasn't mine.

I feel a vague memory return to the surface. Usually if it's pre-Rafe I will force the thoughts back down, unwilling to take a trip down memory lane.

Now, I know I may need to remember if I plan to understand anything that's going on right now, but that thought has fear clawing up my neck.

Closing my eyes, I try to relax myself, pushing past the panic inside, and encourage more of the memory forward.

Slowly, I try to take in what my mind is willing to give me. It feels strange, I don't feel the red haze taking over as strong as usual, is it because I'm choosing to remember?

I can feel a sea breeze on my face, and blowing through my hair, while I'm running as fast as I can. I don't recall where we are, but it feels familiar. I'm dashing through the grass bank, sitting above the beach below, no shoes on, loving the feel of the grass in between my toes.

I must be five at most, a pale pink dress floating around my legs and I can feel my irritation. Even then at such a young age, I'm mad with the restriction the dress is giving me.

I'm laughing, freely, and being chased by someone who is also laughing along with me. My fist is tightly squeezing something and as I look down at my hand to catch a glimpse of my treasure, I'm whipped off my feet and twirled around.

I can't breathe, I'm laughing so hard. God, to be this carefree again, it feels like magic. When my captor finally relents on the twirling, I feel their arms wrap tightly around me in a protective and loving hold. When I finally look through my messy hair I see my father staring back at me, with eyes filled with love and pride.

His brown hair swept to the side, and his green eyes matching mine. Tattoos all over his arms and peeking out under his collar.

"Sweet girl, are you stealing my treasures?"

I shake my head innocently, and my father can't help but chuckle more.

"My sweet Luna, you truly are your father's daughter. One day, in years to come, you will be the greatest of our name. Already outsmarting me so young. I'm going to have to work hard to keep up, ey?"

I just give him the biggest smile my face can hold and hand over the treasure I stole. It's a small broach, a peacock, with bright blue and green gems. That's what drew me to it, it looked so pretty I just had to have it.

My father kisses me sweetly on the cheek and places me on the ground. I instantly start running again, loving the feel of the wind whipping around me. When I look back towards my father he's no longer alone, he's also stood with a smiling Rafe as they laugh together, while my mother is looking up from the sea's edge with menace in her eyes.

I stop myself there, unable to deal with anymore. I have

spent so long pushing memories of my father to the back of my mind, I feel drained. My hands are shaking slightly, and I feel a cold sweat taking over.

I'm too scared to remember even happy times like then, especially when I can vividly remember his death in greater detail.

My father, Bryce Steele, is a mystery to me. Remembering what seemed like such a sweet moment between father and daughter breaks my heart. What would my life be like now if he was still here? It seems I'd likely still be heading to Featherstone Academy, but I'd have been more prepared than I am right now.

I'm struggling with the fact that I'm not in control. I'm used to dominating my surroundings, and right now I don't even have a slight grasp of them. Knowing where to place myself next, who to place my trust in, seeing the danger signs before a situation worsens.

A tapping distracts my train of thought, drawing my attention to Mother. She still has her gun aimed at Rafe, and she's tapping her fake nails against it. Like a little reminder to everyone that she's the one with the power here.

I've been completely caught off guard and I think it

feels worse because Rafe has been holding a lot of this information from me. I trusted him over everyone else. Peering back outside the window, I can see the beginning of dawn touch the sky. We've been driving for some time. Not including the four hours I was unconscious.

I let my thoughts go back to how it would have been possible for me to take jobs from Featherstone without being aware. My profile on the dark web is limited, a lot of my contracts have been done facelessly, and I vetted out the information on who contacted me. Now it seems likely they were told to contact me by Featherstone if what Veronica said was true.

The only person who ever found out, that I was aware of, was West. About two years ago, I'd broken into a CEO's office in one of the many skyscrapers in downtown Philly, specifically looking for some blueprint documents. They meant nothing to me but enough to the guy, who contacted me through my dark web setup, to pay big for the job.

As the job was in the city, I made the trip in my beat-up truck, and parked five blocks away from where I needed to be. After spending a solid twenty minutes driving round in circles, making sure I wasn't being followed.

With all the prep I had done for the job, it was a quick

in and out extraction. I mean really, for a multi-million dollar company, they should have better security measures in place.

When I got back to my truck he was there, casually sitting on the hood, watching me approach. West's excuse for being there was because he'd seen me randomly take off from time to time, and he wanted to see what I was up to. I was so mad at him at the time, furious at him for invading my privacy. It was irrelevant to him what I was doing.

He's four years older, so for him to hold any interest in my whereabouts confused the hell out of me. I almost thought I had another Jake on my hands, but West never tried to overstep the mark, and I never caught any lingering glances.

He promised this was my secret and I believed him.

There hadn't been a time that I did call him, seeing as I was perfectly fine on my own, but on that drive home he kept me on loudspeaker the whole way, and that's when he named me Moon. He would never explain why, but it stuck.

I've never really known what West does for a living, he isn't around all the time and occasionally he'll train with us at Rafe's gym, but he doesn't work at Inked with Jake. He was a bit of a mystery and that suited me just fine, if it meant my secret stayed with him, but now it seems my secret wasn't really a secret at all.

I'm at even more of a loss of who actually surrounds me.

I could cut the tension in this car with a knife. I don't want to be here but apparently that's irrelevant. My arms are completely numb at this point, but I refuse to complain or show any weakness. No one's offered to help me out. Seems it's completely normal to take people against their will and handcuff them like this for hours.

Clearing his throat, Rafe gains my attention. "Luna, we aren't too far from Featherstone and I feel there is still more for us to discuss."

"You've had plenty of time to discuss all of this with me, Rafe, why worry about it now?"

I'm trying to see all of this from Rafe's point of view but I'm still furious with him. As much as it may have been a tough conversation, I would have been more prepared right now.

He sighs but continues, "When we arrive there won't be any hanging around, they don't fuss around like that, so I only have now to prepare you. There is only so much apologizing I can do Luna, and right now that isn't my priority."

He looks me in the eyes, and I can feel him trying to communicate how serious he is. I give a nod and his shoulders relax.

"When we arrive, you should be taken for registration. They'll give you everything you need to settle in, from your dorm keys to a list of materials you may need. Some items can be purchased on site while others hold more value. You should be given access to our bloodline vaults, where you'll have access to heirlooms. Anything else you need, should be provided by Featherstone, otherwise I can get you whatever you need."

He looks to my mother for confirmation of this, who simply nods like it was obvious to begin with.

"There are already cliques amongst surnames here, add in the fact that most of the other students will already know each other, leaves you at a disadvantage," Rafe murmurs, his eyes darkening with the thought.

"Although, with you being a Steele, you are high up in

the ranks, and learning three bloodline skills should help broaden your reach amongst the student body."

He pauses like he's trying to find the right words. "Luna, it's a dog eat dog world here and that includes the tutors too. You are stepping into a world where these kids have been raised to be criminals. Stabbing you in the back, literally, would be like waking up and having a cup of coffee to these people. You need to make sure you are always alert."

"Rafe, always the storyteller," my mother muses, but Rafe doesn't seem to pay her any mind.

"As much as I hoped this would never happen, Luna, I trained you for this. I threw so many techniques at you, pushing you to your limit sometimes, to make sure you could hold your own no matter what."

I usually like seeing the pride in his eyes. I don't want it in this moment, but I do trust him with my life, so I have to set my emotions aside and take in any information he can give me. He looks as though he's going to push on with more insight, when we're interrupted by one of the meatheads sitting upfront in the SUV.

"We have arrived."

Arrived? I glance out of my window to see us pass

through giant wrought iron gates. The perimeter goes on beyond what I can see. Twisting around the best I can, to get a better view, I'm taken back with the size of this place.

From my viewpoint, I can't see much, but guards stop us before we are able to continue down the road. Apart from the road, everything else is nature. Perfectly cut grass, vibrant flowers and large chestnut oak trees.

It's beautiful.

"This is the entry building and where they hold events. The dorms are in separate buildings to the left, classes are held over a few buildings to the right and the shops and cafeteria are in the center. You'll get used to the size of it," Rafe says.

His hands are pointing out in random directions, and I struggle to keep up with him without ending up with whiplash. I hope I get some form of map because I can't remember all of that.

As the car pulls to a stop, I rattle the handcuffs, "If you're so intent on me attending you may need to uncuff me, Mother."

She smirks as she says, "Don't look at me, I assumed you'd come without acting like a child, they're Rafe's."

She wants me to lash out and aim it all at Rafe, but I

won't give her the satisfaction. On the inside I want to rip him a new one, punch him in the throat, and smash his face through the car window, but on the outside, I simply smile.

"The honors, Rafe."

He moves swiftly as he murmurs, "You'd have killed us all Luna and it's not our time yet."

I hum in response as my arms fall to my lap, wiggling my fingers to get my blood flowing again. My mother hands her gun off to one of the guys. Seems it was just an extra precaution to keep me compliant.

"I'm aware we're at Featherstone Academy, but would anyone like to tell me where that is on the map?"

"Not far from Richmond, Virginia."

Oh, so the guy next to me does actually talk, who knew? The guy sitting to Rafe's left opens the door and everyone gets out. The humidity hits instantly and I consider jumping back in the car for the air conditioning alone.

Two people are heading towards us, a man and a woman, who seem to be having a heated discussion. The woman is dressed similarly to Veronica with a tailored pantsuit in black and her caramel hair slicked back in a tight high pony. She wouldn't need Botox with it pulled that tight, that's for sure. The man is a lot more casual in jeans and a leather jacket, and it looks as though he didn't even bother to brush his hair.

As they make their way towards us, Rafe lightly grabs my shoulder and talks softly to me, "Luna, you don't need to hear this, but I need to say it. You've got this. As much as I don't want any of this for you, you were made for this. Don't doubt yourself and don't let anyone get under your skin. If they so much as catch a glimpse of weakness they'll be all over it."

He pulls me into a tight hug, which feels odd as we don't usually show affection, but I squeeze him back all the same.

"Classes begin on the twenty-fifth, so you've got a few days to find your feet. If you need me for anything at all you know I'm only a phone call away. I know I'm not your favorite person right now but that doesn't change anything between us, you will always be my number one priority. I tried to grab as much as possible from your room including your 'Moon' bag, but if I missed anything let me know and I'll get it sent over. I'm proud of you Luna and I love you, no matter what."

I hold him tighter for a moment longer, then step away as the new arrivals stop in front of us.

"Hello, you must be Miss Steele, my name is Barbette Dietrichson and I'm the Head of Featherstone Academy. This is Maverick Miller, our tutor for combat training. If you'd like to follow me, we have much to attend to. Leave your belongings, they will be taken to your room."

She pulls her gaze from mine looking straight to my mother.

"Veronica, a pleasure as always," she says with a smile, turning for me to trail behind her.

The guys are all back in the SUV ready to go again, while Maverick clasps hands with Rafe and they share some kind of man hug, pat, chest bounce thing. No words are spoken between them, but they clearly know each other. I give Rafe a backwards glance as I follow behind Barbette, unaware of where this may lead me, but my instincts tell me nothing will be the same after this.

MY BLOODLINE

FIVE

Luna

I'm led to a large stone building, and to say it is grand would be an understatement. The height alone is powerful, add to that the arch ways, columns, and balconies, it feels like it wants to be a castle. There are intricate carvings around the windows and in the alcoves. Ivy grows up the building, and flower beds decorate the bottom of the stone steps up to the entry.

I wonder what stories they could tell, of what lies beyond these walls and the people that have passed through them. Everything is immaculate, nothing at all like what I expected a criminal underworld academy to look like.

Following behind them up the stairs, I hear the SUV pull away. My heart wants to drown in all of this, yet again being dropped somewhere and left behind. I refuse to be beaten by my circumstances, I've lived through far worse. Feeling out of my depth and a little lost isn't going to be the end of me.

With that in mind, I take a deep breath finding my center, relax my shoulders and raise my head. I'm walking in here whether I like it or not, so I'm going to do so on my terms. Carrying myself with all the confidence I've got, I make sure my poker face is in place and my defensive walls are up.

Stepping inside, it's just as grand as outside. All dark wood and golden framed memorabilia, in all shapes and sizes. Before I can take any of it in fully I'm being led to the left and straight through a door leading to Dietrichson's office.

Her office doesn't match the rest of the building. White walls and modern glass furnishings. Although is that a fucking tiger rug?

"Please take a seat Miss Steele, I don't have much time for this."

I want to yell that I don't want to fucking be here so let's not waste your time, but I don't know who I'm dealing with and it's clear I'm out numbered as a party of one, so I bite my tongue and take a seat.

"Usually this is all done through the administration office but seeing as it's a Saturday that's not possible now is it?" she asks, as she steeples her fingers on the desk in front of her.

I don't respond, that was just a mouthful of snark.

"Here is your ID box, inside you will find the key to your room, a copy of your timetable, a map of the grounds, access to financial funds from your bloodlines, a list of requirements, and access key cards to the vaults you have access to."

She holds a plain wooden box with a piece of paper stuck to the top. Not as fancy as I was expecting for this place. She glances at the top of the ID box and frowns. I look at what's caught her eye and I can see the names of the three bloodlines I'm here for: Steele, Gibbs, and Hindman.

"Do you want to tell me why you've been given access to the Gibbs bloodlines as well?" The venom in her voice is clear as day.

"Is there a problem?" I ask as I lean back in my chair.

I don't know what she wants me to say, I haven't made any of these decisions.

"A problem? You are only given access to your bloodlines, it's impossible to be assigned a third, there must be an error!"

She's flustered by this, but someone must have authorized it, otherwise it wouldn't be happening.

Maverick, chimes in, seemingly bored with all of this already. "Barb, this was approved late last night by the superiors, it was stated in the email."

"I haven't seen any email, I received a call two hours ago to be here for a late arrival, something like this cannot be approved without me. I run this Academy and I won't allow it!"

Wow, power trip much?

I don't know what I'm expected to say here and nothing I could say is going to make this situation any better. Maverick seems to notice this too and takes the box out of her hands.

"I'll take this and sort Luna out while you get your shit together, yeah?"

He marches out of the door, not looking back. It takes me a second to catch on and I'm up and following after him.

"Get my shit together? Are you fucking joking me? Do you even know who I ..."

I slam the door as quick as I can behind me, cutting off her tirade. I've had enough of bat shit crazy women today, thank you very much.

Glancing around I see Maverick leaving through the opposite end of the large hall area that we came in through. Nobody else is around. It feels like I'm trespassing in a museum or something, like that time in Baltimore.

Fuck, I'm getting distracted. I move quickly to catch up with him but as I step outside the box is slapped into my chest and I grapple to keep a hold of it.

"I'm not your keeper. Get your shit and figure it out asap 'cos no one's going to save you here." With that he's gone.

I look around, spotting a bench amongst the trees. I need to figure out where I'm going to be staying so I can figure it all out in peace, without any of these whack jobs catching me off guard.

Sitting, I look inside the box, everything has been organized into specific envelopes. Flicking through I find the slip marked *Dorm Key: Ace Block, Room Two*.

Okay, finding the map layout underneath, I figure out

where I need to go.

I'm at The Hall. Right from here would take me towards the academic buildings. The path in front of me leads to the center where Rafe mentioned the shops would be, so I need to go left for the dorms.

Closing the lid, I make my way to the left down a long path, flowers and shrubs line the edge. It is surprisingly peaceful here, but that might be because I've only seen maintenance staff so far.

Seeing the six buildings come into view, I know I'm in the right place.

Each building is completely different, all the same size but they range from run down to modern penthouse buildings. Some are covered in graffiti and have mud splatters up the sides. Others aren't as bad, but compared to the block at the end they could do with a lick of paint. They were once painted white, I think, but those days are gone.

Why is that?

Looking for the sign for Ace block I realize it's the grandest building of them all. Four stories high, like the others, but there is so much glass I'm not sure there is even any walls. It's ridiculously modern with a water feature outside of it too.

This is flashy, I mean I have money and I've never worried about anything, but I'm not a show-off and all this does is scream, look at me!

Heading in that direction, I notice a few people milling around, nobody is causing a scene. You can feel the tension, it's suffocating, like everyone is on edge just waiting for something to happen.

One thing I do notice is no one is alone, everyone is in groups of at least two. There are bigger masses of people, I'm pretty sure they're more of a gang and you can see who the leaders are instantly.

Especially the group coming up to my right, lounging around a large table. There are maybe ten of them? I'm not willing to count right now, but they are the most relaxed. As if the tension in everyone else stems from that table.

I don't want to make myself a target before I've even made it to my room, so I power on forward avoiding eye contact with everyone.

As I near the water feature I hear people nearby begin to murmur and I know it involves me. Like Rafe said, I'm new here, I'm going to stick out like a sore thumb, and I can feel the target it has put on my back already.

Trying to stay focused on the entry to the building I sense I'm being surrounded, I don't want to show my hand just yet. If I've learned anything, it's to let them think they're making the first move.

I hear a chair scrape across the concrete floor, as I walk past the big group.

"Excuse me." Some girl's high-pitched voice comes from behind me.

I know she's talking to me, but I don't answer her. I just carry on walking.

"Hey, your ears broke? You're being spoken to," a guy says, still behind me but not as close as the girl.

Seems either way this is going to shit, and I won't make it to my room before that happens. I'd just like to catch a five-minute break today, like I've not already been handed enough.

Assessing the situation, I decide it's best to address this here, so I don't look weak in front of so many people. Stopping, I straighten my posture and turn, looking the girl straight in the eyes.

From what I can see she's slightly shorter than me by an inch or two, blonde hair straightened down her back, heavy eye make-up that looks like cement, and a dress so revealing if I crouched I'd definitely see her kittycat.

I don't look to anyone else yet, focusing just on her. Giving her the attention she wanted, but I won't speak to acknowledge her yet. I continue to stare her down while she gives me the once over, she mustn't like what she sees based on the sneer on her lips.

"Care to explain who you are?"

Everyone in the vicinity has stopped what they're doing, that tells me she's a top dog around here, because everyone is listening and the tension has risen, if that was even possible.

She's looking at me like I should be kneeling in her presence, she'll be waiting some time for that.

I tilt my head and keep my voice bored.

"Nope."

My inner bitch loves popping the 'p', but it seems my new friend does not appreciate my sass.

People are definitely staring now, if the gasps are anything to go by, seems nobody stands up to this girl. Noted, but I couldn't give a shit.

I continue to look her in the eye. As much as I don't want to talk to this girl, I also don't want to give her my back.

"You're clearly new around here, so let me catch you up real quick." She smirks.

"I'm Wren Dietrichson and I run this Academy. You were a nobody before you got here and you sure as shit don't have what it takes to survive. So there is no way you are walking towards the Ace honey, it isn't for you. Why don't you run along back to the Joker Block before I show you what we're made of at the top."

Dietrichson? So she's related to the Head, fuck me, like we needed two of them. The group she was sat with chuckle to my left, seems they're all Ace material, from their matching vibes.

Looking around, no one can come at me from the right with the water feature there, no one's behind this bitch, her friends are to my left, and I can't sense anyone behind me. She's not going to like that I am actually in Ace, so I need to be ready for this to go further south without losing my ID box.

"I'm sorry to disappoint you Wendy, but my key says Ace Block, so if you're finished..." I hold the rest of the sentence trying to act indifferent, but I can't help but get her name wrong, sometimes I just can't control my inner bitch.

"It's fucking Wren, you stupid whore. I'm going to enjoy showing you how things go around here."

The words have barely left her mouth and she's already moving towards me, as soon as she gets within arm's length she goes to grip my hair. Damn, I haven't got time for a bitch fight. I drop my ID box at my feet and knock her arms to the right, as she stumbles in that direction I push to encourage her fall. With a splash she falls over the side of the water feature.

Fucking. Epic.

The water is only about knee deep but she's floundering like she's going to drown. I mean I could hold her under if she wanted but I don't think I need to go any further right now. She's screaming bloody murder and people surrounding us are either stunned in shock or laughing, but nobody is actually helping her out.

It's notable that the ones laughing are the group she was sitting at the huge table with.

"You're fucking dead, you hear me? I'm gonna slaughter you, make you wish you'd never been born," she splutters around her frantic coughing.

Seeing as she's so occupied, I take this as my cue to get the hell out of here. I look down to get my ID box just as a guy picks it up. I'm close to losing it now, I do not need another person causing anymore fucking issues. At least let me sleep and eat a little.

The guy looks at the box for a moment before looking at me.

Wow, he's hot. Taller than me, dusty blonde hair, and bright blue eyes like the ocean. A round face with a slight splatter of freckles on his nose. He's trim as hell with bright colored tattoos taking over his left arm. He has surfer vibes, while also looking like he's never seen a board before.

I'm trying to not get carried away with getting my fill of this guy, but they don't make them like this back home.

Sadly, the grin on his face tells me he knows he's hot shit, cocky assholes always gotta ruin it. I hold my hand to take the box back, but he just continues to stare.

"Steele, Gibbs, and Hindman. I'm assuming Steele is your focused bloodline?"

"Yeah," I sigh, hoping this can be over with quickly. He holds the ID box a moment longer, then places the object in my hands. I start moving toward the doors without missing a beat. Just as I get to the door of the building a shout slows my steps.

"Hey, Princess, your bloodline may have you in Ace,

but you aren't one of us." It isn't the hot guy talking, I can tell by the voice, but I'm not hanging around to see who. Stepping inside a short older man with a kind face greets me.

"Hello, you must be Miss Steele, my name is Thomas. Let me show you to your room."

Fuck yeah Thomas, lead the way.

SIX
Roman

What the fuck just happened? One minute Wren's stopping some newbie from entering Ace, the next she's swimming in the fucking water feature. At least it got her out of my personal space so I could actually breathe anything other than her perfume, it's making me sick.

Lavender is no longer a relaxing scent, not when it's strong enough to cause a fucking headache.

"Hey, Roman, who was that?"

I look at Parker, trying to keep my tone relaxed with him, but how am I expected to know exactly who she is?

"I don't fucking know, Parker. Just steer clear of her

until we do, ok?"

He cringes at my language but nods all the same. I've known Parker for three years, he showed up at Featherstone High at fifteen years old. I instantly took him under my wing. He has a solid bloodline, just a shame he's a bastard and they won't give him his surname until he's proven himself.

He looks the part and fits in well amongst us. With his slim frame you could mistake his abilities but he's solid as hell. It's just a shame his head is fucked up. He doesn't seem to understand that people fucking lie all the time and he can quickly be manipulated.

So, I decided to make it my responsibility to guide him in the right direction. Now, he can defend himself and have people backing away in fear. Although, his personality and hatred for cussing doesn't seem to have changed. Which matches his curly brown hair and slim frame if we're stereotyping.

It just doesn't really match the fact that he has tattoos on his hands and a mean right hook.

"Yo, Rome, did you see that? I need me some."

The sparkle in Oscar's eyes tells me that's the truth all right, always thinking with his dick. I'm surprised it's not fallen off.

"What did you say to her? You just let her go into Ace, man." Confusion is in my tone because Oscar loves explaining the hierarchy to everyone, seeing as he's high up. It doesn't make sense to me, unless she's actually meant to be here. But what bloodline?

"Bro, she's got three bloodlines and her major will be Steele."

Three?

Who the fuck authorized that?

I asked for an extra skill set, but even with my father's connections it was declined instantly. Then the fact that she's majoring for Steele? Fuck. This could all go to shit for us because there is no way in hell that is possible.

"Oscar, what were the other names?"

From the smirk on his face I know I'm not going to like what he's about to say.

"Hindman and Gibbs."

My brain mulls this over for a beat.

"Hindman and Gibbs? As in Gibbs being another Ace bloodline? Meaning she just sauntered in there and took two Alpha names and you just fucking let her?"

I'm raging, some bitch is going to walk in here claiming

names that sure as shit aren't hers.

"And Hindman, that's only a step down to Diamond Block, somebody better get me some fucking answers." I'm close to yelling and I've risen to my feet.

Parker squeezes my shoulder reminding me to reign it in. I instantly sit back down and force myself to relax, but this girl just casually walked in here like it might not fuck all my plans up. I've worked too hard for it to go to shit now.

Oscar just winks and saunters off like he has no cares. He probably fucking doesn't, but he should.

I'm ready to get out of here, I need to figure this out in private.

The shrill cries from the water get louder and I hear my name.

"Roman, what are you doing? Stop ignoring me. Get over here and help me out right now!" The fury in her voice is laughable, while she's flapping around in the water like a seal.

She started the whole argument then went into bitch fight mode, who does that?

I think the girl's posture caught her off guard. It surprised me for sure, in the blink of an eye she was defending herself and pushing Wren into the water. Part of me wants to be impressed, but she's a complete unknown and I can't have that.

"Sort yourself out, Wren. You're a fucking mess."

I'm standing and looking for Kai, who's sitting around the other side of the table, in the shade as always. He meets my eyes and gives me a nod. Clearly, he heard what Oscar just said and is already researching like I need him too. He's our tech expert so whatever there is to find on this girl, he'll get it.

I head into Ace and offer a slight smile to Thomas as I pass. I opt to take the stairs instead of the lift, even though I'm on the fourth floor. I can always get a minute to myself this way. The stairs are for the staff really so it's basic green handlebars and magnolia walls, but they serve their purpose.

There are six blocks which form an order for how shit runs around here. Ace is for everyone representing the bloodlines that run The Ring. Followed by Diamond, Hearts, Spades, Clubs and Jokers. In that order. Jokers are at the bottom of the barrel. I don't interact with anyone lower than Diamond, but I get why they're here.

I mean, we need minions to do the shitty skills because

you won't catch an Ace doing them. Then, each building has rooms allocated to bloodlines based on importance. All the blocks are the same size, they just have less and less people in them the higher up the chain you get.

For instance, Joker Block holds up to sixty attendees, all room sharing, and a couple of communal bathrooms on each floor. Whereas Ace holds eight, that's eight fully equipped, top of the range condos. No apartments on the ground floor, that's for our private gym/training area, garage, and private chefs. You then have three condos on the second and third floor, and the top floor holds two apartments. I had the privacy of the top floor at Featherstone High and that's how I liked it.

Now it seems I've gone and got myself a fucking neighbor.

MY BLOODLINE

KC KEAN

SEVEN

Luna

This place is crazy. Thomas walked me to my room yesterday morning and I haven't had to leave since. I'm going a little mad here and I know I need to get out for a bit at some point, but I just needed time to gather myself, to figure out a plan. It didn't take long for me to fall asleep yesterday, once I saw the level of security for my room, and arranged some of my own, I felt a little safer.

Thank God Rafe sent my 'Moon' bag, because it wasn't safe enough to sleep without my switchblade under my pillow and one of my guns under the comforter, but having them was enough for me to relax and let sleep take over for a while.

Once I woke I took the time to check out my new living space. The bedroom is gorgeous, decorated in soft pink and pale grey with a full dresser off to the side. The California King comes with the most luxurious mattress I've ever slept on, and that's saying something, because my one back home is amazing.

The lounge is all navy along one wall, and white accents touch the room. It has two sofas with a wooden coffee table and a giant television. It is surprisingly cozy, to say there are floor to ceiling windows opposite the navy feature, looking out over the entry and the other buildings.

A full kitchen, that is completely stocked, comes off the opposite side of the lounge to my bedroom. Full of high-tech appliances and a big enough dining table for six, but most importantly my favorite coffee machine.

I can't stop staring at the tub in the bathroom. It's a giant whirlpool bath that could easily hold four, and it's all for me. The bathroom also has a walk-in shower with body jets and the largest rainfall shower head ever. Back home I had a good enough shower, but now I had options.

This room definitely softens the blow, but it isn't home.

The technology here is crazy good. From apps I had to

download to let me control the temperature and security from my phone, to touchpads that worked the blinds, the entertainment system, and even place an order for food from downstairs. Not that I'd done that yet, seeing as the kitchen was fully stocked already, I'd been happily taking care of myself.

Looking through the bags that Rafe had packed for me, I was relieved to see some home comforts. I'd stored my 'Moon' bag straight away, even though they seem to know who I am, I don't want my equipment just lying around.

He'd packed every item of clothing I own into two suitcases, apparently I'm a light traveler to say that was all I had. Other than that, he'd made sure I had chargers for my electronics including my phone, thank God. He had even packed my tattoo cases. I just needed some available skin to go crazy on.

My mother on the other hand, when she said she'd had some essentials arranged for me, she was downplaying her work for sure. The dresser came with a beauty table, kitted out with so much make-up I thought it was a full stand at a department store. And don't get me started on all the fancy lights and shit.

There was barely any room in the dresser for my actual

clothes seeing as she had had it filled with dresses and skimpy outfits. She was making it very fucking obvious that she doesn't know me at all. Just to top it all off, nobody mentioned a freaking uniform, and why are there fucking heels with it? In what world do you wear heels as part of a uniform? That shit's just sending me over. The. Edge.

I have to push all this shit out of my mind. I know it's not important in the grand scheme of things. Not when I have classes to consider.

When I finally look at my ID box in more detail, I find my timetable printed and laminated with full color coding. Somebody had too much time on their hands.

It looks as though I have six main lessons: Business, Combat, Weapons, Tech, History, and B.I.C.E, which stands for Bribery, Infiltration, Corruption and Embezzlement.

I mean, it started off normal with the business class but just went off the scales from there.

All this has me a little overwhelmed if I'm honest with myself. I seem to try and wrap my head around one thing and ten more pop up.

There were three credit cards in separate envelopes, one for each bloodline, with bank statements enclosed. All showing obscene amounts of money. Money which

I will not be using. No way. I have my own money that I've earned myself which doesn't come with any strings attached. With that I leave them in the ID box.

I can't get any more familiar with my room. I've scoped out every inch of it and checked it all over for cameras or any form of monitoring device and come up with nothing. So I know it's time for me to check out as much of the grounds as possible before everything officially begins on Tuesday. Seeing as it's already lunch time on Sunday, I still need to visit the vaults and buy a few items, so I know I need to get a move on.

Deciding a jog around the grounds is likely my best option. I throw on some loose shorts and a sports bra since the heat is unbearable, and the humidity is through the roof. I opt to wear my tech earphones, so it'll look like I'm listening to music, but they actually amplify the sounds around me. I'll either pick up some useful information or at least hear an attacker coming at me. With that being said, I opt to pack a razor blade in between my boobs as an extra layer of defense.

Here's to hoping I won't need it.

I've jogged the whole perimeter and there is easily over ten thousand acres of land here, it's huge for the small amount of people actually here. I remember when we had to visit Penn State University with school and I thought that was big, this isn't much bigger but there's a quarter of the people on campus at most. There is so much open space and distance between the different areas.

At some points I felt like I was at a National Park. Barely anyone around, and surrounded by nature, I could forget where I am.

The academic buildings are almost quaint looking, built out of concrete, brick, and stone. It adds character and matches the elegant vibes of the main hall.

Seeing as I stuck to the perimeter I didn't come across anybody except the security and it seems there's plenty of them. I got the occasional nod, but I wasn't interrupted, just how I like it.

The little map they give you does not do it any justice. If anything, it's very misleading. I would have brought extra water if I'd known the campus was this big. I'm definitely feeling it, seeing as I had the fight on Friday night and did nothing at all yesterday. I'm gonna find out who created that map and recommend they add a distance notice. I'm exhausted, but at least the run calmed my mind.

I'm glad I've got a feel for this place a bit more now. I'll need to venture into the center where the shops and food halls are tomorrow since it's later in the day than I thought it would be.

I'm close to the dorms now and there are definitely more people around than there were when I left. From this distance I can see a few groups around, but I don't spot the larger group from yesterday.

No one seems to have caught sight of me yet, so I stop to the side to stretch myself before I head in. Preferring the fresh air and natural surroundings to try and wind down.

I should have known not to when I hear feet shuffling towards me. I'm mid-stretch, touching my toes, when I look to my right and see a girl approaching me. Luckily it's not the same bitch as yesterday, but my guard goes up all the same. I stand tall and look her over. Red hair touching her shoulders, wearing a plain green tee and a pair of denim shorts with subtle make-up, she's rocking the girl next door vibe like a pro.

She looks me over too, she's nervous. I can see it on her face, she wants to say something. I raise an eyebrow at her which makes her blush, it's obvious she isn't going to physically attack me if a raised eyebrow embarrasses her.

"Are you okay?" I ask, hoping my instincts are right. I relax my posture a little to encourage her to do whatever she came over here for.

"Yeah, yeah I'm fine. That's what I actually came over here for. You know, to make sure you're okay." She must see the confusion on my face when she carries on, "Sorry, I err, saw what happened yesterday, and I know you gave her what she deserved but I just wanted to check in and make sure you're alright. I'm assuming you're new to everything Featherstone seeing as I haven't seen you before yesterday, and well, I can't help but worry that you've shown up with a black eye."

Now I'm raising both eyebrows at her, before I can process a response she's continuing.

"I'm sorry, I'm not nosey, I swear. I just remember when I joined Featherstone High and how awful people were then, and I just wanted to offer a friendly smile amongst all of this. And, now I'm talking your ear off. I'm sorry, I have a motor mouth. I'll shut up now."

She literally covers her mouth and her eyes are wide, like deep down there is so much she wants to say, but she really is trying to hold it in. I can't keep the bubble of laughter from escaping and the smile from touching my lips.

"You got a name Red?"

She is practically bouncing on her toes with joy.

"Oh gosh. Silly me, yes. Hi, I'm Jessica," she rushes.

"Luna," I offer in response.

She's looking at me as if she wants to shake my hand, high five me, and hug me all at once. I raise my hands in defense.

"Baby steps, yeah?" I try to keep my voice relaxed and she instantly calms.

"Sorry, I know I'm a bit much, you aren't the first to tell me. I just knew I liked you when I saw you yesterday." She is much more at ease now when she's talking.

"I'm not saying you're anything. I only just met you, that's all." I smile to show her I'm being honest with her. I don't mix well with other girls, they're usually too pretentious and full of themselves, and I haven't got time for it. That and I was always training with Rafe or with the guys at Inked, but this girl, she has a happy go lucky vibe about her, and I feel myself wanting to bask in it.

Catching myself getting carried away, I decide as nice as this all is I need to put a little space between us. I don't want to suddenly rely on this girl just because she's the first person to actually talk to me. Trying to wrap this up without being too harsh, like I usually am.

"Well Jessica, thanks for coming over. I'm okay though, no worries there. I may be new here, but I know how to handle myself," I say, placing my hand to my chest, trying to emphasize the honesty in my statement.

She raises her hand to her cheekbone as if to ask about my black eye without interrupting me.

"Ah yeah, don't worry about that. You should see the other guy."

That seems to get Red more worked up.

"Guy? What guy? Why are they hitting you? Is this an abusive relationship? Domestic violence is never okay, Luna. We need to get you checked over, file a report."

Oh God, I've got to cut her off before she hurts herself.

"Red, calm down okay. I'm fine, I was in an organized fight Friday night. No domestic violence here." I look her straight in the eye hoping to calm her quickly. She's almost got me wanting to rub her shoulder, to console her or something.

"Oh, okay. If you're sure, Luna. Sorry, I get carried away when I worry."

She's worried about me? I don't even know what to do with that.

"No, I'm all good, honest."

Her shoulders relax.

"I'm gonna head back though, I've been on a crazy jog and I just need to shower, eat, and sleep, in that order."

Why am I explaining myself to her? I never explain myself to anyone. I think I've caught her chatterbox. What is it with this girl?

"Of course, sorry for holding you up. If you need a friend for anything I'm in Diamond Block and it's usually okay for Ace and Diamond Blocks to mingle."

What does that even mean? She doesn't seem to fit in here, in the criminal underworld, but she does seem to have experience and knowledge of the hierarchy which could be useful.

"Hey, you want to give me your number?" I ask and her smile is blinding.

Seems I'm not going to be a party of one here. I take my phone out and dial her details.

"Maybe I'll text you tomorrow. I haven't got all my required items yet and you can play tour guide if you're free," I say.

"Yes, I would love that. I'm free tomorrow so let me know."

Stepping back, I start to head towards Ace, but I can't help consider what Jessica has said so far.

She is a ray of sunshine, a lightbulb in this dark world, with her personality, but it seems others here have tried to stamp the sparkle out. How have they treated this girl? For her to feel so strongly about approaching me today.

I never care for other people's feelings or happiness levels, but she deserves someone to brighten her day too, right?

"Hey, Red," I shout. She whips her head around smiling, seems I'm set on nicknaming her. Fuck.

"Thanks for this, it was nice to meet you," I say honestly.

Her blue eyes brighten, and an appreciative smile meets me. I turn and carry on back to my dorm.

Seems I've got myself a friend.

MY BLOODLINE

KC KEAN

EIGHT
Luna

I feel as fresh as a daisy after yesterday. After I made it back to my room, I showered and ordered the best mac and cheese in existence. I did consider the tub in the ridiculous bathroom but ultimately, I needed to power spray that sweat off. Maybe I can try the tub out tonight because it looks divine.

It's played on my mind a little that I've not had any contact with the Head since I was in her office on Saturday morning. Is everything ok now, or is there more for me to be concerned about?

When I was relaxing last night with Queen of the South

playing on the tv, in the background, I made a list of things I really had to get done today.

The plan is to use the access keys from the ID box to go to the vaults this morning, so I can figure out what items I can tick off the list from them. From what I can understand, each bloodline holds a vault with items in them relating to their skill sets.

I have no idea what to expect.

I want to try and find the gym in this building too. Thomas mentioned it on Saturday morning, while escorting me to my room, so I can try and squeeze in a session. Then I can meet Red and venture into the center of campus. I also made a list of questions I could ask her, but I'll play that by ear.

Making sure I have the key cards, I lock up and make my way over. They're on the other side of the main hall. I saw the outer building yesterday, but I'm guessing there is more than meets the eye there, as it was smaller than you'd expect.

I'm out early, it's barely nine, so there isn't really anyone around. The odd student but mainly maintenance staff, none of which make eye contact, strange.

I decide to take the path that leads me in the vaults'

direction, instead of the long way like yesterday around the edge of the property.

When I arrive at the vaults there's a security guard outside, who actually body scans me with his wand. What did he expect me to bring with me? Then he proceeds to check all my access key cards before he lets me inside.

Only for me to step foot inside and another security guard go through the same measures. What did they expect me to achieve in the space of five steps? Once I've met all their requirements, I'm then required to have my photo taken and fingerprints added on to the files for each vault. My God, I wish I hadn't bothered, but there's no use turning around now.

I'm led through to a room that holds a single elevator, nothing else.

"The Hindman vault is on the fourth floor, then you'll need to head down to the seventh floor for the other two vaults," grumbles the security guard.

I'm stunned he can hold a full sentence, everything has been gruff, single word orders. Nodding, I head for the elevator, with the guard following behind me. It feels like a luxury hotel's elevator, all dark wood and golden fittings. Just with high tech scanners to set it in motion instead of all the fancy buttons.

Deciding to start with my mother's family vault, we get out on the fourth floor, and there are doors everywhere. I'm hoping the security guard is here to show me where to go otherwise I'm going to be here all day.

Leading me to the left, we walk for a few minutes when he stops at a door with Hindman carved into the wood. He steps back giving me space and I use the key card to open the door. I don't know what I expected, but it is in no way as exciting as I thought it might have been. There are dozens of filing cabinets running around the edge of the room and two tables in the middle. Walking to the center I see there are microchips, USB's, recording devices, and solid gold blocks.

A little stunned, I walk over to the nearest filing cabinet to peer inside, it's full of hundreds of files all with different names on them. Checking the next cabinet, it's exactly the same. Seems these are all the people who have been affected by Hindman, be it infiltration or corruption, and here sit's Hindman's leverage. Not seeing anything else in here that stands out, I take a USB and microchip seeing as they're on my B.I.C.E list. I don't bother with the recording devices. I have no idea who would have access to the information taken or if someone else can activate it remotely. I have my own devices already. One's I know are safe and only I can access.

Heading out of the room the guard takes the hint and we are heading back to the elevator for the next two vaults. Once we are on the seventh floor the security guard asks, "Gibbs or Steele first?"

I consider this for a minute and opt to hold my father off for a little longer.

"Gibbs," is all I offer in a way of reply.

A nod and we're off to the left, the doors here aren't nearly as close to each other as they were on the other floor, but we don't go too far. I open the door, not really sure what to prepare for, even in the short time I was aware of this place on the ride over here, Rafe didn't mention it at all. I feel like I'm trespassing, as the door swings open into what can only be described as an armory. There are guns of any kind possible to my right, from small pistols to a fucking missile launcher in the far corner.

To the left there are an array of blades, including numerous samurai katana swords, long swords, and even daggers all hanging on the wall. Straight on seems to be a working station for all the weapons stored here, while there is nothing in the center, almost like it's a practice space. Turning, I see the memorabilia on the door wall, for what seems like many generations of the Gibbs bloodline. Walking closer to what seems the newer section, I spot Rafe instantly in numerous frames, never smiling and always with some form of weapon, but mainly a sniper rifle. Well at least he was honest about the gun he used.

Needing to take personal items to the weapon classes, I opt to grab a katana and short daggers as Rafe has shown me how to use them before.

Looking towards the guns, an assault rifle screams for my attention, and I can't seem to say no to it. Grabbing a pistol as well, I leave the next best option of a shotgun behind. At least I know what's here if I need it. The main challenge right now is not getting worked up by the pile of weapons growing in front of me. Finding a holdall, I zip it up and make quick work of getting out of here.

I'm not afraid to use these weapons to defend myself. To survive. But the fact that this seems to be encouraged just blows my mind.

The guard walks me straight to the final doors on the other end of the elevator. My heart is pounding, it hasn't helped being amongst all the weapons a minute ago, but deep down, this is going to open a can of worms in my head about my father. Truthfully, I'll never be ready for this.

Gaining entry, I slowly step in, but I can't bring myself to look up from the floor. Fuck Luna, get a grip. I close my eyes and work to steady my breathing, my emotions are heightened. I can't deal with it. Shit. I hate getting this worked up and not being able to control my emotions. I've shut a lid on anything relating to my dad for a long time, so I could get on with my life.

Rafe had me talk to someone when I was younger. It only made me worse.

I loved him more than anyone else in the world, but seeing him die like he did absolutely destroyed me. Fuck, I'm thinking too much about this again, so I push to clear my mind and find my center. It's hard, really hard right now, especially knowing I'm somewhere he has been and even though I'm not looking around, it makes me feel close to him.

Feeling more prepared and focused again, I glance around to find a mixture of the previous two rooms. There are a lot of filing cabinets lining the back wall, the left side is home to a range of weapons, but nowhere near the amount in the previous vault. Then the right wall is filled with random safes, locks, and devices. It looks as though they're either practice facilities or prized possessions, but who knows.

The door wall is lined with diamonds, gems, and pearls. You name a piece of jewelry and it's definitely here, probably tenfold there's so much of it. Rubies, diamonds, sapphire's, it's all here and my body is itching to grab all the shiny objects.

In the center there are a few files stacked up, and little tech devices dotted around, but the thing that catches my eye the most is the large holdall with my name stitched in the fabric.

I gently trace the embroidery, and my fingers tremble at the feel of the material under my tips. It's easy to tell the bag is already filled. I see the edge of an envelope poking out of the top, and tears prick my eyes when I see it, 'Meu Tesouro' – *My treasured one.*

Two small words that I can't push to the back of my mind like the rest of my memories. As I reach for the envelope, a sob breaks free and I jump back from the bag like it's on fire. What is this place doing to me? Being here isn't a good idea. Do I mean this room or the Academy overall? Overall, definitely overall.

I've never been on such an emotional rollercoaster before and this place is just bringing it all out and leaving me disorientated.

No more.

No fucking more.

I am strong and I am more than this. I steel my back, roughly swipe my face, and grab the bag heading straight out of the vault and to the elevator, not even waiting for the guard.

As soon as I step out of the building with my two holdalls, I'm power stomping back to my room, everything passing in a blur. Unsure of how much time has passed since my emotions are causing havoc in my head.

I need to head for the gym, channel my emotions in the only way I know how.

Getting to my room, I hide the holdalls in the dresser area as quickly as I can, to get away from them as quickly as possible. They're emotionally offending me and I can't take anymore. I check the time, nearly lunch. I've got two hours until I'm due to meet Red. I quickly change into a sports bra and tight training shorts, grab my gym bag and my phone, and head downstairs.

As I walk down the stairs I browse through the notifications on my phone, more calls and texts from Rafe, Jake, and West. Out of the three, right now I'd probably speak to West the most, but we aren't close enough for me to unload on him about all this.

Where do I even begin to explain the last 72 hours?

I can't call Jake, he would take it the wrong way. I don't need the emotional drain of him being overbearing or thinking he means more to me than he does. That just leaves Rafe and he can fuck all the way off, he's on my shit list for the foreseeable.

Red? I guess, but I can't trust her yet. As much as my gut tells me she's wholesome and different, I just don't know her enough.

Feeling a little more deflated I throw my phone in my bag, like it's the phone's fault that I'm dealing with all these issues at the moment. As I go to push the door open, it's opened from the other side.

My hand is raised mere inches from a solid chest, very nicely on display. Olive skin and ripped abs have me drawn to the sexiest 'V' I have ever laid my eyes on. I slowly lift my gaze, unable to stop myself from committing each groove of him to memory. Short brown hair, stunning blue eyes and a square jaw have me speechless. There's a small beauty spot just below his left eye and I need to lick it.

Before I start to drool all over him, I shut my mouth and meet his gaze only to find fury looking back at me.

"Oh good, Princess finally shows her fucking face. Get in here, you've got questions to answer," he says.

Who the hell is this guy?

Before I can even ask, "Did I fucking stutter? Move. Now."

Oh honey, not today, really not today.

"Fuck you, asshole," I bark, angry as hell.

Ready for him to start yelling, I throw my bag down and meet his stare. Damn, a face that good should not look so sinister when grinning, wait ...

Why the fuck is he grinning?

Roman

This girl definitely doesn't know who I am or what I'm capable of. If she did, I wouldn't be listening to her smart mouth right now. She'd fall in line just like all the others, and either bow at my feet or avoid me all together. I can't help but grin with the thought of making her regret standing up to me. It rarely happens these days, seeing as no one has the balls.

Well, except my tight group of friends, they know the real me, not the me I have to be to the rest of the criminal world. This world is all about games and the roles we are expected to play on a daily basis, then comes the violence and the terror.

I spoke to Kai earlier this morning and he promised me this girl's file by this evening, so we won't walk into classes unprepared. When I first saw her walking in here, I couldn't take my eyes off of her face, her green eyes captivating.

But I had to stay focused. I thought I would be able to grill her for answers and she'd give them to me out of fear. Seems I was wrong based on the scowl on her face. Although there is a touch of confusion there too, probably because of the wicked grin I can't wipe from my face.

Good.

I'm glad I've caught her off guard a little.

"Well, Princess, I've already fucked this morning, but if you wanna jump on too I'm sure we can figure it out."

The disgust on her face is instant, but better than that, she doesn't know how to respond. I know she didn't mean literal fucking, but I can't seem to help myself.

I'm definitely making the situation worse. She closes her eyes for the briefest moment and just like that all the emotion is wiped from her face.

Like all of it.

She's not mad, upset, angry, embarrassed, or even irritated. How did she do that so quickly? Her green eyes are suddenly reflective pits of nothingness, like she just made it all go away. Fuck. We all mask our true feelings around here. It's an important part of our world, but I have never seen it shutter so quickly like that, never, and I'm familiar with many people.

If you found Ice Queen in the dictionary right now, this is what she would look like. I don't know where to lead my questions now. I expected to rile her up a bit, not this, but before I can figure anything out she's talking.

"You're the guy from yesterday morning, right? The one I didn't see in the crowd, but who chimed in on the girl's tirade?"

Her tone of voice is flat, no life to it. Where had the feisty girl from just moments ago gone? I want her back. I don't know why, but it feels like it matters right now.

"Where have you gone?" I cautiously say, maintaining eye contact, but not even a blink from her.

"I have no idea what you're talking about, but it seems you have an issue with me being here, like others apparently. Right now, I truly need you to fuck off so I can work out my stress, okay? I'm asking politely, and by all means feel free to collar me later today or preferably never, but right now isn't a good time for me, thanks." I take a deep breath and release a sigh.

Nodding her head, she picks her bag back up and continues further into the gym, breezing right past me.

What. The. Actual. Fuck?

I'm still standing here like a fucking idiot trying to play catch up to what just happened. Obviously I only let her past because of her shift in emotions, it just caught me off guard a little. Internally, I'm slapping my face and pulling myself out of whatever funk this is.

When I finally remember what I dragged her in here for, I see her at the punching bag beside the sparring ring in the center. In the time it's taken me to gather myself she's already taped up and hitting the shit out of the thing.

That's where all the emotion went, pent up inside, and

now she's throwing it all into the bag. This is my usual M.O. To be honest I was down here doing the exact same thing before she arrived, and she's to blame.

Me and the guys constantly come here to de-stress, seeing as the only other person in Ace was Wren, who wouldn't be seen dead in here unless it was a requirement. So we always had the place to ourselves.

I refuse to give her the space she wants right now though, its principle. She needs to understand how it works around here and I do not have enough information on her to be comfortable.

I make my way over, slowly, letting her know I'm the predator and she's the fucking prey.

She's working herself up something crazy right now and the fire in her eyes is hot as sin. She's got me like a moth to a flame and all I want is to feel her burn. The sweat dripping down her chest encourages me to take my time looking over every inch of her body.

In just a sports bra and tight shorts, I can see her usual clothes are hiding a perfect body. Man, all curves of a woman but trim and in shape at the same time. She's not all big tits and ass with a skinny waist like all the other girls are trying to achieve. Princess is completely in proportion from head to toe.

Noticing a tattoo on her arm, my mind wanders to what else she might be hiding. Making my way back up to her face, I fucking stall.

Please dear God, those are not nipple piercings.

Holy shit, they are. This girl is a wet dream.

I'm trying to not pay too much attention, but I can definitely see that one is a ring and the other is a barbell. I've completely lost track of what I stormed over here for, and my dick is rising to the girl in front of me.

I need to get control back. I take a few deep breaths to try and calm myself down. What the fuck is happening? She's playing with my head.

Fuck this, I'm more than what my dick wants. Although I feel like I've never had to work this hard to get it under control before. I storm the rest of the way to the punching bag and hold it still, halting her flow. The storm in her eyes when she looks at me is lethal, but I don't back down.

"Where the hell have you come from?" I demand.

"What the fuck do you want now?" she growls.

She doesn't back down from the aggressive tone I'm using, if anything it makes her stand taller.

She's panting from her workout, but my dick is not

taking it that way.

"Why are you suddenly showing up, out of the blue, at Featherstone Academy?" I push the harshness into my voice.

"What has that got to do with you?" she growls.

"Everything, it has everything to do with me, and the fact that you have to ask that shows how little you know about what you've walked into here."

"It's none of your fucking business unless I want it to be your fucking business. No ego or hierarchy is gonna tell me otherwise, now back off."

With that she makes to walk past me, but I grab her arm and spin her to face me.

"Listen here, little girl, I'll find out what I want to know but you need to fall in line if you expect to live past your first day here," I growl.

I refuse to tell her I know she's a fucking con artist, because there is no way this is the actual Luna Steele. Not after what happened all those years ago.

The look in her eyes tells me she knows I want her anger and fire but refuses to rise to my challenge.

She places her hand gently on my pec, over my heritage ink, and the electricity I feel has me barely holding in a hiss. She leans in close, her lips near to mine.

"No man will ever tell me what I can or cannot do. Proceed to come at me, I don't give a shit, but you don't know me, like I don't know you, and a threat against my life will not end in your favor," she whispers, but it's not a secret, it's a goddamn fact.

With that she pushes against my chest, grabs her bag, and saunters out of here like she doesn't have a care in the world. I don't know what's just happened, but I do know I didn't win.

The real loser here is my dick, it's hard as steel after that little performance.

MY BLOODLINE

NINE

Luna

What an asshole.

I don't know who that guy thought he was, but I sure as shit won't be falling in line. Why are the hot ones always jerks? I wasn't sticking around, the argument wouldn't have led anywhere. We'd have just been going round in circles.

I quickly changed, and now I'm waiting outside of Ace for Red. There are a few people sitting around, but no one is really paying any attention to me.

I'm suddenly wrapped in someone's arms, completely caught off guard. Before I can get into defensive mode,

Red jumps back with a guilty look on her face.

"I'm sorry. Too far, I'll step back now. I was just excited for today is all," she rambles.

She's lucky I didn't hurt her. I check myself over, making sure she didn't do that to place anything on me. I come up clean which has me releasing a sigh of relief.

"Personal space, Red, okay? I could have hit you."

I try to keep my voice firm, but the guilt in her eyes makes my voice a lot softer than I wanted. My God, is this what it's like to have a female friend? I don't know if I'm ready for this.

Glancing over, I hope it's coincidental that we are both wearing denim cut-off shorts and a vest top. At least my top is white and hers is pink. Well and the fact that she's all freshly curled hair and girly sandals. While my hair is in a standard ponytail and I'm wearing my favorite combat boots. Similar outfits but complete opposite ends of the bar.

"Let's go, before you change your mind because you're stuck with me whether you like it or not."

With that she loops her arm through mine and begins to drag me along.

How does she always get me to let my guard down like

this? It blows my mind. It's the whole sunshine vibe she's got going on, and I'd rather be basking in her sun than dealing with that asshole from earlier.

Seems I'd be wise to choose my battles carefully, but he was just a prick. Sadly, a body as hot as that obviously belongs to a jackass. He had my nipples screaming to be touched and my core throbbing for attention. If he'd not been so fucking overbearing and in my face I'd have definitely followed my body's idea. Completely unfazed by the fact he may have been with someone else this morning, but here I am, left unsatisfied.

"So, what's on our to do list then?" Red asks, breaking my train of thought.

"Well, I need a new laptop and a few books for certain classes. That's it really, and coffee, lots of coffee and cake." I smile.

I can't help it, her smile is infectious.

"That's all doable. Do you wanna grab coffee first, then when we've finished getting your things we could get some food?"

I don't miss the hope in her voice and find myself nodding in agreement. She squeals, literally squeals, and I don't know how she manages it with her arm linked through mine, but she's clapping too while doing a little skip.

She drags me along to the center of campus where everything is, and I'm surprised by the layout. There is a full row of shops, maybe twenty in total, ranging from designer brand clothing stores to top of the range electronic outlets. All the buildings are quite small, almost quaint, and the cobbled pathway makes me feel as though I've left the country.

Her hands are going in all directions, as she points things out to me on our way to the coffee shop.

There is a small square of restaurants and cafes with the same vibe, with a small intricate fountain in the center. From Italian restaurants to a Starbucks.

A large building sticks out, which Red said is the main campus cafeteria. It's all glass walls and steel panels, looking completely out of place, too modern amongst the rest.

Red doesn't let go of my arm. I can see her brain working overtime, and I know when we do eventually sit down she's going to bombard me with her own questions, before I have a chance to ask her any of mine.

She's happy to get coffees to go, although her face

scrunchies when I just have a straight black coffee, compared to her Mocha Cookie Crumble Frappuccino.

Cold coffee, who even does that?

Me, apparently. Seeing as I've promised to try one after classes finish tomorrow.

Heading into the electronic store, I picked up a new laptop easy enough, there were limited options but all top of the line. I have my own laptop back in my room, but it's not the kind of thing I can be casually strolling around campus with.

Not when I have access to the black market and the dark web on there. Featherstone knows, but if someone managed to get their hands on it I'd be screwed. I don't know who actually stands behind the Featherstone name either, so I don't fully know who's aware of my extracurricular activities.

The bookstore is the next stop, and after grabbing far too many books for my liking, we are finished. Thank God.

We stroll through the cobbled street, making our way to get food when I see the look on Red's face and it's blatant that she's desperate to say something.

"Go on, spit it out."

She's got the 'dear in the headlights' look.

"Well, erm, I was just wondering if you read the manual fully? I mean you are beautiful, so beautiful as you are. It's just, they can be strict with the rules, and as your best friend it is my duty to help. I don't want you to have issues tomorrow on your first official day, not when I can make sure we avoid any unnecessary confrontations. It's not like you need it. Not at all, but I don't make the rules and ..."

"Red, just get to the freaking point," I interrupt, waving my hand at her.

"Oh, sorry, it's just that make-up is mandatory," she rushes, and it takes me a second to process.

Oh, thank God, she had me stressing with all her rambling then.

"Don't worry I saw, and my mother took the liberty of filling my room with half a make-up store too, so no need to stress. I wear it when I need or want to, it just isn't all that often, mainly because I spend so much time training and it just sweats off."

I never mention how much I train. There I go again, just tell her your life story now, get it out of the way, I scold myself.

"Oh good, I just wanted to make sure in case you needed to buy anything here. Although, make sure you carry some make-up supplies around with you, because they expect it to be reapplied after physical activity," she advises.

Great, just what I wanted. At least she's given me a heads up, because I definitely wouldn't have carted it around with me otherwise.

"It's fine, Red, don't worry about it. Are you ready to eat?" I ask.

"How does Italian sound?" It's the most confident she's been all day.

With just a simple question, I can see she's not trying to please me or tip toe around me, and it makes me smile.

"It sounds like the way to my heart, Red. Lead the way," I respond.

Fuck she's trouble, pity I'm not into women cos she's got me wrapped round her finger. If anyone saw me from back home they wouldn't believe their eyes.

Red leads me to an authentic little Italian restaurant instead of the main eatery, and we decide to sit on the patio outside with the sun still on us. Large red, white, and green canopies shade us as we sit at the classic wrought iron table and chairs, looking out onto the square.

She's grinning ridiculously, more than usual if that's possible, and it has me curious.

"What's got you grinning so wide?" I ask, and that just makes her giggle.

"You didn't deny I was your best friend, and it's too late for you to argue it now."

She sticks her tongue out and picks up the menu attempting to end the conversation there. I'm trying not to laugh at her antics but it's hard and she knows it. I don't know how to argue with her statement, so I don't answer at all which just makes her grin more.

The waiter approaches, he looks to be around our age, does he go to school here too? I don't ask as it seems rude to intrude. So we place our orders, an iced tea each, and she orders a pepperoni pizza while I order spaghetti carbonara, my favorite.

Once we're alone again I try to categorize the questions I have, about this place, about her, about everything.

"So, how did you end up here, Red?" I start, wanting to know more about her first.

"Well when I was 14, my dad sat me down and told me I wasn't going to school with all my friends anymore. I was to attend Featherstone High. He told me the week before I was due to start, and just like that I was thrust out of my comfort zone and thrown into a world I have no clue about," she says, running a hand through her hair, her eyes downcast.

"My dad's not a major part of the underworld, but he's made technology and devices for Featherstone. He says it's so I can have the best education, and nothing is expected of me, but honestly, I think they forced me here. To hold me over him because I learned a lot at Featherstone High, about this world and the people in it, and I don't like it. They placed me in Diamond as a goodwill gesture, I guess. But I'm not a true bloodline, which means nobody wants anything to do with me because my name does nothing for their status." She sighs.

God that's a lot. A lot for her to say and a lot for her to deal with, especially because it's clear she doesn't hold venom in her blood like the others, like me.

"That must have been tough for you."

I don't apologize for her circumstances. It's not my fault, but I feel the need to acknowledge her feelings.

"Yeah, it was. Mostly because it was a boarding school, I've already spent four years stuck with these people, and now I've got another. Can I be honest with you?"

The sadness in her voice has me nodding my head instantly.

"I'm petrified, Luna. Featherstone High was just that, a high school with a standard education plan, but here? Here, I'm expected to learn how to fight, and I'm forced to take L.F.G, too. I'm thankful I was able to take Science, it's my dream, and business isn't too bad. Then they force us to take History, learning their past, and dragging us into their fold," she says, misery floating in every word.

I glance around the square, taking in a few people wandering around, as I consider her words. I made sure to take the seat in the corner so I could see all our vantage points, but nothing is out of the ordinary. Rafe's lessons stay with me, even now, making sure I can see all of my surroundings.

"Have you any experience with combat?"

She just shakes her head, looking down at her hands.

"None at all, not even a self-defense class?"

She shakes her head again, fuck.

"What about the others here?" I ask, leaning in closer.

She shrugs. "There were fights all the time at Featherstone High, and for some it's their bloodline, so it'll only get worse here. Especially for those with access to their family vaults." She sounds defeated.

Holy shit, she's left herself at a disadvantage. I was fine with the combat classes, but that's because I enjoy it. For someone with no experience, it's going to be a shock for sure.

"Okay, well we will start training you then. I'll help you and we can use the gym at Ace for privacy. I know it might not be something you want to do, but it's important we can get you to defend yourself."

I'm not messing around with this. I reach out and squeeze her hand in reassurance.

"Thank you, Luna, I can't tell you how much that means to me," she says softly.

I nod. "We will need to compare timetables and figure out a plan after we've eaten."

She smiles in response.

"What's L.F.G?" I ask.

"Oh, it stands for Laundering, Fraud, and Gambling." She grimaces.

What the fuck, how are there even classes on that? That's worse than B.I.C.E, but I don't say that. I can tell she's struggling enough.

"Well, that'll be an experience I'm sure." I grin, hoping

to lighten the mood, and it does make her smile at least.

This whole chat is completely off course. She has me wanting to help her. I don't help anyone, and I certainly don't care for others, yet here I am. My gut loves her and that apparently means I now have someone else to worry about.

The food thankfully arrives, and we begin eating in comfortable silence, watching the square around us.

"So, Red, is there anything important I need to know?" I ask, once I've finished eating one of the best carbonaras in existence.

"What do you know already?"

I shrug, "Honestly? Very little. I didn't know this was a thing until I was being dragged here."

I don't miss the surprise on her face, but then her brain is working overtime trying to gather what information she thinks I may find useful.

"Okay. Okay, so, this whole place is run on hierarchy. The six dorms, even the way the rooms are allocated are based on it. Jokers are at the bottom and Aces are at the top. That stands in the whole underworld too, they have you learn your place at Featherstone. That way no-one steps out of line and causes chaos."

She barely catches a breath, taking a sip of her drink and carrying on.

"Everyone fears those in Ace. Roman Rivera, Parker, Kai Fuse, Oscar O'Shay and Wren Dietrichson. You had the pleasure of meeting Wren on Saturday and Oscar was the one with your ID box. I don't know if you've crossed any paths since, but they say jump, and everyone asks how high. Now, you're an Ace based on bloodline, but with you also being a new face I don't know where you will stand to be honest. If anybody in Ace shows further conflict with you, after the other day, it's slim they'll side with you. It'll likely put a larger target on your back," she cringes.

The waiter interrupts us as he collects our dishes and leaves us the dessert menu.

Like I'll be upset to be a lone ranger, that's all I've ever been. I say as much, and she simply shakes her head.

"You can't be a lone ranger now you have a best friend, Luna."

She lightens the mood and makes me smile. It's clear we are both out of our depth at Featherstone, just in different ways. With neither of us actually wanting to be here.

"Did anyone at the High school decide they didn't want to be there, and just left?"

Her face instantly pales, and she shakes her head frantically.

"No, Luna, never. You either leave as part of Featherstone in some way or in a body bag. I've seen too many of those in the past four years, Luna. You play by their rules or you die, there's no in between." Fear etched in her voice.

I don't know how to get her to tell me more without her breaking down, but it doesn't matter anyway, as a guy scrapes a chair over to us and takes a seat at our table with the chair backwards.

"Now, this is a three way I can get behind."

He meets my eyes and grins.

"I didn't get a chance to introduce myself properly the other day. I'm Oscar, but you can call me whatever you want, baby."

MY BLOODLINE

TEN
Oscar

Finally, man, I've been keeping my eyes peeled for this girl everywhere since Saturday morning with no luck until now. If you'd have told me a week ago I'd be hot for a girl with no make-up on, wearing combat boots with shorts I'd have told you to fuck off. When she pushed Wren in the water so casually it got my dicks attention and I haven't stopped jerking off to her since.

I just want to jerk in her now, although she doesn't look impressed with my arrival.

What's that about?

Everybody loves me, especially the ladies. She's

clearly not heard about my impressive features and refined skills yet.

"Can I help you?" she asks me shortly.

"What's your name, baby? I only managed to catch your bloodlines the other day." I counter, but she just rolls her eyes.

I can sense that she wants to tell me to fuck off. It's a foreign feeling for me, but it only seems to make me more determined for a change. Usually if you're not an easy target, you're not a target at all. She must be able to see it in my face that I'm not ready to give up just yet and relents.

"Luna. Now can I help you or are you leaving?"

Hmm feisty. I like it. My cock definitely does. Luna, I like the sound of that in my head.

I can't help but swipe my tongue over my bottom lip as I take her in. Pink pouty lips, emerald green eyes, and soft brown hair, long enough for me to wrap around my fist a time or too.

There it is. I saw it. That little sparkle in her eye, only for a moment, but it was there. She likes what she sees, now for me to figure out how to get her up to my speed.

"Baby, I can't leave yet. I don't know enough about

you. I practically know nothing." I purr, but like a lion because I'm a beast.

She glances away from me and looks at her friend raising an eyebrow. How is she not putty in my hands right now? My purr always lures them in without fail. A giggle to my right has me glancing at her friend, is she laughing?

At me?

I look back to my girl of the hour and she's smirking.

"Okay, party boy, you're hot, I'm not gonna lie, but your usual charms mean nothing here. So it's best if you run along, nice to meet you though."

She relaxes back in her chair and gives me a half smile.

What does that even mean? I sweep a hand through my hair, confused with her reaction.

Damn right I'm hot.

I know I am. My looks and my charm are what get me things. Fuck, I sound like a girl, but nobody says no to Oscar O'Shay.

Glancing at her friend again, I recognize her from Featherstone High. I couldn't guess her name, although I'm quite sure she's in Diamond. At least I haven't slept with her, that helps my chances with Luna.

"Luna, baby, I want us to be closer. How about you

let me walk you back? We're heading the same direction anyway."

Fuck her name really does sound good playing on my tongue, I give her my signature grin and ... she just sighs.

"Oscar, right?" she asks, and I nod, as she leans in to whisper in my ear.

"Oscar, you are most definitely my type, but right now isn't a good time for me. I'm trying to have a private conversation, I'm sure you get it. It's just not the best idea for me to lead with my pussy right now."

Oh my days, my heart is beating uncontrollably at her closeness, her voice is intoxicating this close up. She gently places her hand on my thigh. I'm wearing shorts so the skin on skin contact burns me up.

"I like no strings, Oscar, and when the time is right I'm sure you'll be around. But for future reference, don't lead with your mouth. I'm not your baby. You are hot as sin but as soon as you open your mouth it goes to shit," she says with a grin.

With that she stands and grabs her bags as her friend is paying the bill. I was so lost in Luna I didn't even notice her leave the table, and then they're sauntering off, like they haven't just left me sitting here.

Me.

Oscar O'Shay.

An Ace. What the fuck?

I storm my way back to Ace block, taking the shortcut through the trees instead of the path, making sure I don't bump into her again while I feel this confusion. She's already got me acting like a horny virgin and I'm the king of sex.

I head straight for the gym praying my boys are there, I need to vent. Fuck, I'm growing a vagina over all this.

Slamming the door into the gym, both Rome and Parker look up immediately.

"Fuck sake, Oscar," Roman grumbles.

I start to pace in front of the weights where they're training, unable to keep still or sit down.

"You ok, Oscar?" asks Parker, always the caring one.

If it was just Roman here he'd leave me to fester.

"I don't know, Parker, I don't think I am," I respond, but I don't slow my pacing.

"Is anything different about me? I feel the same but am I missing something? Check me over Parker."

He looks at me funny then looks at Rome, who also looks at me confused.

"What the fucks wrong, Oscar? I haven't got time for this." Rome sighs, wiping his face with his towel.

Why is everyone sighing at me today?

"I think I just got turned down, man," I mumble.

"What the fuck are you talking about?" Rome groans.

"I'm talking about the fact that I just approached a girl, laid on the charm, gave her my grin and my full watt purr, and ... well nothing, nothing at all. My dicks weeping here guys, he really wanted in that." I can't help but whine.

They're silent, staring at me like I've grown another head or something. Then Roman bursts out laughing, like full belly laughing, and he braces himself on his thighs to contain himself. Bastard, what the fucks he laughing at? This is serious. I glance to Parker for help, and he's biting his bottom lip trying to hold himself back from joining Rome in hysterics.

"It's not funny guys, I'm serious. It works every time like a charm, and she brushed me off like I was a nobody. Well she did admit I was her type, but then told me to keep my mouth shut, because it ruins what I have going for me. I'm lost here guys, what's wrong with my mouth? I'm genuinely at a loss here guys."

This just makes Rome laugh harder, and Parker fucking

joins him.

My hands are clenched at my sides as I stare them down. Anyone else at this school would have shit themselves at the sight, but it takes these assholes forever to fucking calm down.

"You done?" I growl.

"Yeah, calm your shit Oscar. So you got turned down? It does happen, well not to me but I've heard it does, get over it. Go and use your ... *purr* on someone else," Rome chuckles.

"Fuck you guys, I wouldn't be riled up if it was that easy. I just know she's gonna have the sweetest pussy, man. I mean she barely put her hand on my thigh, near the fucking knee I might add, and I could have jizzed in my pants right then," I state.

It's the God's honest truth and I'm not ashamed of it.

"Man, calm yourself down, go run some circuits, take a cold shower, or take care of yourself. I don't care, but stop acting like a bitch." He grins, as he takes a seat at the weight bench, seemingly done with me.

"Fuck you, Rome. I've been jerking off to her for days and it isn't enough. Parker, help a guy out, I need some advice here," I beg, whipping around to focus on him, hopeful he will be gentler with me, but Parker looks helpless.

"Err, I'm sorry Oscar, nothing I say is going to make you get the pussy, bud. I thought you always said you were the king and I needed to take lessons from you? Now I'm confused," he splutters.

I've clearly tripped a wire in his brain. They're no use to me at all.

"Fuck you, guys," I yell, and storm out of the gym heading straight for my room because my cock needs some attention. At least I have a name to scream in the shower now.

Luna.

MY BLOODLINE

ELEVEN

Luna

Looking at my reflection in the dressing table mirror, I hardly recognize myself. Using a little hairspray, I add extra volume to my standard ponytail, seeing as I've had to apply heavier make-up, to follow their stupid guidelines.

I read the handbook that was in the ID box a few times, to make sure I'd complied with all the make-up do's and don'ts Featherstone had blessed me with. I'm just glad it doesn't force us all to go for the caked-on cement look Wren is rocking. Going with my foundation, a little bronzer and blusher, and a lick of mascara. I'm ready. No full eye make-up or lipstick is required, so I've skipped that, just using a little lip gloss.

The fact that this is a requirement at all disgusts the feminist in me, but it also gives me an insight into where women stand in their world.

Standing from the dresser, I look over my uniform in front of my floor length mirror, it's more of a tailored business suit that flaunts all the goods.

A pearl white blouse without the top three buttons, purposely puts my cleavage on display. My black blazer is edged in gold embroidery and has a blood red emblem on the left breast. The emblem matches the red logo that was on the guys hoodies from Friday night, when I was dragged to this hellhole, with F.A. etched into it in gold. A matching black skirt sits just above my knees hugging my hips, with a dangerously high slit up the back. The whole ensemble is finished off with some four-inch heels with red soles.

How the fuck am I supposed to wear these all day?

I'm not materialistic, but Red promised me it would be noticed if my shoes and bag were basic. I guess my mother's good for something with the amount of designer items in my dresser.

As much as this is not a true form of me, I can already

feel that a lot is based on appearances here. So for now, I'll join the masses and play along.

Red mentioned yesterday that you are taken over to the lecture halls, so I don't have to worry about walking there in these heels. It does mean I have to be subjected to the assholes from Ace though.

Although my run in with Oscar yesterday tipped me over the edge, he really is hot as sin.

He had me touching myself as soon as I got back to my room. I had to picture him with his mouth shut, and I couldn't help but let my brain wander to the guy from the gym too. Between them, I had myself worked up and coming too quickly.

I can tell Oscar's a man whore, but that doesn't faze me. Sex is just that, I don't need emotions or feelings. I just need satisfaction and I can tell he can give me that. Just when I'm more comfortable here, if that ever happens, and needing more than what I can give myself.

Doing a quick run through, I check I have everything I need for today's classes. I don't need much for Tech or Business, but I have Weaponry this afternoon, so I've organized a small cabin suitcase for my guns and blades.

My timetable also had a small notice advising we'd

be given storage at each class, so in future we won't need to cart everything with us. Hopefully, Weaponry has good enough security for me to be comfortable leaving my new belongings, otherwise I'll just bring them back with me.

Hearing my phone chime, I know it's Red and it's time to move. Still refusing to use the lift, I trudge down the staircase. Which in these heels, is proving difficult, as I stumble on the first flight of steps straight away.

"Give me fucking strength," I say, trying to regain my balance. My handbag and cabin case are only making it worse.

Hitting the lobby, there's a group chatting amongst themselves, three girls and four guys. Everyone is lounging on the black leather sofas. The guys include Oscar and the asshole from the gym, as well as two others I haven't seen before.

Fuck me though, is being hot a requirement to attend this school? These guys could make one hell of a Magic Mike setup.

The other girls with Wren must be her puppets, and I'm not in the mood to deal with them.

I have a clear path straight to the exit where I can see Red waiting on the other side of the glass doors. I pop a pair of aviators on, steel my back and walk through there like I own this shit, handbag on my shoulder and pulling the case behind me.

My heels click along the marble flooring and all conversations stop. I can sense their eyes on me, but I don't feel anyone move. I keep walking, not missing a beat. I'm just past them when I hear their conversation pick up.

"Fucking bitch," says a girl, it's not Wren though.

"She could be my bitch whenever she wants."

That comes from Oscar and I hear a smack as if someone just hit him on the head.

"You're going to get what's coming to you, whore, just you wait," shouts Wren.

I don't respond, but I can't help but give her the finger with my free hand over my head. I don't hear any response because I'm already outside walking to Red.

"Hey Luna, you ready?" she asks, rubbing her arms nervously.

"As I'll ever be I guess, you?"

She shrugs her shoulders, but then remembers what I said yesterday.

"You gotta fake it till you make it, Red. Confidence at all times, understood?"

With that she stands tall, relaxes her shoulders, and breathes. Looking to me for confirmation, and I just grin at her.

"Are you ready for later?" I ask.

We compared timetables and we don't have any free periods at the same time. So we have agreed to train on Tuesdays, Fridays, and Sundays. I'll still train everyday but that'd be too much for Red, and as much as she needs to catch up, I don't want to push her too hard, too fast.

She smiles. "Yeah, it's my free period beforehand, so I'll grab the coffee, just let me know when you get out."

I nod and she continues, "You want to get yourself in a car and hope Wren isn't the second passenger?" I grimace, but nod in agreement.

I wish I could jump in the SUV with her, but each block must travel together, no mingling. I can see at the Joker Block there's two coaches, the higher up the chain you get the smaller and more comfortable the vehicle. Red gets a black SUV with three other students and I get a chauffeur driven car with one other passenger, and seeing as there are six of us in Ace, there's no chance of riding solo.

Approaching the first car, I notice it's a Rolls Royce, how ridiculous. I mean its fucking beautiful and the petrol head in me is excited, but it's completely unnecessary.

I'm totally fangirling inside though, I know this baby has a twin turbocharged V12 engine reaching 100 kilometers per hour in 5.3 seconds, and the trims on this thing, damn. Man, I need to see the inside. Walking to the trunk the driver opens it to reveal two separate locked compartments and hands me a padlock and key.

Opening the left compartment, I see that there is a decent amount of space in there, clearly for my weapons or whatever I feel is important enough to be locked away. I place the suitcase in and lock it up, choosing to keep my oversized handbag with my other belongings on me.

Nodding to the driver he leads me round and opens the door for me to enter. I can't help but ask.

"What's your name?"

He looks slightly startled by the fact I'm talking to him.

"Ian, Ian Porter, ma'am" he responds.

"Thank you, Ian," I offer, with a slight smile.

Rafe raised me with manners and respect, no matter what, and the biggest secret to finding yourself on top is befriending the one's deemed 'nobodies'. It's where you can sometimes find your strongest loyalty.

Ian simply smiles in response.

I take a seat and God this is a thing of beauty. Full black leather interior, with the privacy paneling in place, and fitted monitors in the seats in front. I've got leg space for days, and the armrest is open with bottles of water sat waiting. This is my kind of luxury. I'm ready for us to start moving so I can feel how smooth of a drive she is.

I pull my phone out, waiting for whoever gets the short straw to join me so we can get moving. Glancing at my messages, I see Rafe has sent a few more this morning, clearly stressed out with the fact I haven't responded yet.

Rafe: Hey Luna, I know you're mad right now but please spare me a break for five seconds and let me know you're ok. I know that place, those people, and as strong as I know you are, I'm worried.

Sighing, I relent and give a brief response.

Luna: I'm fine.

Within seconds my phone is buzzing again.

Rafe: Oh, thank God. I'm glad you're ok. Try and enjoy your first day, I'm working on what I can, I swear. If you need me at all I'm here.

Rafe: P.S I've arranged for Dot to be shipped to you. Should be there Friday. I'll confirm closer to the time.

Dot? Oh God, I would love nothing more than my motorbike right now. The thought of having freedom, the wind swirling around me, has my heart racing. We're able to leave campus on the weekends, and the prospect of taking her for a spin excites me. Screw all the other shit, my focus is on having my baby here. I'm sure Thomas said there's a garage at Ace when he was walking me to my room, I'll check when I get back.

Suddenly the door opens and one of the guys I haven't met before takes the seat beside me.

I sigh internally, thanking God it's not Wren. I don't need that crazy in here with me. Although there seems to be tension pouring off this guy in waves, and my instincts tell me that it's because of me. Great, I've never met him before, and the extreme discomfort is spoiling my first drive in this hot ride. It's a shame he's not Oscar, at least he seems to like me...well my body.

Looking this guy over, I'm speechless because of how good looking he is. He's not as big as the other two, slimmer, but I can still see the definition around his shoulders. I'd like to see what this guy's hiding under that uniform because he's real eye candy material.

He has Asian heritage in his blood. I can notice it slightly around his eyes, in the chisel of his cheekbones and jawline, and it makes me hotter for him. Jet black hair swept to the side, with his cartilage pierced on his right ear.

I want to lick him.

For fuck sake, Luna, what is wrong with you? I'm not usually so easily attracted to guys, but they make them extra hot here apparently. Not wanting to be caught staring, I glance out of the window and gather myself as the car starts to move.

We've not moved far when the partition rises. I look forward as Ian glances in his rear-view mirror offering a slight shake of his head, letting me know he's not the one controlling it.

That leaves my backseat buddy, and I don't think it's because he wants to get hot and heavy. Shame.

I turn to look him straight in the eyes, letting him see my confidence and complete lack of fear. He stares me down for a few moments, looking for what, I don't know.

"Do you want to explain to me why I'm struggling to find more than the most basic information about you?" he growls, his hands clenched on his knees, tension pulsing off him in waves.

It surprises me that he has it in him. He looks more nerdy than alpha, and as much as he's yelling at me, it's turning me on. I find myself leaning toward him unconsciously.

"I don't know what you mean," I calmly reply, forcing myself to sit up straight.

That does not help the matter.

"I mean, I've searched everywhere, and I mean everywhere, and all I can come up with is a handful of details. Hacking is my game, Sakura. I'm the best, so tell me what you did to erase your records?" He's furious.

I don't think now's the time to ask, but Sakura? What does that mean?

I have no idea what he's talking about, I haven't wiped any of my details. I tell him this and he slams his fist down on the arm rest between us, right next to where my arm is resting, but I don't flinch.

"Don't fucking play with me, it will not end well for you," he grinds through his teeth.

I don't know what he expects me to say, seeing as I'm telling the truth. The venom in his eyes tells me I'm not going anywhere until he has answers. Why is he even trying to investigate my background?

You mister, just lost some of your hotness.

"Look, I don't know you or why the fuck you're trying to look into my background, but I definitely don't owe you shit. I don't know what information you would find either way, because whoever did wipe it, it wasn't me and they didn't tell me either. Now back the fuck off," I growl back at him.

Luckily for me, I feel the car come to a stop and I realize we're outside the academic buildings. With that I swing the car door open, before Ian can even get out of the car, and slam the door behind me. I round the trunk, banging it for Ian to get the hint and open it. He must have a button, because it opens before his door does, and I make quick work of getting my case out of the compartment.

Looking around, I see Red waving and I make straight for her, not willing to glance back.

Great start, fucking fantastic.

Criteria for the males of Ace is to be hot as fuck and a complete dick.

Three out of four confirmed. Ugh.

TWELVE

Luna

Standing with Red, I take in everyone around us. They're all gathered in groups and cliques in the open space between the two academic buildings. Both are the same size with classic brick walls and large stone steps leading up to the entries.

I can feel a lot of eyes on me since I stormed out of the Rolls. They don't know what to make of me and it's clearly unsettling them that I'm not standing with the others from Ace. Red wasn't wrong when she said they rule over everyone, no one dares stand too close to them, but every student here is aware of their presence.

Out of nowhere a bell rings, gaining everyone's attention. Red jumps comically, like a few others, making me chuckle. She tries to give me a stern look, but it just causes a bubble of laughter to burst out of me.

The group of girls next to us are looking our way with wide eyes. I can't tell whether they're scared I'm laughing because I'm crazy, or because they think I'm about to hurt them, but I don't pay them any attention.

Red gives me a small nudge and nods in the direction of the entrance where Barbette Dietrichson stands, at the top of the steps, glaring at me for all to see.

Fantastic.

I don't react, I just continue to stare in her direction, but with my sunglasses on she can't truly know if I'm actually looking.

"Good morning, everyone. Introductions aren't really required. I know you're all well aware of who I am, but for formality's sake, my name is Barbette Dietrichson. I'm the Head here at Featherstone Academy. You may address me as Mrs. Dietrichson."

You may address me? You're not the fucking Queen of England.

Fuck off.

I'm glad my eyes are covered because I can't help but eye roll at her shit.

Sadly, she continues, "I hope you all use this opportunity to the fullest. Featherstone has bred some fine graduates who lead powerful and fulfilling lives once they have graduated. That being said, you are all here for many different reasons, those reasons are your sole focus. Know your place, follow the rules and you will succeed, it's simple really, but not all of you will survive. Hopefully, we'll be able to say you died trying though," she sweetly finishes, with her eye's locked on me. Watching for my reaction to the possibility of death, but she won't get one.

She holds her stare long enough for others around us to follow her line of sight.

She's just painted a target on my back, and she knows it. I can literally feel hundreds of eyes tearing me apart, but I won't back down. Instead, I raise my glasses to the top of my head and continue to stare at her. Letting her see she has my attention, along with the fact that I'm not afraid, and I'm not backing down.

That earns me a sneer as she saunters down the steps, climbing into a nearby car.

I could do with a minute to gather myself, but I won't

get it surrounded by all these people who are still staring at me. I drop my glasses back down to hide my eyes from them all and nod my head in the direction of the entrance, for Red to follow.

She takes the hint and we walk through the sea of people, oozing confidence. I make sure to put extra sass in my hips when I climb the stairs. As fake as it may be, these people don't know that, and they step back giving us space.

As we enter the building Red steps closer.

"What the hell was all that?" she whispers.

"I don't know, she was furious on Saturday when she realized I had a third bloodline, and I hightailed it out of there. This is the first time I've seen her since."

I gave her the short version of how I ended up here on the walk back yesterday, but I didn't mention Dietrichson. She's clearly not happy, and this is all just a mind fuck.

Looking at the sign post, I see that Tech is on the third floor while Science is on the first. Red pulls me towards the elevator and I don't put up a fight. Stepping in, Red takes care of the buttons while I'm trying to piece together anything I may have missed with Barbette, but come up short past the third bloodline.

I'm not taking in my surroundings or the layout of the building. I spot the elevator and that's what I'm focused on. I'm sure it's the same over the top decor as the rest of this place.

Luckily, before anyone else can join us the doors shut, and we're moving. It's spacious in here and it looks bigger because the walls are all mirrored.

I agree to meet Red outside the main doors so we can head to Business together after this. She seems unsure about leaving me alone, but I offer an encouraging smile and she gets out on the first floor. Hopefully, this girl will realize she doesn't need to waste her worry on me, I can handle myself just fine.

Arriving on the third floor, I'm met by a woman with a clipboard. She takes my name, confirming I'm here for Tech and directs me to the far wall, where lockers are lined up. Dragging my case across the hardwood floor I find my name. These are next level, my locker back home didn't come with a touchpad, or a plaque with 'Steele' on it.

Reading the instructions she gave me on a slip of paper, I quickly run through the process of setting up my fingerprint, and store the belongings I don't need until later.

There isn't a lot of space where the lockers are, so I'm

pleasantly surprised by the size of the actual Tech room as I head inside. A board is set up at the door, advising us to wait for our seat assignments. So I hover at the front, taking in the rest of the room.

All the walls are bright white, with a standard blue carpet throughout. There are two separate desk layouts positioned opposite each other. One setup with computers, while the other is bare. Behind the desks are tall benches filled with different electronic devices, some dismantled, and there's even a small freakin' robot.

Crazy. Looks like we aren't working on spreadsheets here then.

People begin to step in around me, and a guy greets us. He's wearing casual jeans and a band t-shirt. Light blonde hair falls past his ears, with giant framed glasses covering his eyes.

"Hi, I'm Derek Griffin, please just call me Derek. I'm your Tech tutor and this is our workspace. I prefer old school seating assignments because I'm classic like that. For the time being I'd like it to run off first names. So, when I call your name in a group of three please take your seats, starting from the front row. This will also be your team when group exercises are required. We'll be on the computer side today, but please take notice of the board, at the beginning of each lesson. If that's not too complicated for you, I'll begin."

He starts to reel off names, and people begin shifting through the small crowd, taking their places. Who knew a class of trainee criminals could listen so well?

"Kai, Luna, and Parker please," he calls.

I don't know anyone else here, so I don't bother to look for who I've been assigned with.

I take the middle seat on the next available table, set my bag down and try to get comfortable. I'd be better without all this shit on and a proper pair of shoes for God's sake.

Shadows on either side of me take a seat. Fuck, whoever is sat on my right smells delicious, a gentle woodsy scent with a slightly sweet accent. I could definitely envelope myself in a shirt from this guy.

Looking in his direction, I stall when I notice it's the last guy from Ace that I haven't met yet. He gives me a small smile and faces forward. Glancing to my left, I can't help the sigh that leaves my lips. There sits my favorite car buddy, with a scowl in place, glaring daggers at me.

For fuck's sake, can't I catch a break for five minutes, please?

What names did the tutor say? Kai and Parker.

Well Parker is my current favorite Ace guy, I can't help but look at him from the side. He has short curly brown hair, and I want to reach out and run my fingers through it. Dark eyebrows frame stunning hazel eyes, but my gaze is frozen on his full lips.

Not only has he got hot nerd vibes going for him, he didn't open his mouth, and the small smile he blessed me with was pure. I admire him for a moment, then prepare for him to be an asshole, just like the rest of them.

That's their new name, Aceholes.

Derek explains to the class that we will be completing an assessment this morning, to understand what we are capable of. With that he turns his back on us, proceeding to play around with the gadgets upfront. Great talk, Sir, thanks ever so much.

I click start and proceed to fill in my personal details to begin the assessment, clicking through I hear a frustrated sigh from my right. Glancing over I see Parker is a little flustered, red in the face and his leg is bouncing.

What has him all worked up? I check Kai but he doesn't

seem to have noticed, so I lean closer to Parker.

"Hey, are you okay?"

I don't know why I'm asking though, it's nothing to do with me. He lifts his head back, looking at the ceiling, and takes another deep breath. I'm about to move back when he turns his gaze to me.

His eyes are captivating, I wouldn't be able to look away even if he was gutting me with a knife. He holds my stare for a moment longer then slowly, he raises his hand to the monitor. I follow what he's trying to show me, but the confusion is clear on my face. He's still on the first page, entering his personal details, I don't understand.

I look back to him, but his head is down and he looks defeated, so I look back at the monitor because I'm clearly missing something.

Scanning over his details again, I pay closer attention. There's a red asterisk next to an answer box which is preventing the assessment from continuing, because he hasn't filled it in. I look to see what details are required and it's for his surname.

Why has he left it blank?

He's clearly not missed it by accident otherwise he wouldn't be so worked up over it, he'd have just filled it in and carried on. It doesn't make any sense.

Pulling away from the screen I look back to Parker, this has really hit him, something so small to me and he looks beaten. He's still looking down, and if he can feel my eyes on him he doesn't react.

I gently place my fingers under his chin and raise his eyes to meet mine. What the fuck am I doing? Get off him Luna and get back to what you were doing.

I don't like how sad he is, and I really can't figure out why I give a shit.

Looking into his eyes, he looks lost. I know that look, that feeling in the depth of your soul, like you don't know where you belong, and you're just sinking further and further into the abyss. Maybe that's what's pulling me towards him, making me want to take it away, because I know what it can do to you.

Keeping my hand under his chin, I lean in a little so I can keep my voice low.

"Talk to me, let me help you."

He's got to make the decision within himself to pull himself back up. He continues to stare at me. I can see he's in there, and he's searching my eyes like he's looking for an answer.

I try to keep my facial expression open, moving my hand round to stroke his cheek and his jawline. Don't fucking ask why, because I don't know, I just know I don't want to stop either.

It seems to have an effect, because his eyes crinkle for a moment, before he tenderly leans into my hand. I don't speak, I just continue to look into his eyes and wait.

I feel locked in place, this moment right here is so raw, so real, so intimate.

It's intoxicating.

I'm freaking out a little, but I can't back away. We wouldn't be any closer right now if we we're having sex.

We're peering at each other's souls.

I shouldn't let him see, I don't let anyone ever see but there is nothing I can do about it.

It's getting too much. Why the hell does it feel like my heart is about to break out of my chest? He must see it on my face that I'm trying to force myself to move away, and that makes him finally talk.

"I don't have a surname," he barely whispers.

Huh?

"How can you not have a surname? Especially in a place like this when it's apparently all we stand for?"

He tentatively lifts his hand and places it over mine on his cheek, like he's afraid what he's about to say will make me move it.

"I have a strong bloodline, but I'm a bastard son, and bastards don't usually attend here. My biological father didn't produce any more children and requires an heir. That's where I come in, but I don't get the name until I prove myself," he says softly.

What the hell? How am I even hearing this right now?

Parker must confuse the frown on my face and he drops his eyes.

"I'm not frowning at you, Parker, it's your circumstances that are making me mad," I say, encouraging him to look back up, and it works.

For some crazy reason I want to make this all better for him. He's worse than Red, all under my skin without even trying.

"You want my surname? I'm here on three bloodlines and I'd be more than happy to sacrifice one," I whisper.

I don't think he was expecting me to say that with the shock on his face, and it makes me smile how innocent his face looks compared to the rest of his masculine appearance.

"I can't do that," he shakes his head.

"Okay, well when you usually give your name, what do you do?" I ask.

"I just give Parker. If they don't know about my situation already, Roman usually stares them down until they back off."

By process of elimination I assume Roman is the asshole from the gym, after Red gave me the lowdown the other day. Seems he has a soft spot for this guy too, huh?

Considering our options here, I nod at him and remove my hand, feeling the loss instantly, but I push on to try and solve the situation. I lean over his keyboard and type, happy with myself I click continue and his name comes up in the top right corner. I look at him but he's looking at the screen.

"Parker Parker?" He raises a questioning eyebrow at me. I smile and nod in response.

"Yeah, why not? You have to just be you Parker, fuck surnames and bloodlines. Besides, it has a nice ring to it."

He smiles at me and I nod before returning to my screen, attempting to catch up on my assessment too, but I don't miss Kai staring at me out of the corner of his eye. He clearly saw our interaction and it leaves me a little unnerved.

"Thank you, Luna," whispers Parker, but I just nod my head in response without looking away from the monitor, needing to break the hold he has over me.

I need to lie down. There must be something in the water here. Fucking with me.

Well it can fuck right off, thank you very much.

MY BLOODLINE

THIRTEEN
Luna

Time is finally called as the bell rings. I finished fifteen minutes ago, but I chose to stare at the monitor to avoid making eye contact with either of my table buddies.

I feel like I don't know anything about myself at the moment, my mind and body are doing things completely out of character, and I'm drained trying to figure myself out.

At least I made it through the assessment. It was based on knowledge, from data input to coding and understanding gadgets. I considered my skill level with tech and decided I wanted to downplay my abilities, choosing to get a few questions wrong or just leaving them blank on purpose. Seeing as the Head is after me I need to hold my cards as close to my chest as possible.

Grabbing my bag, I'm up and making my way across the room as quickly as possible, when I hear Parker.

"Luna, wait up," he calls, but I carry on.

He's messed with my brain enough for today. I head straight for my locker, making quick work of the finger recognition, and grabbing my suitcase. I climb into the lift with a few others, praying for it to start moving. With my current luck, the doors are stopped by Parker, who is closely followed by Kai and who I believe to be Roman.

This is why I should always take the stairs.

Roman wasn't in our class so why is he even up here?

"Hey, I was calling you," says Parker, standing closer to me, making me look up to meet his eyes.

I don't know what he wants me to say so I continue to stare, but I don't need to say anything anyway.

"Everybody out," shouts Roman.

Yes please, I make to get around Parker but I'm all out of luck.

"Not you, Princess." Roman says, stretching his arm out in front of me.

For fuck sake, I sigh but stay where I am. When everybody gets out it leaves me with Parker, Roman, and Kai in the elevator. Roman waits until the doors shut and we're moving before he suddenly smacks the stop button.

What the hell?

"So, who wants to catch me up to speed?" asks Roman.

The three of us just look around at each other. Not knowing what he wants, nobody says anything. He shakes his head at us and sighs heavily.

"Okay, I'll be more specific. Parker, you wanna tell me why you're chasing this girl down in front of everyone, when I specifically told you to stay away from her? We know nothing about this bitch, Parker ..."

Parker's back straightens and his jaw tightens.

"That's enough, Roman," he growls, his hands clenched at his side.

I'm stunned, like my jaw is literally on the floor, I didn't think he had a growl in him.

Glancing around the elevator it seems I'm not the only one surprised by his outburst.

"The fuck, Parker?" fumes Roman, but Parker doesn't back down.

If anything, he's moved slightly to block me from

Roman's view. This is getting out of hand and it's only going to get worse if I don't calm the situation down.

I gently place my hand on Parker's arm to gain his attention.

"Hey, it's okay. Don't argue with your friends, he's just trying to protect you, alright?" I calmly say, because as rude as Roman is, that's what he's trying to do. I get it with Parker, and I barely know him.

I get the pull to want to protect him, even though it seems he doesn't need it. So as much as Roman is a dick towards me, I can't fault his protective nature.

"No, Luna, you don't get it."

He quickly glances my way before returning his stare to Roman.

"I had an episode, a bad one Roman, over the smallest of triggers, and Luna...She helped me climb back out of the black hole, okay? So, I get that you don't know her, but I know enough, and you will not use your crude language towards her." He grits through his teeth.

Crude language? Who is this guy?

Everyone seems frozen, I don't think it's my place to say anything just yet, so I take in the others. Roman looks like his brain is trying to process what Parker just said, and Kai is looking up at the ceiling as if he'd rather be anywhere but here. Me and you both, buddy.

"It's true, Rome. We've been assigned seating together and I hadn't even noticed anything was wrong until I caught sight of Luna leaning towards Parker," Kai offers, pausing to look me over, before continuing to Roman.

"It was bad, Rome, his leg was bouncing, his face was blotchy, and he wasn't responsive. I was trying to figure out how to intervene without drawing attention, but before I could do anything she had the color back in his eyes, and within minutes he was talking. Then, just like that, he carried on like nothing had happened," he breathes out.

This has Parker nodding and Roman drilling holes into my head like whatever he wants to know will just pop out, sadly that wasn't going to happen. He must decide that I'm not a current threat because he presses a button on the panel and we're moving again. He steps closer to Parker and they talk quietly. As soon as we come to a stop and the doors open I'm out of there without a backwards glance.

I spot Red waving at me like a lunatic, and race over to her.

"Hey, bestie, how was your first class?" she asks.

"It was fine, Red. Drama as always though. So, let's get

over to Business so I can avoid everyone," I say, pulling her along to the other academic building.

"Will it make you feel any better to know there is a coffee shop in the Business building?" She smiles at me, and I move faster.

"Hurry the fuck up then! What the hell are you waiting for?"

She needs to lead with this stuff in the future, not my feelings and shit.

Parker

Luna storms out of the lift like her tail is on fire. Part of me wants to check she is okay, but I've got no chance of that right now with Roman checking me over.

Everything Kai said was true and I'm just as surprised as Roman. I remember lifting my arm to the screen, and the next thing I know she's stroking my cheek and I couldn't get out of my head and to her quick enough.

It was strange for me. Sometimes it can take over an hour to come out of it and, when I do, I still go into a slump that can last even longer than the episode. Yet she had me out and pushing through like it was nothing, but it was something, and the guys knew it.

When the lift started up again Roman started peppering me with gentle questions to make sure I was alright. Roman was normally the person who helped me out of the darkness, so I'm sure he will baby me for the rest of the day.

Not that I'll complain about it really, it makes me feel cared for, which is something I've missed out on in my life. These guys are my family and Ace is my new home, just a pity Wren is there because she really gets on my nerves.

Leaving the building, we make our way across to the other academic building for Business.

"Are you sure you're okay? You can head back if you need too, we don't need to fucking explain to them," he grumbles.

It has definitely thrown him that I don't seem like I've had an episode.

"Roman, I'm fine, honestly, and no I can't explain any of it. Apart from the fact I had a meltdown over the surname error, like an idiot."

I should be used to it by now, after all these years, but apparently it's a trigger.

"Hey, at least it had the hot new girl caressing you," Kai says with a wink.

"What's that about the new girl? Why is she touching someone that's not me?" whines Oscar, as he joins us.

That earns him a clip around the head from Roman like usual.

"Shut the fuck up, Oscar," mumbles Roman.

He's short tempered right now, seems he's not happy with Luna, but he's trying to process that she helped me, which leaves us with a grouchy Roman.

"Anything else happen in Tech?" Roman asks.

I didn't notice anything, but Kai must have.

"Yeah, she purposely didn't answer certain scenarios or clicked the wrong thing. I still believe her this morning, that she doesn't know anything about her information being wiped, but she knows more than she answered on the assessment. Considering Dietrichson this morning though, I can guess why she would hold back her skills."

Nobody says anything to that. Luna is an enigma. She doesn't act like the other girls here and she keeps herself closed off so nobody can figure her out or get too close it seems, but it's only been a few days.

When we enter Business, the room is quite big, with dark wooden tables that seat four scattered around. Magnolia walls and an old school chalkboard make me feel like we've stepped back in time.

I spot Luna with her friend, Jessica I believe is her name. She's always been quiet and overlooked, never really fit in here. Looks like Luna is attracting all the strays apparently, and I'm enjoying being one of them so far.

She sat as far away from me as possible, over by the windows. I made sure I was sitting facing her direction, but with all the other bodies in here I can only see her face.

I can't help but look over to Luna here and there. I can't explain why she settles my soul like she does, I think it's because she knows what I'm feeling. I saw it in her eyes, and she knows I did, and I can tell she doesn't like it.

The class goes quickly with the tutor, Penny, flirting with Oscar the whole time and barely holding a lesson. I definitely didn't learn anything here today.

Before we head over for lunch, everyone with Weapons this afternoon has to drop their gear off at the training center. We're chauffeured over and I want to grab the car with Luna, but I think that'd upset Roman, so I climb in with him and see Kai get in with her. He better not grill her like this morning, not after she helped me, she doesn't need his crap.

The lockers are top of the range here and a lot bigger, they're practically mini versions of the vaults. They are fingerprint access, so once we've got it set up and have stored our things, we are on our way for food. Thank God because I'm starving. Out at the cars, Oscar tries to push Kai out of the way to climb in with Luna, but Kai shoves him back.

Huh. I didn't think he'd bother, but I guess it's Luna or Wren, and I know who I'd choose.

Walking into the cafeteria, I can't help but let my eyes follow Luna.

I think I'm a lost puppy.

Joining the guys at the order station I notice I'm not the only one tracking her. Of course Oscar is, but even Kai and Roman are. She takes a seat with her friend, near the full-length windows and I glance to where we're expected to sit with Wren in the middle.

I can't control my frown which Roman catches, and he pushes me to the front to order first, as if it's hunger that's got me worked up. I barely notice I'm ordering a pizza, but

I grab my slip to scan at the table anyways and a bottle of water.

What do I do here?

I know what I want to do. I know it'll upset others and that's where I'm stuck. I hate causing more issues than we're already dealing with, but if Roman has taught me anything it's to do what I want, not what others want of me. Well... when I can, and my life doesn't hang in the balance, and right now is one of those times.

It'll be making a statement...

Fuck it.

If I care enough to internally cuss then I care enough to suit myself. I don't look back at Roman, because if he seems mad I'll change my mind to please him, and this isn't about him.

I make sure to keep myself relaxed as I walk through the crowd, like I'm not breaking code, but we're not in high school anymore. I approach Luna's table, and I'm petrified she's going to tell me to get lost. So I try to make it less overbearing, and take a seat next to her friend with her across the table instead, scanning my ticket at the end as I pass.

The tables are long with matching benches, with a

machine at the end to scan your receipt, so they know where to bring your order.

Whatever they were talking about is paused as she stares me down, while her friend observes her with me. I think we're both waiting for a bomb to go off. Trying not to spook her I give her a smile and turn to her friend.

"Hey, Jessica, right?"

"Err, yeah."

She's surprised I'm sitting here right now, but she also has a look of fear in her eyes. I get I'm an Ace, but I've never been cruel to her. I can't help the confusion on my face, which she registers and leans toward me shaking her head.

"Not you, but the silence in here has me believe it's about to kick off, where do you stand when that happens, because it's going to?" She murmurs, folding her arms on the table.

It's deadly silent in here, I hadn't noticed because my mind was focused on getting here. Trying not to blatantly look around, I see that all eyes are looking in one of three directions, waiting on a reaction.

If they aren't looking at me sitting with Luna, they are staring at the guys who are standing at the order station assessing me and the situation in front of them, or worse, they're staring at Wren because if this blows up it'll start with her.

I look Luna straight in her eyes, while responding to Jessica.

"I made my decision when I walked over here. Luna's done more for me this morning than Wren has in four years. There's a lot of Featherstone politics around here, but where I eat my lunch isn't one of them. Is that okay?" I have to ask, to make sure she's not going to kill me.

She takes me in for a moment, bracing her elbows on the table and resting her chin on her clasped hands, finally she nods her head at me. Thank God.

I smile at her as I relax back into my seat, sipping my water so I can look over at the guys without being obvious. As I do I see Oscar pat Roman on the shoulder and saunter over like he's amazing, and right now? Right now he is, because he just backed me. It might be because he's hot for Luna but the why doesn't matter.

Looking back to Roman, he's staring at me already with a raised eyebrow. Code for 'are you sure about this'? I nod and that has him moving in my direction with Kai behind him. I look back at Luna.

"I apologize in advance, it's about to get busy over here." I smirk.

Her confusion only lasts a moment before Oscar arrives, scanning his ticket, and sitting next to her.

"Hello beautiful, you miss me?" His grin on full display.

I can't help but laugh when she doesn't answer him, just rolls her eyes, but there's amusement in them.

Roman arrives, scans, and pushes Oscar clear down the bench, taking his seat next to Luna.

"Fuck off, Roman. I got here first," Oscar sulks, banging the table like a child.

Jessica starts laughing, as Kai joins us and sits on my other side. Luna's not laughing, she's not doing anything, and I think that's because Roman is sitting next to her. She's waiting for his shit.

"Roman, can you not be overbearing? It's food time. I want to relax, which is why I sat here, but your brick walls are bumping Luna's concrete walls and ..."

Before I can finish my sentence there is a screech so piercing my ear drums hurt.

"Shit," calls Oscar.

"For God's sake," groans Kai.

The girls are looking at each other, aware of what's coming. I look to Roman, this is my fault, but it's Luna that's going to get the backlash. He must see the pleading in my eyes because he nods, and leans into Luna, whispering in her ear. Whatever he says doesn't relax her, but she does nod.

Fuck me, they're the same person with their own nodding language.

"What the fuck are you doing, Roman? Get your guys and move your asses," Wren yells, as she stands at the end of the table, hands on her hips.

It's laughable, how she thinks we're just Roman's puppets.

"Wren, fuck off will you? We're busy," Roman responds, as he tucks a loose strand of Luna's hair behind her ear.

It's intimate for Roman, he doesn't do PDA. So it'll rile Wren up, because she's always throwing herself at him with no success.

"Roman, I'm not playing around here," she yells, flicking her hair back.

God her voice is like nails on a chalkboard.

"Neither am I Wren. Now. Fuck. Off."

I think steam is about to come out of her ears. Wren does not like it when she doesn't get her own way, but I don't care about pleasing her. I see the moment her eyes lock on Luna, and this is about to get out of hand.

"You, you fucking bitch ..."

She swings her arms at Luna, who is standing within an instant and smashing Wren's face to the table. The thud is almost drowned out by Wren's scream, but it doesn't stop Luna. She cages her in from behind, with her hand gripping Wren's hair, keeping her in place.

"I thought you might have learned from Saturday, but clearly I was mistaken. Every time you try me, it'll get worse, do you understand? I couldn't give a shit who you think you are, you have no idea who I am and what I'm capable of. I recommend you keep that in mind for future reference," Luna growls.

With that, she stands tall with her hand still wrapped in Wren's hair, lifting her up off the table and shoving her back in the direction she came from.

"Pepperoni pizza and meat feast pizza for Steele and Watson," a waiter approaches with a tray loaded with food.

Luna doesn't even spare Wren another glance.

"Yeah, perfect timing. Thank you," she answers calmly, like none of that just happened.

Wren goes straight out of the cafeteria with her girl group chasing after her.

The girls start eating. Is this another universe?

Are we not going to address anything that just happened? Jessica glances around the table noticing all of us staring at Luna with our jaws slightly loose, and she just giggles breaking the silence at the table.

"Fuck me, beautiful, you can gladly have me by the balls. As a matter of fact, I insist. I'll even buy a pretty jar for you to put them in, yeah?" Oscar says out loud.

Everyone just looks at him when Roman bursts out laughing.

"His fucking purr," he chuckles, and the table breaks into a fit of laughter.

Except Oscar.

"Luna, baby, tell them," he pleads, holding his arms out wide.

She takes one look at him and grins.

"Well if they're as small as I think they are, I can wear them as earrings, *yeah, baby?*"

KC KEAN

FOURTEEN
Luna

I don't even understand what happened at lunch. As if I've not dealt with enough already, and it's not even been four days yet. My life back home was easy, simple really, how I like it. There is so much going on here that I can't control.

When Parker took a seat, I didn't really consider the repercussions until Red mentioned it. When Parker responded, it was clear in his eyes that he meant it. I'm not sure what I actually did earlier, to make him stand his ground with his friends, but he seems happy about it.

I could see he hadn't meant for it to cause such a stir.

It shouldn't be a big deal for him to sit where he wanted, but it caused a power play. One that left me in the shit, yet I still couldn't bring myself to be mad at him.

From the way Wren screamed it's obvious Roman is the leader, and his presence brought the power. That thought has me remembering Roman's whispered words.

"You better not make me regret trusting Parker about you. I know you're a little liar, and it won't be his fault when you fuck up. Now, she's about to cause a scene, and you, Princess, are gonna show me you can handle it. For Parker, because he's never paved his own path before, do you understand?"

I'd simply nodded, this was a big deal, bigger than me, and usually I'd say fuck that and run, but I felt the need to validate Parker's confidence in me. Roman seems adamant I'm a liar, and I don't have the care to understand why.

I seriously needed to lie down, but sadly I was sitting in the Rolls heading back to Weaponry. Wren was nowhere to be seen, so I managed to jump in a car on my own. Luckily, Ian was the driver and he was happy to help.

See what I mean? Ian is already on my Christmas list.

Arriving at the main building, where the lockers are, I gather my belongings and head to get changed. From what

I can tell, this building is just to hold the mini vaults and the changing rooms.

I kick my heels off and feel instant relief.

Bliss.

Hanging my uniform, I change into a loose black top over my sports bra and a pair of tight black shorts. Popping my combat boots on I feel like me, this girl in the mirror I know. Taking a few minutes to just sit, on my own, in silence, is just what I needed, seeing as I was on my own in here.

I sat on the bench, back straight against the wall with my head tilted up slightly. Taking a few deep breaths I find my center, relax my mind, and the weight of the world doesn't feel so heavy again.

A knock on the door gains my attention.

"Sakura, you ready?" called Kai.

There goes my silence.

I lock my uniform away and grab my suitcase. Stepping outside, Kai is alone, offering me a quick smile and then he's leading the way. Since our screaming match this morning I've found that isn't really his character. He's very quiet and observant, which I like.

He offers comfortable silence, no small talk, it's perfect.

He leads me out of the main building and towards what looks like a giant circus tent, all blue and white stripes. It looks odd compared to the rest of the campus, but out here there is only the Combat building as well, so it doesn't look as garish as it could.

Kai holds the door for me, and I step into a massive space which is laid out with different target practice areas, for both guns and blades, around the outside, and a small seating area in the middle.

Following Kai's lead, we head to the center. The rest of the guys are here, along with the guys from Diamond and Hearts. I read that all men from the top three blocks are required to attend weapons while only the women from Ace were. Although, there's still no sign of Wren.

The seats are spread out enough to not be sat touching anyone else, but there isn't much room. I find myself following Kai further, and I can feel a lot of eyes on me. I don't know whether it's because they're checking me out or because of what went down at lunch. Either way I look to the board instead of meeting anyone's gaze.

Mr. Morgan – Weapons Expert

Is written boldly on the board. Huh, I know a Morgan. At least I know how he wants to be addressed.

"Luna, baby, sit closer to me, you're too far away," Oscar says with a pout.

He's ridiculous, but I can't help but find him entertaining. So I give him the finger, which just makes him stick his bottom lip out, and the guys laugh.

"Sit, Luna," grunts Roman, moving his bag off the chair next to him.

I'm not sure that's a good idea, but glancing around I catch Parker's face. His face is light with joy, seems he likes Roman being nice to me. Which then means I can't decline and the smirk on Roman's face tells me he knows it too.

Fucking Acehole.

As I go to take a seat there's a large bang from a door shutting.

"Sorry about that, guys. I was held up for a moment, but we'll get to it now."

I assume it's the teacher, heading towards us. But...I know that voice.

I turn to get a better look at the guy when all the color drains from my face, and I think I'm going to be sick.

This is the devastation that broke the camel's back. This is definitely the cherry on top of my fucked-up situation.

"Hey. Luna. Hey," Roman calls, shaking my arm, but I'm frozen in place.

I couldn't have hidden these emotions even if I'd tried. I don't look at him, I keep my eyes trained on the apparent fucking tutor, who has stopped at the edge of the space. The guilt is written all over his face, but the worst part is, he's not surprised to see me.

"Luna, can you give me a minute please?" The silent plea etched in every word.

Is he fucking joking? Is this whole thing a fucking joke?

I remove the emotion from my body language, I'm angry enough now to overpower it.

"I don't think that's a good idea West, do you?" I growl, at the very same Morgan I just remembered.

I try to contain myself, but I need to pound my fists into something, anything.

I just need to let my emotions out.

"Luna, you need to let me explain, okay?" West gently speaks.

Like if he talks too loud it'll set me off, but his fucking calmness is riling me up anyway.

"I think you've had plenty of time to explain, don't

you? Now, it's a bit too fucking late."

My hands are fisted at my sides, but the need to lift them is becoming hard to control.

"You want to explain what's going on West?" It's Roman, the confusion is clear in his tone.

I'm glad he's not asking me to explain right now, because he'd likely just get a punch to the face.

"Rome, it's between me and Luna, okay?" West answers, looking at me. "Please, Luna, I can't do this in front of all these guys. There's a lot you don't know."

You're fucking telling me, apparently I don't know anything, but right now I'm not in the right frame of mind to listen.

"Right now, West, it isn't going to work out well for you," I state calmly.

He must hear the truth in my voice.

"Okay, but we do need to talk, Luna," he says softly.

I just nod and take my seat. I can't process anything right now, I need to tuck it all away for later. West starts talking to the group about what we'll be doing today, but I'm not paying attention. I feel Roman lean in.

"What the fuck, Luna? How long have you been fucking him?" He growls in my ear.

What the hell? Who does this guy think he is?

"Fuck you, Roman," I grind through my teeth.

I don't owe him shit, and definitely not an explanation. Any progress to calming down I'd just made is gone now. Fuck men.

Fuck. Them. All.

The shrill sound of a bell draws the class to an end. I pack my case up as quickly as I can, and head for the door.

"Luna, wait up," West shouts, drawing everyone's fucking attention.

I don't slow my pace, not even a fraction. I just continue to head for the exit.

"Luna," he calls again, only this time he grabs my arm, forcing me to slow down. He just can't take a hint, can he?

I'm not fucking around. Using my free hand, I make a fist and punch him straight in the throat.

He instantly releases my arm, his fingers wrapping around the pain in his neck. He's bent over at the waist, trying to keep himself upright as he coughs and splutters.

"I told you right now wouldn't end well for you, West, and I fucking meant it," I grind out.

Without wasting anymore of my time, I avoid everyone's gaze and storm out. I'm in a foul mood, I have been the whole fucking class and I couldn't give a shit. Today has been a rollercoaster of epic proportions and I'm real close to losing my shit.

The lesson was for West to see how everyone handles a gun, there was a mixture of experience in the group, a few thought they were bad boys because they know how to play a video game, but couldn't actually take the safety off. While others had precision and skill, including myself, and I should, seeing as West fucking taught me how.

I can't, I shake my head and stop my train of thought. It'll do me no good right now to think about West, does Rafe know he tutors here? No. Stop. I'm at war with myself, my brain is gonna break if I don't get a punch bag real soon.

Getting to the locker room, I quickly change and send Red a text.

Luna: Grab me any coffee. Meet at Ace in an hour.

I can't even bring myself to fluff it up a little more

for her. It's not her fault but she'll have to get used to my shortness if she plans to stick around.

Red: Yes Captain!

Fucking captain, I can't help the smile, but my current mood quickly stomps it out. Heading to the lobby, I store my belongings in my mini vault and head outside. As quick as I thought I might have been, I wasn't as quick as Roman apparently.

"Get in," he grumbles.

I don't respond, just climb in. I'm ready to get the fuck away from this building. The whole fucking place in general really.

Roman is clicking the partition up before we've even begun moving. I can tell he wants to trample me for information, but he can also see that I'm close to feral. His eyes are burning holes in my skull, making me want to scratch the spot.

"You seem stressed, Princess," he murmurs.

You think? He doesn't even deserve a response, so I continue to gaze out of the window.

"You want to talk about it? I'd love to hear all about

how long you and West have known each other. It'll help clear some things up for me," he pushes.

Fuck. Off.

If I wanted to talk, it wouldn't be to you. Yet I say nothing, I do nothing, and he gets the message, leaving me be for the rest of the drive.

Arriving at Ace, I don't have time to mess around, I'm out of the car in a flash. I need to be in the gym, now. I just need to change as quickly as possible, so I'll be calmer when Red shows up.

Hitting the lobby, I make for the stairs when I'm grabbed by the arm and dragged past them.

What the fuck?

"What the hell is your problem with manhandling me? Get the fuck off, Roman!" I yell, but he ignores me.

Thomas the doorman can see us but does nothing.

Great. Thanks.

I try to dig my feet in to stop his pull but with these heels on I've got no chance. He shoves into the gym doors and whirls me around, pushing me in the direction of the ring. I spin to face him, fire burning in my eyes.

I'm furious, unable to mask my emotions.

"There she is," he says with heat in his eyes.

Of course he gets off on me being so worked up.

"What's that supposed to mean?" I sneer.

He stares me down, from head to toe, and it feels like he's touching me. I can feel everywhere his eyes land on my body.

"It means, you're incredibly good at playing the Ice Queen, but the real you. The person you hold in, is fire. The emotion in your eyes could burn a man, and they'd love you for it."

He says it so casually, I'm left speechless.

"Take your heels off," he says, as he pulls his blazer off

"Why?" I demand, but he just smirks.

"Because I'm not gonna let you take your anger out on me with those ridiculous heels on."

He what? He can't be serious, but the look in his eyes tells me he is. I would much rather spar with someone than a punching bag, so I'm not going to turn his offer down. I kick my heels to the side.

"You expect me to do this in my uniform?" I ask, resting my hands on my hips.

He looks me over and just nods.

Okay then. I can't keep the blazer on, so I throw it on top of my heels and climb in the ring. He's watching me like a hawk, like I'm his prey and he's just biding his time. He stalks towards me, ripping his shirt clean off in the process.

Fuck.

Just fuck.

His body is a dream, and those eyes. God, those eyes.

He fucking knows what he's doing. His smirk says so. Acehole!

He climbs in the ring pulling two sets of light gloves off the table as he does. Muscle memory has us both set to go in no time at all. He stands in the middle of the ring with his arms outstretched and I bump gloves with him.

No words are spoken between us, we just follow routine.

He's not surprised when I make the first move, he instantly responds and we begin feeling each other out with light jabs, but then it's game on. I need to beat this adrenaline and anger out of me. A pace is set, and we block back and forth. He's not afraid to come at me.

I need that. I need someone to see that I need this, and not shy away because I'm a female, and he must, because he's giving it to me willingly. No one's made a move for submission, that's not what this is. We are just pushing each other to our limits. The sweat trickling down my back helps ground me. Fuck, this feels too good.

I see it, the moment he decides to charge me, and I use his momentum to continue rolling him when we hit the floor. I know I can't pin him down, but he lets me hold him down for a second before I'm jumping back up. He's glistening with sweat too, and I can't stop myself from looking at his forearms, they're bulging and completely distracting.

I can tell I've done enough beating if I can think about anything other than hitting shit.

"I'm done." I breathe, pulling my gloves off.

"Nah, Princess, you're not done till I say so," he murmurs, before he's launching himself at me again. I'd turned my back to him, so he grabs me and turns me midair to face him before we crash to the floor and his mouth is on mine.

Or mine is on his.

Who knows.

I hear a soft thud, beside me. It must have been his gloves too because his fingers are slipping into my hair.

If he thought my eyes were burning earlier, my core could set him on fire.

I don't melt into him, that'd mean submitting, and neither of us are built to do that. We're consuming each other. He lifts up slightly to meet my eyes, the want clear on my face. In the next breath he's ripping my blouse open. Buttons actually fly off, he doesn't attempt to pull it down my arms, he's given himself the access he wanted.

He pulls my white lace bra down, letting my nipples free, and his hands are instantly tweaking my piercings, and I can't hold back my moan.

Oh fuck.

He drops his mouth to my pebbled nipples, swirling his tongue slowly, while squeezing my breast hard. The burn goes straight to my pussy, which is rising up off the ground trying to gain some friction.

"Please."

I don't know what I'm asking for, I just need…more.

His teeth latch around my nipple and the pain has me gasping louder.

I need him in me.

That's what I need.

And I need it now.

I start to fiddle with his pants trying to undo the button, but the lust filled haze I'm caught in, has me struggling to process how to do it. Roman grips my wrists and holds them above my head, pinning me to the mat.

Fuck, being in the ring is making me melt.

"You'll touch when I say you can, Princess," he purrs, stroking his other hand down my chest to my navel.

I'm about to put him in his place, he doesn't run the show, but then he's lowering his hand under my skirt, heading straight for gold, and I'll be damned if I stop him.

He palms the inside of my thigh, teasing me, before a single finger ghosts over my clit and slowly strokes down to my entrance.

He does it again.

And again.

And again.

I'm going to explode, but I'm too proud to cum with just a light touch. He must be able to feel the frenzy taking over my body as he thrust two fingers inside of me on the next turn. I can't help it, I scream in pleasure, my orgasm hitting me instantly, and I continue to ride it out on his hand.

Oh my God.

Fuck.

I'm too far gone to be embarrassed with coming so easily.

"Fuck me, you're going to have me cream my pants from your moans alone, Princess," he pants, as he lifts my skirt around my waist and drops his pants.

His cock springs free and I can't help but gape at it. Fuck. It's a good job I'm drenched before he comes at me with that thing.

I lift my gaze, hearing him chuckle.

"Don't worry, Princess, I know how to use him," he winks as he rolls a condom on.

I couldn't care less where it came from but I'm glad he remembered, because I'm useless right now. He leans down taking turns pulling my nipple piercings with his teeth, and I'm putty in his hands.

He slips inside me so slowly, I'm close to screaming, but I can't get a single sound to pass my lips, I'm so full.

When I'm close to wondering if I'm splitting in two, he pulls out and slams straight back in.

"Fuck yes. More. I need more." I'm panting.

God, I'm so full, but this feels like ecstasy.

He doesn't disappoint and picks his pace up. Ramming me into the mat, like we're fucking animals.

Over and over and over again, he doesn't relent.

His thrusts are brutal but addicting and I can't quit chanting more. His thumb finds my clit and as he thrusts in I feel his cock pumping with release, forcing my pussy to clamp around him like a vice, sending me over the edge again.

Fuck.

It feels like the aftershocks aren't calming down, as we continue to ride out our pleasure together.

He gently slips out and I'm left trying to gather myself. I could slip into an orgasmic coma right now. I'm that blissed out.

I'm trying to work out how this just happened, but my brain isn't willing to switch on.

As I slowly rise I consider how I am going to get back to my room like this. I'll just have to hope no one's around.

Roman clears his throat, gaining my attention.

"So, this doesn't really change shit. I don't trust you, and I don't commit. This was just us caught up in the moment, nothing more," he says, as he's pulling his shirt back on.

His face scrunching like he's ready for me to kick off, but I can't help but laugh.

"Roman, those are the best words you've said to me yet. I don't have any expectations because I don't want any. I love sex, not commitment. Besides, I like dick too much to just settle for one."

Just to wind him up further, I wrap my arms around his neck, lick his cheek with a chuckle, and head for the door.

His chuckle has me glancing back and when I do, I finally catch a glimpse of his back.

My God.

His whole back is covered in a skull tattoo, it makes me stop my movement. I've seen plenty of back tattoos at the shop, but none have been as stunning as this piece. The silence must have him glancing around because he hasn't heard the door go.

Catching me gawking, he raises his eyebrow at me in question.

"No, no, no, Roman. Turn back around. In future you always greet me with no top on and with your back to me, do you understand?" I say, swirling my finger for him to give me his back again.

My outburst catches him by surprise, but he still has a grin on his face.

"That shits hotter than your face, and especially your

mouth. In future you should lead with that." I wink and exit through the door.

As I step out of the gym, Red is there, arm raised, about to push open the door.

Shit.

She looks me over, a smirk on her face.

"Roman?" she asks, as she passes me a cold coffee concoction.

My silence is answer enough and it just has her chuckling.

"Come on, you can show me your room while you shower because I'm not taking any self-defense classes with you smelling like sex," she laughs, as she links her arm through mine.

Completely unfazed by my bra on show.

My legs aren't ready to climb the stairs right now, so we take the lift, and I take a sip of the shit she bought me once we're inside.

Oh my God. It's almost as good as the sex.

Almost.

MY BLOODLINE

FIFTEEN

Luna

God I feel good this morning. After training Red last night, I ordered a steak from downstairs, showered, and slept like a dream.

Good sex will do that for you.

Sadly though, it can't happen again. I got carried away, lost in the moment. I don't know these people and I'm just letting them crash down my walls. No more.

Red promised we would be able to get another Frappuccino at lunch today. It's vital. I need them more than oxygen.

I feel a little more on edge today, having not seen

Wren since lunch. So I've got to keep myself on high alert because I know she's going to strike again.

I enter the lobby and it's like déjà vu. Four guys and three girls, all sat around making small talk. Sounds like the start of a joke. Wren is practically wrapped around Roman like a second skin, and a foreign feeling washes over me.

Am I...Jealous?

Fuck, no. I don't need to be dealing with that as well. Keeping my gaze fixed on the door, I head in that direction.

"Luna, baby, wait up," yells Oscar.

I don't want to stop while Wren is behind me. So I step outside, walking to Red, and I turn to watch him approach.

"So, how's my favorite girl this morning?" he asks.

His cheese is next level and as much as I want to cringe, it has me smiling.

"Depends, Oscar, am I your favorite girl this morning?"

My hands lift to straighten his tie. He brings the flirt out in me, I can't help it, and I didn't say no flirting. Which is good, because with him standing this close, surrounded by his scent, he's intoxicating. He almost smells fruity, but with a woodsy undertone and the tiniest hint of vanilla.

The grin that spreads across his face is hot as sin, but I

love downplaying his effect on me.

"Baby girl, you're my favorite girl in the morning, in the afternoon, in my dreams," he purrs.

Raising his hand to stroke my throat, it sends a shiver down my spine at the skin on skin contact. These guys have me playing with fire. I probably shouldn't be giving Oscar my attention after yesterday with Roman, but I was honest when I said I like more than one partner. After Tommy, I decided not giving all my time and attention to one person would keep the emotion and commitment out of the mix, and so far so good. I get the sex and occasional date night, but nothing serious.

"So, I just wanted to let you know that Rome told us about yesterday, and ..."

"What do you mean he told you about yesterday?" I say as I step back out of his space, making his hand drop away.

I glance at Red to make sure I'm not the only one hearing this. The shocked look on her face and her hand to her chest tells me he really did just say that.

"I mean, you can see there are more guys than girls here, and it's always been that way. So, we always keep each other in the loop with where our dicks are going. Plus, within Featherstone it is very common to have multiple parties in a relationship. Securing connections between families and all that."

Is he fucking serious? The scowl on my face has him spluttering some more.

"Honestly, baby, it's all good. We've shared before, and I just wanted to let you know it doesn't change anything between us, okay?"

Change anything between us?

There is no us.

This guy.

His mouth always has to fucking ruin it. I can't help the grim chuckle that escapes my lips.

"Every time, Oscar. Every. Fucking. Time. You start off so well, then your mouth ruins it. Now, fuck off," I grind, linking arms with Red and moving away.

He looks like a wounded puppy, but I couldn't give a shit, he will be wounded for real if he doesn't learn to shut his mouth. Glancing over my shoulder, I can see him trying to think of something to say, but it'd be pointless right now.

"What's going on out here?" Kai asks, as he walks towards us, he can tell from our faces the conversation went south.

"You want to comment on my private life too, Kai?" I ask, blunt as hell.

He holds my stare for a moment, his body language remaining relaxed, with his hands still resting in his pockets.

"Nope," he replies, heading towards a Rolls.

"Are you coming, Sakura?" he calls, with his back to me.

Red squeezes my arm and nods in his direction. I don't need to be told twice.

Kai holds back letting me climb in first. The door shuts and the partition is already up. We pull away and I'm happy to bask in Kai's silent company, but it seems he's talkative today.

"So, what did Oscar say exactly?"

"Does it matter?" I sigh.

"Well considering the size of his mouth, things could be...misinterpreted." A knowing smile touching his lips.

"He just wanted to let me know that you're all aware I fucked Roman yesterday, but not to worry because he isn't put off by it, seeing as you guys share anyway."

Wait.

When it comes from my mouth and not Oscar's, it

sounds like my kind of fun, and hot as hell.

"See how it sounds so much better when it's not Oscar saying it?" Kai says, raising an eyebrow at me. I can only bring myself to hum in response.

"Rome mentioned you were anti-commitment because you like dick too much to just settle for one."

I did say that to him, and I wasn't lying, but I didn't realize it would be hot gossip.

"I don't like being a hot topic, Kai. I think that's my issue here."

"Surprisingly, Rome didn't give any details other than you fucked in the ring. Which is hot by the way. Usually Oscar can get him to dish plenty of spank bank material, but he was very tight lipped."

I can only nod in response, unsure how true his words are.

"I'd also be careful of Wren today. She has a crazy glint in her eyes, and whenever she does, things can go to shit."

Great.

We pull up outside Combat and I get out without a word. I'd just like a drama free day. Just one, but it doesn't look likely.

Red is waiting by the entrance for me and we head to the changing rooms together. She's quiet today. Not in a 'be worried' sort of way. More, 'I'm comfortable and confident in your presence so I don't need to make noise' kind of way.

I'm obviously growing on her. I just hope it's not a bad thing.

We are such a stark contrast in gym clothes; me rocking the all black as always, while she has pink shorts and a white tank top.

All flowers and shit.

Wren's in here but she talks quietly in the corner with her friends, and it has my guard up. I expected her to be in my face by now, I can feel it building.

Joining everyone in the main space, it is literally a massive room with the floor completely covered in different colored mats, and the occasional ring dotted around the large space. The open space above us gives the feel of an old warehouse, you could probably add three more floors in here and still have high ceilings.

The guy who met me on arrival is the teacher here. Maverick was it? The guy who helped drop me in the shit. Fabulous.

"Morning, I'm Maverick Miller, you can call me whatever, I couldn't care less. The track around the outside of this hall is a kilometer. Let's start off with two laps, see how you do," he grumbles, and claps his hands to encourage everyone into motion.

A run around this place sounds like a dream right now.

I look at Red as she says, "Don't worry about me. Go. Run your brain out."

I offer an appreciative smile and do what she said.

I can't tell whether people are lagging on purpose to drag this out or if they really are that unfit, but I'm not waiting around. I zone out and just feel the rhythm of my arms, the bounce in my step, and the beating of my heart. I love this feeling.

I make quick work of going round twice, followed quite closely by the Aceholes.

I slow as I approach Maverick, who doesn't seem ready to begin anything else yet.

"Err, you can go again or take a seat," he says dismissively, waving his hand at me.

I don't hang around and make for another lap.

I hear footsteps approach and hover to my left. Glancing, I see its Parker.

"I hope Oscar's mouth didn't ruin my chance of you being my friend," he says softly.

Taking in the slight crinkle of stress on his face, I continue my pace as I answer.

"Parker, I never make a decision on friendship based on someone else's actions, and I don't think I could judge anyone except Oscar based on that goddamn mouth of his. Okay?"

The sigh of relief is instant, and he smiles genuinely at me.

"Sorry, I won't say anymore. I love running, and now I know you don't hate me, I can get my rhythm again."

With that we jog together in silence. I know he's there, but he isn't a distraction and it actually feels kind of...nice? Who knows, but it's not something I'm familiar with.

Once Maverick has everyone's attention, he decides to split us off into groups so he can see what we already know.

"Each group can take a blue mat to sit on, around the large red one in the middle. Then we can work through some moves, see where everyone's at. That will then allow me to better group you at the same levels in future classes."

Wow he actually sounded professional for a moment there.

Split into six groups, we each take our spots. I'm not familiar with anyone I'm with, but I notice Red has been grouped with Wren. Fuck. Roman is also there too, so hopefully Wren will want to partner with him, and not fuck with my girl.

We slowly make the rounds throughout the groups, some know nothing about defense and can barely throw a mock punch, while others are more aware. No-one has been at Ace level though.

Oscar, one to always show off, bragged the whole-time shouting encouragement for his opponent, only to block every move and land every mark, and to be fair his opponent would have been decent against anyone else.

Kai's moves were so smooth and practiced there was no possible way to fault either his attack or defense. It was hot, seeing his body move.

But nothing…nothing could have prepared me for Parker.

I don't know why I feel so protective of him. Maybe it's because I saw a vulnerable side to him, and now I can't see past that. See the Ace everyone knows him to be.

Holy shit.

When he attacked, he was beyond precise, and his

skill level exceeded my expectations. His guard was likely stronger. The power he demonstrated blew me away. I already liked his mind, his soul, but God help me, that body could cause havoc and it had me burning up.

Nope.

Stop letting these guys get under your skin with their knockout bodies.

I'm called next, my opponent being a guy named Tyler, who I believe is in Diamond, and he's built like a house. The sneer on his face makes him look like a thug, especially with his buzz cut and neck tattoo of a gun.

How original.

"Tyler attack first, Luna defend," Maverick guides.

Tyler is coming straight at me, grabbing around my waist. Having me instinctively shove my elbow into his neck harshly, while kicking the inside of his thigh. He releases his grip quickly and we go again.

This time he's coming at me with his height dropped a little, grabbing my waist from the side and lifting me off the ground.

Fuck.

He makes the rookie mistake of tilting me over his back, thank God, so I can wrap my arm around his neck and pull as hard as I can. It catches him off guard and he topples backwards, taking me with him.

"Okay. Okay," calls Maverick. "I don't think we need to see anymore from either of you, please take a seat."

"What? Let me defend," demands Tyler, smacking his chest as if he needs to be clear on who he's talking about.

"I've seen enough of both of your fighting skills, and that's what this is about. Now, sit down," Maverick responds, moving on to the next pair.

"Fuck you, bitch," Tyler growls at me as he passes, but I don't even offer him a response.

I haven't got time for this dick at the minute. It's not my fault if he's got little man syndrome.

The final group is Red's, with Roman and Wren.

"Wren and Becky please," Maverick calls.

Before I can even release a sigh of relief Wren is interrupting.

"Actually Mav, I think my skills would be better portrayed against Jessica, right Jess?"

Mav?

She's talking to 'Mav', but her eyes are fixed on me, sly bitch. She isn't a match for me so she's trying to fuck with my friend instead. Jess can see what's going on but doesn't move or offer a reply. I'm ready to storm their group when I hear Roman.

"Maverick, I'm pairing with Jess, move this shit along."

I could fucking kiss him right now.

Don't let me down Roman.

She's my sunshine.

"Don't be silly, Rome, baby," Wren sweetly interrupts, placing her hand on his chest.

Maverick looks between the three of them, and a single nod from Roman conveys how serious he is about this.

"I won't repeat myself Wren, get a move on, or I can call this class a fail," Maverick calls, turning his back to the dramatics.

She glares at everyone as she steps on to the mat, a wicked glint in her eyes. She plants herself in front of me and signals for Becky to attack first.

I go to get to my feet, but I'm not quick enough. Becky is leaping in my direction as Wren drops and rolls. I lift my feet in the air as my defense and brace for the impact, making contact with Becky's chest forcing her back onto the mat.

"Fucking bitch," Becky growls.

I don't know what she expected me to do. It's not my

fault her friend is a dick, and she's happy to play minion. So I just shrug at her.

They take their positions again, but away from me this time. I don't take my eyes off them though. Wren shows off, throwing Becky over her shoulder as she attacks. Becky has no clue what she's doing and is useless at defending herself.

Final move and they're moving closer to me, and I refuse to remain on my ass. Standing, I remain in the same spot, refusing to step back. I won't show weakness. Not to this bitch.

Everyone around must also feel something is coming, because any small chatter has gone, all eyes focused on the mat.

Becky turns her back to Wren, allowing her to attack from behind. She sneers at me, telling me I was right to stand.

"Now," yells Wren.

Becky quickly moves to the side letting Wren charge at me. I don't have a chance to consider what to do, I just have to move. I know I need to hit her from a distance, otherwise she'll take me down and there's less chance of me landing on top.

Letting my instincts take over, I place my right leg in front, turning slightly, as I crouch a little, holding my weight on my back foot.

I see it. In her eyes, she knows she's fucked, but it's too late for her pace to slow.

I raise my right leg and extend it with force, straight into her face.

Crack.

The contact has her head snapping back, the rest of her body going with it, and she's out cold.

A part of me wants to feel bad, but she fucking deserved it. I was just defending myself, and I did warn her it'd get worse every time she came at me, but this time it's in front of a tutor. Shit.

"What the fuck have you done?" Becky screams, and a few other girls stand and join Becky in shock.

I don't look at anyone but Maverick, I don't care what anyone else here says. I shouldn't care what he says but his take on this situation has the most impact on me. He pulls a small device out of his pocket, which he pushes, and a small bell sound comes from the speakers around the hall.

Suddenly, three people rush towards us with a stretcher. They don't look at anyone, just load Wren up gently.

"Knock to the head, clean out," Maverick says and then they are off.

He stares me down and everyone is watching what happens next. To me.

"Rafe sure as shit showed you how to move, huh?"

He smirks and walks towards me with his hand raised.

Is he fucking joking?

I don't know, but I high five the shit out of him anyways. While managing to hold in my smile of relief.

"What the hell, Mr. Miller! Did you not just see what she did to Wren?" Becky screeches.

"Of course I fucking saw. What do you think you're here for? This world isn't flowers and rainbows, sweetheart."

Turning to address everyone, he continues.

"This world is death, it's corrupt, cut-throat, and complete darkness. If you want any chance at surviving, I suggest you learn to see in the dark."

His words hit me deep. Everything he said, he knows to be true, the loss in his eyes confirms it. Without wasting anymore time he's back to it.

"Rome and Jessica then."

The stress is clear on her face and I don't know how I can help from here. Roman whispers in her ear, and whatever he says brings a little color back to her drained face, and she nods frantically.

Red stands in the middle of the mat taking the neutral stance like I showed her, she looks relaxed and unaware. Perfect.

Roman grabs from behind allowing her to show elbow use in a few spots. Then he steps back to come at her from the front, letting her show some small leg work.

I'm relieved she took onboard what I showed her yesterday. I can see Roman's not gripping too tight as well, happy to let her show that she can defend. When they step back Roman looks to Maverick.

"You already know I can defend too, showing you now is irrelevant."

With that he takes a seat. The gratefulness on Red's face is clear to see, she can't attack, and we don't need any of these assholes to know that.

Maverick doesn't argue, he simply moves on to the next pairing. When he eventually calls time, everyone breaks off heading back to the changing rooms. Red links her arm through mine, and I can't help but like the connection.

This girl is the sister I never wanted.

"You okay?" I ask.

"Yeah, I'm just glad Roman was watching us last night, so he knew what I could do."

How is she even saying that so casually? What the hell does she mean he was watching us?

I ask her this and she just laughs, resting her head on my arm.

"He said next time, he wants a real invite, to our girl on girl session."

"I wish I could tell him to suck my dick instead, but, well, I don't have the facilities for that now do I?"

The cackle that leaves her mouth has me breaking into laughter too, and some of the people around us frown.

Keep trying to break me and I'll just stand taller, laugh louder.

Fuck you all.

MY BLOODLINE

KC KEAN

SIXTEEN

Luna

Business class is just as useless as yesterday, with the tutor fawning over Oscar the whole time. Wren isn't here which doesn't surprise me, but it still leaves me unnerved. Her mother is the Head, and she already seems keen on making my life hell. I'm likely making things worse for myself, but I refuse to let someone trample all over me.

We decide to avoid the main cafeteria, I don't need any more drama today. So Red and I decide to relax in the sunshine, sipping cold coffees and eating burritos in the square. With barely anyone else around, perfection.

Heading to History together, I'm glad there aren't many students here. Red explained that a lot of students are taught history by their parents when they are younger. This class is for anyone who didn't get the memo.

It's their legacy.

Seems I could unearth information about my family history, and I'm not sure if I'm ready for it. Walking in, I spot Parker immediately. It makes sense for him to be here, after what he told me.

God, how was it only yesterday?

It feels like a lifetime ago.

He pulls the seat out next to him, and I can't help but comply. Now I'm sitting between my two soft spots. I'm screwed.

"Hey, I missed you at lunch," Parker says, as I relax into the seat.

"Yeah, I needed cold coffee and sunshine."

"You do not drink that frappuccino stuff, do you?" He grimaces.

"Hey, blame Red over here. I was more than happy with my black coffee until she forced her unicorn sprinkles and rainbow dust at me. Now I'm addicted," I declare, pointing straight at her.

They both just laugh at me.

"Red, huh? Do you give all your friends nicknames when initiated into your group?"

"Who knows. She's the first," I reply with a frown.

I can't help but be open with him and it irks me. I should be keeping my guard up with everyone, but these two just don't give me a choice.

"Good afternoon everyone, my name is Gina. If you aren't already seated, take any. Where you sit in here is irrelevant, and sadly will not change history." She is softly spoken.

Naturally blonde hair and a button nose, her vibes remind me of Red. Not fit for this world, but who's to really know.

"You will find that we spend quite some time watching the big screen in here. This is because actual footage has been preserved for many important events in Featherstone's history, which will offer better insight than a textbook. I have to warn you that some of what you will see is not for the faint hearted, but you are unable to leave this room." She ends on a sigh, looking down at her feet, as a soft click of the lock can be heard.

Fuck. We are going to be forced to watch it unfold,

and they've locked us in from the outside. How bad is this going to get?

The lights drop and the screen flickers.

"Welcome to Featherstone Academy. Founded in 1925 to bestow our code of conduct, loyalty, and family skills down our bloodlines. To ensure we are always on top, always stronger, and always ruling. There are many parts to Featherstone and you are all here to further our reach with the skills you have inherited. The criminal underworld is Featherstone, never the other way around. Featherstone Academy stands for:

Fraud
Embezzlement
Assault
Torture
Human Trafficking
Extortion
Racketeering
Sexual Exploitation
Theft
Obstruction of Justice

Narcotics

Espionage

Over the years we have followed the trends and expanded to additional outlets, but these were our core and will remain so."

I glance around the room, there are less than twenty of us here, and we're all staring in confusion at the screen. I'm glad it's not just me. The screen shows old photos but nothing specific, while the voice over is eerie through the speakers.

"For eighty-three years we grew as one family, pushing for greatness. There was hierarchy, but it was never obvious as we all knew our importance to the greater cause. Eighty -three years from Featherstone Academy opening takes us to 2008. 2008 was the year many things within Featherstone changed, and these changes impact you today. Catastrophic events changed our course, our structure, and our values. All because of one man. A man who attended this Academy as a bloodline for running drugs, but in years to come decided he wanted more. More power, more control, more money. He would go on, over

the course of six months, to overlook our code of conduct, our loyalty, and murder innocent bloodlines in hopes of becoming the King of the Criminal Underworld."

I was six when all this happened, but I don't recall anything, likely because it coincides with my father, and that leaves me blank.

"You will learn how we behaved before this time to understand our behaviors after this devastation. The man who changed all our lives was named Tony 'Totem' Lopez. He earned his name 'Totem' from the disaster he caused and his ability to elude justice. Because to this day Tony Lopez has evaded death, and we will continue to prepare for his return."

I look at Red, and she glances back offering a shrug, because she knows as much as me about this.

"We will begin with an overview of our current structure. The six buildings enforce the hierarchy ensuring everyone knows their place and does not attempt to overstep their reach, but continues to honor their bloodlines and commitment to Featherstone.

There are eight bloodlines who hold access to the top, known as The Ring. Rivera, Steele, O'Shay, Fuse, **BEEP**, Dietrichson, Gibbs, and Morgan.

What the hell was that beep? I couldn't hear the name.

Wait.

Shit.

I glance in Parker's direction and his hands are clenched fists on the table in front of him. How degrading to publicly ensure his surname is not uttered in his presence.

They are not worthy of him.

Not a single ounce.

I can't help but want to offer him my support. Placing my hand on his arm I squeeze gently. He slowly relaxes his tensed posture and places his hand on top of mine, crushing it like it's a lifeline.

He slides my hand down his arm, allowing him to clasp it between his.

This isn't good. I didn't know what I was doing last time, it just happened. Now I feel pressure to make him better, but I don't know how.

I look at him, and I'm surprised he tilts his head in my direction. His eyes are dark, but he's not lost in there, not fully anyway, like yesterday.

"Phone," I mouth to him and he just looks down at his blazer.

I take that as my hint and use my other hand to find his

inside pocket, pulling his phone out. It's locked, so I press the phone against his thumb, unlocking it.

I pause a moment, his home screen is a picture of the four guys. They're relaxed, smiling, and they look happy.

That is some photo.

Remembering what I'm actually supposed to be doing, I search for Romans number and type out a text with my left hand, fuck this could take forever.

Parker: Hey, it's Luna. Parker needs you. He's not as bad as yesterday, but I don't know what to do without drawing attention to him.

The response is immediate.

Roman: What happened? What color are his eyes? Is he fidgeting at all?

Fuck, right erm…

Parker: They were listing off the eight names of Ace and when it came to his family name there was a really loud beep played over it.

Parker: I can't really tell his eyes because they've got the lights off, but they're dark, not as dark as yesterday, but close.

Parker: He isn't fidgeting. His legs are still, his hands were clenched but now they're gripping my other hand like his life depends on it and I think I've lost feeling.

The video's still playing but I have no idea what's going on. Yet again my focus is on something it shouldn't be. I'm my own worst enemy here.

Roman: Do not let go of his hand. You're clearly keeping him grounded even if it's the smallest amount. I'll be there ASAP, but it may be the end of class before I do.

I don't bother to respond, it's too hard and he's on his way anyway. Parker seems content on squeezing the life out of my hand, but otherwise he isn't doing anything.

I look to my left at Red, she can see something is going on. Questions of concern float in her eyes, and I offer her a small smile, before trying to focus on the screen.

That is why we have The Ring. They control the head of Featherstone, ensuring the right decisions are made, but even their bloodlines do not just get instant access to sit at The Ring's table. Featherstone laws state that for a chance to stand for The Ring you must first compete in The Games. The Games determine the strong from the weak, and in a controlled environment other names can make a play, but it's life or death inside there. You may enter up to groups of six, or solo, or not at all. Unless you are an Ace, then the bylaws state you MUST enter The Games.

What the fuck was that? What does that even mean? I don't want to enter any games. I don't want to be forced to fight for a place at a table I want to be as far away as possible from.

The video stops and the lights are turned on.

"Thank you very much class, that is all for today. Your assignment is to learn something about your bloodline that you did not previously know. Be it from the library or asking them directly, but I want it for next week. Dismissed."

I look at Parker and he manages to offer me a half smile.

"Hey, you think we can make it outside, or do you want

to wait here for Roman?"

"Move out of my fucking way you idiots," roars Roman from the other side of the door.

"Never mind, the grumpy bastard's here now," I say with an exaggerated eye roll, and it actually earns me a small chuckle.

I squeeze his hand back and relax a little. Roman storms over and crouches down on the other side of Parker.

"Hey buddy, you okay?"

He doesn't move his eyes from me but grins a little, it's almost like he's drunk.

"See, Roman gave me a nickname," he says, barely a whisper, and I laugh.

"You gonna be okay with the big bad wolf?" I ask.

"I'm his favorite, of course I'll be okay."

I give his hand a final squeeze and stand, turning to see Red waiting patiently with concern in her eyes. Roman manages to get Parker up but the minute he does he grabs my hand again.

I look to where we're connected. It's foreign to me to hold someone's hand. I have always been way too independent to want to hold a guy's hand, and I'm not very affectionate anyway, especially not in public. Yet, here I am again unable to bring myself to say no.

I look him in the eyes.

"You are a little shit, Parker Parker, don't make me give you a mean nickname," I warn, but inside the contact gives me tingles.

I feel almost delicate in his hands. I could get lost in this feeling.

He doesn't respond, he just kisses me gently on my forehead, and slowly starts walking to the lift, like that light touch didn't melt my walls away.

Like it didn't impact my life.

I let him drag me along, with Roman and Red behind.

"Fair warning, Princess, when he sucks you in, you're screwed," Roman whispers, as he places his hand on the small of my back.

No shit sherlock. I'm screwed already.

After making it back to Ace, I decide to change and head for the gym to work off some steam, so I can try and figure my head out. As much as I like the way Parker makes me feel, I shouldn't be allowing it to happen. I don't know what's going on around me enough to let myself get distracted, and they are all trouble.

I change in my room, grab a water, a towel, and my phone to take with me. My phone buzzes in my hand and I see Rafe flash across the screen. I don't really want to talk to him, but if he's getting Dot to me then it's a necessary evil. While I have him on the phone, I could mention needing something for History too.

"Hey," I answer, as I make my way down the stairs.

"Hey, Luna, how are things?"

I don't know how to answer him. I've been thrust into a world I do not truly understand, and I still haven't had time to process everything.

"I don't know, Rafe. I didn't know anything about this place this time last week, and I haven't had much time to process everything that's going on."

"It'll take time, Luna, that's all. You're made for this," he praises.

"What if I don't want to be made for this? I don't want this life Rafe and I certainly didn't ask for it," I fire back.

I take a breath trying to calm myself down. I don't like letting my emotions get the better of me, and this conversation is just riling me up.

"I know, Luna, I know. Any trouble?"

"Plenty. The Head wasn't impressed from the moment I stepped through the door with an extra bloodline, and it doesn't help that her daughter is a first-class bitch gunning for me too." I sigh.

"Dietrichson? She's always been a bitch. I'll never understand how she was given the position to begin with, always wanting more power and thinking she's superior. If they weren't so much alike, she would be perfect for Veronica."

I can't help the chuckle at that. He's definitely on to something there.

"Rafe, did you know about West too?" There's a pause on the other side before he responds.

"Yeah, Luna, I did. There is a lot going on in the underworld, there are few you can trust, but you can trust West, I swear. When you finally talk to him it'll be clearer, okay?"

"But when you dragged me out of the Warehouse, you wouldn't let the guys in, you said they don't know what they're walking into, was that a lie to force me here?"

I squeeze my temples, this is all just one big giant headache.

"No, no, Luna. It was Jake and Tommy banging on

the door, and they know nothing at all. When West's fight finished, he saw a message from me telling him to get out of there, because no one knew he was with us, Luna, and we couldn't risk them finding out."

More information for me to absorb, I can't keep up. I'm silent for a moment as I walk through the lobby. I've had enough of this talk, so I try to change the subject. "What are we looking like for Dot's arrival?" I ask.

"Oh, that's what I was actually calling for. What time do you finish Friday? I was hoping you would be okay for me to follow the truck, maybe hang around for food..." He trails off hopefully.

"I have a free period after lunch so anytime from say 2 o'clock? As much as I'm mad at you right now Rafe, I'd really appreciate a catch up. I'm lost Rafe, I don't know if I'm swimming or slowly sinking, and seeing your ugly mug would help, and you can answer all my questions without the presence of my mother," I say with a smile, trying to force myself to feel more positive.

Making it to the bottom of the stairs I head towards the gym, when the lights suddenly go out and its pitch black.

"Shit, Rafe I'm gonna have to go. I'm at Ace, near the gym, and the lights have just cut out."

"What? Luna, that shouldn't happen."

"Well it has, don't stress I ..."

I feel it. My senses heighten.

I'm not alone. This is an ambush.

I try to figure out how many people are here and prepare for an attack. Someone's charging me from the front. I drop my phone, and punch straight forward. I can't guess how tall they are, but I'm going to make contact there at least. My fist meets someone's stomach and they grunt.

It's definitely a guy based on his body and the noise that just came out of his mouth. I try to focus on my surroundings, and I feel someone approaching me from behind. I decide to crouch quickly, which has them tripping over me and stumbling into the guy in front.

I go to step back from them when, SMACK!

Fuck. I'm smashed on the side of the head with fuck knows what and knocked to the ground. Trying to clear the fuzz from my head, I can feel blood trickling down the side of my face and a pounding in my head has me at a disadvantage because all I can hear is the ringing in my ears.

"Fucking bitch, you're gonna wish we were given the all clear to kill you."

It's a guy's voice, but with the pounding I can't place it.

Following his words comes a kick to the face, crashing me to the floor.

Fuck.

Just fuck.

Someone grabs me by the hair and smashes my face into the floor. I manage to grip whoever has hold of me round the wrist and I squeeze as tightly as possible, I don't know how I manage it, I'm barely conscious, but a girl screams in pain when I do. Blows to both sides of my ribs have me releasing her and curling in on myself. I'm out numbered and disadvantaged enough to admit I just need to block myself.

The hits don't ease up, but I fight to keep my face covered, they've hit my face enough already. I can barely keep my mind processing let alone keep my eyes open. My body is trying to shut down, but I'm holding on with everything I can.

The pain is barely registering, there's that much of it. My whole body is numb, but throbbing at the same time.

"Beg, fucking beg for us to stop," a female voice growls.

I'd rather they finish the job before I beg for anything. My silence earns me a blow to the back of my head.

Fuck, maybe I could close my eyes for just a minute.

"Shit, someone's coming, we need to move," a guy whisper yells.

I'm gripped by my hair and lifted off the ground, like a rag doll.

"You listen here, and you listen good. You need to learn your place. Do you understand me? I'm going to make your life a living hell. You and anyone who tries to stand by your side. You're not going to make it out of here alive, I can promise you that," a female voice growls in my ear.

With that she spits in my face and drops me back to the floor. All I hear are the sounds of their footsteps inching further away.

I finally succumb to the pain and the sleep trying to take over my body. In the distance I hear my name being called, but I don't have any fight left in me.

MY BLOODLINE

SEVENTEEN

Luna

I feel like I'm floating. On a floaty, gently swaying with the waves. I try to open my eyes but it's too bright, so I shut my eyes tighter and drift back off.

I feel myself coming round but I'm no longer floating. I feel like I can't move, every inch of my body is screaming in pain. What the hell is going on? The pounding in my head is unbearable. I try to lift my hand but it's too heavy. Instead I focus all my energy on opening my eyes, it feels like it takes forever, but eventually I pry them apart and try to take in my surroundings.

I know I'm in my room at Featherstone Academy. I feel like I should be up and out though with the sunlight coming through the closed blinds, but I'm struggling to move a muscle. A creak from the door has my eyes shifting in that direction.

West?

Why the hell is he standing inside my room right now?

What's happened?

"Hey, you're awake," West gently says, as he approaches the bed.

I try to respond but my throat is like a desert. West must be able to tell, because he reaches for the bedside table for a glass of water and a straw. I feel like a child letting him help me have a drink, but I need water more than I need my pride right now.

"How are you feeling?"

"Like I've been hit by a bus that happened to reverse too, what happened to me?"

"What can you last remember?"

"Err, I remember Combat, Business, and History, then I came back and changed to workout. Rafe called and we were talking when ... the lights went out ... then I woke up here. I'm confused," I say, trying to sit up but everything hurts too much.

"Luna, while you were on the phone to Rafe someone cut the power to Ace and proceeded to attack you. Rafe could hear commotion over the phone, so he rang me from the Inked phone line screaming down the phone that something was happening. By the time I got here they'd already gone, but they beat you bad Luna. There were at least four different footprints on your body, and they used a weapon too," he offers, crouching down beside me.

I try to process what he's saying, and it makes sense with the way I'm feeling right now. I try really hard to focus on what happened when the lights were cut. I can't remember the feeling of any of the blows to my body, but I do remember what was growled in my ear.

"You listen here, and you listen good. You need to learn your place. Do you understand me? I'm going to make your life a living hell. You and anyone who tries to stand by your side, you're not going to make it out of here alive, I can promise you that."

I look at West.

"I remember what someone said to me, but I can't place the voice, it's all muffled."

Who would do this? I can't think of anyone past the Dietrichson's, either the bitch or her mother, but my head hurts too much to try and piece it together.

"It's likely because you took quite a few blows to the head. What did they say?"

"Oh, just the classic I'm going to ruin you and anyone close to you speech, and threats against my life."

"Fuck, Luna, I'm sorry I couldn't get here quicker."

I just roll my eyes, it's not his fault I was targeted.

"What time is it?" I ask, changing the subject.

"Nearly lunch."

"The next day?" I'm taken back. Still unable to lift myself up, I change tactics and lift a hand to my head, tentatively trying to feel for damage.

"Yeah, I had a doctor come here to check you over. Two cracked ribs and a solid concussion are your main injuries, luckily the rest is a lot of swelling and bruising, with a couple of cuts thrown in for good measure too."

"Oh great, I feel really lucky."

"I don't miss your smart mouth, Luna. Nobody knows what happened except the doctor, Rafe, me and whoever did it. Word will travel but it's better to keep as much as possible private. Someone called Red has been blowing your phone up, anything you want me to do with that?"

I just shake my head, she's better off away from me. I just bring drama and she doesn't deserve it.

"Could you help prop me up a little better?" I ask, resigned to the fact I'm in no state to do it myself.

He just offers a smile, helping lift me up and stuffing more pillows behind me. My body is aching so bad. I can't help but groan in pain.

"Try and get some rest, okay? You need to eat too, so I can give you some more pain meds, any preference on food?"

"Whatever you can get your hands on," I reply, trying to relax.

"Oh, and West," I call, which has him looking back, hand resting on the door frame.

"I hate you right now, but I'm not too proud to say thank you. So, thank you. You didn't have to rescue me, especially after the last time I saw you I punched you in the throat, but I'm grateful that you did," I whisper, as I feel myself drifting back off.

"I'm quite sure I deserved that if I'm honest. I will always come when you need me Luna, no matter what," he replies before clicking the door shut.

I'm in between being awake and asleep but hearing him say those words, I feel like I've heard them before.

"Hey, pretty lady, don't cry. West is here okay? I'll always come when you need me Luna, no matter what. I will always protect you, my little Luna moon."

BANG. BANG. BANG.

"I swear to fucking God, I'm about to bust this fucking door down if someone doesn't fucking open it. Right. Now."

What the hell? Is that Parker?

It sounds like Parker, but he doesn't cuss or yell. And why the hell is he trying to break in?

"Hey Luna, what do you want me to do?" asks West, from my bedroom door.

BANG. BANG. BANG.

Rolling my eyes, I nod.

"Let him in, but could you give a slight overview before he steps in because I can't deal with any more shouting."

With that he runs off to stop the banging at the door.

"What the fuck are you doing in her room?"

God, the yelling isn't getting any better, and is that

Roman as well?

"Roman, I swear to God, calm him down. He's not helping the situation and I won't let him through like this, she doesn't need any extra shit right now."

He's damn right I don't need this.

"West, I'll calm him down when you tell us what's going on. We've been trying to get hold of her all day, since Jess said she'd heard nothing. Now we finally get in here to find you, West, a tutor, you need to tell me what's fucking going on."

Oh God, between these two it could turn into a pissing match.

"West." I try to shout but it comes out weak and gravelly.

It must be loud enough because it stops all their noise, sadly it just makes my bedroom door swing open. The first thing I see is Parker's concerned face, he's followed by Roman. I must look bad because the shock is clear. I expect West to follow them in, but instead in walks Oscar, followed closely by Kai and Red.

Great. It's turning into a goddamn party.

Eventually West walks in and I look at him with pleading eyes. Luckily, no one starts getting in my face or demanding answers from me.

"West, I need you to start explaining to me. Right. Now," Roman growls, pacing at the bottom of the bed.

God if I could feel my lady parts, I'm sure they would have appreciated that tone. Sad times.

"I can tell you what I know, if Luna is happy with that, but you have to remain calm. This is only the second time she's woken up and she needs to eat. So, calm yourself or get out. Understood?"

West remains firm until everyone offers some form of sound in agreement. Looking at me to confirm explaining, I just give a small nod.

He goes over the last twenty-four hours, being jumped and the extent of my injuries.

"Okay, now can you explain how you ended up involved in all this?" asks Kai.

"She was on the phone with Rafe as a group attacked her. He could hear shit going south so he called me. I brought her up here and I've stayed ever since, problem?" he responds, staring him down.

"Rafe?" Roman questions, but I can't deal with all this testosterone right now.

Again, when my lady parts are working it'd be different,

and minus West, but right now I need it to stop.

"First one to pass me some water is my favorite." I say it as a joke to relax the atmosphere, but everybody fucking moves like meerkats, seeking the closest water.

Kai and Parker spot a fresh bottle on my bedside table and run at it together. Kai manages to grab the bottle first, but Parker grabs the straw. I can't help a little bubble of laughter that escapes my lips at their antics, but I cringe because my throat is raw. They make an efficient team and in seconds I'm sipping water, which is a little awkward with everyone staring at me.

"Can you all give me a minute, I need to use the bathroom," I say with my head lowered, not really liking the need to explain myself.

No one says a word and I prepare to try and lift myself up, when the cover is gently pulled back and Roman is tenderly placing an arm under my legs and one round my back. Lifting me as delicately as possible he heads to the bathroom. I don't argue, as much as each step he takes causes me pain, I do quite like being enveloped by him.

He walks me into the bathroom and slowly places me on my feet, making sure I'm steady before he steps back a little.

"Which side of the door do you need me on?" he asks, like it's not a big issue.

Glancing down at myself, I'm wearing an oversized t-shirt that hits me mid-thigh, and I know I've got panties on, so that's all I'll need to take care of.

"I'll be alright if you can just give me a minute. Please," I murmur, not willing to meet his eyes.

He doesn't respond, just does as I asked.

My body hurts so much, every part aching from the attack, they didn't leave a stone unturned that's for sure. Once I've finished, I prepare myself for the large mirror over the sink. I turn the faucet on and slowly raise my eyes.

God. I don't even recognize myself. There's a cut on my forehead and another on my right cheek, two black eyes, and my whole face is swollen and colored black and blue. I look at my arms too, which are covered in bruises, and my legs match.

I raise my t-shirt to check over my ribs, it's fucking hard trying to get my body to comply. I've got the top half way up when Roman pushes the door open, he must be able to tell what I'm trying to do, because without a word he stands behind me and raises my t-shirt, stopping just below my breast. I obviously can't see the cracked ribs, but they are by far the worst marks.

"How bad is my back?" I ask, meeting his gaze in the mirror.

"As bad as the front."

No sugar coating, just the honest truth, and that's what I need right now. I feel weak enough in my physical abilities, I don't need my mentality to be babied too.

Roman releases my t-shirt and goes to carry me again.

"I really appreciate it Roman, but could you maybe help me walk back? You don't have to, but I need to do it for myself, even if it hurts like a bitch."

He takes me in for a moment, then holds his arm out for me to link. It takes a lot of effort and energy, but I eventually make it back to my bed. Nobody questions it, which is likely to do with the stern look on Roman's face as a warning not to.

"Baby girl, I ran back to my room and brought some of Roman's mama's stew for you. It's the shit I swear, and it'll have you feeling better in no time." Oscar approaches with a big bed tray loaded with other snacks too.

I smile appreciatively at him, as he places the tray over my lap. He bends to meet my eyes, and there is a softness there. Amongst all his jokes and ego, he can be a nice guy?

Who knew his mouth wouldn't get him in trouble for a change?

"Do you need any help?" he asks, tucking a stray hair behind my ear gently, but I shake my head.

"I can only allow myself to be so weak, but thank you for offering."

"You can be as weak as you need to be Sakura, we are here to help," Kai responds.

"I do appreciate that, but I don't know you guys enough to hold that level of trust. Too much has already happened in the space of a week. My trust has been broken by too many people already," I reply honestly.

Nobody responds, they can tell I won't believe any different right now. I take my time, but I consume every last drop of the stew. He wasn't lying, it was to die for, literally. Thick with vegetables and beef, I don't know what is in the sauce, but I need to ask Roman how I get some more.

The silence in the room makes me feel a little awkward, with me in this state. Parker must sense my discomfort.

"So, word of the day guys," he says, trying to relieve some of the tension in the room. He looks Roman, who just rolls his eyes.

"What's word of the day?" I ask, happy to encourage a conversation.

"Parker likes to learn a new word every day," Oscar adds with an exaggerated sigh.

"That sounds like fun. From the Urban Dictionary though? That's the best," I say, looking at Parker, who just frowns back at me.

"What's the Urban Dictionary?"

"What do you mean? The Urban Dictionary is the funniest. It's an online dictionary for slang words and phrases," I chuckle.

"I need to see this," he says, pulling his phone out.

There's a knock on the main door, which West must take care of because in walks Red, when did she even leave? I'm clearly a shitty friend for not realizing. Then I see what she's carrying.

"You did not just go get me unicorn sprinkles and rainbow dust," I cry out, and she smiles at me holding out the icy cold goodness.

"I wanted to get something to make you smile," she whispers in my ear, as she gently wraps her arm around me in a side hug. I feel like I could burst with tears.

Always my fucking sunshine.

I need to figure shit out, after what the attackers said, I don't want to put anyone in harm's way.

"So, the only thing I actually remember is their parting words. Which were basically threats against my life and those choosing to stand with me. I don't even know what they think I'm standing for, but I'm sure you all know I'm a stubborn bitch and they won't be able to keep me down. So, it's probably best you all keep your distance, okay?"

Confusion is written on everyone's face, like my unicorn sprinkles created an actual horn out of my forehead.

The first to speak is Parker.

"Luna, I've remained calm since I got in here, like West asked. For your sake, but do not push me with that shit, do you understand? This is the world we live in, someone's always going to want to attack us, if we're with you or not. So don't insult me by taking away my choice. Understood?"

My mouth is going like a fish. I'm stunned, I want to say something, but I have no idea what. Who knew I could be silenced.

Parker with his surprising firmness again. Hot. Everyone chuckles at my expense and the guys all pat Parker on the back. Aceholes.

West steps into the room, with his phone to his ear.

"Rafe," he mouths.

I expect him to hand me the phone, so I'm surprised when he ends the call.

"Did he not want to talk?" I'm surprised, because that's not like him at all.

West chuckles.

"Of course he wants to talk to you, he's been out of his mind, but we don't need the phone. Not when he's just driven on to campus."

He doesn't say anything else, he just saunters out.

Give me strength to deal with all this pain along with all this babying because I'm gonna fucking need it.

EIGHTEEN

Luna

Rafe had stormed in and roared for everyone to leave. Taking over as always. I couldn't help falling back asleep before we could talk though. I'd burned through all my energy already.

The next time I woke up, my curtains had been drawn and the silence was welcoming. Refusing to ask for any further help I brought myself to sit on the edge of the bed. West was getting good at keeping fresh water ready for me, with some pain tablets on the side. Bringing myself to stand, the pain ran through me like a wave, but it was a little more bearable compared to last time.

What time is it?

Glancing around, I couldn't see my phone anywhere, so I slowly made my way into the lounge. My two sofas looked tiny with both West and Rafe laying across them. That must be uncomfortable. The television was playing quietly in the background, casting shadows around the room. Looking at the clock I see it's 06:10. Damn I slept for a long time again.

I turn on the coffee machine and head to the bathroom to freshen up. I hate how long such simple tasks are taking me. I'm stronger than this, but my body is telling me otherwise, and I don't want to push myself too hard. I need to shower or finally relax in that beautiful tub, but even I know it's not a good idea right now. I'll likely need someone awake just in case.

A knock sounds at the bathroom door.

"Hey, Luna, are you okay in there?" calls Rafe.

I open the door to see a sympathetic smile on his face. I don't need anybody's pity, but then he gently wraps his arms around me. Protecting me from the world around me and I can't stop my walls from crumbling, and the tears begin to fall. He holds me like that for what feels like forever, while I let my emotions take over. I haven't cried since I was six years old, but so much has just happened in such a small amount of time that I just can't hold my emotions at bay.

Last Friday was the perfect day I'd wished for. I'd spent the day at Inked and headed for my first fight. The only way it could have been better would have been some hot sex afterwards, but instead my life was tipped upside down.

Forced to join an Academy I had no care for, an Academy for the criminal underworld, and I knew we hadn't even scratched the surface with how dark this all was. Then to meet people who are breaking my walls so casually, forcing me to care, and making me enjoy their presence.

Then I get attacked by people who know this world better than I do. I need to catch my breath.

Finally calming down, I step back from Rafe, who wipes my face with his t-shirt like I'm still a little child, but I can't help the smile it brings me. I know there is a lot for me to learn, and there is a lot Rafe has held back, but I'm glad I can still feel safe enough in his company to relax my walls, even if only for a moment.

"Come sit, I'll make us something to eat," Rafe says,

as he guides me into the kitchen.

He pulls a chair out and I see a cushion there ready for my bruised body. Fuck. I hate that he babies me, but I do appreciate these small gestures to help ease my pain.

"You want some eggs and bacon?"

"Rafe, let's not ask silly questions, okay?" I respond, making him chuckle.

He pops a black coffee in front of me and proceeds to take over the space. I have so much to ask and I don't know where to start, and I'm sure he wants to know more too. While he cooks away, I relax before we ultimately start grilling each other.

The smell of bacon soon takes over the room and has West walking into the kitchen. He doesn't say anything, he's barely awake, if the drag of his feet or the wiping of his eyes is anything to go by. He just grabs a coffee and takes a seat at the table.

Rafe soon joins us with the food, and we all just devour the heavenly goodness before we bring ourselves up for air.

"So, I'm sure we all have a lot of questions and explanations between us, so where do you want to start, Luna?" Rafe asks, as he sets the coffee machine going again.

Huh, I'd spent all this time thinking it over in my head, and I still had no idea.

"I guess I really need to understand what I'm expected to do here. I was literally taken out and told to know my place, but I have no idea what my place is supposed to be," I say, raising my hands to air quote 'my place' because I'm not buying into that shit.

I look between both of them, seeing as they both know much more than me.

"Featherstone Academy will expect you to leave here with your skillset heightened and with job leads that fall in line with your blood. Both mine and West's are best around weapons, just in different ways."

"Okay, so it's correct to assume you attended here too?" I ask. I know Rafe did, but I need to hear it from West.

"Yeah," West quietly responds, looking down at his hands.

"What outcome does Featherstone expect of me?"

"Well, because you have been given access to three bloodlines you will likely take on numerous jobs between what they offer to the organization," replies Rafe, placing a fresh coffee in front of me.

"So, for your father's bloodline it will always be to steal in some way. For your mothers, it'll refer to infiltrating legitimate businesses to benefit Featherstone or ensuring solid connection through bribery. Mine will likely be the worst, I'm afraid Luna. I never thought you would have to take my bloodline, and I would never have expected your mother to push this through. So it likely came from someone else higher up. With my bloodline, death is always involved. I'm hoping they train you in my skill set but only as a defense to your other skills." He sighs.

We all remain silent with that hanging in the air for a moment.

"So, I'll be expected to kill people?" I ask, the words feeling foreign on my tongue.

Neither of them respond, and that answers my question. The shiver that runs down my spine is uncontrollable. Mulling that over I consider what that means. I could never bring myself to hurt innocent people, no matter what, but if I could get my hands on the people who did this to me I would likely kill them. I just know, deep down it would hurt my soul all the same.

"Is there any way out of this world for me?" I ask,

wrapping my hands around my mug, needing the heat.

"I'm trying, Luna, but this is higher up the food chain than I originally thought. I'm at a loss and I can't overrule The Ring, including our families. Someone wants you here Luna at all costs, I just don't know what for," Rafe offers.

I thought we were in 2020, I thought we had freedom of choice, freedom of speech, but apparently that doesn't apply here.

"Okay, so I'm supposed to just go along with this, accept this is my life now?"

Rafe and West stare at each other, communicating with their eyes. It's clear I know nothing here and it isn't helping me that they are still considering keeping things from me.

"Can you not do that?" I slam my hand on the table. "I'm at a disadvantage already and I don't need you keeping any more secrets."

"It's not that, Luna, this is bigger than all of us. There are so many rumors you can never really know the truth in this world. We don't want to tell you too much too soon or tell you wasted lies." This comes from West.

"Well, I think you need to tell me something to expect, fucking top tips, anything because I literally have nothing to go on, and the people attacking me know much more.

They've gotten me once. I refuse to let them beat me twice." My determination is clear, and I fucking mean it.

"Right, well a lot of the battles between the bloodlines are based around Totem, have you heard of him yet?" Rafe asks.

"His name came up in History yesterday."

"Well, he is the devil himself. He's always wanted to control Featherstone as a whole and was never satisfied with the drips they fed him. Everyone knows he's still out there but impossible to find, and even harder to kill it seems. The main rumor is that he has an heir, an heir willing to follow in his footsteps. Now, of course they would never name that child Lopez. So if it is true, we do not know who they are, or even how old they may be."

I nod in understanding, but I don't really know what to say, likely because I don't truly know the extent of this man.

"In the same lesson they also mentioned something about Ace students having to compete in something called The Games, and it's mandatory?"

I have my response as soon as I mention The Games and the color drains from both of their faces.

You ever asked a question, and regretted it the second

the answer isn't what you want it to be? This is mine. I think I would have rather been oblivious. I can't bring myself to ask more about it right now.

"Okay then, how am I supposed to survive this world?"

"Luna, there are a lot of cold-hearted people here, who won't think twice to do things you wouldn't usually consider. You need to keep your wits about you, and they need to fear you by whatever means necessary, otherwise they'll make you a toy," West sighs.

"Honestly, right now though, make them think you're obeying their orders. Until we can figure out more details about what's going on within The Ring. That'd also mean us keeping a distance still, because nobody knows of our connection," he continues, running his hand through his messy hair.

"You're asking me to not stand my ground and be true to myself West? You tell me they need to fear me, but you don't want me to retaliate or show any dominance. On the other hand, I still haven't forgiven you so keeping a distance won't be hard at all," I fume.

"I know, Luna, but you really are going to get a lot thrown at you from the Academy itself, never mind other students." He reaches over and clasps my hand. "I will help you wherever I can, okay?"

"I'll try this your way, but the second I know for sure it isn't working, we go back to my way," I say, pulling my hand back. I can't help the yawn that escapes.

"Is Dot still arriving today?" I'd completely forgotten.

"She is, but you're joking if you think you're going anywhere near her for the time being, Luna," Rafe laughs at me.

Acehole. No, Asshole. Wait? He was an Ace, so he damn well is an Acehole.

Dot will make me feel tons better, although right now I wouldn't be able to lift my leg over.

"How long will you be staying for?" I ask them both.

"I'll be leaving tomorrow as long as everything is okay here, is that alright?" Rafe asks and I nod in response, looking to West.

"I'll head out for a while if that's okay, then I'll come back when Rafe is leaving."

It's not a question but he's asking.

"We'll see how I am, I don't need to be coddled."

West smiles and starts to gather his things while I rise to my feet and prepare to go and lay back down. I'm tired again and the sleep will help my body heal.

I'm almost to my door when a question touches my lips.

"Hey guys, what's with Parker not being allowed his surname? What's the other bloodline for Ace?"

Rafe shakes his head. "Honestly, Luna, it's better no one knows because if that boy finds out before he's privileged, his father will kill him before the sun rises the next day."

The shock that washes over my body has me believing every word, and it makes my stomach turn.

This isn't the catch up I envisioned, let's not do this again anytime soon.

Roman

I've been sitting with my front door open for hours, waiting for him to leave. West left a few hours ago but I wasn't interested in what he had to say. It's mid-afternoon when her front door finally opens, and he shuts it behind him quietly, which tells me she is sleeping.

Good.

When he finally turns around, he stops at my presence, but the look in his eyes tells me he's not surprised to see me. I don't stand, I just hold my hands out in question. He raises his eyebrow at me, forcing me to push, Luna must have picked it up off him too.

"Fine," I sigh, "Did you ever consider giving me a heads up? I was having Kai run checks on her and we kept coming up with nothing, I assume that is because of you? I thought there was an imposter."

A simple nod is all I get.

"Does she have any idea what she's walked into here?"

"No Roman, she doesn't, and if we tell her too much all at once she'll snap, she needs baby steps, okay?"

"Have you not seen the state she is in? Nobody around here gives a fuck what she needs and you're leaving her blind-sided," I fume, he's so fucking stupid.

"Roman, I'm warning you. You keep your mouth shut, this is more than all of us and you damn well know it. I trained her with everything, gave her all the skills she will need."

"All the skills, Rafe? What about her fucking mind? What about how you feel after you kill someone for the first time? Or that fact that she'll have to continue to do so to save herself, huh? This is going to blacken her soul just like the rest of us," I growl through my teeth.

He looks to the ceiling, like he might find some answers there, but he fucking won't.

He can't answer me, because he knows I'm right, but there is nothing any of us can do about it. Not yet anyway.

"She needs to rest right now. A lot will be going on with your skill-based assignments in the next few weeks. That'll be hard enough for everybody, but it will hopefully take some of the heat off her. For now, that's all we can do."

He means, do nothing.

Fuck.

I nod in understanding.

He holds a moment then makes to take the stairs, but I call him before he leaves, having him glance back at me.

"Is that really her? Meu Tesouro?" my voice barely above a whisper, memories floating in my mind.

"Yeah, she likely won't remember though, she doesn't remember West. When she saw her father die, Roman, she locked those first six years of her sweet life away. I see her shut herself down when a memory tries to float to the surface, it causes her a lot of pain. So, don't expect her to remember that you were chasing her around even as babies okay?" He lightly chuckles, trying to make light of the situation.

I close my door without responding.

When Rafe stormed in yesterday, I'd already pieced it together, with West being in her room and the mention of Rafe being on the phone to her. Assholes had kept more secrets than they let on.

When she first arrived, I was scared she may have been Totem's heir. Three bloodlines were crazy enough for it. It was made worse when we got nothing on our background check.

Then Parker floated to her like a moth to a flame, and he's our best judge of character, but now, now I know.

Meu Tesouro, her father always called her. His treasured one, and I remember from such a small age that she was my treasure too. Shaking my head, I push the memory away. If she refuses to acknowledge anything from that time it'll do me no good to accidentally say the wrong thing.

I just can't believe it. They said she was dead. Gone with her father, yet she's sleeping across the hall from me right now.

Needing to take my mind off everything, I send a

message to the group chat with the boys, looking for a sparring partner. They all respond quickly, seems we're all on edge with things at the minute.

I only wish there was a chance it would get easier.

NINETEEN

Luna

The weekend goes too quickly, probably because I spend so much of it sleeping, but it was definitely for the best. Even though the bruising hasn't eased much, the pain is a lot more bearable.

Rafe left on Saturday evening, giving my keys for Dot to West, to make sure I didn't go riding before I should. Assholes. It didn't stop me going down to the garage to check her over. Seems someone else in Ace had a thing for bikes too, seeing as there was a Suzuki Hayabusa parked in the garage too. The speed of that thing had me leaning towards Oscar, he seemed the craziest.

I refused to let West continue to stay, I can take care of myself. If they wanted to keep it low key that I knew him, then it'd be better if he wasn't seen staying, especially as he's a tutor. I just had to check in every five fucking minutes, but at least it got him out of my hair.

He also encouraged me to reach out to Jake, he'd been bombarding both Rafe and West with questions about me, but I didn't really know what I was supposed to say to him. Jake isn't high up the list of my priorities.

The guys and Red had popped in and out, always coming together to save me the effort of constantly getting up. It feels strange, other people caring. I don't know what it is about these guys, but it feels like my soul needs them, and it's clear I might need their help surviving this place.

Everyone encouraged me to take longer to recover, but come Monday I was dressed and ready to go. I refused to apply any make-up, even though the guidelines actually come with a section on covering bruises, like it's completely natural. I want them to see their damage, and I want them to see I'm not afraid to hide. As much as Rafe wants me to hold back, I won't completely lose myself to a fake persona. How is the worst part of all this, still having to wear these stupid heels?

Red came by early this morning, and we enjoyed breakfast together in peace. A knock at the door tells me the guys are here and we need to get going.

"Are you sure this is a good idea?" she asks, again.

"Red, I'm not spending another day in this room, okay?" I sigh, fed up with having to repeatedly answer the same question.

She raises her hands in surrender with a guilty look on her face, before opening the door. I don't let them hover long enough to try and step inside, because they'll likely join Red's tactics and force me to stay here.

Oscar tentatively wraps his arm around my shoulder, leading me to the elevator. No one says a word until the lift closes behind us. Roman goes to open his mouth but Red interrupts.

"Don't bother, I already tried. I think if one of us asks her to stay here again, her brain might explode." She's saying it to the guys but looking at me.

I offer her a smile in thanks. She might not agree with me, but she'll stand by me no matter what. It'll be interesting to see if the guys do too.

Roman stares me down, and I hold my gaze right back at him. Eventually he releases a sigh and offers me a small nod. The tension I was holding in my shoulders relaxed. He would have put up the biggest argument, so I'm glad it was avoided.

Kai steps in front of me and gently cups my chin.

"Whatever you need, Sakura, just say the word," he murmurs, and kisses my forehead. I love his delicate touches.

Oscar offers me a squeeze, with his arm still around my shoulder.

"We got you, baby girl."

I roll my eyes, ready to explain to him exactly how independent I am.

"Luna, we know you don't need us, before you start your lecture. Just humor us, okay?" Parker says with a slight grin on his face. Pleased with himself because he can read me so well.

"Fine," I say, giving him the stink eye and sticking out my tongue.

The elevator doors open to a surprisingly quiet lobby, even the guys are glancing around for Wren and her puppets. Linking my arm through Red's we head for the exit, my pace slows as we near the glass doors.

"What the…" Oscar murmurs behind me, as we all

take in the sight outside.

I step outside, to see the entire student body standing nervously around the water feature, all crammed in. With Wren in the center, her bitches and a few guys I recognize from Diamond with her, including Tyler from the last combat class.

Red squeezes my arm tightly, as I feel one of the guys step up to my other side. I hold my hand out though, to stop them from going any further. I wanna see what this smug bitch thinks she's going to achieve here.

"I'll lay them all out, Princess, with pleasure," Roman murmurs. I should have known it'd be him to step up for a battle first, but I refuse to move my gaze from Wren's.

"I know, but we need to be smarter, not that it'll be too hard. Now just isn't the right time."

Before he can respond, Wren starts clapping.

"Guys and girls, I gathered you all here today, to show you what it looks like when a whore doesn't know her place. Please take a look at exhibit number one," she says grinning at me. I can feel hundreds of eyes taking in my bruised face and legs, but nobody utters a word.

I loosen Red's grip on my arm and push her behind me toward Roman as I step forward. I can feel the guys burning holes in the back of my head, not wanting me to get close to her, but that's just not who I am.

I stop about a meter away from her. I can see it in her eyes, she's surprised I've taken her on and not shied away, but it'll take a little more than assault to truly break me.

"Exhibit one, is what someone looks like after some sly fuckers outnumber you, and jump you in the dark," I say, looking around the crowd.

Tyler goes to step towards me, but Wren holds him back.

"As long as you learned your place, whore," he growls at me, and I can't help but snicker.

Oscar doesn't find it funny though, as he steps up beside me and places his hand on my shoulder.

"I suggest you keep your dog on a leash, Wren. Wouldn't want me to have to put him down now, would we?" he sneers, pure venom etched into his words.

"Fuck off, Oscar. Put your bitch in her cage, or worse will come," Wren spits out, before turning and climbing into the closest Rolls.

Everyone is silently taking in what just went down. Her little puppets climb into a nearby SUV and sped off, but the Rolls doesn't move, because it's waiting for someone else to get in too. I look at the driver and it's Ian.

"Ian, if you don't take her alone, someone won't make it to the destination, do you understand?" I say honestly.

"Of course, Miss Steele. I'll be back as quickly as I can." I offer a nod in thanks, and turn to face the crowd that's still lingering.

"Shows over people," I say, and everyone is quick to disperse.

Glancing back to Red and the guys, I see they're all standing waiting for whatever I say next.

"Oscar, can you make sure Red gets in an SUV safely, without any assholes please? Then we can get to Combat," I ask.

Red's gaze lingers a moment longer, making sure I'm okay. I'm a fucking Ace.

Literally.

I take one step into Combat and Maverick's eyes bug out of his head.

"Oh, fuck no. You're not sparring on my watch. Forget it. Rafe will murder me," he shouts, which just riles me up.

"Have you always been such a pussy, Maverick?" I ask, goading him.

"Luna Steele, you've got Rafe's mouth on you for sure,

but I'll be damned if you think you're getting in a ring this week," he says, before turning to address the rest of the class.

I'm standing here, gawking at his back. This was my piece of normality for the day, what the hell?

"Come on, Princess. I'll let you punch the shit out of me on the mats in the corner, okay?" Roman asks, as he strolls past me heading for the corner he just mentioned.

I could fucking kiss him. So I pick up my pace to get to his side, stalling his steps to plant a quick kiss on his lush lips.

"You're gonna hit back though, right?" I ask excitedly, but he just shakes his head at me.

"Don't push it, Princess, or I'll leave you over here alone," he warns, with his eyebrow raised at me.

"Fine. Acehole," I sulk.

"What was that?" he asks with a grin on his face.

"Nothing. It was nothing," I squeal in response, walking in front to get away from him.

How embarrassing.

MY BLOODLINE

KC KEAN

TWENTY
Luna

The next week passed by in a blur. I spent the days sitting in classes with tutors pretending not to see my injuries, and my spare time with Red and the guys. I'd never felt this close to a group of people before. I was getting too used to them being around. I felt like I was waiting for the other shoe to drop, but it hadn't yet. I was learning more about them every day.

How Roman was the leader of the group, always taking on everyone's troubles, especially mine and Parker's. He was all Alpha and I loved it. To the outside world he was a wall of arrogance, but the care and attention he gave in private had me addicted. Always willing to give me what I needed, even if it was a rough sparring session.

Oscar was all about a good time, however it came, and he didn't shut the fuck up. Although his mouth didn't get him into trouble as much, for now. His fun attitude is infectious. I don't think I've laughed this hard, and so often, in a long time. He brings out a side of me even I'm not familiar with.

Kai is so smart, but quiet. Sometimes too quiet, I can see loss in his eyes occasionally, but I don't want to ask. He is beyond observant, it seems he always knows what I want before I do myself. I could sit in his company for hours, and when he did offer me one of his rare smiles, it warmed my soul.

Parker, when he wasn't lost in his head, was the gentlest of souls. The shine that surrounded him, full of hope, was addicting and I wanted to bask in it. His physique did not match his soul. It was as if his body had transformed to match what Featherstone wanted but his soul had remained the same.

Red was starting to live up to her nickname. In private she was all fiery and willing to stand her ground with the guys if they disagreed on anything. Her sunshine vibe rubbed off on them too, making them protective of her as well. She was my biggest supporter, and I made sure I was hers. It blew my mind how she had changed, I just needed her to have that confidence in public.

By Friday I was ready to kick back and relax. We'd been given a few assignments this week, almost like this was a legitimate place. I'd tried to keep on top of them so I could spend the weekend relaxing.

I was fucking pissed that West and Rafe still refused to hand over the keys to Dot. I'd pleaded and screamed at them so much my throat hurt, and it didn't get me anywhere. I was so frustrated, so I planned to spend the weekend in the gym and practicing with my ink kits. With only Business and B.I.C.E today I'm even happier with an early finish for the weekend.

Sitting in the back of the Rolls, like it was completely natural now with Kai. I was relaxed, while I could be. Kai had argued with the others that he had the most calming influence on me, so he should get to ride with me. I don't know how he got them to agree, but I'm not complaining.

"You heard Parker's word of the day yet?" he asked.

I can't help but smile. Since I'd mentioned it, he was addicted to telling everyone his new word and their dirty meanings. It was brilliant, even if everyone else thought I was a bad influence.

"No, not yet, is it good?"

He just hummed with a grin on his face. His fingertips stroked my hand on the arm rest between us.

Huh, this is new.

Yet I couldn't bring myself to move my hand away. I look from where he's touching me to his face, and I see the question there, whether he's going too far or not. I offer a small smile in return, which has him continuing.

"Did you know, a Dirty Kai is a couple who sixty-nine each other's toes?" he asks, trying to keep a straight face, and I can't help but chuckle.

"You think that one's funny?"

He pulls a packet of Doritos out of nowhere.

"A Dirty Luna is when you give a hand job for a bag of these bad boys," he says with a smirk, and I just laugh harder.

"These are brilliant, any other good one's?"

"Roman's was a dick sword fight and Parker's had Oscar jealous, because his own was gross."

"Why?" I ask, caught in the magic of his words.

"A Dirty Parker is the act of splitting a girl in half with

a huge cock," he grins.

I could do with a Dirty Parker right now, and the look on Kai's face tells me he knows where my head just went.

I don't know what's going on here, with any of the guys, but there is a connection that I just can't deny. None of them have complained I fucked Roman, but it's probably because they do things like this, stroke my hand or kiss my head, which can be just as intimate and leave me grasping for control.

Red just laughs, especially because she isn't used to seeing them be gentle either. Roman continued to train her this week while I've not been able too. I'm glad they're taking care of her, she comes more out of her shell around them every day, and even though our circumstances are difficult I see the happiness on her face that she's not alone anymore.

We pull up outside the Business building, and as much as I could sit here and let him draw gentle patterns on my skin all day, we head out. Stepping out of the car I have to take a minute to compose myself, putting the walls back up that he just melted away. My mind doesn't fully trust them yet, but it seems my soul does, and it's a constant battle internally, which usually leaves me on edge.

Heading towards Red and the other guys, I notice all the tutors are standing around and it looks like they're organizing documents. I'm not sure what's going on, so I ask the group. Everyone, including Red, looks to Roman to answer, which doesn't sit well with me, because that means he's the only one with the balls to tell me.

Releasing a sigh, I prepare myself for what's about to come out of his mouth. When even he doesn't know how to say it, I start to get frustrated and raise an eyebrow in question.

"Fuck, okay. I didn't realize it would be today, otherwise I'd have given you a heads up, but it looks like they're going to be handing out tasks," he says quickly.

The confusion is clear on my face because I have no clue what he's talking about.

"Shit, they're going to give us a different type of assignment. One's which match our bloodlines."

"You mean they're going to be handing out criminal activity assignments?" I'm surprised, but deep down I know I shouldn't be. As much as we'd been learning about this world, it was only a matter of time before we were expected to begin being more active in our roles. Just over two weeks in, and they're already throwing it at us.

"Yeah, pretty much," Roman responds quietly, rubbing the back of his neck.

Before I can ask anything else, a tapping of a microphone gains everyone's attention.

Just like on our first day Barbette Dietrichson stands at the top of the steps waiting to address us.

"Good morning, students. I'm sure you're all thrilled about your next assignments. I remember this day when I attended Featherstone as a pupil, and the excitement I felt when I was able to finally contribute to the greater organization. It still lingers with me to this day."

Fuck, she sure loves the sound of her own voice.

"We've decided to spice it up a little this year and instead of giving you set tasks we're going to give you the chance to choose, a little like Russian Roulette if you please."

How fitting.

"We will present to you three envelopes, two of which represent tasks based on your expected skill set and the third is...a wild card shall we say," she chuckles, but it's sinister and has everyone on edge. I can feel the tension rolling off everyone.

"You will pick an envelope for your main bloodline,

and if both of your parents attended, you'll pick a second. The wild card is the same for everyone. If you happen to choose that envelope, you will participate in that assignment all at once. Understood?"

She looks around then claps her hands.

"Fantastic lets begin, there are six tables set around, one for each block."

I look to Red who squeezes my arm and sets off to find the Diamond area, I wish she wasn't on her own.

"Oh Ace's, if you'd like to come up here, I'll be assigning you personally," she calls gleefully, but it's so fake, and it feels like a trap.

Wren is standing at the front waiting and the guys line up behind her, with me trailing at the back. It's crazy how Ace is so small in student numbers, but holds the most power. I feel my phone buzzing in my bag and sneak a glance, a message has just come through.

West: Avoid the middle envelopes, they're the wild cards.

I don't respond, there isn't time if I want to pass it onto the others. I quickly fire a text to Red, hopeful she will get it in time, then pat Oscar on the back frantically.

Once I have his attention I lean in and whisper.

"Not the middle envelope, tell the others, quickly."

He searches my eyes a second then passes the message on. I see it reach Roman just as Wren begins choosing hers. He looks at me and I can only nod. Let's hope this wasn't a shit game of Telephone.

Wren takes two envelopes, from the outside. Ahh, so her mother doesn't want her taking part in the wild card. Which has me consider the fact that if she represents her mother's bloodline, who was her father? It soon leaves my mind as I watch Roman step up to choose his. He takes the two from the outside and moves along, thank God. I watch Parker reach for one when Dietrichson intervenes.

"Oh Parker, your father has asked for you to take two, you know, to prove your worth."

Fucking bitch.

I can't control the growl that leave's my throat. Parker looks to Roman who nods, and he picks another. I watch as she switches the envelopes around and I panic. Luckily, Parker caught the move too and picks the right envelope.

I'll kill her. I swear to God.

Parker quickly moves away from her and I know she's

just dampened his mood. Kai takes one, and Oscar pulls the two from the outside like Roman.

That just leaves me. I hate being this close to her, especially when I'm mad because I really want to strangle her. She holds the three envelopes out as she did the others and I go to take the two ends, when she pulls them back.

"How silly of me, if you think you can attend this prestigious Academy representing three bloodlines, it would only be fitting for you to take all three, don't you think?"

She tries to thrust them all at me, but I step back a little and glance around trying to remain calm. I hear someone swear, and I lock eyes with West who gives a slight nod. I can't get out of this. I have no choice but to accept them, but the wild card can't be good.

I'm not prepared for anything that lays inside these envelopes, but I refuse to let her see that. Placing a sickly sweet smile on my face, I hold my hands out.

"Of course, I would be honored to complete the *THREE* assignments for the bloodlines I represent, thank you for giving me the opportunity," I say, grabbing them out of her hands. I hold her stare as I place them in my handbag, offering her a wink before slowly stepping back. Leaving her stunned in silence.

That makes a change.

I don't want to open them near her. I refuse to give her the satisfaction of seeing my response. So I make my way to Red.

"You okay?" I ask her, seeing the frustration in her eyes.

"Yeah, it's something I'm completely capable of, I just hate being a pawn for these criminals," she responds, holding out her card.

FEATHERSTONE ACADEMY

WITH YOUR SKILLSET WE WOULD LIKE TO OFFER YOU

THE OPPORTUNITY TO:

CREATE GAS EXPLOSIVES

WE WANT TWO DOZEN

YOU HAVE SIX WEEKS TO COMPLETE

FAILURE TO COMPLETE IS NOT AN OPTION

GOOD LUCK

What the hell? I look at her.

"This is why you take Science, huh?" I say, waggling my eyebrows at her, trying to ease her tension. She nods and her cheeks turn red.

"Red, are you blushing?"

I can't help but tease her, and it has her grinning back and smacking my arm.

"Hey, if this is what you have to do to survive then we make it work, okay?" I say wrapping my arm around her shoulders.

"Yeah."

I feel the guys approach, all of them frowning, which must be because of their assignments. Before anyone can say anything, Dietrichson's at it again.

"I'm sure you'll all need some time to consider what you have been assigned, and with that in mind Business is cancelled this morning, for you to begin organizing what has been asked of you. All other classes for the day will continue. On a final note, I want to make it very clear that failure to complete your assignments will mean you are no longer able to attend Featherstone Academy."

She surveys the crowd before continuing, hoping a pause will build anticipation. "You won't ever leave these grounds, if you catch my meaning." With that she walks straight to a waiting car and leaves.

Did she really just tell everyone if we didn't complete

our tasks, we're as good as dead? Fuck. If we were unsure how dark this world would get, she just told us. If we're no use to Featherstone, we're no use at all.

Looking around our small group, I sigh.

"I'd rather not read these so publicly, so I'm going to take a car, read it on the drive and grab a coffee."

"I'll meet you there, if that's ok?" Red asks and I just give her a nod.

I'm too focused on what my assignments will be.

Stepping into the closest Rolls, Kai follows. I raise my eyebrow at him, and he just shrugs his shoulders.

"We all know I have a calming effect on you, and I think you're going to need it, Sakura," he says quietly.

I don't respond. When the car starts moving, I begin opening the envelopes that are burning holes in my bag.

FEATHERSTONE ACADEMY
WITH YOUR SKILLSET WE WOULD LIKE TO OFFER YOU THE OPPORTUNITY TO:
ACQUIRE THE BLUEPRINTS FOR DCM TECH HEADQUARTERS
WE EXPECT ALL OF THEM
YOU HAVE SIX WEEKS TO COMPLETE

FAILURE TO COMPLETE IS NOT AN OPTION
GOOD LUCK

Fuck. This has Moon and Steele written all over it. This I can deal with. Opening the second a picture of a man also falls out too.

FEATHERSTONE ACADEMY
WITH YOUR SKILLSET WE WOULD LIKE TO OFFER YOU THE OPPORTUNITY TO:
SECURE SPECIAL AGENT DOMINIC BRIDGE ON OUR PAYROLL
BY ANY MEANS NECESSARY
YOU HAVE SIX WEEKS TO COMPLETE
FAILURE TO COMPLETE IS NOT AN OPTION
GOOD LUCK

What the hell? Any means necessary? At least that doesn't mean death if they want him on the payroll. This sounds like a Hindman skill set. Preparing myself, I open the last envelope, the one I know is the wild card.

> FEATHERSTONE ACADEMY
>
> WE WOULD LIKE TO GIVE YOU THE OPPORTUNITY TO TRIAL A BRAND-NEW SEGMENT OF THE GAMES AMONGST YOUR FELLOW STUDENTS
>
> YOU ARE HEREBY CALLED TO PARTICIPATE IN THE PYRAMID
>
> YOU WILL BE ADVISED AT LEAST TWO HOURS AHEAD OF COMMENCEMENT WHEN WE SEE FIT
>
> FAILURE OR SURVIVAL IS THE GAME
>
> GOOD LUCK

I re-read it a few times and I can't seem to figure it out. What the fuck is The Pyramid? I was unsure if I was going to show the others my assignments, but I think I'll need to with this one. I sink back into my seat massaging my temples, feeling Kai glancing at me from the corner of his eye.

I know I need to give this my all now. There's no option anymore, to blend in like Rafe asked me to, that much is clear. I need to learn everything I can because I need to if I want to survive.

And I will survive.

TWENTY ONE

Luna

"Hey Luna, is everything okay?" Rafe answers the phone, echoing around the kitchen on speaker phone.

"Well, have you spoken to West at all? They handed out assignments today," I ask, swirling an empty glass on the kitchen table, it's oddly relaxing.

There's a pause before he answers.

"I had a missed call from him earlier, but I haven't had a chance to respond." He goes quiet. "How bad is it?"

I recap the whole 'spice things up' shit, and the fact that I had to take all three envelopes even after West's warning text.

"What the fuck is going on? You're only supposed to be given one for the time being, and another one next month if required, but three? Talk me through them," he grunts.

So I do, word for word I read each card out in the order of which I read them myself. The first I'm confident with, I've stolen documents and intel before, I just need to start doing the prep work for it.

The second card, forcing someone into this world doesn't sit well with my heart, but I can't fail if the result at the end is my death. I explain the third card.

"The last Rafe, the wild card, has me for a loop. It's so vague I'm on edge," I sigh, resting my head in my hands.

"Tell me."

"Okay, it reads, we would like to give you the opportunity to trial a new segment of The Games amongst your fellow students. You are hereby called to participate in The Pyramid. You will be given at least two hours' notice prior to commencement when we see fit. Failure or survival is the game, good luck."

I wait for him to say something because I don't know what to even say. He's quiet for so long, I start to wonder if we've lost connection when he suddenly thunders.

"Are you fucking telling me, that they plan to force you to take part in a new segment of The Games? Before the actual games? This is a joke, it fucking must be. I know people have participated in trials before, but out of choice not force. I have no idea what The Pyramid is. Press whatever buttons on your phone to get West on here as well Luna. Right. Now," he grits out.

Shit.

I fumble with the buttons, and West's voice breaks through the phone.

"Hey, I tried to call after the assignments, but you mustn't have gone home," he says casually.

"This isn't my fucking home, West," I say, picking at the most ridiculous of things.

While Rafe yells, "Did you know anything about this West? Because if you did and didn't give me a heads up, I'm going to beat the shit out of you, do you hear me?"

Fuck, I thought I'd heard Rafe mad before, but I was definitely wrong, if this is anything to go by.

"Rafe, calm down, I don't know what you're talking about," West defends.

"The fucking assignments, did you know what the wild card was?"

"No, I just knew whatever the wild card was, made Dietrichson smile. So I knew it couldn't be good, how bad is it?"

"Bad enough for Featherstone to be trialing a new fucking segment of The Games on whoever picked the fucking card," Rafe spits out.

I feel like I should just end the call, let them yell at each other.

"What? They can't do that. Can they?" West asks.

"You fucking tell me. Luna can you take a photo of each of them and send them to me, use your own laptop so it can't be traced, okay? Then I can forward it on."

"Yeah sure. What am I supposed to do with all of this Rafe?"

His sigh is heavy down the phone.

"For now, focus on the first two cards while we look into the third. Hopefully we'll have answers before they spring it on you."

"Okay." I don't know what else to say.

"Luna, we'll figure it out, just make sure you take it easy while you're still recovering, alright?" Rafe says, which just has me rolling my eyes.

"Alright, keep me updated on what you find out though,

okay? I need to know as soon as you guys do. Remember, no secrets."

"I swear, Luna, send me the photos." With that Rafe hangs up.

"I'm sorry, Luna, I didn't know," West says quietly.

"It's okay, it's not your fault," I pacify, but I really don't have the effort for this.

"I better go send these photos over before he's calling me back."

"Yeah, of course. If you need me, call okay?"

I hum in response and end the call, staring at the phone like answers are about to pop out of it. I make quick work of getting the pictures over, the quicker I can start the process, hopefully, the quicker we get answers.

I decide to take my mind off everything by tattooing flowers into grapefruits from the fridge, because I'm cool like that. I need to ask Rafe to sort out some pig skin for me. I've tattooed people already, but I love how therapeutic it can be, and that will give me a bigger surface.

I'm completely zoned out when I hear a knock on the door. Unsure who it might be, I put all my stuff away before I answer. Checking the security system on my phone, I see it's Red. That's me not practicing anymore. Although, her company is worth it.

"No bitches allowed," I yell through the door.

I see her giggle and stick her finger up at the peephole. Shit, my girl grew some balls. I love it. Swinging the door open I pop my hip, all attitude.

"You touch your mamma with them fingers?" I ask, putting on a bad attempt of a southern accent.

She hip checks me and saunters in, anyone else would be thrown to the floor, but it just makes me laugh.

"What are you doing in here all alone?" She quizzes, looking around the lounge, and back to me.

"Minding my own business, you want to try it?" I sass back, which just gets me an eye roll.

"Well to save you from being beyond boring we can either go to a little party, or I can have a sleepover here. What will it be?"

How do I actually not get a say in any of this? The determination on her face tells me I can argue but I have no chance of getting rid of her, and a small part of me doesn't want to. Deciding I like her a lot more than having to over socialize, I opt for the sleepover.

"Perfect, so you go choose what movie we're watching in your swanky lounge and I'll get the pizza ordered while

I run and grab my bag." She doesn't even give me a backwards glance as she heads back out again.

Bossy bitch. Although I am loving her newfound confidence.

She didn't even shut the door properly. As I go to shut it, I see Roman come out of his room, and he spots me straight away.

"Hey, we're going for a few drinks at a party just off campus, you up for it?"

As tempting as his black fitted jeans and loose white tee are, I already chose sleepover, so sleepover it is.

"Thanks for the offer, but we're apparently having a girl's night," I smile, as I wrap my hands around my throat pretending to choke myself out. Roman just laughs at my antics.

"You mean Red cornered you, and you went for the easiest option?"

Acehole. I just stick my tongue out, because apparently I can be playful, who knew?

"You sure I can't tempt you? I could get Parker involved to convince you?" He grins, as he steps in closer, leaning against the door frame.

Oh, he thinks he's funny, I see how it is. Placing my

hand on his chest, I find myself leaning towards him, but before I have a chance to respond Red comes waltzing out of the elevator.

"Nope, no, no way, go away Roman. She's mine tonight, no dicks allowed. Now shoo. Go on. Get," she shouts, as she starts flapping her hands around for him to leave.

Fuck, she's feisty tonight, towards Roman too. I'm proud. Even Roman's surprised if his jaw hanging open is anything to go off, but he nods his head.

"Fine, don't get comfortable though, I'm letting you have this one night," he says with a wink, as he reaches his hand out and squeezes my waist. Fuck, such little contact and it has me hot, but he's already stepped back and heading for the stairs.

"Have a good night, ladies." He salutes with a grin, and then he's gone.

"Please tell me you've chosen a guy already?" she calls as she saunters past and into my room.

"What?" I can't help but squeal. "You always been this nosey, Red?" I fumble, completely caught off guard with her question.

"You bet your ass I have, you just help my confidence.

You're stuck with me either way though, because you never declined the best friend statement. So, no takesy backsies, but you didn't answer my question," she giggles.

Shutting the door, I turn to meet her gaze seeing the humor in her eyes, and I can't help but grin.

"Why choose?" I say with a wink, and she just laughs out loud.

"That is such a Luna answer right there," she chuckles, as she saunters into the kitchen. Apparently the conversation is over.

As hard as life is right now, I find myself able to embrace some happiness amongst all the darkness. The guys and Red being a big part of that. So, I'll accept this best friend business, even though she's crazy as shit. Tricking me with her innocence, but secretly she's as feisty as her nickname.

"I swear to God, Luna, all this food in here, I better find some good snacks," she continues yelling.

I think I'm going to enjoy girl's night.

Monday rolls around too quickly. Probably because I struggled to get a moment's peace with Red around, but I must have enjoyed myself as it went by so quickly.

She allowed the guys entry on Sunday afternoon and we relaxed, binge-watching Power on TV for hours, like normal people. Not people set to commit crimes to survive this crazy place.

The guys always wait in the lobby for me in the mornings, but they still haven't been able to get Wren to back off. She's still hovering round Roman like a fly to shit, and her bitches are clawing at my other men. I refuse to show my green monster though, there are bigger battles to fight here.

Monday mornings are slightly different, seeing as I have a free period to start the day, although I can't help but worry about Red having L.F.G with Wren. Who knows what the crazy bitch will do next?

I finally went down to the gym this morning and did a slower workout. My body is screaming a little, especially around my ribs, but I feel amazing. I feel focused again, and ready to work on my assignments. I'm going to go full Luna 'Moon' and get the blueprints first, while I figure out how on earth I'm going to force a Special Agent onto Featherstone's books.

I'm almost ready for classes, when I hear a knock on my door.

The feed I see on my phone is my own CCTV set up, so I'm not relying solely on Featherstone's facilities. Especially if Dietrichson has any access. I wouldn't put it past them to mess with it. It's not noticeable unless you're really looking, and it's so small I've never had one register when someone's been scanning for bugs. They're what I usually use when scoping out locations I'm about to loot.

Checking the screen, I see it's the guys and head to let them in.

"Good morning, senorita. How is my little lady today?" Oscar greets as he barges through the group, wrapping his arm around my shoulder.

I can't get used to his touchy-feely personality, but I let him squeeze me for a moment, before I step out of his space. Which has him giving me his puppy dog eyes.

"What are you guys doing here?" I ask, glancing around them all.

"We were hoping to compare our assignment cards with you, seeing as all of ours interlink somehow," Roman responds.

I don't really want people to know what I have to do, but I could also use the back up and their thoughts as well. I think I'm more scared that they're going to screw me over, and I don't want to admit how much that would actually hurt.

"Okay, let me grab them. I read all yours first though, understood?" I ask firmly.

"Whatever you need, Princess," he says, holding his hands up in surrender.

There he goes with that nickname again. Never has anyone even remotely considered me a princess, but it doesn't seem to grate on me like it used to do.

Dashing off, I grab all three cards and walk back into the lounge where they are all sprawled out, like it's their place and not mine.

"Make yourself at home why don't you," I say sarcastically, which just gets me snickers in response.

"I'd be much more comfortable with you sitting on my lap, baby girl," Oscar says with a grin, which earns him a smack on the head from Roman.

Parker and Kai are sitting on the other couch which leaves me having to choose which pair to join. I opt to sit closest to Parker.

"No fair, baby girl," whines Oscar.

"Oh, boo hoo Oscar, Kai gets to carpool with me, Roman gets me for B.I.C.E and you can be my partner for combat." I counter without even looking up, but my tummy does a little flip at the fact that I just organized myself for everyone to have my attention.

I will not get embarrassed. I will not.

"But, baby, I want to show you what I can do in private," he begs, but I pretend I haven't heard him which has Parker chuckling beside me, as he slips his arm around the back of my neck.

I hold my hand out and they all become more serious, handing their cards over.

Parker: to create six fully working grapplers and design an undetectable tracking device

Kai: hack into DCM Tech systems

Oscar: create stimulus shots to leave temporary paralysis (minimum of two hours) and destroy a safe house for the Agency

Roman: confirm a business contract with DCM Tech and provide surveillance of Special Agent Dominic Bridge

Holy shit, the tasks really do interlink. I wordlessly pass my cards to Parker for him to read and pass along, nobody mentions the third card until everyone has read it.

"What the hell is The Pyramid? My father has never mentioned trials like this being run here before," Roman says, but I don't know how to respond because I have no idea.

So he gets a nice shrug from me.

"I'll put some feelers out to him okay? Mention that I saw a few people get it, but I won't name you," he offers, and I nod in thanks to him.

"West and Rafe are looking into it too."

"Good, the more ears to the ground the better."

We all take a moment to further connect the dots between our assignments, and Kai is the one to give us a run through.

"So, they want grapplers, tracking devices and stim shots from us."

"Oh, Red's is to create gas explosives too," I add, remembering her card.

"Okay, then in regards to DCM Tech, they want me to hack into the systems, their HQ blueprints stolen and a business contract of some kind confirmed."

We all nod in agreement.

"Then, they want surveillance of a Special Agent, who they want on their books. Which could be linked in some way to the Agency safe house they want rid of," he finalizes. "How do you feel about this Luna?"

"Honestly, getting the blueprints is fine. I just don't know how I'm going to force someone into joining Featherstone, but I'm going to have to figure it out because I refuse to give them a reason to beat me," I answer honestly.

"What do you mean the blueprints are fine?" Roman questions, a frown on his face.

I sigh not wanting to give too much away, but I also need them to know I don't need to be babied.

"You're forgetting my bloodline, I have experience. You don't need to worry about that." Keeping my voice relaxed. I feel them all staring at me, trying to figure out what I just said.

"How much experience?" asks Parker. Typical of him to ask, he's the best one for getting into my head.

"Enough experience that when I was being dragged here, I found out I'd already completed jobs for Featherstone."

Parker's eyes go wide, and he looks to the others. Me and my big mouth. I need to learn to shut the hell up.

"Holy shit," yells Oscar, gaining everyone's attention.

"You're Moon," he splutters, shaking a finger in my direction.

"What did you just say?" I can't help the defensive snarl. What the hell does he know?

"I remember during the summer, my father was on the phone discussing some documents he'd acquired. He specifically said, it'll be better when we have Moon fully integrated. Keep me up to date on her arrival at the Academy."

His eyes took me in with a new light. What does his father know about me?

"I think you need to leave," I say flatly, heading towards the door.

"Hold up, Luna, it's okay. Calm down," Roman says, jumping up to stop my march to the door.

"Believe me, they have had every single student here do something without them knowing. My father says they call it the right of passage, so they can see what level you're already at," he adds, as he gently strokes my arm.

It's clear I'm a deer caught in the headlights. I'm frozen to the spot. I don't know how to handle that they know about my secret, and that it's completely the norm for this place.

Roman turns me to face him, stepping closer into my space, and cups my cheek.

"Luna, it doesn't matter what you did before here. It doesn't matter what you have to do here. What matters is that we survive, understood?"

Searching his eyes, I see nothing but the truth to his words, and I find myself nodding in agreement. His phone starts ringing and I move to step back, but his hand moves to the back of my neck, holding me in place.

"That's my alarm, we need to start heading to Combat," he says to everyone, but his eyes don't leave mine.

"Now let us help take your stress away," he murmurs, as he inches closer, touching his lips to mine. As demanding as ever he tightens his grip and devours my mouth, having me claw at his shirt in retaliation.

Just as quickly as it started he steps back, with a wicked gleam in his eye, and motions with his hand. In the next breath, Oscar has his hands on my waist and his lips against mine. Wow, to say his mouth gets him into shit, his actual lips have me melting. I can't help but raise my hands to his face and graze his bottom lip with my teeth, and the moan he gives me hits straight to my core.

Fuck. As soon as it escapes his lips, Roman is pulling him away from me.

"Share, Oscar," he orders, and before I can see his response, Kai is in my space.

He raises his thumb, tracing my lips and it has me mesmerized. He searches my face ensuring I want this, and it's definitely clear in my eyes because my body is screaming for him. For all of them. I grab him by the lapels of his blazer, lifting my lips to meet his. Kai's kiss is tantalizingly slow, but I follow his lead, such a contrast to the other two.

He steps back and makes space for Parker, who rests his forehead against mine. He looks into my eyes, seeing my soul as always, it's so willing for him to peer in. Our noses brush slightly as he gently moves where we are connected. His lips touch mine in the softest caress I have ever felt, but it wraps around my heart and squeezes. I have to hold on to him to keep myself upright. Damn, I could get lost in this.

As soon as the thought crosses my mind Parker is stepping back too, and I can't help the pout at the loss of contact. The lust in all of their eyes lets me know I'm not the only one. Roman wraps his arm around my shoulder and moves us towards the door. Stopping to grab my bag he leans in to whisper.

"Parker doesn't like kissing, he finds it too personal. He's different with you." With that he steps back and leads everyone out.

Parker's hand finds mine and I can't help but enjoy this. This is a completely different level of intimacy and it has me wanting more.

KC KEAN

TWENTY TWO

Luna

Heading over to the academic buildings, I'm relaxing in the Rolls after our brutal session in Combat this morning. I'm ready for a nap already, Wednesdays are always the longest.

I enjoy riding with Kai though, loving our newfound foreplay, where he caresses my hand between us like I'm a delicate flower. What I'd really like to do is get on my knees but somehow this is more. I've hinted for him to caress me elsewhere but he just smirks.

Ian holds the door open for me to get out, and I'm surprised to find posters and flyers everywhere. The bright pink and yellow splashes of color dotting every surface, look like someone set off a giant confetti cannon.

Stepping towards a giant poster, I'm handed an invite, Ace scrawled in gold boldly at the top of the card. I continue to read, so I can see what the deal is.

FEATHERSTONE ACADEMY

You are cordially invited to attend this year's

Fall Ball

25th September 2020

19:00 sharp

Monte Carlo Themed

This fantastic event will be held in the ballroom

of the Main Hall

Attendance is mandatory

Fantastic, another event to look forward to. I flip it over, seeing that it stipulates the dress code requirements, and the menu that'll be served. It's just a load of fancy shit; caviar, white truffle, and foie gras. I hope I can order food when I get back to my room.

Red's suddenly wrapping her arm through mine, all bouncy with excitement. I can't help but roll my eyes.

"You're going to love this aren't you?" I sigh, as we walk up the steps to our Business class.

"Yep, it's going to be brilliant. It's only two weeks away so we can go dress shopping this weekend," she offers, but I couldn't think of anything worse.

"Or, we can look through all the brand-new shit in my dresser that my mother bought."

That has her eyes lighting up.

"Yes, definitely that, they'll be extra fancy and free," she giggles, as she gives my arm a little extra squeeze.

"So, which of the guys do you think will ask first?" she asks, trying to be innocent, but she just loves the easy drama of the boys bickering over me.

"That's irrelevant, you'll be my date, Miss Sunshine. I'll stay for the shortest time possible and have a party for one back in my room, deal?"

"Deal, but boy talk isn't over." She fake scowls, as we walk into Business.

Wren is sprawled all over Romans desk, making a nice show of herself, boobs in his face and her fingers running through his hair.

It makes me want to smack a bitch.

But I can't, I have to keep myself out of it, even though

the green-eyed monster is rearing its ugly head. Technically, we are anti-commitment and I need to remember that.

"Come on, Roman baby, the dance will be amazing. I need some alone time with you, it's been forever. I'll make it worth your while," she purrs, for everyone to hear.

"I already said no, Wren. So you can move now," Roman responds, keeping his tone uninterested.

The glare she sends around the room has everyone on edge, except me because I know my name is about to be dragged into it. I can see it in her sneer as she catches sight of me.

"Is it because of that dumb bitch?"

She doesn't say my name, but everyone knows she means me. I don't comment or cast my gaze her way, I just take my seat and pull my phone out like I'm oblivious to the whole thing.

"Wren. Back. Off," Roman growls.

"No, Roman. She shows up, and suddenly I'm a used doll and I won't stand for it. Over my dead body will you go to the ball with her, do you understand? I'll make sure it doesn't happen, you've been spending enough time with that whore. I refuse to let it continue!" she screams, but I refuse to rise to her bait, even though it's really fucking hard. My fingernails are cutting into my palm, I'm trying so hard to hold myself back.

Instead, it's Parker that slams his chair back and plants his fists on the table.

"Fuck off, Wren, now. I've heard enough of your shit." He's practically spitting, and she just cackles in his face.

"So, whose is she then? Because we all know she's not yours, Parker. You like dick too much for that, don't you?"

WHAT. THE. HELL.

He can like whatever the fuck he wants, and she should not be calling him out in front of everyone like that. I'm ready to get involved now, not for myself but for Parker, but his menacing snicker has me glued to my seat.

"Wren, don't kid yourself, I'm Bi. I was just never interested in your pussy and fake tits, don't confuse the two."

A few people can't contain their chuckles at his dig, including Red beside me, who has to cup a hand over her mouth.

"Whatever. I'd never let a guy inside me who actually let someone tattoo the word minge on him anyways," she sneers.

Nobody responds because she's a petty bitch trying to

embarrass Parker, and she's not liking that it doesn't have the effect she wants.

Glancing at Parker I can tell he's not fazed by what she's said, but there is a little worry in his eyes when he meets my gaze, like any of it would send me running for the hills. I offer him a wink in reassurance, as Wren walks in my direction.

I can't control my own petty bitch, as I kick my bag out from under the table. She trips over it and the room breaks out in laughter. By the time she's got back to her feet, I'm back to playing on my phone, pretending I'm unaware of the situation.

"You fucking bitch," she screeches, just as Penny walks in.

"Wren, please take your seat, you're wasting time."

With a final sneer at me, she storms off. I can almost see smoke coming out of her ears. Oscar sends me a wink like that was hot shit, but I don't take him on. Instead I'm processing what she just spilled about Parker. Bi. That's hot, I'm not afraid to admit I love me some man on man action. Please tell me with at least one of the other guys because that's gonna make my day. How do I ask to watch? Is that rude? I need it to not be.

Shaking my head to stop myself getting carried away in my sex induced mind, I consider what else she said. Who the hell tattooed my Parker with the word minge?

I need to fix it.

Last lesson is History, so I have a chance to chat with Parker. I'll wait till after class, because as open as he was happy to be in Business earlier, I don't like the thought of pushing him again. I've already told Red I'm busy after classes and she just smirked at me like she thought I was going to get it on with four sexy men. Not today, sadly.

Gina walks in and the door is locked behind her, as always.

"Good afternoon class, we'll start off with a few of you telling us what new things you've been learning about your bloodline, then we'll get on to the projector."

She calls a few names out and they tell her random facts, all of no significance. It's as if the families are trying to give as little away as possible. I asked Rafe for some information, and he told me it was best to stick to my mother's family for the time being. Seeing as they weren't Ace level, the information would be softer.

"Luna Steele please," she says, but doesn't look at me.

"I learned that my mother, Veronica Hindman, infiltrated a well-known company and embezzled over a million pounds in a two-week period," I respond blandly.

She nods with her head still down, continuing through her list of names.

"Jessica Watson."

Red's back straightens instantly.

"Err, yes. I learnt that my father created the toxic chambers for The Games," she sounds queasy as she says it, but she pushes through.

There are a few gasps around the room, and I'm not sure if one came from me. What's the toxic chambers? I won't ask her though, I'll find out from someone else.

The rest of the class is spent watching another film about life before 2008. They talk like it was long ago, not the twelve years that it's been.

I make sure Red is okay before she gets into her SUV. There's only one guy in our History class that's also a Diamond, and he's already seated waiting for her. She seems okay, just a little ruffled having to openly say what her father has done for Featherstone.

I climb into the Rolls and kick off my heels, they're

always the worst on the days I've had combat. Before I have a chance to protest, Parker is lifting my feet into his lap and forcing me to turn sideways in my seat. His thumbs go straight to the ache and the pressure is pure bliss, I can't contain the moan that escapes.

"God, Parker, that feels so good," I groan, with my eyes closed.

"Hmm, I'm glad you think so, but I need you to contain those moans for me, okay?" he says, while gripping tighter. This has me biting my lip as hard as I can, because staying quiet is not easy.

"In future, when I offer a foot massage, I'm going to bring headphones and look out of the window because you're killing me," he groans.

I force my eyes open and take him in. The lust in his gaze and his rapid breathing make him even sexier, and it turns me on.

Fuck.

I can't let this progress, yet, not before I have the chat I want. He must see something switch in my eyes.

"You want to talk about what Wren said, huh?" He doesn't look mad, so I slowly nod my head.

"Okay, do you mind if I grab a quick shower, then I'll

head up?"

I want to offer for him to shower in my room, but I don't. I think he needs a minute to himself and it'll help clear my head too.

"Yeah, of course. Want to order food too?"

My heart pounds a little, the last time I was alone with one of them was Roman, but that feels almost circumstantial. This time I want to talk and understand him a little more, and I want to help.

"Only if it's pizza," he grins as the car pulls up outside of Ace.

I slip my heels back on and we walk in together. I head for the stairs, but he steers me to the elevator. He must feel my shoulders tense because he's instantly soothing me.

"I got you, Luna."

He fucking better, he's slowly making me have trust in him. He takes the elevator up to my floor with me before he heads back down.

While he's not here I jump in the shower too, changing into a pair of leggings and a khaki green off the shoulder top. Throwing my hair up in a bun, I wipe all my make-up off and feel instantly relaxed. Hopeful that I can tempt him, I pull out my ink kit but leave it in my bedroom.

A knock on the door has me checking the camera feed, it's Parker. I wipe my hands on my leggings nervously and open the door. The feed did him no justice. He's dressed in a pair of fitted grey joggers with a simple plain white tee, and his curly hair is still damp. He's a wet fucking dream.

I'm not sure if I'm drooling or not, but he steers me inside and shuts the door with a mischievous grin on his face. Lifting my jaw off the floor, I whack him on the chest and head for the lounge.

"I'm starving Luna, what pizza do you want?"

"Meat feast, please."

"I think I like you most based on your pizza choices," he says with a wink as he calls it in.

What is it with these sweet ones getting all sure of themselves? Between him and Red I feel well and truly conned.

I hold up a bottle of water and some iced tea, hinting for him to choose, and he nods at the iced tea. I pour us both a glass and get comfortable on the sofa, pressing a few buttons on the sound system and the Imagine Dragons – Evolve album comes through the speakers. This is my artistic go-to, the beat thumps through my veins and I love it.

"So you want to talk about me being bisexual, huh?" he

says as he sits next to me, shaking his fingers through his hair.

The confusion on my face reflects back at me from Parker's.

"Err, I mean we can. I do have questions if you're open to answering them, but my main focus right now is the other thing Wren mentioned," I say, lifting my legs under me so I can turn and face him better.

"So you're not upset about my sexuality?" he asks, tilting his head at me.

"Fuck no, if anything it's a turn on, but you're distracting me from the point." I fake glare.

The grin on his face is part appreciation, part predator. Seeing it on Parker's face has me melting. This guy. There is so much I don't know, but I can't help but want to find out. I point at him sternly and he sighs, but relaxes back into the cushions.

"I didn't think that tattoo would be an issue for you."

"Issue? When did I say it was an issue?" I can't help the scowl on my face and the defensive tone, but maybe he needs to not assume he knows everything.

"Then I'm confused why you want to talk about it." I can feel him getting defensive too. This really isn't going how I wanted.

"Do you want to tell me the story behind it?" I ask cautiously.

"It's not really a big deal. When my father's men found me, a part of my process was for them to mark me, and they thought it would be funny to print the word minge instead. I was barely fourteen and I'd lived a sheltered life before, so I didn't really understand at the time. Since then, I've had the crosses on my fingers done but no one has been willing to cover up my arm."

Wow. That's not what I was expecting the story to be. What vile men. It's not like Wren said at all, but it shouldn't surprise me that Parker never told her the truth. Yet he told me, and that means something to me.

Before I can ask anything else there's a knock. I let Parker answer it as I checked the monitor on my phone, as much as I'm trying with the guys I don't want them to know about this. This is my security from everyone.

The greasy smell that fills the air has my tummy growling, and I snatch a box from Parker. Luckily it's my meat feast, otherwise I'd have to apologize or something. Instead I smile wide at him, making him shake his head.

We eat with just the music in the background for a little

while, happy to enjoy each other's company and the good food. When I'm done, I place my box on the coffee table and anxiously look at Parker.

"Can I show you something?" I ask.

Happy to go along he nods, and I run to grab everything I pulled out earlier. I can tell he's slightly confused with what's going on, but sits quietly waiting for me to wheel my setup over.

"Right okay, I know I don't really talk about anything prior to being here, except that I had no choice, but I was never going to college. I'd already chosen my career path for as long as I can remember, it just took a long time to get Rafe to agree."

I pause.

"Sorry, I'm rambling. You can say no, that is completely fine, but I just wanted to offer."

Why am I so nervous? I know I can do this for him.

"You're still not telling me what you're offering, Luna." He smirks.

Acehole.

"Right, I've been a trainee tattoo artist for the past two years," I rush out.

The shocked look on his face makes it clear I just talked

a lot of shit, and he had no idea what I was getting at. I sink my head into my hands. What an idiot. Forget it.

"You know what, forget I said anything okay." I stand to wheel everything back, but Parker grasps my wrist gently.

"Are you serious?" he asks quietly, like he can't believe what I'm offering.

I simply nod, which has him pulling me closer to stand in between his legs. He holds my waist tight and rests his head against my stomach. I don't know what I'm supposed to do, but I think he needs a minute. Wanting to convey that I'm here for him I gently rub his shoulders, but then my hands are itching to run through his curls.

Tilting his head back, he rests his chin against my stomach and stares up at me. He looks so vulnerable right now and I can't look away.

"Please, Luna, make it go away," he murmurs.

Without saying a word, I pull everything over and meticulously clean and prep like my life depends on it. He sits quietly, looking through the portfolio I hand him. When I'm sure everything is perfect, I look at him.

"Have you decided what you want to go for?"

He nods and takes his top off revealing small lettering on his right bicep. I'm trying really hard to not get lost in those abs he's been hiding, and focus on the job at hand.

"I can't believe these are all your work, Luna, they're amazing," he praises.

"Thank you," I breathe in response.

I've never been good at compliments.

Bringing the portfolio over he turns it round and points dead center, to an intricate feather, with Aztec detailing and strength scribbled in the spine. I feel like I can't breathe.

"I drew this, but I didn't actually do the tattooing," I mutter.

"That's okay, I just know this is the one I want," he says, determined.

Lifting my t-shirt I show him high up on my ribs, always hidden by my sports bra at a minimum. He looks at what I'm showing him, then meets my eyes.

"Even better," he says as he leans in to give me a lingering kiss, not long enough though because he's soon stepping back.

"Let's get to it then, angel. I've always wanted a matching tattoo with someone."

MY BLOODLINE

KC KEAN

TWENTY THREE

Luna

I'm so ready to get to Weaponry this morning, because West has promised me the keys to Dot today. I'm Red's level of giddy and I can't help it. Ready to go, I'm surprised to see the guys hovering outside of my door when I open it.

"Err, good morning, everything okay?" I ask, eyeing them all.

"Yeah, apparently Parker wanted to show us all something this morning. Which includes you, and he didn't want to do it downstairs. So, here we are," Kai answers.

God I clearly need to clear out some private time for myself, because these guys have got me all hot just from standing near me.

"Good morning, angel," Parker says as he kisses me on the side of my head.

My eyes close instinctively, embracing the touch. When I finally remember to open my eyes it's to a knowing grin on Roman's face. Acehole. Parker takes off his jacket and hands it off to Oscar, proceeding to undo his shirt buttons.

"I didn't realize we were about to get sexual in public," Oscar jokes.

Which reminds me, we didn't get a chance to discuss the questions I have about Parker's sexuality last night.

Like if I can watch or not?

Parker must think the same because he sends me a cheeky wink. Seriously, who is this guy? Next thing I know he'll be as cocky as Oscar, and I can barely handle one of him.

"Fuck off, O'Shay," calls Parker, as he reveals his new tattoo.

I take in my work, beyond pleased with myself. While mine is horizontal, Parkers is more diagonal to make sure I could cover that cringy word. If you look hard enough you'll still see it slightly, but that was always going to be the case without lasering it off first.

The guys around me are all silent. Jaws to the floor, staring at his arm like it's a brand new one. Kai is the first to move, resting his hand on Parker's other arm.

"Parker, I'm pleased for you my friend." A man of few words as ever.

Oscar's next in line jumping on Parker's back.

"Woo hoo, my boy is winning at life right now." He laughs.

Before getting shoved aside by Roman. Roman stares at his arm up close for what seems like forever. When he lifts his gaze to meet Parkers, there is a lot of emotion there for his friend. They all know how important this clearly was to him, but Roman feels it for him the most.

"This is real right? No jokes," Roman whispers to Parker.

I feel like I'm watching a private moment, not meant for us to see, but the others aren't fazed.

"It's real, had it done last night."

Roman rests his forehead against Parkers and cups his cheek.

"You fucking deserve this. Do you understand? This is you taking a part of yourself back. This is a reminder to you, that they can't take everything, okay?"

Wow. His words hit me deep. This clearly meant more to them than just covering a crappy word up. Parker nods in response with a smile on his face and a single tear trickles down his cheek. I think my tear ducts are about to burst, but I contain myself because this isn't about me. The fact that something I did has given this level of happiness for Parker, will warm my soul forever.

Roman returns Parker's smile before placing a delicate kiss on his lips. Nothing more, but the connection between them is real. Eyes closed and embracing each other. How are all small touches with Parker so intimate? I'm burning up watching them.

"Parker, who did you even convince to do this?" Roman asks, as he steps back so Parker can get his shirt back on.

Parker doesn't respond, he just looks straight at me. The gratitude in his stare has me unable to move. It takes a moment before the guys realize what he's saying without using his words.

"Holy shit, baby girl, you did this?" screeches Oscar, pulling me from Parker's stare.

I can only nod in response. All the emotions around me have me stumbling for words. Kai kisses my forehead lightly in thanks for his friend, while Oscar continues.

"Baby girl, can I have one next? Pretty please, ice cream sundae with my dick on top?"

I can't help but laugh at him as he breaks the heaviness around us.

"Sure thing, just let me get a start on these assignments, okay?"

"Whatever you say, baby girl. I just want your hands on me, have you ever tattooed a cock before? I'm open to being your first try," he grins, while he ducks down, knowing a swing from Roman is coming, and the whole thing just makes me laugh.

Glancing at the time, we need to get moving.

"Not to break up the party, but I really need to get to Weaponry."

No one disagrees and we make our way down. As soon as we step into the lobby Wren's scowl is there to greet us, along with her bitch friends. Oscar throws his arm around me and steers us around them.

"Fucking bitch," someone sneers.

I'm close to done with their attitudes. I want to slaughter them all. Make them learn their place instead, but I'm trying really hard to do this Rafe's way. I just don't know how much longer I can cope.

Making it outside to the cars I step into a Rolls, and I'm surprised when it's Roman who climbs in with me.

"Take the long way round," he barks at the driver and lifts the partition.

Fuck.

Is he mad about the tattoo?

It's Parker's body, I shouldn't have to run everything by him.

Before I can open my mouth to defend myself, his hand is gripping the back of my neck and pulling me to his lips. He's not soft with me, not like with Parker. He devours my mouth, keeping complete control and taking all of my air. I'm wound up tight, especially thinking about how his lips had only just been on Parker's. He pulls back slightly.

"You, Princess, have been a very good girl," he purrs.

Fuck.

His fingers trail up the inside of my thigh slowly, my legs parting for him on their own accord. He's taking his sweet ass time but finally touches my soaked panties. He teases the outline but doesn't slip under them.

"Please."

I'm too needy right now to care that I'm begging. Removing his hand, he pushes my skirt up and rips my panties clean off.

Holy shit.

Before I can complain, he's thrusting two fingers inside of me, my head falls back and a moan passes my lips. He thrusts a little more, then circles his fingers inside me. Oh God. I can't stop my pussy clenching around his fingers, wanting more.

He retreats before I can cum, leaving me frustrated, but he just grins.

"I want your fire, Princess, and to get that, unfortunately, I'm going to need to piss you off."

"Or I can just take what I want," I rasp.

"Oh yeah, you think I'd just let you?"

"You will."

I don't say anymore as I throw my blazer off. Keeping my skirt around my waist I lift myself over and sit on his lap, his hands instinctively caress my thighs, but otherwise he remains still, grinning at me.

"What you got, Princess?"

Seeing as these uniform blouses are so low cut, I only need to undo one button to release my breasts, showing him I'd gone without a bra today. Sometimes I liked to tease myself with my nipples scratching away at the material all day. Luckily, today happens to be one of those days.

The surprise on his face, and the heat instantly in his eyes has me grinning instead.

"Roman, we both know how much you like tugging on my nipple piercings," I whisper seductively.

No further encouragement is needed before he's biting down on my right nipple hard.

"Oh fuck." I can't help but moan. I register that we're not really alone here, but then he's twisting my other nipple and everything else is forgotten. His dick is like steel beneath me.

"I forgot how rough you can take it," he mutters, as I grind against him. Making him follow up with a moan of his own.

Remembering this is about taking, I lean back. My nipples just out of reach, and cup my chest, rolling my thumbs over my taut peaks. He can't take his eyes off my hands, until I release a moan drawing his attention to my face.

"You're going to let me take now, and you're going to love it, yeah?"

He nods slowly in response, like he has no control over it.

"Good, I need you to sit on the floor with your head leaning back on the seat."

I lift back over to my seat while he does exactly as I said without question, which just makes me hotter. Moving back across, I position myself with my knees on either side of his head. Understanding dawns on his face and a wicked grin takes over.

"Fuck. If this is what you taking charge looks like, count me in."

"If only the guys could see you now, huh?"

"They'd still want to be me. They're gonna be sad they missed the show."

"I'll be sure to make it up to them," I say, as I lower my pussy just enough so that he has to reach his tongue right out.

Fuck.

He goes straight for circling my clit, and I gasp.

Not wanting him to think he's still in control, I go for exactly what I want. I grind my pussy against him, and his tongue is perfection. I drag my clit from his chin across his tongue and stop at the tip of his nose, before dragging myself back down again. The friction is divine, but I still need more. Cupping my breasts, I squeeze my nipples.

"Roman, get those thick fingers of yours back inside me," I groan, not stopping my motion.

He doesn't disappoint, holding them just right, so that when I drag back his fingers penetrate me. Oh God, I'm so close, as I drag back up his teeth latch on to my clit with his fingers still rooted inside me, and I feel him push another finger inside my ass.

Oh God, there's so much happening, I'm lost to it all.

Fuck.

I explode, biting the headrest in front of me, to contain myself from shouting.

I ride out every last ounce of pleasure, and he laps it up like he can't get enough. I move back, allowing him to sit back up on his seat. I go for his pants, but he stops my hands.

"No, Princess, this was about you, not me," he says as he crushes his lips against mine. Giving me a taste of myself on his lips.

"We're here," he murmurs.

Glancing out of the window I see we're just pulling up outside of Weaponry. I push my skirt back down and fasten my button. Roman hands me my blazer with a grin on his face.

"I'm going to enjoy knowing you've got nothing on underneath that skirt for the rest of the day," he says, and I can't help but grin along with him.

I go to open the door, when he places his hand over mine. All humor gone.

"Thank you, Luna, for what you did for Parker." I nod, the understanding clear between us.

I can see he wants to end on a lighter note when he gives me a sly grin.

"So, little Luna, likes a finger in her ass, huh?"

Oh. My. God.

It's something I'd have expected from Oscar and been prepared for. So the grin on his face tells me he knows he's caught me off guard.

Acehole.

So I lean in and whisper.

"Baby, anal is my favorite."

With a wink I climb out of the car and saunter off. I see all the guys staring at me with raised eyebrows, clearly you can tell I've just been enjoying myself. The heated stares are having me question whether getting the keys to Dot is worth it, but I quickly grab Red's arm and rush off before I change my mind.

"Can you two not be left alone?" Red questions with a giggle.

I just laugh along with her, when West stops in front of us, my keys outstretched. I snatch them up before he can play jokes on me. My smile is even bigger. Not wanting to draw attention to our interaction I carry on heading for the changing rooms.

Orgasms and motorcycles. Today is my kind of day.

I take it back, today is not my day.

I decide this as I'm walking through the doors for lunch, and Wren literally throws herself at me. Arms swinging.

"I fucking know what you were doing in the car this morning with Roman," she yells.

This girl is beyond crazy. She manages to catch a slap to my jaw, and that's when I decide.

Fuck it.

I've done this Rafe's way. I played nice, I didn't get involved, I didn't push back or stand my ground and it didn't mean shit. I'm done trying to keep everything at bay for other people, when this bitch just doesn't know when to quit. I've had enough of her catty antics, it's ridiculous.

The fact that she just came at me and it was with slaps? Featherstone be damned.

She raises her arm to do it again when I go straight for her throat. I'm not fucking around. Wrapping my hand around her neck, I swing her into the wall next to the door I had barely just walked through. The shock on her face has me sneering.

"You always have to underestimate me. I love it." I squeeze and I see the panic set in. Instead of backing off and letting go, I lift her off the floor. Not much, not even a foot, but I have her attention now.

"I've played nice, Wren. I let you and your mother attack me, and I did as I was told, but I've had about enough of your shit now," I growl.

Her face is bright red now and I can't bring myself to care, especially after her outburst at Parker yesterday too.

I feel a hand wrap around mine that's around her neck. Looking to see where that arm leads, I find my attention drawn to Oscar.

"Baby girl, I need you to let go of her now, okay?" I can't help but frown at him. She deserves everything she gets, why is he siding with her?

"I'm not siding with her, but I think you're pretty close

to killing her."

It's as if he's reading my mind. Had I said that out loud? I look back to Wren and as hard as it is, I find the strength to let go. Letting her slump to the floor gasping for air. Stark reality washes over me and I realize Oscar just stopped me from going too far.

How far would I have gone? My heart is pounding now. I feel like a loose cannon, completely out of control. Frantically glancing around, everyone is staring in our direction. The other guys are holding others back and Red has Becky pinned to a nearby table. What the ever-loving shit just happened?

Suddenly, West is in my face.

"Get the fuck out of here now, cool down. You're done for the day."

"Fuck you, West. Were you here when she came at me? I've had enough. I tried, okay? But I'm done with their shit. I'm done for the day, and I'm done with you constantly fucking telling me what to do. I don't see this as you protecting me, understanding me, looking out for me. Do you?" I growl.

Fuck this shit.

Fuck all of them.

Fuck. Fuck. Fuck.

West steps towards me, but I just can't. Shaking my head I step outside, taking a moment to feel the sun against my face. Heading for the closest Rolls, I'm ready to get out of here and clear my head. I see the driver is Ian, thank God. He looks concerned but doesn't utter a word.

"Hey, Ian, is there a quiet spot around here? I need a timeout," I say it as a joke, but it falls short.

"Of course, Miss Steele, would you like me to stop off at the coffee house on the way?"

See, this is why Ian is my favorite, he gets it.

I nod in thanks, and offer a small smile which he returns. Once I'm in he settles in up front, and just as we're about to leave the back-door swings open. I'm about to protest when Kai climbs in. He doesn't utter a single word he just grabs my hand and laces our fingers.

Fuck. Part of me wants him to know how much I needed this from him, the other doesn't want him to know how he impacts me. Ian looks at me, and I nod to continue on as planned.

We pull up outside of the coffee house, and without a word Kai gets out with Ian. Leaving me to stew in my own silence.

Would I really have taken her last breath?

My instincts tell me no, but she continues to push, and it feels like kill or be killed at the minute. I know I've overreacted, but she pushed past my limit. I've ignored all her sneers and taunts for nothing, she hasn't backed off, and I had to put my foot down. Just probably not that hard.

The guys are quickly climbing back into the car and Kai hands me a frappuccino. Ian drives as if he's going back to Ace, but he turns left at the library. He pulls to a stop next to a row of hedges.

"Miss Steele, there is an entrance just round the side, I'll stay here as long as you need."

Stepping out, I follow Kai's lead through the gate. Oh my God. This place is like a different world. Not big at all, but perfect cut grass leads a small path amongst pretty flowers and vibrant plants. In the center of it all is a little gazebo with a picnic bench.

Ian strikes a home run again. I just found my new favorite place.

I kick my heels off and leave them at the gate. Feeling the grass between my toes, smelling the flowers around me, I feel much more centered than I did just moments ago. I take my time walking around, taking it all in before I sit on the bench. Kai has followed quietly behind me the whole time, and as happy as I usually am with his comfortable silence, I can't take it right now.

"Are you waiting patiently to discuss what just happened?"

"Is that what you want to do?" he asks, always so calm.

"I don't really know what happened, or how to process any of it right now. So no, not really, but I feel something in the air that isn't usually there in your silence," I reply honestly.

He sits down next to me, "I promise you, Sakura, nothing is between us."

I nod, relaxing a little more.

"Would you like to put our efforts elsewhere right now? Distract your mind?"

This is what I was hoping for, why I didn't stop him from coming with me. He knows he relaxes me, and I'd hoped he would be able to help.

"Yes, please."

He offers me a rare smile that warms my insides and proceeds to pull out his laptop.

"Fantastic, I thought I could use my assignment for DCM Tech to help you with yours."

I can't help my grin.

Now that's what I'm talking about.

Unable to restrain myself, I plant a quick kiss on his lips, I lean back and clap.

"Lead the way, handsome."

MY BLOODLINE

KC KEAN

TWENTY FOUR

Luna

I sat with Kai all afternoon running through surveillance and finding hot spots. By the time my tummy grumbles, I have my plan laid out. That was Thursday. I decided to show a big fuck you and skipped all my classes Friday, avoiding calls from West and the guys. Red had been texting me still, making sure I'm okay, and she was about the only person I had the energy to entertain.

Now it's Saturday morning and I'm rolling Dot out of the garage, helmet in hand, ready to get my bike on. It's not too hot today, but I can still feel the heat in my leathers. Which is why I've only got a bikini on underneath.

"Hey, baby girl, what you up to?"

Turning I see Oscar strolling towards me, looking hot as hell. "Hey Oscar, I'm getting out of here for a while," I say nodding at Dot.

"Can I join you?"

"I want a relaxing ride, Oscar. Feel the wind in my hair, maybe head towards the coast, get away from all the drama."

"I can do that. No big mouth Oscar, I swear. Besides, I know the best place to go," he pleads, and the puppy dog eyes he gives me are hard to say no to.

"No big mouth Oscar and you've got yourself a deal."

"Whoop."

Did he just kick his legs in the air like he's the lead in a jolly Broadway show? I shake my head, he might have a big mouth that gets him into trouble, but he can always put a smile on my face.

He pulls a helmet out of thin air and climbs on the Suzuki. Ready to go, just like that.

"No leather?"

He's wearing shorts and a top, no other protection. At least he's wearing a helmet. Back home I never wore protective clothing, but Rafe made me promise to if I wanted to ride.

"Nah baby girl, where's the danger in that?" He winks.

"Lead the way then tour guide."

I can see him go to say something, but he thinks better of it shoving his helmet on and starting a slow crawl through the blocks.

Once we're off Featherstone's grounds he floors it and I'm right behind him. The winding roads are a dream, nobody is around, and it's just what I need. I've missed this, it's only been a few weeks, but I rode Dot daily before all this. Feeling the rumble between my legs and having full control of the bike always made me feel better.

I continue to let Oscar take the lead, enjoying just following his path and not having to worry if I'm going to end up lost. I hope he does know where he's going though.

Just over an hour and a half later and I can smell the sea in the air.

So good.

I follow him through the busy town, along the road next to the promenade. I'm hoping he knows a quieter part seeing as this place is brimming with people both on the sand and along the sidewalks. He drives for another ten minutes or so and pulls off. I follow him although I'm confused when a house comes into view and he parks in front of the porch.

It's a big house and I can see the direct access to the beach from here. He pulls his helmet off and steps off his bike. I follow suit with my helmet but hold my seat until I figure out why we're here specifically.

"Baby girl, I promise to not let my mouth run and I didn't say anything before we set off, but damn, you look sexy as sin in your leather, and the way you handle your bike, fuck. So good," he purrs as he strolls towards me.

"Where are we?"

"Oh, no stress. This is one of my parent's properties. Featherstone High School is only about forty minutes from here, so I always come for the vibes."

Staring him down, I try looking for something that tells me to turn around, but I find nothing, and instead climb off my bike, grab my bag, and follow him inside.

This place is all floor to ceiling windows with stunning views and modern touches.

"Do you want a tour?" he asks, like it's a requirement.

"I'd rather not, the water is calling me," I answer honestly, which just makes him grin.

"Thank God for that." He smiles. "Do you need help

getting out of your suit?"

The question is valid, but the mischief written all over his face just has me rolling my eyes at him. God he makes me do that so often I'm gonna get eye strain. I step out onto the deck and unzip my suit, enjoying the cool breeze against my skin.

"Holy shit," he whispers, and I glance in his direction.

He's staring hard. "I'm glad I didn't know that was all you had on underneath there, otherwise I'd have never made it here alive."

I can't help but chuckle at him.

"Please, Luna, I need a picture. I can't promise it won't go in the spank bank, but its purpose is to send to the guys and have them all jelly because they hate my Susie. They call her a death trap, but look where she led me," he gushes.

Fuck, it was a straight up no, until they called Susie a death trap. Instead I'm nodding my head in agreement to fuck with them.

"For real?" he screeches.

"I'm about to change my mind, Oscar. What did I say about that mouth?"

"Shit, I'll shut up. I'm sorry."

Getting on with it before I do actually change my

mind, I walk towards him and slip one arm out. Leaving me with my bikini and bare skin showing on one side and my leather on the other. I press myself against him, and his arm instantly goes around my waist.

"Fuck, baby girl."

"Take a selfie, Oscar."

Standing with my bare side closer to the camera I raise my hand, wrapping my fingers around his throat and rise on my tip toes to lick his cheek as he smirks at the camera. I hold myself there for a few seconds then lean back, finding myself actually missing the contact.

He grins down at me and shows me the phone and the picture he sent to a group chat.

"Shit, I'm biased but that's a hot picture, baby girl."

He pockets his phone and slowly drops the sleeve off my other arm. Leaving me standing with my suit hanging off my waist and my little blue bikini top on full display. His eyes are heating my skin from his attention.

"Let's get you a drink and some sunscreen before I hump you like a dog, yeah?"

He chuckles as he adjusts himself and leads me inside.

He makes quick work of grabbing a cooler and filling it with water bottles and snacks as well as grabbing blankets, towels, a windbreaker, and sun cream. I take my leather off fully and slip an oversized t-shirt on over my swimwear. I try to grab something off him to help with the load, but he just swerves around me.

I follow him down the steps and stop the second my feet touch the sand. Sinking my toes in, I close my eyes and lift my face to the sun. God I love this feeling. I let myself get lost for a minute, I just appreciate my surroundings and let all my problems fall away. When I open my eyes again, Oscar is standing closer to the water but he's facing me, taking me in like he can't look away.

As I near him he starts laying the blankets down.

"Can you not stare me down like that, baby girl. I was just trying to embrace my surroundings, and you had to put me off with all that need in your eyes."

I falter until I see the grin on his face, and see he's trying to make light of the fact it was actually him staring me down.

"I'm sorry, I just couldn't help it. All that man meat on display, my mind went into overdrive."

"You haven't seen man meat yet. Now sit, while I set the windbreaker up, then I'll take the unfortunate job of creaming your back," he says with a wink.

Doing as I'm told I sit down facing the water and relax into watching the waves. A light thump behind me catches my attention, and I see cushions stacked behind me. Damn this guy has beach skills for sure, I don't think I've ever been this comfortable on the sand.

Once I've applied the sunscreen he silently takes it from me and sits behind me. Legs alongside my own, I can feel his body heat and my body is at attention, aware of his every slight move. He's so gentle with his hands. I don't think it's because he sees me as delicate but because he knows what kind of effect it can have. He takes his time, wanting to drag the contact out for as long as possible, and I can't seem to stop him.

His hands move to his knees, but he stays seated. I shouldn't be aroused just by his proximity to me. Deciding to drag out this sexual tension for a little longer, I stand, letting my hair down. I shake it out, then bend in half at the waist, catching his eyes between my legs.

"Last one to the water is a bitch," I shout, before taking off.

Fuck, he brings out a fun side of me I didn't even know I had.

MY BLOODLINE

KC KEAN

TWENTY FIVE
Oscar

Fuck me, she is pure perfection.

I could have sat with her bent in front of me, with her ass in the air, for all of eternity. Or with her sat between my legs like she was. It felt...I don't know. I don't know how to place it, but I liked it. A lot.

As much as my big mouth can get me into trouble with her, I can't help wanting to tell her everything, and my mind doesn't always process what I'm trying to say in the right way quick enough. I just catch verbal diarrhea around her.

Whenever I'm not putting my foot in it, she gets my

jokes or she's laughing off my advances. No in between, no fakery, just pure raw emotion. She's either happy with you or she's not.

Which is why I think she went off the rails so much at Wren the other day. The minute she stepped foot on Featherstone she stood her ground, refusing to let anyone push her around. Then she gets attacked and everyone's suddenly telling her to play a game she has no interest in. Well, screw them for underestimating my girl. She's a fucking Queen, and I'll have her back no matter what she does.

This place isn't as real as she is. It's all dark and fucked up. I can see the darkness a little in her eyes too but only because it was placed there. Nothing she has said has been a lie or just some shit to tell you what you want to hear.

Do you know how many girls have told us they're all about sex and no commitment, then turn right around and start going bat shit crazy? Far too fucking many. Do you know how many girls have said the same thing and actually followed it up with actions to prove it? Just one, and she's running towards the water playfully, wanting me to chase her. And you bet your damned ass I will, and I'll even lose just to see her move.

Whipping my t-shirt off I stroll towards the water, taking in every inch of her. She looks different with her hair down, all carefree and fun, with no stress weighing on her shoulders. She's standing knee deep in the water letting the waves crash into her. This woman is addictive.

I come up behind her and lightly graze my hands over her waist, dragging my fingers against her stomach. I feel the shiver run through her and it runs straight to my dick, but she just made me a bitch for losing. So while she least expects it, I tighten my grip on her waist and lift her off the ground. The squeal that escapes her lets me know I definitely caught her off guard, and before she can whip out one of her brutal moves on me I throw her further into the water.

She sinks under for just a moment, then her face bobs just above the waves.

"You're trouble," she calls, and I can't help but grin.

"You love it."

She doesn't respond and I don't expect her to either. I didn't think it was possible for her to look sexier, but the wet look suits her. When I near her she splashes water at me out of nowhere and stuns me, I didn't think I would get to see a playful side of her like this.

Wanting to make the most of her letting her hair down, I drench her back. We relax and goof around in the water until we can't take anymore. It feels amazing to not have to be serious for a while.

It's still just warm enough to be happy for the sun to dry you off so we sit and devour the snacks I threw in the cooler. I lay back enjoying the windbreaker and the privacy it offers us, not that there are many people around this part of the beach, but it feels like we're in a bubble.

Checking my phone, I've missed numerous messages off of all of the guys and I can't help but smirk, jealous fuckers. Luna catches my grin and raises an eyebrow at me, she doesn't even ask but I show her anyway. Below the picture we sent, the guys have been going crazy.

Roman: Where the fuck are you?

Parker: Is it normal to be jealous of your cheek?

Kai: Fuck.

Roman: Where

Roman: Are

Roman: You?

Parker: Is it normal to be jealous of a motorcycle?

Roman: I swear to God Oscar!!!

Kai: Roman we all know you're acquainted with her. Leave him alone.

Roman: Fuck off, Kai. Oscar, you better not let your mouth make her mad, I swear!

Kai: Green is not your color my friend.

Parker: Okay, it's official. I'm jealous of Oscar. Oscar! Who knew?

Parker: It saddens me to admit this. Send help, or Luna. Preferably Luna!

The laugh she releases is infectious.

"You guys are crazy, and I think your group chat just scared me," she manages when she catches her breath.

"Best have another selfie, you know, so they don't worry."

I'm going for the innocent look, but I know it's not working, yet she still entertains me.

This time I take a picture of us both squished in, hair slicked back, smiling wide at the camera. This picture is happiness. Joy, that's the feeling I've been struggling with since we got here. Joy. Fuck, I like it.

I keep the phone held between us waiting for their responses, and we don't have to wait long.

Kai: How beautiful. Not you asshole. She is incredibly beautiful with that smile on her face.

Roman: You better make sure she stays smiling like that or it's all your fault.

Roman: Don't think I haven't figured out where you are.

Parker: Wow. Why did you have to stand so

close I can't crop you out of the picture!

She smiles and rolls her eyes at their antics, while I respond.

Oscar: You can fuck off, she's mine right now. Don't make me keep her.

She steps back and leaves me to banter with them. As she lays back on the cushions I take more notice of the tattoo on her ribs.

Holy shit, that's …

"Fuck, you and Parker have the same tattoo, huh?"

Her eyes go wide, and she looks panicked.

"He chose it out of my portfolio, while I was setting up. I showed him that I had it and that seemed to make him even more determined."

"Calm down, baby girl. No need to explain, but do I get matching too?"

She can't tell if I'm joking or not, and secretly, neither can I.

"What do your tattoos mean?" I ask.

She looks me over, all coy.

"You have to tell me about yours first."

"I can do that, no problem."

Stretching out my left arm, which is covered in a tattoo sleeve.

"Every single tattoo on here represents a video game. Pacman, Crash Bandicoot, Sonic. They're all games I played as a child before I found out about the real world I was living in. This is a permanent memory of when I was truly happy and allowed to be myself, before all the obligations came."

Pointing to my chest. "This is my only other tattoo, and it is my bloodline symbol."

It's a Celtic symbol that every heir to the bloodline has had to get over the years. I hate it.

"So, now you show me yours."

"You've seen my feather. Not many people know that a feather can represent strength. It's underestimated, like me," she whispers, making me itch to touch it.

She flips over showing me her back. Lifting her hair off her neck I see three arrows and an upside-down crescent moon.

"This is the symbol for Diana, Goddess of the hunt. I actually didn't choose it, Rafe did, and with you saying you have a bloodline symbol it does make me wonder." She sighs.

I trail my eyes down her spine where she has five symbols trailing down delicately.

"And the symbols are a saying an old friend would say all the time. Then she left and I got this to remember her."

I can tell she doesn't want to explain further so I don't push.

Instead, I lay down beside her and she turns so we are facing each other. I could get lost in her eyes, which blows my mind. I'm usually good at getting lost in pussy then bowing out, but there is something about her that makes me feel more.

Today was everything I didn't know I needed. By chance I was exactly where I was meant to be. Now, I didn't want to push and end up in trouble, but I wanted her so bad.

As if sensing my thoughts, she props herself up on her elbow and glances down at me. She doesn't say a word, she just stares into my eyes as she lifts her hand to trace my lips. Girls never make the first move, and that's my rookie mistake because she's clearly all woman. She nudges me on to my back and eases herself on to my lap.

Fuck.

I like her there. Teasing my hands up her thighs slowly, I watch them trail up her body. When I come to rest my hands on her hips I stretch my fingers out, trying to touch as much skin as possible. Her skin is fire against mine.

Her hands trace my shoulders as she lifts my face to meet hers. Her tongue swipes out tasting my bottom lip. That's hot as hell. Taking and teasing however she wants. The only thing Roman told me when they both stumbled out of that car the other day was that she took.

She took what she wanted from him, and he'd let her do it again. Now she sits before me ready to do the same, but there has to be an agreement first, before I lose myself in her touch.

"Baby girl, make your decision carefully. If you take charge here, now, there will be a round two before we leave and then whatever I say goes. Either way, before we leave, we'll have both submitted a little," I breathe out, bare millimeters away from her lips.

She pushes down on my erection and her pussy feels like lava, even through all the material between us.

"So, what you're saying is we have to compromise?" she asks, and I nod in response.

The grin that takes over her face tells me she likes this push and pull between us.

"If that's the case, who's turn will it be when we need to shower off?" she purrs, and I've reached my limit.

I can't hold back any longer. Flipping us over she's under me in seconds, her legs wrapped around me and my dick nestled perfectly in between her legs.

Neither of us speak now. The time for that is over. I crush my mouth to hers, trying to consume each other, fighting for control. It's hot as fuck. I pin her hands above her head as I use my other hand to untie the strings on her bikini top, slowly, wanting to drag this out forever. As she fights against my hold to free her hands, I finally let her nipples come into view. Piercings? Roman didn't warn me about these.

Fuck. I might come in my pants like a horny teenager.

I need them in my mouth. I need two mouths so they can both have my attention. Shit, that gives me a vision of me inside her pussy while the guys take care of her nipples. Fuck. We've never really shared someone like that. We've let a girl go round and give us all blow jobs in the same room, but she makes me want to give her more.

Diving down I take her nipple in my mouth swirling

my tongue, forcing a moan past her lips. I switch to the other as my free hand finds the string to her bottoms. I want her naked, in the open. Free for me to explore and I love the adrenaline from the prospect of being watched.

As I pull away her bikini bottoms, I release her hands so I can sit back and take all of her in. She is a beautiful sight. My eyes don't really know where to focus more. She likes me looking, and it seems she has a show for me. She cups her breasts, running her thumbs over her peaks giving me little moans. I stand and drop my shorts, wanting nothing between us.

Her eyes fall to my cock and go wide when she takes in my Prince Albert. Her hand trails down over her stomach heading straight for my prize and I'm mesmerized by her movements. Her fingertip touches her clit and she shivers, swiping down to her entrance, and dragging moisture up to circle around her clit, eliciting little cries of pleasure.

I can't help but pull on my dick at her little show, she's fucking stunning.

"I can't decide if I want you in my mouth or your mouth on me right now," she whispers.

"There's a special number for that, baby girl," I respond.

The lust in her eyes tells me she's involved, then she rises to her knees joining our lips. I slowly sink down and lay on my back, trying not to break our connection. She trails kisses down my body until her lips are hovering over the tip of my cock, blowing lightly, and I barely contain my moan. Licking from the tip to the base, I hum in pleasure. Just a tease, then she's raising above me and lowering that sweet pussy to my face.

She is a literal dream.

My mouth instantly comes into contact with her core, my hands gripping her ass cheeks and pushing her into my face, as she takes me into her mouth.

This is heaven.

Holy shit.

She rides my face, using my tongue, as she takes me deeper and deeper. Dropping a hand back, I spear her with my fingers as my tongue circles her clit. Her movements become erratic and I know she's close, so I maintain the exact tempo I've got going, and in minutes she's releasing me from her mouth as she cries out in ecstasy, coming all over my face.

Still on her hands and knees, I lift her hips so I can come out from under her. Placing myself behind her I tighten my grip on her hips. Glancing behind me, I look for the blue cushion. I quickly unzip it and search my hand inside, pulling out the rubber I stored in there.

"You did not just pull a condom from that cushion."

I turn to see an exasperated look on Luna's face at my antics, I just wink as I roll it on and position myself at her entrance.

"Aren't you glad I did?" I tease as I stroke myself against her folds.

"God, yeah," she moans in response.

Then I slam in, all the way home.

Fuck.

I have to hold for a minute to give us both a second. Tightening my grip on her hips I slowly pull out and slam back inside. I can't tell whose grunts are who's right now, I just know we are lost in bliss together. I don't speed up, wanting to drag this out. I cover her body with mine, wrapping myself around her, gripping her tits as I rut into her like a beast.

I need more, and I need her to come again before I do, so I lean back bringing her with me. Looking out over her shoulder I see a couple far out in the water taking us in.

"Baby girl, it seems we've got an audience. Why don't

you cup those titties of yours while I ravage you, show them what we're rocking, ey?"

I don't wait for her answer as I find her clit, pinching it as I thrust into her faster and harder. One of her hands cups her boob as the other lifts back, gripping me on the back of my neck.

Holy shit.

That is a show. Fuck, I'd love to see this played back.

I'm close, and the second her pussy clamps tightly around my dick I'm pushed over the edge, coming for what feels like forever, making sounds I've never made before.

Best fuck ever.

I slowly pull out and take care of the condom, she lays down beside me and I use one of the towels to clean her up.

"What are you doing?" she asks, looking at me strangely.

"I honestly have no idea. You make me do crazy things, my Goddess."

"Goddess huh?"

"Yeah."

I lower myself over her, meeting her lips.

"You're addictive, Luna Steele," I murmur.

"Right back at you," she replies. "Now feed me so we

can go again."

Yes please.

Marry me?

MY BLOODLINE

KC KEAN

TWENTY SIX

Luna

That was the best weekend I've had in a long time. We ended up spending the night at the beach house, having sex everywhere possible. We couldn't get enough of each other.

We're heading back to the Academy early on, I needed to figure out where I stood after everything with Wren, and Oscar wanted to head into the lab while it was empty. He pulled into a small diner near campus and I followed in behind him. I'm glad I packed a pair of yoga pants in my bag yesterday with my oversized tee, as a 'just in case', because I definitely needed them now. I wouldn't be able to walk in here with just a bikini on, and I'd opted to pack my leathers away too.

Following his lead inside I was starving and ready for something with actual substance. He held the door open for me thinking he was a gentleman, bowing and shit, and I should have realized then that there was a reason for it.

"Oscar, I'm about to knock you out, just get over here," rumbles Roman from the corner booth.

I raise my eyebrow at Oscar who looks sheepish.

"I was worried that if I told you this was our Sunday tradition you wouldn't have come."

"You would be right."

I wouldn't have, but I'm here now and I'm not mad.

"But I'm starving, Oscar, so I can deal for now."

Worried I might change my mind he places his hand on the bottom of my back and guides me towards the others.

As we near the table they stand, motioning me to sit in the middle of the booth with Kai and Parker on either side, and Roman and Oscar taking the ends.

"We haven't ordered yet," Kai says, breaking the silence, and hands me a menu.

"What's good here?" I say, not raising my head from the pages.

"You," they all say in sync.

Oh my God. I'm actually fucking blushing. I do not blush. I lift the menu to cover my face.

"I meant to eat."

"Still you," calls Oscar, making the others chuckle.

Even Roman isn't clipping him round the ear.

Aceholes.

I don't think it's possible to sink any further into my seat. I can actually feel the heat in my face. Parker peeks his head around the menu, taking me in.

"Luna Steele, are you blushing?" he asks with a chuckle.

The glare I send him has him back pedaling. He lifts his head looking around the table.

"Nope, no blushing around here guys," he says with a shit eating grin on his face.

I'm starting to think he's the worst of the group. I go to pinch his leg, but he catches my hand before I even get close. Threading his fingers through mine and raising my hand to place a gentle kiss on my knuckles.

How does he always get away with so much PDA? I don't usually like it, but his innocent face has me unable to reject him. It should feel strange holding his hand after I spent the night with Oscar, but it really doesn't. A hand on my thigh also gains my attention, and I look to the source, meeting Kai's eyes that are already on me.

"They do the best pancakes here, Sakura," he says, then plants a kiss on my cheek.

"I feel left out," grumbles Roman, and I can't help but chuckle.

I arrived with Oscar and now have physical contact with both Parker and Kai. The other guys chuckle, which seems to make it worse. I lean forward over the table, and hint for him to move closer too. Which he does in an instant. Without needing to do or say anymore, he's forcing his tongue into my mouth, branding me in front of everyone. Fuck, it's even hotter with Kai and Parker touching me, even though it's light petting. Turning it up a notch and adding Oscar to the mix would be a dream.

God, I need to calm down.

My stomach grumbles in that moment, and Roman leans back growling at Oscar.

"Have you not fucking fed her?"

Guilt takes over his face, looking between me and Roman. I just roll my eyes, and look at Kai.

"What pancakes do you get?"

"Always the chocolate chip," he responds, not missing a beat.

"Then I'll have some of them, and a coffee."

As if hearing my words, the waitress approaches to take our order. All her attention is focused on Roman and the glare I get tells me she saw him kiss me, and she is far from happy about it. Roman reels off what everyone wants.

"And you'd do well to remember your place and who we are. She's an Ace."

The color drains a little from her face and she scurries off.

Always drama wherever I turn.

Parker squeezes my hand, gaining my attention.

"So, we wanted to talk to you about something."

He looks nervous, so I just nod for him to continue. He hums and stutters a moment trying to figure out how to say whatever's on his mind, when Kai takes over.

"We want you to try a relationship, with all of us."

As serene as ever, he calmly drops that in my lap.

I look at each of them and they're all staring back with some level of unease in their eyes. As if sensing a rejection coming, Roman jumps in too.

"I know after the time in the ring you said no commitment, but that was just me. We're asking you to explore this with all of us. That's four dicks, plenty more than one, like you said."

He thinks he's so clever with his thought process. I still don't know how to answer. I'm enjoying what there is between us individually, and how relaxed we can feel as a group still. I'm just worried I don't know enough about everything going on around me still and this could be a huge distraction.

"We're just asking you to give it a chance, Luna. It'd be just like this, the rest we can figure out along the way. We just want it to be the five of us, nobody else," Parker adds.

Always Parker getting involved, playing with my soul and making me agree to whatever he says.

Before I came here, I was adamant I didn't want any commitment at all, but I didn't have a best friend then either. My life is up in the air, death knowingly waiting round the corner, yet these guys make me forget all that.

"Okay, I'll try," I sigh out, not sure if I already regret saying it.

"You won't regret it, Sakura," whispers Kai as he

kisses my neck.

Damn, I could get used to this level of attention.

Heading back to Ace, we each go our separate ways, which earns me a quick but passionate kiss from Kai, Parker and Oscar when we get to their floor. Leaving me and Roman to ride to the top floor alone. The second the elevator shuts he has me pinned in the corner.

"So, how was your day at the beach?" he huffs.

"It was exactly what I needed." He stares me down searching for something.

"Did he take good care of you, Princess?"

Err, am I supposed to answer that? I guess if we are being open about this I should.

"Yeah he did," I answer honestly, and for some reason his shoulders relax like he's pleased with that answer.

"I want this to work between us all, Luna. If you start feeling yourself backing away you need to tell me what the issues are so we can try and fix it, okay?"

The determination on his face tells me he's serious, and I nod in response.

Stepping out of the elevator, I stop in surprise when I

see West sitting outside my door. Roman looks between us.

"You want me to get rid of him?"

"No, I'll be fine."

Before I can make for my door Roman wraps me in his arms tightly, and brings his lips to mine, devouring me. It feels so good I can't even bring myself to care that someone is watching.

"If you need me you know where I am, or hit the group chat," he says, as we step back.

I nod in response, it was weird that we hadn't traded numbers until today, and now we have a freaking group chat. My head needs a minute, but instead I get West.

Stepping around him I open the door, leaving it open for him to follow.

"You can put the coffee machine on while I take a quick shower," I say, looking over my shoulder at him, and he nods in response.

His silence tells me he knows I've had enough.

Jumping out of the shower I slip into a fresh pair of leggings and a knotted crop top. Deciding to let my hair dry naturally, I leave it loose down my back. Walking into the kitchen there's a coffee waiting for me, so I take the seat opposite him. I don't know what he wants me to say, so I wait for him to go first.

"Dietrichson tried taking what happened to The Ring. Told them you were feral and not fit for this Academy, and she wanted authorization to kill you, after your attack on Wren."

He leaves that hanging in the air. I knew this place was fucking crazy, but the fact that the Head actually wants permission to kill me, sets like rock in my stomach. I have no words right now, so I nod for him to continue.

"Do you know who the members of The Ring are?"

"No, I know the names in Ace represent the names in The Ring, but actual names seem to be on your 'I'll tell you another time' list of things to do." I'm being snarky but I just can't help it. He doesn't take me on, he just nods, still not divulging the information.

"Well, Barbette's father is one of them. He stands for the Dietrichson name in The Ring, and lucky for us when he heard the actual story from an eyewitness, he was disgusted to hear that his granddaughter was attacking someone over a boy to begin with. Said she deserved whatever she got, for playing playground games in a big man's world."

Huh.

My words exactly.

"That being said, he does not like his bloodline to seem weak, and agreed that he wanted to push for authorization."

Asshole, I was starting to consider that the Dietrichson's weren't all fucking idiots, but never mind I take it back.

"So, what's the verdict?" I ask, he's weaving a story and it's getting on my nerves.

"The verdict stands at 6 v 2 in your favor. It was agreed that something like this, in a lower block, wouldn't have even reached their ears, and would have been left to be resolved between the main parties, not bloodlines as a whole."

"What aren't you telling me?"

I can see it in his eyes. I know him, and Rafe said there was a lot I didn't know, and they agreed no more secrets, but it seems I'm still the bottom of the barrel when it comes to being in the know.

"A lot, and for right now it's for your own safety," he responds, so casually it grates on me.

"Okay then. Well if I'm not being targeted and you feel no need to tell me anymore, you can leave."

I can't keep the emotion out of my voice, but I'm frustrated with all this shit. I rise from the table encouraging him to leave.

"Luna, there is a lot you do not know because it is safer for you. You may not believe or care to hear it, but everything we are doing is for you. Can I be honest with you?" He sighs and I nod in response.

"If we aren't telling you something for your safety, we aren't telling you because we believe it'll trigger you about your past. It seems you still aren't ready to open your mind back up to it yet."

My brain kicks into overdrive.

"West, what would you know about my past?" I can't keep the ice out of my words. He realizes he's said more than he probably should have, because he clearly knows things about me. Things I refuse to visit, things I just lock away from even myself.

"I remember all of it," he whispers.

Remember?

What the fuck does that mean?

"What the hell do you mean, West?"

He just shakes his head like he knows it's pointless having this conversation with me, and it likely is. He goes to walk around me, but I push against his chest.

"I said, what the hell do you mean?" I growl.

I'm shaking. I don't know whether it's with fear of

what he is going to say, or because he simply isn't saying anything at all.

"Were you in my past, West?" I scream, needing something, anything from him.

He looks down at his feet, still giving me nothing.

"You're a fucking coward, West. Get out. Get the fuck out, I'm done," I scream as I swing the door open.

He looks pained as he walks towards me. I can see his hands itching to reach out and touch me, and his brain working overtime to try and say the right thing.

"You were my moon." Barely a whisper, and with that he raced out of the door.

I was too stunned to chase him. My moon he'd said. Like when I felt that sense of déjà vu when I was injured. The place it took me...was real. He'd really said that. Why?

My fear of having to open my mind to my history was right at the surface and the shake to my hands told me I wasn't ready for this. Shit, I needed to get myself under control. I needed to channel my emotions. I needed to hit something.

Prepared to head to the gym I stare out of my open door and a better idea comes to mind. Barefoot I step out and knock on Romans door, he instantly sees the struggle on my face.

"Where the fuck is he? I'll kill him," he growls, venom laced into every word.

I just shake my head frantically.

"I need you to spar with me."

Fuck even my voice is jittery.

"Are you sure?"

I nod, not wanting to hear my voice like that again.

"Let's go," he says as he grabs my hand and pulls me to the stairs.

It isn't until we're halfway down that I realize we are both barefoot, and somehow that seems to settle me slightly. Knowing that I went to him when I needed him, and he dropped everything so quickly that grabbing his shoes didn't enter his mind. Just wanting to give me what I needed. He doesn't even realize it's these small things I need most.

It frightens me how much he gets me, but I crave it.

KC KEAN

TWENTY SEVEN

Luna

The next two weeks go by quickly, with no further drama from Wren or her mother, but if glares could kill, I'd be dead and buried by now. Everything with the guys is no different than it was before. They're more than happy to give me the space I need, yet shower me with affection at the same time.

It's weird how they each have found a role in my routine. Kai is my car bestie, his eyes always holding me captive as his fingers graze mine. He's also helping me focus on my assignments, so I can get it done as seamlessly as possible.

Roman is training with me every day, no questions asked. He jumps in that ring with me and spars like I need him to. He doesn't go soft because I'm a girl, he pushes me. Knowing the world we are in but not actually knowing what is coming up next, it's exactly what I need.

Oscar is my motorcycle guy. Eager to get on his Susie, like I am to get on Dot. He knows some good roads around here and I'm actually happy to let him lead me. It's not something I would have done before, but after the beach I trust he'll take me somewhere fun.

Parker, he's my movie fix. He wants to just hide inside from the shit storm around us and get lost in another world, and I can't help but join him. Our souls are familiar and that's what holds us so close.

I didn't think it would be possible for us to relax into this, but we have. Surprisingly, I have. I don't feel pushed or pulled, it feels like they're just right for all my crazy sides. While Red makes me want to be a kinder, gentler person. Well to her at least.

Now I'm getting ready to go to the Fall Ball and I told them all to get fucked, because Red's my date tonight. Of course they'll be there, but I don't want her lost to this crowd under the influence, it has also made sure she's sat at my table.

"Okay, Luna. I've narrowed down these dresses to the top three for you. Now choose so I can do your hair and make-up," she calls, bossy as ever.

Walking in I notice she's hung three dresses near the floor length mirror for me to try. All are floor length, there's a green, deep blue, and dusty pink option.

"I'm not wearing green this bright," I say, sounding like a bitch, but please, that's not me.

Red just chuckles like she did it just to wind me up.

"You can do my hair and make-up first then I'll try the dresses," I say, which makes her clap with glee. She's already done her own, sexy smoky eyes and her shoulder length hair half pinned back. I don't know how she has the effort for this stuff, but she looks gorgeous.

"Fabulous, sit. Are you sure you don't want me to go a little crazy with this?"

"I'm sure. If you give me an over the top look I won't go," I warn, but she just rolls her eyes.

She turns me away from the mirror and gets to it. I relax back while she tugs my hair around, doing whatever she pleases. As she pulls the make-up out I give her a warning glare, which has her raising her hands in surrender.

When she finally steps back from me, I'm nervous to find out what she's done.

"If I do say so myself, Captain, you look stunning. Now choose a dress, we've got about half an hour until the guys get here," she says, before sauntering off to get herself ready.

Glancing in the dresser mirror, I take myself in. She's curled my hair, then twisted it loosely round one side, and fitted it all into a messy bun at the back of my head. I actually love it. It looks classy, but not stuck up. She's done my make-up beautifully, my skin looks flawless. My eyes are a gorgeous blend of bronzes and golds, and my lips are a glossy pink. My girl did good. This is why she's my favorite.

Looking between the two dresses, my make-up will suit both so that doesn't help narrow down my choice. I try the blue option first then the dusty pink. As soon as I look in the mirror, I know the pink dress is the one. It's stunning. Floor length with a small trail, spaghetti straps leading to a low V that stops in between my breasts. It hugs my hips tight accentuating my assets, and the back is completely bare except for the straps around my shoulder blades. I consider using some tape to hold everything in place, but everything is so tight, nothing is close to slipping.

Accessorizing with the jewelry pieces Red left out, and the black strappy heels and matching clutch, I'm ready to go.

Stepping back into my bedroom Red isn't there, but I hear noise coming from the lounge.

"Nope, no way, Jessica. You are not leaving this room until you go change. Tell her Roman," Oscar's shouting. What the hell is he shouting for?

"Shut up, Oscar," calls a bored Roman.

"No way. Guys are going to be staring at her and getting dirty thoughts, and I won't allow it."

"Fuck off, Oscar," Red shouts.

Oh shit, I better get out there. Stepping into the lounge I observe the scene before me. Everyone is sat casually on the sofas except Red and Oscar who are glaring at each other. I want to get involved but he looks hot as sin in a fitted deep blue suit and tie, and he's got me all tongue tied.

Looking at the others Roman and Kai are both kitted out in fitted black suits, whereas Roman has a black shirt and tie too, Kai is wearing a white shirt and a bow tie.

Tracing my eyes over Parker he's wearing a grey fitted suit with a bow tie too. My brain has officially short-circuited, and my body cannot deal with this amount of hotness at once. I think I'm going to self-combust from the sexual tension alone. Remembering why I rushed out here I shake my head ready to stop the shouting, but there is no shouting. Everyone is staring at me with their jaws hanging loose, even Red.

Clearing my throat, I try to find something to say.

"Why were you yelling in here?"

Nobody responds, they just continue to stare and it's starting to make me feel awkward. Getting frustrated with them I march past them all, heading to the kitchen. When they're behind me I hear curse words and turn to see what's going on now.

"I think I just came in my pants," gasps Oscar.

The confusion on my face has him pointing at me, but he doesn't expand.

Fucking idiots can't even hold a conversation now apparently, so I waltz into the kitchen and grab a water, I don't want to let my guard down around so many threats tonight. A finger traces down my back gaining my attention, Kai is staring at me like I created heaven or something.

"You look truly beautiful, Sakura, no words can truly do you any justice," he murmurs.

Playing with his bow tie I smile at him as a way of acknowledging his compliment.

"You look very handsome Kai, a bow tie suits you," I whisper.

In our own private bubble like this I could stare into his eyes forever. With my heels on I can touch my lips to his easily, so I don't deny myself the connection. We easily lose ourselves and the caresses of his fingers down my spine are electric. Before we can escalate too far, he pulls back slightly.

"Fuck, Sakura," he murmurs. Did he just swear?

"What does that mean, Sakura?"

Finally willing to ask what he has called me since the beginning.

"I grew up in America, my father is American while my mother is half Japanese, half Danish. She taught me that every word in the Japanese language was beautiful, but cherry blossoms were just something different. They're level of beauty is unparalleled, just like you."

I melt at his words, in such a small sentence I learned things I never knew while he simply complimented me. I kiss him lightly this time, as his fingers continue to trace patterns on my skin.

"Stop hogging her, Kai," Roman grumbles, as he enters the room. Making Kai step back, offering his spot to Roman.

Before I can mourn the loss of contact Roman is offering me a different touch, one I crave just as much.

"You are the most beautiful Princess I have ever seen," he says, as he cups my face and hip at the same time. Slowly tracing my hands over the front of his shirt, I take him in.

"You'll do, I guess," I say with a grin which he returns before joining our lips. No issues that they have just been touching someone else's moments ago. The passion is different, yet it sets me on fire exactly the same.

"Get off her, the car's here and I'm not redoing her make-up," Red calls from the lounge.

The need in Romans eyes is raw, making me question if the ball is even worth it. Seems it must be when he steps back offering me his elbow.

Stepping into the lounge everyone is ready to head out. Parker pushes Roman out of the way and takes my arm, while Oscar takes my other side. I think everyone's a little surprised by Parker's force, but it's hot as hell, and Roman doesn't even grumble. I'd love to know more of what's there between them, but now isn't the time.

Oscar and Parker both lean in kissing me delicately on the cheek, whispering sweet compliments in my ear. God they sure know how to express themselves once they pick their jaws up off the floor.

A quick trip in the elevator and we are stepping outside to a waiting limousine, which catches me by surprise. I thought we were just travelling as normal. I look at the others, and it's Oscar who answers the question in my eyes.

"We didn't want to fight over who rode with you, and we didn't want to leave you and Jess in a car alone, so we compromised on a limo."

Shaking my head at their antics, we climb in, and I take a seat next to Red.

"You look gorgeous, don't listen to any of that shit Oscar was spouting. I actually think you have him all protective," I whisper.

"I know, don't worry. Who knew he had it in him huh?" she chuckles as we climb in.

As we pull up to the main building, I'm taken back by how beautiful it looks. With little lights and a red carpet forming an entrance, it's exactly what you would expect from this place.

Parker helps me out of the limo and leads the way with Roman, while Kai and Oscar take up the rear behind me and Red.

"Jeez they're like bodyguards. Guys didn't come near me before because I was a nobody, now being seen with these guys puts me out of reach. I can't win," she grumbles.

"Red, you are beautiful, and if some guy isn't willing to stand tall for you no matter what, then they're not worth your time anyways," I say, like I'm the queen of advice. Yeah right.

Entering the Main Hall, I'm surprised at the space with all the furniture removed. There are people milling around everywhere, waiting for the rope to drop and to be led upstairs. Glancing around I take in everyone else. I feel people's eyes stare back at me, but I don't maintain eye contact. Although I do plaster a half smile on my face to make myself look approachable.

That's been my new tactic, no resting bitch face. If I'm going to prove to these people that I'm not a pushover, and I won't take their shit, then I need to show that I'm a leader of people. For that, I need the people to like me.

Feeling a hand on my hip, I know it's Oscar, his thumb unable to refrain from stroking my skin. "Baby girl, I have never in my life been turned on by someone's back before, but I just can't keep my hands off of you," he murmurs against my ear, sending shivers down my spine.

Holy shit, it's a good job this dress came with padding, because I'd likely poke someone's eye out with how hard my nipples are. They don't like my bare skin getting all the attention.

I look over my shoulder at him, loving his attention. In a room full of people, who the hell am I?

"Don't give me that sexy coy look, baby girl. I'm struggling enough as it is, and I can feel Roman glaring daggers at me too."

I can't help but grin at him, he's trying to be serious, yet he always makes me smile. Seems he actually listened when I told him to shut that big mouth of his. Before he can say anymore, a bell is rang gaining everyone's attention.

"Good evening, ladies and gentlemen. It is my honor to be able to invite you into this year's Featherstone Academy Fall Ball. If you would be so kind to follow me, we may begin." Some guy I've never seen before announces to the room and drops the rope.

Everyone starts pushing like it's a race, but this dress was not made for that. I'll get there when I get there. Red links me and the guys surround us as we make our way, at the back of the crowd, up the stairs.

The ballroom is gorgeous. Large tables take up a lot of the space, with gold satin tablecloths and large floral centerpieces. The chairs are all vintage off white, while the chandeliers are black wrought iron, surprisingly it looks classy. I'm mostly on edge with all the amount of cutlery and glasses on the tables. A stage and dance floor fill the center of the room, while a few drink stands are dotted around the edge.

I'm surprised to find that there are two tables filled with teachers and another table filled with people I haven't seen around here before.

"Shit," Roman grunts. I whip my head to see what the issue is, but he's too focused on Parker.

What's going on? What's wrong with Parker?

Then Kai is leaning in to whisper in my ear.

"The Ring is here."

The Ring? As in, top of Featherstone elite.

Wait shit, as in their families? I'm not ready for that.

Wait.

No one's here from Steele though, right? Because I definitely can't deal with that.

Fuck, I may need a drink after all.

KC KEAN

TWENTY EIGHT

Luna

The food has come and gone, and I barely touched anything in front of me, let alone looked to see what it actually was.

I'm on edge.

I forced everyone to move the place cards around, so my back wasn't to the table The Ring were sat at, yet I hadn't dared look in their direction in case it drew attention to me. Add to the fact I've had to deal with Wren and Tyler for the past hour at our table, and I'm ready to call it quits.

They've sneered at me all night. I want to gut Tyler with my knife, I know he was one of the guys that helped

Wren jump me. He's sneering a lot at Roman too, seen as he got the short straw of sitting on Wren's other side and she's been all over him like a dog in heat.

My green-eyed monster is definitely close to the surface. I want to pluck her away from him and cut her fingers off for touching what's mine, but I refuse to look like a fool. Especially when he knows he's mine and he's not even glanced her way, keeping his attention solely on me. Well, unless he's staring daggers at Kai for getting the seat beside mine. Red has been giggling at their antics the whole time, not fazed in the slightest by our guests this evening.

"So, Luna, tell me. How many dicks have you had at this table already?" Wren brazenly asks across the table. Seems she's willing to go to any lengths to try and get a reaction out of me with The Ring nearby.

I don't breathe a word, I just offer a smile, while Oscar steps in.

"What's the matter, Wren, jealous? How many times in the High School dorms did you sneak into Roman's room, lay naked, and hope he'd be willing to stick his dick in you?"

He chuckles like it's a joke, which just makes her go

red in the face. Fucking creeper.

"My mouth was just fine for you wasn't it, Oscar?" she retorts, glancing to see if I give a reaction.

Which I don't, on the outside anyway. Inside I'm screaming that this bitch touched him, and my nails are digging so hard into my palms, I think I may have broken the skin.

Before me. It. Was. Before. Me.

Kai squeezes my thigh in knowing comfort and I let his relaxing aura surround me. He nods slightly towards Oscar for me to follow his glance, and I see Oscar with fear in his eyes. Fear that I'm furious at him. I offer him a half smile which has him visibly relaxing back into his chair, before he turns back to Wren.

"Yes, Wren. Your mouth, when I was black out drunk did the trick. Yet I still couldn't force myself to stick it in your skanky pussy now could I?" Fuck his big mouth, I'm so close to cringing at his choice of words.

Wren's face is beetroot red, but before she can respond a man approaches the table.

"Miss Dietrichson, your grandfather wishes to see you, alone," he says, then turns and leaves just as quickly as he arrived.

The color drains from her face, but she still manages to glare at me like it's my fault. As she stands, I see her actually trembling, I don't care to watch her near them.

"Fuck off, Tyler. Formalities are done with for the night, and I do not need any more encouragement to beat you to a pulp," Roman grumbles, and Tyler actually does as he says.

Clearly, it's the female population he doesn't like being above him. Maybe that's why he's lurking around Wren, being with an Ace will boost his reputation.

I want to ask why the members of The Ring are here, but I don't know where to begin. A singer is now on the stage with a live band, and I'm surprised when they start singing up to date music. Pairs take up the dance floor as I feel a presence behind me.

"Luna, it's really important," West whispers, before leaning back and talking louder. "May I have this dance?"

He holds his hand out for me and I consider my options. As much as I hate the fact that West is a part of my past, he may also be able to help me understand what to do with The Ring being here. I place my hand in his, seeing the frown on Roman's face. I can tell he's not happy, but it won't stop me following West, although I do try to offer a smile of reassurance. Which just seems to have him curse under his breath.

West takes us to the center of the dance floor, surrounding us with the other dancers. He places his hands on my hips leading me to place mine on his shoulders. We sway for a moment, it feels so odd to be in this situation with West. We'd spent time together but never really alone or this close unless we were training.

"What's so important then, West?" I ask, straight to the point as ever.

I don't want to waste time dancing for no reason, especially when it's not with one of my guys.

"Rafe is on his way, about thirty minutes out," he says in my ear.

"What? Why?"

"The Ring weren't supposed to be here tonight. They showed up about an hour before this thing started, surprising everyone."

"Okay, and what does that have to do with Rafe being on his way?"

"Because, Luna, they're likely here to look you over in person. You can't let them catch you alone, do you understand me?"

"What on earth is going on, West?"

He won't meet my eyes and it's driving me crazy.

"I need you to not keep secrets if it's putting me in danger, West. How am I supposed to defend myself?"

He finally looks at me.

"Fuck. Okay, when you went to live with Rafe, it was because an agreement was always in place that if anything ever happened to your father, Rafe would get you off the grid," he says slowly, as if I'm going to freak out.

"Off the grid?" I ask, confused.

"A lot of shit was going down at the time, and you aren't ready for all of that and we both know it. It was everyone's priority that you were to be kept safe. Again, a lot you have locked away and now isn't the time, but Rafe got you and ran. No one found you for a long time, not even your mother, until you were twelve."

He checks my reactions, and proceeds when he sees I'm not having a breakdown at his words. Simply because I can't yet process them.

"Rafe broke a lot of rules to do what he did, and a lot of manipulation and blackmailing on his side kept them at bay. Until now."

He's right, now isn't the time to try and make me

remember things. Rafe ran with me? What did he sacrifice to honor his agreement with my father? I feel a little sick. West must see it on my face.

"I swear, Luna, he would have done it again in a heartbeat," he declares as he cups my cheek.

"A lot of things would be very different if your father was still with us, and I'm sorry that he's not. When you are ready, I will talk to you about anything you wish, but right now I need you to trust me. Rafe will be here soon to distract them, but they can't know that I have contact with him."

I nod understanding the seriousness in his eyes.

"What about them seeing us right now?"

"They wouldn't be surprised, Luna, and that's also for another time, okay?"

"Okay," I breathe, confused with all of this.

"Who exactly is sitting at that table, West? I feel unprepared and I need to know who's who."

He contemplates what I'm asking for a moment before he sighs and nods in agreement.

"Okay. Dietrichson's father, John, is the oldest with the moustache and blue suit, place him and I'll go clockwise from there."

He turns us slightly so I'm looking in their direction as discreetly as possible. I nod once I have who he described, who is still grilling Wren from the looks of it.

"From there it's Patrick O'Shay, Travis Fuse, Reggie Rivera, Juliana Gibbs, Maria Steele, Betty Morgan and Rico," he whispers.

My heart is pounding in my chest. There is a Steele here, someone with my blood and I can't even bring myself to look at them, for fear of it crushing me.

"Who is she to me?" I ask quietly, he knows what I'm asking.

"She is your grandmother. To be completely honest with you Luna, there are three others up there that were also very fond of you too."

He doesn't say who or why and I don't know if I want to know, but I've left myself at a disadvantage refusing to acknowledge my life before the disaster.

Trying to push past all this emotion, I focus on the fact that Parker's father is here. Even West doesn't give his surname to me. Looking at him, I want to tear his throat out for what he's done to his son. That soon has me under control again, just filled with rage instead.

"Thank you, West," I say as I step back and make my

way to the table.

Taking a seat everyone's eyes are on me checking me over.

"I'm fine guys, he just wanted to apologize," I say as I smile, but no one is convinced.

I'm ready to leave now, done with the tense atmosphere. I can't stop glancing at the door watching for Rafe, when the same man who approached earlier stands beside me.

"Miss Steele, Rico has requested you for a moment." Huh, still no surname? Asshole. He definitely doesn't deserve the privilege of being an Acehole.

I glance at Parker whose face is white, while Roman's is red with fury.

"Thank you for letting me know, but if you could be so kind as to pass on my decline, I would be grateful," I reply sweetly.

"Miss, please, I don't believe that'll be in your best interest," whispers the guy frantically.

"I'm not going, now unless something will happen to you for passing on that message, that is all," I respond, determined, but the guy is shaking.

"Will something happen to you?" I ask quietly, and he nods with fear.

Fuck.

I glance around the table again, and nobody knows what to say or do. Nobody wants me to go, but everyone seems to know it'll not go down well if I don't do as I am told.

When will these guys learn?

I make my own rules.

Raising my hand to make the guy wait, I pull my phone out and dial Rafe.

"Luna? Luna, are you okay?" he answers instantly.

"Yeah, West told me you're near. How far out? I've got Rico the dickhead wanting my attendance and there is no way I'm going, but if I send the messenger back with a no it won't end well for him. What do I do?"

"Shit, send the guy to West, he'll take care of him. As for Rico, over my dead body. I'm outside, it's probably best you prepare to leave." The line goes dead.

I send the guy in West's direction telling him to explain exactly why, he doesn't look close to tears anymore but he's still shaking.

"I hope you don't mind guys, but I think the party is about to be over. Want to head back to my room?" I ask.

Everyone nods in agreement. Parker doesn't know

what to do, he likely hasn't disobeyed his father before, and I don't want him to get caught in the middle of this.

"Roman, get Parker out of here first, he doesn't need the backlash. Do you understand?" I'm not fucking around, and the determination is clear in my voice.

Parker tries to protest but whatever Roman says soothes him, and they head out just as Rafe steps in the room. I sigh deeply inside at his appearance. I stand as he approaches, and he wraps me in his arms.

"You look beautiful Luna, everything okay?"

"Yeah, there are bigger things going on here, but we need to address the fact that you own a suit. You're lucky I recognized you," I say with a chuckle, trying to lighten the mood.

He gives me a small chuckle, pacifying me.

"One of these days, Luna, I'll get to actually come down here to just see you, not because there is an emergency," he says with a smile. "Now get yourselves out of here before it gets too crazy, okay?"

He places a gentle kiss on my temple, but before he leaves, I have to ask.

"Rafe, does she know much about me?"

The understanding on his face is unmistakable, "West?"

"Yeah."

"He say anything else?"

"Not very much because he said I wasn't ready, but he said you broke the rules to run with me," I whisper, fidgeting with the buckle on my clutch.

His face softens.

"I can see the question you don't want to ask in your eyes, Luna. I would do it again and again to keep you safe." He squeezes my shoulder in reassurance.

"As for your actual question, she was one of two people in the whole world who knew where we were the entire time. She loves you fiercely, Luna, enough to keep away to save you."

I nod, not sure how to process any of this really, but I had to ask.

Kai puts his arm around my shoulder and guides us out of here, as Oscar does the same with Red. As we near the stairs I hear a smash, followed by screams and raised voices. I know it's Rafe, but Kai refuses to let me turn around and it's probably for the best, because I would want to step in, but I know I'm helping by leaving. I just don't actually understand how.

The night air greets us as we head for the limo.

MY BLOODLINE

I'm ready for that drink now, or two.

KC KEAN

TWENTY NINE

Luna

Pulling up outside of Ace, Red pulls me aside.

"Hey, I'm going to bow out, get my book boyfriend out and relax," she says as she side hugs me.

"Are you sure? You don't need to leave," I explain.

If she wants, I'll ban the guys and we can have girl time. As much as it weirds me out to admit that.

"No, honestly. I had fun tonight, getting dressed up and all that, but now I need some me time. Besides, I'm itching to finish this book."

I nod, giving her a quick hug. Completely out of character, to be the one initiating the contact.

Kai offers her his arm to walk her back to her room. I love how they take care of her too, she's important to me. I smile in thanks to Kai, and head inside with the others.

Stepping into the elevator Oscar whips a bottle of tequila and a bottle of bourbon from behind his back, wagging his eyebrows.

"Got us a little treat out of the limo, who's ready for some fun?" he cheers.

I grin at his antics. I need to let my hair down a little, and I'm trusting them enough to do it around them.

Heading straight for the kitchen I look through the cupboards and find some glasses perfect for shots and shorts. I carry them back into the lounge where the guys have put an action movie on in the background, and rearranged the sofas so everyone's closer.

We've done this a few times after classes, but it feels different tonight.

Hotter.

Part of me wants to change into something more comfortable, but the guys are still wearing their shirts and I like the idea of someone else getting me out of this thing, so on it stays.

A knock at the door has Oscar letting Kai in while I grab

some snacks. When I step back into the lounge, they're all staring at the door, waiting for me. Want in everyone's eyes.

Oscar breaks the tension.

"Baby girl, come sit down we're playing drinking games," he says with a wink.

"Is that so?" I ask with a smirk, but it sounds like fun for a change.

He just nods at me while biting his lip, distracting me.

"Okay, what are we starting with?" Kai asks.

"Never have I ever, or truth or dare?" Oscar asks.

"Really?" Roman sighs.

"Yes, really. Luna, tell him." Oscar pouts. "It'll be fun. Watch. Luna, truth or dare?"

I just roll my eyes at him trying to force me into taking his side.

"Luna, truth or dare?" he repeats.

"Fine, truth."

"Is it true you want to kiss me right now?" he grins all sexy at me, but I can't help but rile him up a little.

I shake my head.

"I'll take dare instead," I respond, thinking I'm funny but he just widens his smile.

"Perfect, I dare you to come kiss me," he purrs.

He looks to the others then returns his stare to me, beckoning me over, and I find myself on my feet making my way to him. He slouches back in his seat and spreads his legs wide, getting comfortable. Resting his arms out wide, he looks like sin.

If I roll my skirt up and sit on his lap right now then it's game over already, and I'm not ready for that. So I stand behind him, making him lean his head back, and touch my lips to his.

Fuck, it's sexy like this, especially with the feeling of the others watching. I pull back too soon, but we're only just getting started. Parker pours everyone a shot of tequila and Roman fetches salt and lemon from the kitchen. Counting down we lick, gulp and bite together, and I shiver at the tequila burning my throat.

"Never have I ever fingered myself," calls Oscar.

Shit we're getting straight to it apparently, and I'm already outnumbered. Giving him the stink-eye, I take another shot raising the heat in all of their eyes.

"Never have I ever had my dick pierced," calls Kai making Oscar groan, but I can't help but smile that this didn't just turn into the fuck Luna over show.

"Never have I ever come in a Rolls Royce," calls out Roman.

Acehole.

I take another.

"You never did explain what happened in that car," Oscar shouts but neither of us respond.

"Never have I ever fucked in the ring," Parker carries the game on.

Bitch, I'm screwed here, but at least Roman has to drink this time too.

"Okay, never have I ever had a blow job," I cry out, feeling rather proud of myself when they all take a shot, and I don't have too. Then I realize they've had blow jobs that weren't from me, and I struggle not wanting to strangle a bitch, like Wren.

"Never have I ever had my nipples pierced," Oscar teases, pulling me out of my head, and making me take another shot, as Kai and Parker stare at me open mouthed.

I wink, the tequila having me playful.

"Never have I ever had sex outside," Kai adds.

Fuck. Oscar's fault and the grin on his face tells me he's pleased with himself, and Roman drinks too, although not meeting my eyes, because it wasn't with me.

"Never have I ever had anal," Roman shouts.

He's fucking worse than Oscar, I take a shot and the shock is clear, even on Roman's face. He was trying to catch me out after what I said after the Rolls incident, but I wasn't lying.

"Never have I ever seen a more beautiful woman than the one in front of me right now," Parker says, making all the guys drink.

Usually I'd be embarrassed but the Tequila is working its magic.

"You guys need to stop, I can't think straight with you all right now, you're getting me all hot," I fake glare, but end up laughing at myself for no reason, throwing my head back.

"God it's been a long time since I've let myself feel tipsy," I say to myself.

I look to Oscar and see him palming himself, fuck. That's hot.

"Show me," I whisper, eyes glued to his movements. When he doesn't move, I look to his face but he's looking around at the others.

"Please, Oscar," I whimper.

I'm so turned on I can't think about anything else, the

alcohol is making me want it more.

Oscar stares into my eyes.

"Sit on Kai's lap facing me and I will," he orders, making my core clench.

Fuck.

Yes please.

I slowly stand and move to Kai, he turns me and drops me on to his lap. Right on his dick. God yes. I tilt my head back on his shoulder as he squeezes my hips, letting a moan slip past my lips. I glance back at Oscar and true to his word his dick is in his hand, and he's pulling slowly giving me a show.

I can't help but grind myself on Kai, needing the contact, and making him moan quietly in my ear.

"I want more," I say, not to anyone specifically just to the room.

"Are your nipples hard, princess?" Roman asks as he unbuttons his shirt.

I can't form words, so I just nod.

"Prove it," he pushes.

Fuck. I'm not backing down. Not even a little bit. This is beyond hot.

I lean forward slightly so I can drag my spaghetti straps

off my shoulders slowly, releasing my rock-hard nipples to them. A few groans are called out around me and it only has me hotter.

"Parker, taste them," Roman orders and Parker follows through.

Kneeling between Kai's legs he slowly brings his mouth exactly where I need it. The sharp bite catches me off guard, and I gasp feeling the tingles go straight to my pussy.

"Ahh, God yes," I cry.

He brings his hands forward cupping my breasts, testing the weight of them in his hands.

"Fuck, Luna, you're perfect," he whispers, as he leans back in to swirl his tongue around my taut peaks.

My core is throbbing with the need to be touched, and I have my guys teasing me. My guys. Why does that make me clench just that little bit more?

Both Oscar and Roman are gripping themselves, and I see the slight shine of pre-come making my mouth water.

"Please."

Fuck, I don't even know what I'm begging for.

"Stand up, Princess," orders Roman.

Parker doesn't remove his mouth as Kai helps me stand

and my dress falls to my feet. Leaving me stood in only my heels.

"Fuck, had I known you had nothing on under that thing I'd have had you stripped before we even left," curses Oscar.

"I need more," I repeat

"You want a show huh?" asks Roman, and I nod in agreement.

"But if someone doesn't touch my pussy soon, I'm kicking you all out." I'm past the point of pleasantries now, it's all about pure need.

Behind me Kai's hands tease over my ass, this guy and his fingers are everywhere but where I need him. He kicks my arousal up a notch, especially with Parker not relenting. Add to the fact two out of four dicks are visible, and I want to explode.

"What do you want, Princess?"

"I want your lips on Parker's again," I answer boldly, and completely honest.

His eyes widen in surprise, but the grip around his cock tightens. Fuck he wants that too. Parker lifts his gaze to mine, he must be happy with what he sees, because he's crushing his lips to mine in an instant.

Kai chooses that moment to tease a finger around my entrance making me whimper against Parker, before he steps over to Roman.

Oscar drags the coffee table over, taking a seat and pulling me down to sit between his legs, offering me the perfect view of where Roman and Parker stand staring at me. Kai crouches down between my legs as Oscar squeezes my breasts hard, and I fucking love it.

Roman grabs Parkers chin and pushes straight in past his lips, just like he does to me, and it's a fucking vision. Parker's hands are all over Romans bare chest and I can't get enough of it. When I think I can't take anymore Kai swipes his tongue against my clit.

Oh.

My.

Days.

This is what heaven feels like.

As I watch the most erotic scene I've ever witnessed before me, Oscar pulls my piercing close to the point of pain and I can't control my cries of pleasure. Kai wants in on the action and finally. Finally. Pushes those fingers of his inside me.

"Fuck, you're drenched, Sakura," he growls.

Fuck, the growl only enhances everything. He doesn't hang around, thrusting three fingers inside me like an expert, as Oscar finds my nub with one hand while pulling my nipple with the other. My hips instinctively rise and grind against their hands, electricity zapping my core. Then Parker is kissing down Roman's chest and taking his massive cock in his mouth, forcing Roman to throw his head back with ecstasy.

I explode.

I scream.

I ride the never-ending waves of pleasure being fed to me from every single one of them.

Looking at Parker, on his knees in front of Roman, the lust in his eyes as he takes him deep over and over again, has me ready to go again, but I want to taste them too.

I find the strength to stand only to kneel straight away. The need in my eyes must be clear to Oscar and Kai as they both stand before me. Kai finally releases himself and I get to see all of him. He's long just like his fingers, but not quite as thick as the other two, which is perfect, and I'm already envisioning him in my ass. For now, I need him in my mouth. He doesn't grab my head, letting me set the pace. I switch between them both as Parker continues to work Roman, who's watching it all unfold.

"Fuck, fuck, fuck."

I have no idea who's cursing or if it's all of them. I'm lost in my other senses. I need my mouth fucked, I place Oscar's hand on the back of my head, encouraging him. Fuck, he likes that, his thrusts become frantic, and he's coming down my throat making me swallow every drop.

He releases my head and I blindly search for Kai, who thrusts to the back of my throat making me gag, and I fucking crave it. Gripping his ass to hold him in place. I swallow around his dick and it sends him over the edge, spilling inside me as he rides his own aftershocks.

I look to Roman who is already looking at me, and I find myself standing and forcing his lips to mine as Parker continues his pace. I don't even consider the fact he'll be able to taste the others on my lips, but it doesn't stop him devouring my mouth and finding his release, which I catch a glimpse of Parker swallowing down.

I take a second to look around, is it bad I need a little more? That's when I realize Parker is yet to cum. Meeting him on the ground, his eyes are blown, he's never looked sexier. I need some of him.

Resting my forehead to his I whisper, "I need you

Parker."

He considers what I said for a moment before he's whispering in my ear. I stand instantly pulling him to his feet, dragging him towards my bedroom. Remembering the others, I glance back and they're all staring confused.

Shit.

I push Parker into my room.

"Strip," I purr at him and he grins in response.

Looking at the others I shout, "This is important, can you drag Roman's mattress across and we'll drag mine out soon. I don't want anyone to leave tonight."

Roman knows, he nods and forces the others to follow his lead without question.

I slam my bedroom door shut and spin to find Parker stripped like I asked.

"Are you sure about this?" I ask.

"One hundred percent," he responds. No hesitation, just the truth.

I nod.

"Good, because you're all mine, Parker," I murmur.

Goosebumps rise all over my body.

All mine is right.

My hot as shit fucking virgin.

Parker

My brain is going a mile a minute and if I don't calm down this will be over too quickly, and I'm not going down like that. The look in her eyes tells me she has questions first.

I lean back bracing myself on my hands and her eyes are locked in between my legs.

Fuck the lust in her eyes is driving me crazy, from the second I whispered, it flicked up a notch.

"Luna, I want this with you so bad, but not like this. I haven't done what I can see you want to do in your eyes."

I never expected her to order everyone around and give us some privacy, I expected her to run for the hills. God, watching her out there she was so sexy, a real fucking Goddess.

"There's no going back from this?" she states.

She doesn't ask if I'm lying, she knows. I don't respond, giving her a nod instead. She moves towards me slowly, she's a black widow and I'm caught in her web, yet I don't want to be anywhere else.

"What experience do you have?"

I thought I would be embarrassed talking about this, but it feels natural with her.

"Everything but actual sex. I'm quite happy for just about anyone to give me head. I need a little more to reciprocate, but I've never held enough of a connection with someone to want real ecstasy," I murmur honestly.

"Have you ever done that with Roman before?" she asks, and I can see her remembering his dick in my mouth and it turns her on.

"Yeah, rarely but yeah," I answer, again happy to be honest with her.

She lowers between my legs, fingers gliding up my thighs but not touching me, driving me crazy.

"I've never been someone's first before," she whispers.

Fuck.

"Then it was meant to be like this, Luna," I reply confidently.

She gives me strength in so many ways, she'll never truly understand.

Not only that but tonight she refused to meet my father. Stood up to him. Stood for herself. She's always had my attention, but in that moment she had me fully. Then she makes Roman get me out of there, caring enough to see the repercussions I could have faced, because I wouldn't have been able to just stand my ground too. Not yet anyway. She's making me want to.

I cup her face and bring her lips to mine. I want her. I need her.

She pulls back too soon, to slowly graze her lips down my chest, like I did to Roman. Her tongue lightly swirls around my tip and I throw my head back, fuck she's a little tease.

"Luna, you might be my Queen, and this might be my first time, but don't fucking tease me. We've had our foreplay already." I grunt as I squeeze her breast and she shivers.

She can't talk, just nods.

"Have you got any condoms?" I ask because I sure as shit didn't even consider bringing any.

She climbs on to my lap and stares at me for the longest time before she finally answers.

"I do, but I'm on the pill, and for your first time I want us to feel each other skin to skin, remember this between us forever. I've never done that, it'd be a first for both of us."

Fuck, I want that. I trust her especially when I see the vulnerability in her eyes. I nod and that's the only permission she needs as she's dragging her pussy against my cock, bringing it to her entrance and slowly sinking down on me.

Fuck. This. Is. Incredible. All I can process is the feel of her heat surrounding me, taking me deeper and deeper. When she's fully seated, my hands find her hips holding her in place. She's so tight. My dick has never been strangled like this before and I want more of it. Remembering to breathe, I finally release a groan trapped in my throat.

Her hands force my head to lift from looking at where we are joined.

"Fuck, Parker. I've never. Oh God," she cries out as she tries to grind against me.

I loosen my hold so she can move, and I lose it.

Lose myself to her movements, to all these sensations.

Keeping one hand on her ass as she grinds over and over, I use the other to bring her nipple to my mouth. She curses when I flick my tongue again and again. The drags of her pussy get frantic as her core clenches tight around my cock, and I can't help biting her nipple, which only sends her further over the edge.

If the guys are out there, they definitely heard her and that makes me hotter. Letting them know I'm taking good care of her.

Deciding I want control I flip her on her back, swiping my tongue between her legs, tasting my Queen before I thrust back inside of her.

Fuck.

She wraps her legs tight around my waist as I thrust deeper and deeper. Her cries get louder and I can tell she's close again, finding her clit with my thumb, I don't relent on my pace or brutal pounding.

"Parker. Fuck. Parker," she screams as her pussy locks tight around me.

I can't hold off anymore coming harder than I ever have before, as I continue to ram myself inside her, riding out our aftershocks together.

I drop my head to her shoulder trying to catch my breath as we both come down from our high. She strokes my hair back and I lift to glimpse into her eyes. I kiss her with all the passion I feel for her instead of using stupid words, she responds just as fiercely, and my soul feels settled, yet close to exploding at the same time.

Not wanting to leave her laying in our mess, I stand

off the bed and she follows, although she pauses to look down her body. I see it. My cum running down the inside of her leg.

"Fuck, I like that," I groan, and she smirks at me.

"You want me to set the shower or bathtub for you?" I ask and she wraps her hands around my neck.

"You, Parker Parker, are too good to me. I would die for a lie in that tub right now."

I smile, unable to hide her effect on me.

"Are you okay going like that or do you want my shirt?"

"I would have been fine naked, but the thought of your scent on me is too hard to deny," she purrs.

Fuck. She knows what she's doing to me. I hand it over to her and she fastens just two of the buttons, hot as hell.

She goes to open the door, but I can't help but pick her up to carry her to the bathroom. When we step into the lounge a different movie is playing on the tv and whatever the guys were talking about has been forgotten as they watch us.

Luna's head is resting against my shoulder, so she doesn't see we have their attention. I'm halfway walking her through when Oscar finally opens his mouth.

"Fuck me, Parker, did you manage to last more than six seconds on your first time or what?"

Roman whacks him round the head as Luna calls, "Don't be a dick, Oscar."

"Baby girl, I'm not, I'm only making sure he treated my girl good," he defends. Asshole.

"He can give you details while I have a bath, seen as his cum is trailing down my leg still, okay?" She replies, eyes on me and a grin on her face. She knows what she just did.

"Wait? What? Why would that…oh man. You lucky bastard, Parker, my dick's hard again now," he groans.

Yeah.

I could live in this moment forever, as the luckiest bastard alive.

MY BLOODLINE

THIRTY

Luna

Monday morning, yet I'm not in my uniform. I'm all set to get my first assignment done. West signed me off to leave campus for the next two days, without questions which surprised me. I think I expected him to kick up a fuss, but I'm glad I didn't have to deal with any of that. I've got Dot beneath me and I'm heading to Washington, which is where DCM Tech headquarters are. I've got my own tools and a few new tech ones from Kai so I'm all set.

I'm ready for my phone to start blowing up anytime, since I sent a group text letting them know I wouldn't be around for the next few days. I just know at least one of them is going to be unhappy that I'm alone, but I've done this many times on my own before. Red knew I was setting off this morning, so someone knew where I was going to be. I knew she wouldn't put up a fight about it like the guys will.

I left before six this morning so I could make good time and have the day to set up before I hit them tonight. It's almost eight as I pull into the Four Seasons. It took a lot of research to find out which hotels in Washington weren't influenced by Featherstone, and typically it was either the most expensive or run-down guest houses.

I park Dot a block away, making sure no cameras are on her and keeping her away from being linked to me at this hotel. As I enter the lobby in my skinny ripped jeans and leather jacket, I feel slightly underdressed, and I wonder if I should have tried to blend in better.

Fuck it, I'm sure they have Rockstar's stay here too, just not right now.

Heading to the check in desk, the girl looks at me like I've walked shit in. Great.

"Can I help you?"

"Yeah, I've got a reservation under the name of Gibbs,"

I reply, trying not to rise to her shitty attitude.

"I think you're at the wrong place, hun."

Is she joking with me?

"I suggest you bring your system up and check me in, Laura," I say reading her name on her badge.

She sighs as she clicks around a little, then her face drops.

"Gibbs as in the Royal Suite reservation," she asks, gulping.

I want to whack her head into the wall in frustration at her shitty girl antics, but I don't.

"That'd be me," I say with a smirk.

She nods quickly and gives me everything I need.

"I hope you have a wonderful stay with us, Miss Gibbs. Your parcel was received on Friday and is now waiting in your suite for you."

Fuck off, Laura.

I hope you get genital warts.

Judge that.

I'm on the second floor so I take the stairs. There aren't many rooms on this floor, because they are so big, so I'm quickly inside. Fuck if I thought adjusting to my room at Featherstone was something, this is next level. When I saw they had rooms with private fitness space, I jumped at it. I can literally do everything except scope and actually enter DCM all from here.

This room is bigger than some people's houses. The entry space alone is the size of my lounge back at Featherstone, all marble floors and high-end furnishings. Are those star lights in the ceiling? The whole space is a mixture between modern and traditional. The lounge is about the size of the Main Hall, it's crazy. I'm loving the deep purple sleigh bed in the bedroom too. While the outdoor terrace makes me wish I hadn't come alone, because you could throw one hell of a party out there.

The suite even comes with a conference room which could easily seat ten people, with projectors, monitors, and memory boards hung on the walls. So I decide to set all of my stuff up in there.

I had everything that wouldn't fit with me on the ride down shipped here in preparation. A lot I'll leave behind, still set up to continue my checks after I hit them, the rest will either be thrown away or shipped back.

It would have been easier if I'd just brought a car, but fuck that.

I need to set up my cameras outside of the building,

everything else I'll have access to by hacking into their surveillance. I'd always done this, it would take me forever, but Kai helped me out this time. He's basically done all the work, I now just need to open a secure folder on my laptop and bam, I'm in.

I've been watching them at different times of the day and the shutdown process is always the same, no one ever stays later than eight in the evening. The blueprints are casually stored in the admin office, easily accessible. I just need to get in there.

I place a few cameras around my suite in each room because I can never be too careful, and at least while I am out, I can still see everything.

I consider taking a nap, but I haven't eaten yet and I can see my phone flashing from here, screaming at me to answer the guys before they explode. Unlocking it I see over twenty missed calls and too many messages in the group chat. I also have a text from Red too, so I look at hers first.

Red: Hey, just checking you've arrived? I already miss your sassy ass. Get it done and get back here girl!

Luna: I'm here. You would die for this room. Makes me think we need a trip! The guys are blowing up my phone, wish me luck.

Red: Girl, that sounds like a plan! You don't need any luck, you have those guys wrapped around your pinky. Ha ha. Love ya bitch!

She makes me chuckle to myself, always brightening my mood. Now onto the shit show that's about to be in the group chat.

Roman: What the fuck Luna, you're joking right?

Roman: Luna, I swear to God, answer the phone.

Oscar: Baby girl, you're crazy. Where are you?

Parker: I'm not happy you've gone alone Luna, please answer.

Roman: I'm close to having Kai track your mobile, don't make me!

Kai: Sakura, please just let us know you are okay.

Oscar: Baby girl…

Parker: I'm worried guys, it's been nearly three hours.

Roman: I'm speaking to West, he's obviously the one to give her an off-campus pass.

Oscar: Get us off-campus passes, she shouldn't be alone.

Kai: Luna is a grown woman, but I agree, I am worried.

Parker: Roman? Any luck?

Roman: He's a dick. Says she needs to do this

alone. Give it twenty minutes then I'm leaving here. Fuck the consequences.

Oscar: Me too.

Parker: Where are DCM Tech based?

Kai: Washington

Oscar: At least we know where we're headed.

Fuck these guys are crazy. I'd like to send a quick text so I can eat and sleep, but I know that won't be enough. I make quick work of ordering some food to be sent up and call the group chat, putting it on loudspeaker and stepping back from the table.

It barely rings once when Roman's voice comes through the line.

"What the actual fuck, Luna? Do you know how worried I've been? We've been? You can't just fucking do this," he growls.

He's mad, but he needs to learn I'm my own person and I got by just fine in life before I agreed to this, whatever this is with them.

"Are you done?" I ask.

"Done? Fucking done? You don't even have a clue do you?"

"I get your concern, Roman. I get you guys not liking that I'm off doing this by myself, but the second you start shouting at me like I'm a child is the same moment you get cut off. Now, you're either going to show me some fucking respect when you talk to me or this conversation is done, what'll it be?" I growl.

I'm probably acting overly defensive, but I am who I am, tough shit.

I'm met with silence, looking at the screen I can see the other guys names are also showing as in the call, but no one says anything.

"He's done, Luna. Please don't end the call," Parker quietly calls through the phone.

"Hey babe," I respond, like I'm a completely different person, all soft and full of joy.

He brings it out of me, has me calling him nicknames, and well, he wasn't an acehole just now.

"Hey angel, are you okay? I'm worried about you," Parker responds.

It's as if he knows he needs to do the complete opposite of what Roman just did to make this work better and it makes me smile.

"I'm okay, just at the hotel, waiting on some food. Then I need to set up my cameras outside the building and take a nap, I just haven't decided what order to do those in yet. Are you okay?"

"I'm better now I've heard your voice, but I'd be far better if you weren't alone."

"I know, Parker, but this isn't about you guys. This is my assignment. An assignment almost identical to jobs I've done before. I'm not out here trying to prove myself to people who don't deserve that level of effort from me. I'm out here fully aware of myself and my skills. I'll be back tomorrow night," I offer, like I should even need to pacify them.

"It is about us, Princess. We care about you and you aren't letting us do that," growls Roman, clearly still not able to control his frustration.

"Shut up, Roman," calls Kai, which makes me silently chuckle.

Someone using Roman's classic line back on him. It should have been Oscar who said it for a complete role reversal.

"Sakura, are you sure you can't make room for just one of us?" Kai asks, I don't respond for a moment trying to figure out what's for the best.

"Please, baby girl, compromise with us. Just one of us, whoever comes won't be in the way just there to keep us from going any crazier," Oscar begs, finally joining the conversation.

Compromise? Is that what this is? I'm still not used to thinking of others. When it was Tommy, I never took him into consideration, not once. Now I'm having to think about four others, like that's completely normal.

This is different though. It feels different. I'm different, and I want to make this work. Especially after Saturday night. Not the sex, although that was phenomenal, but after all of that. Both mattresses pushed together on the floor in the lounge with the sofas behind us. Curled up and relaxed in each other's company, I felt like I belonged there in that moment with these guys. That's what I wanted more of.

"Okay, I'll compromise. Just one, and don't push me. I swear if any more of you show up, be prepared for a shit show. I'm at the Four Seasons, don't park at the hotel. Royal Suite, second floor, room 200. Decide amongst yourselves who's coming, my food's here and I deserve a fucking nap after being ganged up on."

I put the phone down. I don't think that was too harsh. I wanted to be harsher, but I compromised as much as I could bring myself to do.

God give me strength to deal with four bossy assholes. I'm gonna need it.

Roman

For fucks sake, how do I convince these guys to let me be the one to go? Selfish, I know but I don't care.

"I feel like we just achieved a huge milestone convincing her to compromise, so we can't mess this up. Well done, Oscar, for a change your mouth didn't make the situation worse," says Kai, making Oscar grin like a Cheshire cat.

"That means I get to go then right?" Oscar nods.

"No it fucking doesn't. I need to go so I can make it up to her," I add.

The others stare at me with a frown, considering my

words and deciding whether or not to agree with me. This is my moment to come clean with them, I can feel it coursing through my blood and it starts my heartbeat off at a thundering pace.

"There are also other things I haven't talked about with everyone, including Luna, and I need the chance to do that. It involves her, and I'm worried if it gets too late there will be no coming back from it," I confess.

"Talk about what?" Parker asks.

"Parker, I swear I will explain everything to you guys, but I need to talk to Luna first," I plead.

I know we are all invested here, and I know even if it's by omission or not I could ruin all of this and we've barely begun.

They stare me down.

"Fine, you go," Oscar agrees. "But I swear to God, whatever it is, you better make it perfectly clear that we don't know shit, because if you sink this ship I'm not going down with you."

All I can do is nod.

"And make her video chat us when you get there, I miss her face already."

Fuck me, Oscar is the most pussy whipped for sure,

although we're really not far behind him.

Not wanting to waste any more time I head for the door, as Kai places an envelope in my hand.

"It contains a tracker. It'll give us a solid two hours on her, it's super discreet but you need to make sure she doesn't find it, understand?" he whispers.

Fuck yeah I understand, this is why he's the best tech guy around. I pat him on the back and head out. With the two-hour drive ahead of me she'll have plenty of time to nap, while I figure out how the fuck I broach the fact that we knew each other as children.

My palms sweat thinking about it. If what Rafe said is true, it's going to look like I've kept it a secret on purpose, but I followed his advice to keep her from breaking down. Now a lot is happening around us and from the snippets my dad has given me, it's only going to get worse. I don't want this weight between us, and I want to be there to support her through it.

Together we are stronger, no matter the past. I just need her to see that.

Arriving in Washington, I drive past the hotel, finding somewhere to park. Ten minutes later and I'm knocking on her door. It takes her a minute to answer, and when she does, she's in her training gear. God, every time I see her she gets prettier. I think it's because every time I'm around her she gives me another little piece of herself. Reminding me of when we were young, and I followed her every word then too. I might be a cranky asshole most of the time but if she asks me to jump, I'm going to do it.

"Huh, I thought for sure Oscar would have convinced you all that he was the one to get me to compromise, so he was the one who got to come. He'd have nagged so much you'd have sent him just to shut him up," she says as she leans against the door frame.

"You'd be right. He did do that, except I thought I'd get better silence if I were the one here with you." I can't help the grin.

She's learning our dynamic. Pulling her towards me I crash my lips to hers, loving the feel of her against me.

Pushing her inside, I shut the door behind me. Taking in this place, I raise my eyebrow at her in surprise.

"Don't look at me like that. I've never stayed anywhere like this before. Did you know the Four Season's is the only hotel in Washington with no connection to Featherstone?" I shake my head, surprised that she researched so deeply before coming here, I'm impressed.

"Then when I was booking a room I found out the Royal Suite comes with its own private fitness room and I just couldn't say no to that level of luxury," she winks, forcing a chuckle past my lips.

"How girly and materialistic of you," I joke, making her whack me as she leads the way.

"So, you can be my food buddy if you like? I have time to eat, then I need to get the last of my equipment set up, which shouldn't take more than a couple of hours. Then I'll need to head out around ten to be on the safe side," she calls over her shoulder.

I hate that she has to do this, but whether we like it or not, this is our world.

"So I'm here to provide company while you eat, huh?"

"Well you wanted to be here remember?"

"Don't try and sass me, Princess, otherwise you don't get any dick for dessert." I fake pout at her, hands on hips too.

The whole works. It actually fucking works too.

"You wouldn't dare," she says, but she's lacking the usual confidence in her voice.

"Try me," I offer.

I just issued a challenge, I can see it written on her

face. She somehow manages to stand taller and her grin is all kinds of fucked up, but I love it. She whips her sports bra off, and she knows she's got me. I can't say no to them babies, all fancy with their jewels.

"You win," I murmur.

"I'm glad you said that, now come christen the mattress with me, handsome," she purrs and I'm like a fucking puppy following after her.

We'll talk later.

I need a taste of my girl first.

KC KEAN

THIRTY ONE

Roman

She left for a few hours to get her surveillance set up, leaving me to browse around. Her tech set up is impressive. I can tell what came from Kai, but even without it she knows what she's doing here. She was fucking made for this world, she just doesn't know it or seem to want it.

It's close to ten. I know she's going to be leaving soon and I still haven't figured out where to put this God damn tracking device. I send a text to Kai.

Roman: Can you distract her for a while? I can't place the tracker.

He doesn't respond but within twenty seconds Luna's phone is going off with a video chat waiting with the guys on the other end. She rolls her eyes as she answers.

"Are you calling to annoy me before I need to leave?"

No greeting or pleasantries, just Luna. Perfection.

As they hold her in conversation, I head out of the conference room she's been holed up in, so I can figure out where to put this thing. This is why these guys are like my brothers. No questions asked, we're always willing to go to bat for one another.

I find her boots and place it in the slight arch on the bottom. The tracker is ultra slim, almost like a screen protector just a lot smaller. I stick it on and hope that's it. I head to the kitchen and grab a bottle of water, downing half as I make my way back to her, as if this is what I left for.

They're still chatting away, but I can see her glancing continuously at the time. As much as we don't want her to have to deal with any of this, she does, they've done what I needed them to do, now she needs to focus.

Standing behind her, I rest my chin on her shoulder, glancing at the phone.

"You fuckers done harassing my Princess?" I say, as I kiss her cheek.

I see her blush slightly. She's not used to all this attention, but she likes it.

"Screw you, Roman, I should have been the one to go," Oscar pouts, but no one takes him on.

"She needs to focus now." I order, "say goodbye."

They've barely gotten their words out when I'm snatching the phone and ending the call.

"Acehole."

She glares but there's no real anger in her voice. I love her little nickname for us when we annoy her, so I can't help but smirk at her.

"What's left to do?"

"Nothing, everything's ready to go, I just need to actually leave now," she says, as I wrap my arms around her, bringing my lips to the top of her head.

I've never been one for showing affection with small gestures and touches, but she brings out the side of me I once remember as a child. With that in mind.

"Hey, when you get back or in the morning, I want to talk to you about some stuff," I murmur.

"What about?"

"It's not important right now, you have all this to deal with and I want you to focus on that, but afterwards, please. It's important afterwards."

She looks me in the eyes with concern, but I offer her nothing, I'm not joking when I say I want her to focus. She must be able to see that I mean it because she nods and moves along.

"You don't need to wait up, I'm not sure how long it'll really take."

"Screw that, I'll be sitting watching these monitors until your sweet butt is back here, understood?"

She doesn't answer because it's not really a question.

She throws on her boots and a black hoodie, before grabbing her small backpack carrying everything she needs.

"I'm not going to lie, Luna, it doesn't feel right to me staying here while you do this, but I'm trying my hardest to respect your wishes."

"I can't tell you how much it means to me that you are going against your own internal instincts to give me the room I need to do what needs to be done," she responds with a smile. "Now kiss me so I can go and get back."

She barely lets me give her more than a peck before

she's moving towards the door. She smiles then she's gone, and I'm left feeling a little lost.

I dial up Kai as I head back to the conference room.

"Hey, she just left. I stuck it to her boot."

"Yeah it signaled on my laptop when you activated it. I'll send a copy of my screen to Luna's laptop until she comes into focus on everything else," he says as he ends the call, and does exactly what he just said.

She's moving slowly. She must be walking, fuck I should have offered to drive her or something. Now I feel like even more of a dick.

Kai: I can feel your stress from here. She'll be walking to blend in and keep in the shadows.

His text calms me a little, but I still don't like it.

About twenty minutes later I see her come on to the feed from the cameras she set up outside the building, she also has access to them on her phone so she can see as much as possible. She goes to the staff entrance and pulls out an access card. Where the hell did she get that from? Clearly because this isn't my assignment, I've not actually considered how any of this will go down.

I'm a fucking idiot.

A couple of digits on the keypad too and the green light above the door flashes and she's in. Simple as that. I flick to the monitors showing inside the building and I don't see her anywhere, not even a shadow. Then one of the cameras flickers for a moment before it returns to normal.

What the hell.

My phone is ringing, and I answer without glancing.

"Are you seeing this?"

Kai calls down the line.

"I didn't even know she had this kind of tech."

"What do you mean?"

"She's literally keeping to the shadows like a ninja. But when she can't, she's jamming the surveillance feed where she is, allowing her to still get by unseen," he whisper shouts, in awe of what he's seeing.

Fuck me, she really is good.

"I know she said the files were in the admin office which is on the twelfth floor, so she'll likely take the staff stairwells," I say.

He stays on the phone, yet we say nothing at all just watching the surveillance screens for absolutely nothing except the occasional flicker here or there. To anyone else this would be some crazy shit, but fuck me, it's hot.

Suddenly the camera in the admin office cuts out, for all of twenty seconds then it's back on again, like nothing happened.

"She's amazing," declares Kai down the phone. "You better treat her good when she gets back, she deserves nothing less."

"Yeah," I respond as I cut the phone off.

Not needing any further acknowledgment of how amazing she is. I just need to talk to her first then she'll hopefully give me a chance to make her feel like the Goddess she is.

She's not out of the building yet when there's a knock on the door. Why the fuck is someone knocking at the door? I walk to the entry hall and glance at the intercom which has been blacked out.

Shit.

Something isn't right here.

I quickly throw a text into the group chat then set it to silence. A knock sounds again as I'm pulling the handgun I'm glad I brought out of my coat pocket.

"I know you're in there, Rivera. It's best you answer the fucking door now before I change my mind and grab her first instead."

Holy shit.

Rico.

I don't have a chance to send a follow up message before the door is opened by a maid, who is instantly shot before my eyes. Raising my gun, I steady myself.

Fuck.

Don't come back Luna.

Luna

As I step away from DCM Tech, I slowly release the tension from my shoulders. Getting out of there unnoticed with a meter-long tube is a little more difficult than it was on the way in. Checking I've not got any of my devices still running, I hide in a nearby alley and put all my stuff away.

Fuck the adrenalin is going to take some time to wear off. Maybe it was a good thing Roman came down after all. I just want to know what it is we need to talk about first, it has my mind in overdrive worrying.

I walk back the exact way I came running through what I needed to do before I could sleep. I'd scanned the main overview already before I actually swiped all the papers, but I need to take copies of the rest when I get back to the room. Then I can ship it back to me in the morning.

I would never usually take a copy of documents I'd stolen before, but this time I wanted to know the why behind all of this, and I'd get a better picture once we'd all collated the information. Kai had already hacked into all of DCM's systems, which is how he gave me the passages I'd been digitally using.

I knew Parker was close to completing the tech he was required to make. Oscar said he's done everything except destroy the safe house, and Roman had a good surveillance feed on the Agent but hadn't sealed a deal yet with DCM tech. Although he still hadn't explained in more detail what the deal was for.

This was all just a mind fuck and clearly part of a bigger plan, which I refused to be blind too.

Seeing the hotel come into view I pick up my pace, ready to let Roman work me over, and pull me back from my veins exploding with this rush I was still riding. I take the stairs and pull my phone out of my backpack, remembering it'd been on silent while I was out.

Holy shit.

There were messages and missed calls from all of the guys, even worse than this morning.

Fuck sake.

We need some ground rules because this is getting out of hand. Getting to my floor I decide to get in first and talk to them all at the same time, because this is ridiculous. I thought there was an understanding after earlier, but clearly I was wrong. Glancing at the messages as I near my door, I stop my next step.

Roman: PINEAPPLE

Kai: Where?

Oscar: What's going on?

Oscar: Roman what is going on?

Parker: Where's Luna?

Kai: We're on our way.

Parker: Luna. Do not go back to the hotel.

Parker: Luna?

Oscar: Answer the fucking phone, baby girl.

Oscar: Stay away from that hotel Luna.

What the hell is going on. I hear something smash from the other side of my door in front of me and I know whatever I'm about to walk into isn't going to be good. I can't walk away though, not with Roman inside. Dropping the blueprints, I pull my gun from my hoodie pocket and check my blade in my boot. Taking a deep breath, I lift my room card and the click is loud, whoever is here, knows I am too. I push the door with my foot and step back with my gun raised.

"Don't be shy, little Moon. If you want Roman to live longer than the next five seconds I suggest you show your face," someone growls from the other side.

I can't place the voice, but I know this isn't good.

Keeping my gun raised I step into the room and my insides are screaming.

Parker's father.

Flanked by four men with Roman tied to a chair.

I'm going to fucking kill him.

"What's going on here?" I ask casually, like my heart isn't pounding in my ears.

"Well, you refused to meet me at the party on Saturday, and as hot as Rafe likes to think he is, nobody, and I mean nobody, says no to me. That would include you, Miss Steele, now wouldn't it?"

The sneer on his face is menacing, and the look in his eyes is crazed. He's definitely got drugs running through his veins, which makes him even more unpredictable.

"Well now you have my attention, so say what it is you want to say and fuck off."

I try to keep my voice even, but I don't think it's a complete success.

"Ah, ah, ah Chica. You do not make the rules around here. Understand? I have so many questions for you so we will be here a while. Take a seat," he demands.

No fucking way.

"How long have you been here?" I ask, not moving an inch.

"I've waited rather patiently for you for the past half an

hour, now sit," he growls, but I still refuse to move.

"You have about ten minutes before this quickly turns against you. I'm going to be polite and offer you to ask me five questions, then you can either leave or be forced out. It's your choice."

He thinks I'm calling his bluff. Let him fucking come at me.

"Is that so, little moon?"

"It is, so would you like to start with question number one?"

I offer, but he just cackles like this is all a joke.

"Fuck, Chica. You have some balls, I'll give you that," he leers at me. "Fine. I'll play along."

He taps his chin considering what to ask, and I pray I'm not wrong here. I look to Roman and the fury is evident in every breath he takes. I think I've made it worse by showing up.

"Six months ago, you stole a pouch of blood diamonds, I need details on that trade," he demands.

I run what he's saying through my mind and I remember it clearly. It is obviously linked to Featherstone somehow, and if I want to survive this moment I'll happily give him the details.

"I stole the pouch from a vault in a small-town bank about forty minutes outside of New York and dropped them at a locker set up in Boston," I answer honestly, and he can tell it's the truth.

"I'm going to need the exact address of the drop off," he warns, and I just nod in response.

"Now, would you like to tell me how you are alive? Do you remember me?"

Remember him? The fuck?

Shit. I really need to grow some big fucking ovaries and open my mind to the past because I'm caught off guard now.

"I have no recollection of you, or know any reason why you would assume I was dead." I give him the truth again, and it just makes him mad that I haven't got all the answers.

"Not good enough, little moon. I see you and Roman are cozy again, just like when you were children. Two peas in a pod wreaking havoc all around you. You can't tell me you remember him but not me, Chica. I don't buy it," he yells, as he raises his gun toward Roman as a threat.

What the fuck does he mean? I didn't know Roman before I came here. Someone would have told me that, I'm sure of it. But the look on Romans face tells me a different story.

I knew him? From the time in my life I'm too scared to remember?

He knew me and didn't say a single word?

Every ounce of trust I had begun to place in him was gone, evaporated. I feel my emotions shutting down, and my walls building back up in an instant. The look in Roman's eyes tells me he sees the shift.

"Where did the fire in your eyes just go, little moon?" Rico asks.

"I don't know what you're talking about," I say, void of any emotion. Which just makes Rico snicker.

"Although I'm surprised you've allowed my bastard son into the fucking mix. The bloodline agreement was always for you to unite with Roman and West to solidify your names. Had I known mine was up for discussion, I'd have brought Parker home sooner," he mocks.

He's giving me too much information I'm not aware of while pointing a gun around. A bloodline agreement? I can't fucking deal with this right now.

"I'm going to need you to agree to my way of business, or I'm going to have to off you, and your lover boy too."

"That'd be a hard no from me, but thanks," I respond as I hear it.

The one, two tap.

Seconds later the door is busted open and the room gets a whole lot more crowded. Six men walk in that I've never seen before followed by…my grandmother.

Holy fuck.

"Rico, explain to me why I shouldn't just kill you right now?" her voice booms around the room, like she isn't the oldest one in here.

"Maria, how nice to see you. How did you know we were here?"

"It seems my granddaughter picked up technology just like her father did. You want to explain to him dear or shall I?" she asks as she meets my eyes, winking, and the pride I see there nearly brings me to my knees.

Gun still raised at a very confused Rico, I clear my throat.

"Well, I'm a little obsessed with security. So no matter where I am I always set up my own. It's a closed circuit, which has never been breached or detected by scanners," I say, making sure not to glance where it is.

"I set up facial recognition telling it who is and isn't

safe in my space. Unfortunately for you, you're not on the authorized list." I glance to my grandmother who nods for me to continue.

"When the system detects someone not authorized in my space it sends out a distress signal to Rafe, who promised me a forty minute timeframe for backup wherever I am in the states, if I don't answer his call."

The shock is clear on his face, as it is on Roman's. Hating that I just had to explain myself, I want this to be over.

"Are we done here, or is this going to get messy?" I ask, maintaining eye contact with this dickhead.

"I don't think you're strong enough to use that big weapon, little moon," he goads me, but enough has happened now and I'm not outnumbered, so I swing my arm round without moving any other part of my body, and shoot one of his men in the shoulder, while my eyes stay focused on Rico.

"You want to try me old man, because next time I'll aim higher," I growl, as his soldier falls to the floor, screaming in pain like a little pussy.

His rage has him red in the face and shaking.

"You're going to regret that, you little bitch," he growls

as he storms out of the room, his men behind him.

One of the men with my grandmother slams the door shut behind them as another pulls the gag off Roman's mouth, but my eyes stay fixed to the lady in front of me.

"Hello, sweet Luna, I'm pleased to see you have your father's spirit and not your mother's rat for brains," she says with a smile, and I can't help but grin back.

The first time someone has mentioned my father's traits in me, and I haven't turned into a tornado of fists.

Progress.

I just need a fucking minute to deal with all this, or a fucking lifetime.

MY BLOODLINE

KC KEAN

THIRTY TWO

Luna

I close the door behind my grandmother and slowly slide myself down it, unable to keep myself on my feet any longer.

She was...amazing? I think.

She stayed a little while, having her men clean up while she fussed a little. Rafe called and spoke to her, but I declined when she extended it to me. I had enough to deal with, I'd offer my thanks when I had gotten my head around everything.

Trying to occupy my mind I find the blueprints that someone had brought in, and begin scanning the prints I hadn't got yet.

"You don't really need to be doing that now Luna, come lie down. A lot has happened," Roman says from the doorway.

I can't even bring my head to look at him, my emotions are too close to the surface and I will not let him see the pain I feel from the secrets he's kept.

Before he can say anything else there's a knock at the door.

"It's the guys," he murmurs, as he makes his way to let them in.

I'd heard him on the phone to them earlier explaining exactly what had happened, but I was too busy with Maria to get involved.

Parker comes charging into the room, relief on his face when he sees that I'm okay.

"Oh my God, Luna. I'm so sorry he did this," he cries, as he makes his way towards me.

The others are not far behind him, but I hold my hands up for them to stop. Confusion takes over their faces, but they stay where they are.

"Hey, baby girl, it's okay. We're all here now, it's going to be alright," Oscar says softly, he has no clue.

Not responding, I look to Roman.

"Do they know?" I ask, void of any emotion.

He shakes his head as Parker interrupts.

"Have you spoken to her yet?"

Before I can call them out, Roman finally speaks.

"I got to be the one to come down here because I told them I had something important I needed to talk to you about. They didn't know what it was, and if you give me a chance I can explain everything Rico didn't."

"You've had all this time to talk to me and you suddenly wanted to right after someone brought a few secrets up? Bullshit," I growl.

"It's true, Sakura. He promised he would explain to us what was going on after he spoke with you here first," Kai adds.

"Yeah, and he promised to explain that we knew nothing about whatever this shit is about," Oscar throws in with a glare at Roman.

"Is what he said true?"

"Luna, we were children. I remember a lot, but not conversations that were had by adults, I..."

"I didn't ask for your bullshit excuses. It's a simple yes or no question. Is. It. True?" I grind out.

"Yes," he responds barely a whisper.

I nod subconsciously, trying to understand what emotions I'm feeling here.

I feel stupid for letting my guard down, more fool me for taking a chance.

"Who said what? And what's true?" Oscar shouts, trying to keep up.

"Did you know that I watched my father die?"

I ask the room and everyone but Roman shakes their head in shock.

"Did you know that my brain refuses to acknowledge that moment and any moment that ever came before it?" I ask louder, and they just keep shaking, no one daring to speak.

"Did you know that if random things are mentioned from that time, they act like a trigger for me and send me into destructive mode, uncontrollably?"

I'm on a roll now.

"Did you know that Roman fucking knew who I was? Knew me as a child? Was apparently my fucking betrothed, like that's actually a thing? Oh, and West as well, apparently I was always destined to be a whore. Let the adults use my pussy to solidify this fucked up world.

You know any of that?"

I'm shaking with rage.

How dare these people do or say any of these things.

"Please, Princess, let me explain better. Let me call Rafe."

"Fuck you and fuck Rafe. I don't believe a word that passes your lips," I sneer.

"Princess, we can get past this."

"We? We? Roman there is no fucking we now. You shit all over it. I'm done. With all of this, all of you. I need you to leave." I end on a calm note, pushing down my feelings.

Roman sees it. Me, putting up my walls, locking them out in the cold.

"Wait a minute, I'm not going down with him. I had nothing to do with that," yells Oscar.

"This isn't about you Oscar, it's about me, and right now I don't even want to be in the same room as anything that links me back to this fucktard. Now. Leave."

"Luna, I'm not leaving you like this," Parker says standing firm, but it's too late.

My mind needs a break from everything and that includes them.

Right now, all I need is Red.

Fuck it, I'll leave.

I start unplugging all my tech, throwing it into the suitcases they were shipped in.

"Sakura, leave all of this. I will organize it and take it back in the car," Kai orders.

Well I won't say no to that if it means I get out of here quicker.

I grab my phone and small backpack, ready to go.

"Luna, please don't leave like this. We can sort it out," Roman pleads, but it's all too much for me.

"I need fucking space, from you, from all of this. You need to respect that," I sigh.

He stands in front of the main door blocking me from leaving.

"Roman, you're only making this worse right now."

"Please, Meu Tesouro, don't leave," he begs, but I don't hear the end of his sentence.

I don't hear anything.

I don't feel anything.

I don't see anything.

Except pain. It's ripping through every inch of my body.

"What did you just call me?" I cry in rage.

He's white as a sheet. He knows he just fucked up and made this worse, but I don't care. Not about anything right now.

A vase on the table near the door finds itself in my hands and I'm launching it across the room, making everyone jump in shock. Including myself, this is like an outer body experience.

I'm not in control of myself right now. I hate this.

What this does to me. I can see the pain in their eyes, and I don't give a shit. They can all rot in hell for all I care.

"I'm so sorry, Luna, please," Roman cries as I see him hit Rafe on his phone.

Before I can knock it out of his hand he's speaking.

"I just lost her. I called her his nickname, I didn't mean to. It just came out. Rafe, tell me what to do, her eyes are black pits of nothing. Fuck," he screams. Keeping his frantic eyes searching over me, as he swipes a hand down his face in desperation.

The others are still standing in shock, but only concern is in their eyes. I just can't connect to that emotion right now. I can deal with pain and pain alone.

"You'll do well to stay the fuck away from me. All of you," I roar, as I charge out of the room.

No one stops me. I'm on autopilot.

I'm slightly aware when I'm riding Dot, but everything is muscle memory because I'm not aware of my surroundings.

I don't know how long I'm driving for when I finally pull up outside of Ace.

I feel like I've not been here for a long time when it was barely twenty-four hours ago that I left. I consider going to Red, but in this state I'll probably just ruin her in the process.

Heading up to my room I'm stopped by a sign on my door, and if I wasn't in the middle of a breakdown already, this sure as shit would have sent me over.

FEATHERSTONE ACADEMY

THE PYRAMID

YOU ARE REQUIRED TO ATTEND THE TRIAL GAMES TODAY AT 12 NOON.

ATTENDANCE IS MANDATORY

YOU MAY BRING ONLY ONE WEAPON OF YOUR CHOOSING, BUT IT MAY NOT BE A GUN.

YOUR SACRIFICE FOR OUR ORDER IS HONORABLE

What the fuck do I do?

I've been asking myself that question over and over again and it's almost eight. In my current state asking for help would be worse than sawing my own hand off, but I need to know if Rafe found anything out about this or not. He's been trying to call me non-stop after Roman called him, but I'm nowhere close to calmed down since then, so I decide on a message.

Luna: The Pyramid is today at noon. Did you find anything out? Do not call me.

I attach a picture of the notice as well. At least they gave me more than the two hours' notice they could have done, but I don't know how to prepare to make the most of this time.

Rafe: Fuck. I'm already on my way.

Rafe: Nothing solid. Let me push and see if I can come up with anything.

I don't need any of these secretive assholes near me

right now, they can all go to hell.

A knock on my door catches me by surprise. I pull up the feed on my phone and see Red outside.

"Luna, I know you're in there. Open the door right now," she shouts.

"Now's not a good time, Red," I shout back, walking closer to the door.

"Don't give me that shit, Luna. If one more person rings my phone I'm likely to launch it. Now let me in so I can help."

"No."

"Now, Luna," she yells with a bang against the wood.

"I'm doing you a favor, Red. Be grateful I can see through all this fog in my brain to recognize your importance to me. I can't promise the same when you're in here," I answer honestly.

"Luna Steele, open the fucking door now," she screams.

Making me swing the door open to shut her the fuck up. Yet when I do. she smiles at me sweetly and barges past me.

The fuck just happened here?

She has the notice in her hands as she walks into the kitchen, flicking the coffee machine on. Raising her eyes to mine she looks me over.

"Your eyes aren't the same," she murmurs.

I don't know what she wants me to say to her, so I say nothing.

"What will be better for you, catching a few hours' sleep or powering on through?"

"I've been awake since I took a nap yesterday morning so about twenty-two hours, but my brain isn't going to switch off right now," I answer honestly, she nods and hands me a coffee.

"I won't ask if you're okay because I know you're not. You don't even look like you right now. It's weirding me out a little," she says with a smirk, but I don't respond.

I'm still in the same state of mind. Only pain registers, nothing else.

Maybe today is a good day for whatever this is.

Another knock on my door and I've about fucking had it with everyone interfering.

"You want to be my best friend? Then you get rid of whoever is on the other side of that door. I'm done with all of this shit," I growl as I lock myself in the bathroom.

I don't even bother looking at my phone.

Taking a shower, I try and find some control over

myself, but it's pointless. I'm lost to the sadness inside of me and I'm not ready to be pulled out. I didn't think to bring fresh clothes with me, so I wrap a towel around myself and head for my room.

Stepping out into the lounge it's quiet. Too quiet.

"Red?"

Nothing.

Is she still dealing with whoever fucking showed up at the door? I head that way but stop in my tracks when the door is wide open. I don't sense anyone in my apartment but I'm not really aware of any of my surroundings. Opening my surveillance on my phone, I head to the door slowly, but I haven't got a weapon on me and only a towel covering my skin. So my current attack will likely be to jab them in the eye with my fucking nipple or something, but I still go like an idiot.

No one is there, just another card stuck to the door. Fuck sake, what now?

COMPLETE THE PYRAMID TO SAVE YOUR FRIEND

Ah shit. They've fucking done it now. The rage that already consumed me is tripled in ferocity.

I'll burn this fucking place to the ground.

MY BLOODLINE

KC KEAN

THIRTY THREE

Luna

I'm operating on autopilot, lost to it completely. I dress in my classic black ensemble of sports bra and shorts with my boots. It hasn't stated anywhere what kind of situation this will actually be, but I'm not stupid enough to overlook the fact that this is some form of trial for The Games. To take my friend as some form of threat or incentive for participating, I don't know, but I can feel the war inside of me.

I braid my hair down my back as I would for a fight back home, only this time I need to choose a weapon to take with me. I decide on the daggers I brought from Rafe's vault, but who knows what I'll be up against.

My phone has been going off with calls from the guys, but fuck them. I check every time because if Rafe does call I'll have to answer, any form of a heads up would be useful.

I stand in my lounge letting the rage consume me. I've decided against trying to gain control of myself because I haven't a chance in hell of that happening in time, and the fury in my veins will take all of the emotion out of whatever is about to happen.

I warm my body up and practice moves around the open space. I'm firing on all cylinders. My body ready to go and my mind focused only on the fact that they've taken Red.

I attach the blade holsters to my shorts, and I feel as ready as I'll ever be to get this over with. I don't even know where I'm going so here's hoping someone does.

Grabbing my phone in case Rafe calls, I'm heading out. Outside a Rolls is waiting for me and I'm thankful Ian is the driver.

"Miss Steele, I'm here to take you to the event when you're ready," he says quietly, as if he wishes he didn't have too.

"Anything you can tell me, Ian?"

He considers me for a moment before he opens the car door for me. Thinking that's a big fat no I begin to climb in as he whispers in my ear.

"I don't know what's going on inside Miss Steele, if I did I would tell you. All I know is that people are going to die today. I pray you aren't one of them."

With that he leans back and shuts the door.

Settling into the chair, I imagine I would usually feel sick to the pit of my stomach being told something like that, but all I'm focused on is survival and the fact that they took Red.

"Miss Steele, I'm also aware that Rivera, O'Shay, Fuse, and Parker were stopped on entry back into the grounds and forced straight to the Combat building," he adds.

So that's where I'm going, and apparently there will be an audience.

"Are there many others there?"

"The whole Academy. Miss Steele. And another driver just mentioned The Ring are here, although some do not seem too happy, as they were unaware of these events."

Okay, this is way bigger than I thought, which is a clear indication of how crazy this is going to get. I don't ask any more questions and he doesn't divulge any more information. We ride in complete silence.

When we pull up outside the Combat building there are a few people milling around, but the sight of the Rolls has them rushing inside. Probably to get a good view of the shit show that's about to go down.

Ian opens the door for me, and I'm greeted by West. Before I can tell him to fuck off he's guiding me by the arm while turning the screen of his phone in my direction.

I'm wired to make sure I don't tell you anything. I'm sorry this is happening. You will get through this Moon.

Fuck him and his apologies. I know my brain has closed my past off to me to deal with the pain, but he's just like the rest of them keeping secrets, there is no difference. They can give me whatever excuse they want.

I knock the phone away discreetly, saying nothing just letting him drag me along. As we get to the main doors, I can hear everyone on the other side. West lifts my chin forcing me to meet his stare, but he must be able to see that something has triggered me, because he strokes his finger near my eyes, knowing why they look so different, so bleak. He places a gentle kiss to my head, and I've had enough, pushing back from him.

"Are you ready?" he asks and all I can do is shrug my shoulders.

Am I ready? No.

Do I need to do whatever it takes to survive and make sure I have Red with me? Yes.

With that he opens the door and the screams of the crowd fills the air. I don't know where to put my eyes first.

The students are sitting on bleachers, like this is a fucking sport. Adults mixed in among them with fear in their eyes as they stare at the center of the room. Below them are two boxes with The Ring members split between them. Dietrichson, Rico, and my fucking mother in one, with Wren sat with a smug grin on her face. Why the hell is my mother not sitting with my grandmother? Why is she sitting with the enemy? I shouldn't be surprised with her shit.

In the other box is Maria, Juliana Gibbs, Betty Morgan, and Reggie Rivera. I don't know where Mr. Fuse or Mr. O'Shay are, but their sons are with Parker and Roman who are in the box with my grandmother, along with Rafe. The grief on their faces is visible from here, but I don't feel it. I still can't see Red though.

The main attraction in the room is literally a pyramid of fighting rings. Three going up both sides with a final one on the top. That one is set back from the crowd with something covered in front of it. There is someone in each ring except the final one. Is that where I'm supposed to fight?

Before I can try and run different scenarios through my head, the tap of a microphone rings out in the air drawing everyone's attention.

"Good afternoon, ladies and gentlemen. Thank you very much for joining us here today, for this special occasion."

Barbette Dietrichson greets the room, that fucking name fuels my fire.

"It isn't very often a new addition is added to The Games, but it is our greatest honor here at the Academy to run the trials when the time does come," she says, so sickly sweet I want to vomit. I think I hear West make a noise beside me too, but I don't turn my gaze away.

"In previous years, the Academy has allowed people to put themselves forward to be a part of such an event, but this year we decided to take a different approach. If a student pulled a wild card, it entered them into the trial. Today we have eight students who were lucky enough to pick those cards, and I'd like you to give them a round of applause please."

She doesn't even clap herself. I wish she would just get on with whatever it is we're supposed to be doing here.

"As you can see we have a pyramid formed out of rings. In the three rings either side of the pyramid you will find a student present, and behind the curtained top is another ring which is currently empty."

Get to it for fucks sake.

"We have two additional students who are standing towards the sides. I'd like to introduce Miss Luna Steele and Mr. Tyler Bishop."

At the sound of my name my back straightens.

"The aim of the game is for both Luna and Tyler to make it past the three rings, to fight it out at the top. The winner then must complete the final act before winning The Death Pyramid," she shouts with glee.

Death Pyramid? The gasps around the room are audible even to me, trapped inside my shell of a body right now. I'm glad I'm in this current state of mind otherwise I don't know how I would approach all of this. Instead, I let it wash right over my head and crack my neck ready to go. I don't bother looking at Tyler, that'd be pointless.

"In each ring they must battle to the death, or at minimum one of them must be unconscious before they can move on to the next ring. The third ring is where their weapon of choice will be coming into action and not a ring before. If a pupil who is already in the ring defeats our main runners, then they will continue the trial for survival instead. Everyone's lives are literally at stake. Isn't it fantastic?"

She begins clapping, but very few follow suit. Even those who do aren't sure why they are following her lead, likely out of fear. Looking over to the boxes I see Rico and my mother clapping profusely, and I'm not even surprised.

A bang sounds from the other box gaining everyone's attention. It's Parker, red in the face, screaming and yelling but I can't hear what he's saying. It's most definitely to me or about me. Rafe has to pull him back and calm him down. The smallest part of me registers that he's hurting right now, but I don't care enough in this state and look back towards the bitch.

"To add extra incentive for the main runners to win,

I would like to now remove the cover from the top of the pyramid," she pauses, waiting for them to drop the sheet.

A few screams sound around the room and I reluctantly raise my eyes to see what was hidden.

These vile pieces of shits.

I'm going to fucking ruin them.

Tied to a pole is Red and Becky. I couldn't give a fuck about the latter, but the fear in Red's eyes fuels my anger. All I can see is Red, both literally and figuratively.

"The final act I mentioned earlier is to save someone who matters to them. We pulled both Jessica and Becky from our runners' rooms earlier today, in the exact state we found them in. And would you look at that Wren, Becky was naked in your boyfriend's room. Aren't you glad they were fucking behind your back, so you didn't have to take to the stand?"

Looking at Wren she's white as a ghost, but she nods along with her mother's joy.

She's an evil bitch.

"As the battle commences below the two girls at the top will slowly start to be hung. They must reach the top and cut the rope in time. Now I think I've covered everything. Shall we begin?"

I take one last glance at the box where everyone is and Rico catches my eye, blowing me a kiss and a wink like he had some involvement in all of this, but I don't respond.

I keep my focus on Red now.

Her life is in my hands, and I'll destroy everyone on my path to her.

Parker

"Somebody better fucking explain to me why the hell this is happening, right now?" I scream as they drag me away from the glass.

I'm thrown into a chair furthest away from seeing the pyramid, but I'm never going to forget this. She's been thrown in the deep end for no reason at all. I hear everyone scream and I smack Rafe's hand away so I can see what's going on.

Whatever little color was left in my face is drained now, as I look up to see Jessica tied up.

Rafe tried to explain the shit my girl has to deal with in her mind, which led to her getting triggered, because

Roman called her a nickname her father used. It guts me when I look at her and see nothing back, it's as if she doesn't recognize me. My beautiful angel is in there somewhere, I just can't see her on the surface.

Rafe said it usually takes a day or two for her to come round, but putting her in this situation, while she's in this mindset, with her best friend strung up, who knows what'll happen.

I just wish I could be with her to ease some of the pain, but apparently my association to Roman gets me on the shit list. West said everyone will be on her shit list right now, irrespective of involvement, but I know when she pulls herself out of the dark hole she's in it won't make a difference. She's done with us, with me.

All because Roman is a fucking idiot.

I can't even look at him right now, none of us can.

I get some of this wasn't his story to tell, but omitting that he was her childhood friend and they're bonded by bloodline agreements. No wonder she fucking stormed off.

"Who fucking created this damn game?" I ask the room.

I don't really expect an answer, but Luna's grandmother looks at me with pity in her eyes.

"Your father did."

My heart stops, I'm sure I'm dead. If not I may as well be.

The blood that runs through my veins is the same blood cruel enough to come up with this, and put my Queen through it in the process.

"None of us are saints, Parker. We have all added our sins to Featherstone, as we will all continue to do. It is the way of this life, and whether you like it or not, you are a part of it. You have to decide what your sins look like, and what values the people around you believe in," she offers.

"Rules set before us are difficult to change in this world, unless every member of The Ring are in sync with each other. As you can see, that is not the case here, so we must follow those rules or we all lose our heads," Romans father adds.

"I can hear a lot of words, yet none of which are telling us how to help Luna," Roman growls.

"That's because she has to do this herself, whether we like it or not. It was destiny when she chose the wild card," Maria Steele murmurs.

As though she understands that those are the rules, but deep down she doesn't like this.

"Destiny?" fumes Kai, catching everyone off guard.

He hasn't said a word since Luna walked out of the hotel room.

"There is no destiny in this. They forced her to take all three cards because someone decided it was a good idea to push three bloodlines on to her."

"Fuck," curses Reggie Rivera, as he looks to the other members of The Ring in here.

"It was all a setup, wasn't it? Her bitch of a mother came in convincing us it was the right thing to do, to strengthen Luna in a world she didn't yet understand, and we agreed, expecting it not to pass all the members anyways."

Another lady I believe is West's grandmother slams her hand on the table next to her.

"Those imp bastards. They agreed because they wanted to force her into this trial. Cut her out before she could make a difference, I'll fucking castrate them wankers myself."

"That still doesn't get her out of this," adds Oscar.

"It won't my dear, we can't stop what has already been set in motion here today. We can only hope she has the strength and will to survive," Luna's grandmother murmurs, but her posture is rigid and her hands are clenched.

"So, I'm just clarifying that you want us to stay in this

box while our girl has to face four other bloodlines? She pretty much has to fight to the death to survive while also trying to save her closest friend from dying? And I repeat, we stay here and do nothing?" Roman furiously questions the members of The Ring.

It is completely silent, no one mutters a word, and that there is our answer.

"Is that what it is like in the real world of Featherstone? Constantly attacking and defending alone?" Kai asks.

"No, it is not, but it can be like this in The Games. Unless you have already gained allies, it is very lonely in there. Every man for himself. And as this is a trial, only members chosen can participate. She has to stand alone, unless anyone in those rings are her allies," answers Mrs. Morgan.

"If she gets through this I want a full list of who can and can't be trusted here at this Academy, do you understand? If she doesn't survive it won't matter because I'll burn the whole place to the ground," Roman explodes.

Luna's grandmother stands tall and glares at Roman.

"Let me make something very clear, Mr. Rivera. There are no if's around here. If you do not believe in Luna then she is better off without you anyway. I sacrificed a relationship with that girl to avoid all of this, all for her mother to screw everyone over anyway. Yet I looked in her eyes last night and saw my son shining back at me. There is strength in her heart, determination in her eyes, and the will to survive in her soul. Do you understand me?" she grits out.

Nobody speaks, taking in her words. We have to be positive, for Luna and ourselves.

Finding my voice, I look Maria Steele dead in the eyes.

"Luna Steele is my Queen. I will always give her my strength, even when I'm not close enough to touch her, she will know."

A small smile creeps over her lips, but she says nothing at all. She doesn't need to.

A siren calls and everyone turns to look to the center of the hall, seeing Tyler and Luna make their way to the first ring.

My blood is pounding in my ears and I wish it was me in there, fighting for her, but I wasn't exaggerating when I said she was my Queen.

She has the strength to rule us all, and I'll happily follow her to hell if I have to.

KC KEAN

THIRTY FOUR

Luna

I haven't even seen Tyler, he's blocked by this monstrosity taking up the space around us. It doesn't matter anyway, it seems I have to kill or be killed. What a lovely day.

West is still standing with me, I can feel him constantly trying to get my attention with subtle nudges, but I'm not interested.

I just need to focus.

I need to survive this.

Yet still be able to find myself at the end of it all.

"Please, our two runners if you could step up to the first ring in preparation," Dietrichson calls, and the rest of the room goes silent.

Watching, waiting for this to all unfold.

I slowly step up to where she is asking me to be. West stands in front of me so I'm unable to block him out any longer.

"I believe in you, my moon. In more than just this challenge, in life, I believe in you. I always have, I always will."

He squeezes my shoulder and places a swift kiss on my forehead. With that he walks away, I don't know where to because my eyes are set solely on Red.

"May the best bloodline win," Dietrichson declares, as a siren sounds in confirmation this shit show has begun.

Climbing into the first ring, a girl I don't recall stands rigid in a fight position. Fear written all over her face, but I can't let it get to me. There are more important things on the line here.

She attempts to circle around me a few times, but it's clear she has no clue what she's doing. As lost as I am right now I can still recognize that at least this round doesn't have to be brutal.

"What's your name?" I ask quietly.

She considers me a moment before she whispers back.

"Trudy Byrnes."

"What block are you in Trudy?"

"Clubs," she answers, still keeping her stance in place.

She may not know what she's doing but at least she isn't dropping her guard. A Club won't be missed by these people, they won't see her for the person she actually is.

"I don't want to kill you, Trudy," I offer, which causes her to shiver behind her guarded arms.

"I don't want to have to kill you either."

I raise my eyebrow at her.

"Let's be honest here, Trudy, we both know that isn't going to happen."

I'm not trying to be rude, but there's no point trying to sugar coat this. Her eyes are searching mine frantically, she's petrified.

"How about this, Trudy, I can knock you out with one hit. It'll hurt for that first second then you'll be out like a light, but the most important part is, you'll wake up."

She's trying to take in what I'm saying, but she doesn't trust me enough to believe in my words.

"Trudy, my friend is slowly being hung up there. All because she is my friend and they needed an incentive for me to do this. Now you're out of time, what'll it be?" I ask, losing the gentleness to my tone.

"Okay, you're right," she whispers.

Thank fuck for that.

"I promise you after all this, there will be changes around here and you'll be standing beside me, do you understand?"

She barely nods in response but drops her arms. I step into her space and before she can change her mind I raise my fist connecting it full force into her face and she drops to the mat.

Simple as that.

Pity they won't all be this easy.

Before I move up to the next ring, I look around for anyone, and that's when I see Maverick. In all the encounters I've had with him he's been barely tolerable, but I believe in him enough to help this girl. I pick Trudy up and walk to the edge of the ring. He understands the silent communication as he moves to the ring.

"She's unconscious, I want her awake by the time I'm out of here. Keep her the fuck away from anyone vile enough to change that. You got me?"

He doesn't question me or consider his options; he just holds his hands out to take her through the rope.

"Don't let me down, Maverick. She doesn't deserve to die. But if you let something happen to her, well, I won't say the same for you."

A part of me is fully aware of the fact I'm speaking to a tutor like this, but the lines are blurred in this place and I'm passed giving a shit. He nods once, then marches off. I haven't got time to see where he is going. I need to get a move on.

Climbing up to the second ring, I'm barely in when someone's trying to rain punches down on me. Fuck, definitely not going to be the same in here then.

By the grunts coming from my attacker I can tell it's a guy, and he seems quite keen to power through so he can claim my victory.

Not today.

The fact that he caught me off guard has me on the floor, but he's not covering me professionally, so I raise my knee straight to his groin and he keels over a little in pain.

"Fucking bitch," he spits out, but I haven't got time to chat.

Standing, I gather myself for a second, and while he's still caught off guard I bring my elbow down on his face, causing him to cry out.

Blood drips down onto the mat from his busted nose.

I hold my fighting stance now, ready for him to move my way. He doesn't disappoint. He is too focused on putting me down and not thinking things through properly. His stance is poor and even after I've landed two blows to him already he doesn't raise his arms to defend himself.

He charges low towards my waist, lower than I prep for, and he's toppling me over.

Fuck.

I keep the momentum going so he can't hold me in place. I rise quickly and he just sneers at me. He comes at me and I can see by the hold of his arms he's going to go for an uppercut. Fucking amateur. Before he can get close enough for that, I extend my left fist straight for his defenseless face. It ricochets his head back, but not enough to floor him.

I've caught him off guard slightly, so I continue to follow it up with a few jabs to his ribs.

He goes to make a swing at me, but I duck and punch him straight in the dick.

He's not going to have any manhood left by the time I'm finished with him. He leans forward and this time I move quickly. My fist connects with the side of his head before I wrap my arms tightly around his neck and throw all my weight backwards. As we fall he's not prepared, throwing his arms out to try and break his fall, exactly what I need him to do.

The second my ass touches the mat I'm wrapping my legs around his upper arms, pinning him down while I tighten the pressure around his neck. He bucks a little and throws his legs around, but it does nothing to help him out.

I can't think about him now. I just continue to add as much pressure as I can until he goes lax. I'm not waiting too long before he's not moving. I slowly rise and stand back. Not wanting to see the damage I've actually done, I roll him off me and stand.

Shaking myself off I give myself a second to catch my breath and check my body over. My ribs are hurting, he's likely busted whatever progress my recovery has made there, and my jaw aches, but otherwise so far so good.

Not wanting to waste any more time, I climb up to the next ring. I prepare myself for a blow straight off the bat again, so I'm surprised when I'm given the space to stand. When I do, I see why, there's a referee here. He's holding the daggers West had to take off me before I entered. He also holds a crowbar which must be my opponent's choice of weapon.

Looking to the referee he holds out our weapons to us. My opponent is another guy but he's shorter than me, not by much but his frame is small too. Probably why he's chosen a giant fucking crowbar as a weapon, so he can attack from a distance.

Fuck.

Once we take our weapons the referee leaves without a backwards glance, leaving me to stare down this guy. He doesn't make a move. He just observes me.

"I don't know what to make of you," he says, catching me by surprise. I just raise my eyebrow at him, if he wants to expand on that he can but I won't push.

"I saw you talk to the girl, I don't know what you said to her, but she suddenly drops her defense and lets you knock her clean out. Then you get a tutor to help her before you move up."

He still doesn't move a step, he's not talking to distract me, he's assessing me out loud.

"Then you get in the ring with that guy, who doesn't give a shit and you pummel each other. You didn't even check him over before coming up here. You handled them both completely differently and I'm trying to figure out why."

"You really want to have a conversation about this right now?" I ask, bewildered.

He just nods in response, waiting for me to continue. I don't know this guy and I don't need to explain myself to him, but something tells me I should.

"Well that guy was a dick, coming at me before I was fully in the ring to get the advantage. He would have happily wiped me off the face of the earth without any care," I sigh. "But Trudy was different. The fear in her eyes reminded me of my best friend, so I offered her a deal."

"What was the deal?"

"I offered to knock her out as quickly as possible, instead of death being on the table," I answer honestly.

He stares me down. I don't know what he's looking for, but he eventually speaks.

"She's my sister." I frown, making him continue.

"Trudy, she's my twin sister."

I can't keep the surprise off my face, they look nothing alike. He must know what I'm thinking.

"I know, complete opposites right? Are you offering that same deal up here? I mean, I'll do what I need to do to survive, but I can't leave Trudy to survive this world alone."

The stark honesty in his words surprises me, and I find myself nodding.

"If you don't mind, I'd rather you use my weapon than yours," he murmurs, extending the crowbar to me.

I slowly wrap my hand around it still expecting him to attack, but he doesn't. I think this is me forming alliances in difficult situations. Let's hope I fucking survive to make good on my word.

Not wanting him to second guess his decision, I swing the crowbar at his head, wanting to knock him out but not write him off. He falls to the floor with a thud. I land on my knees beside him, checking his pulse. It's still there, but I want him out of here. Standing, I glance around but I don't need to go far. Maverick is already climbing into the ring. Wordlessly he feels for a pulse then lifts the guy in a fireman's hold over his shoulder, and they're gone.

I think I owe him a thank you once this is over with.

I climb into the final ring, taking my daggers and leaving the crowbar behind. Rising to my feet I'm alone so far. I can't look at Red right now, being this close and unable to do anything yet is ripping my heart out.

Looking down the other side of the pyramid Tyler is in the top ring. The carnage left in his wake is devastating.

The bodies laying lifeless in the first two rings tells me what I'm up against. The way their bodies are laying tells me they won't be waking up.

In the next ring down he's clearly won, he just hasn't stopped butchering his opponent. I don't notice his weapon of choice until he raises his hand back, brass knuckles. That explains the blood splattered all over him, he's definitely up close and personal with his weapon.

He's wasting time now. Beating a dead body while Red needs me. I need to speed this the fuck up.

"Hey asshole, you fucking done?" I yell.

He slowly rises to his feet, spitting on the dead body before slowly turning to sneer at me.

The evil in his eyes is visible from here. I feel grateful for my journey up here so far because I'm going to need my strength to survive this guy. When I was against him in Combat it was in a controlled environment. Whereas this, anything goes here and he's making the most of it.

"Bitch, you'll do good to remember what happened the last time I jumped you," he snarls, confirming my suspicions that he was part of my attack.

He says it to scare me, but I'll take fucking pleasure in destroying him, because that's what I'll have to do to survive this final ring.

Against my better judgement I step back allowing him the space to enter the ring. He takes his bloody t-shirt off using it to polish his dusters, trying to intimidate me.

"I've heard stories about you being a crazy bitch," he grins.

"Is that so?"

"Yeah, I've heard you trigger if someone upsets you with ghosts of the past," he sneers.

I can tell where this is heading, but I think he's not fully aware of what that trigger means.

"I think I'll take great pleasure fucking with your mind before I kill you. Then I think I'll fuck your dead body in victory," he taunts.

I don't respond, instead I twirl my daggers ready to get this show on the road. He just smiles wider.

"Have it your way, my treasure."

I want to fucking laugh. The nerve of this guy. He thinks he fucking knows me.

He doesn't know shit.

It fuels my anger.

I'm fucking done with these cunts thinking they can fuck with me and manipulate me, all while underestimating my strength.

It ends now.

He's staring at me like he's waiting for me to break down, but he'll be waiting forever. I throw a dagger straight at his thigh, catching him completely off guard, dropping him to his knees. Before he can process what's happening, I'm darting towards him, grabbing the dagger and wrenching it out. I'll bleed this fucker out, bit by bit.

"Bitch," he screams, his face red in anger.

"Wrong language asshole," I hiss, referring to his attempt to trigger me.

He charges me and I let him knock me down, as I stab a dagger into his back and use the other to puncture another hole in his leg. He yells, but smashes me in the face with the brute force of his fist wrapped around his brass knuckles.

Fuck me.

The pain across my face is excruciating. I can feel blood trickling down my face, but I can't waste time focusing on it. Instead, I tear the daggers from his skin and stab him again. This time just below his rib cage on both sides.

He punches me in the side of the head again as he rolls off me. I'm able to keep the daggers with me and the angle he pulls away at makes it worse for him.

He's seething. My face is pounding, and I can barely see through all the blood running over my eyelids. He's staggering from the pain, but he still launches himself at me, and I catch his movement too late. The force behind him has me dropping one of my daggers as he pins me to the mat. He's sat above me with his hands squeezed around my throat. Enough to hold me in place but not enough to cut my air flow off, he wants my attention first.

Picking up my fallen dagger with his free hand he raises it to my chest. I don't squirm away from it, I refuse to show weaknesses to this psycho. He drags it down my chest, piercing my skin ever so slightly, slicing a line down between my breasts, cutting open my sports bra in the process.

Fucking pig.

"For a bitch you sure have good tits. Maybe I'll fuck you now and again when your dead. No one can see up here, so I'll have all the time in the world. I'll make sure they can recognize you by your teeth though, don't worry," he whispers as he continues tracing the dagger down, lifting it from my skin at my navel.

The mark burns, from my collar bone all the way down, but I don't move. He's too busy staring at my tits.

Dropping the dagger his hands raise to my breasts. My skin is crawling but if it keeps him distracted I'll push through it.

"Pretty little nipples with pretty little piercings," he murmurs to himself. I don't want to give him too long, he'll probably enjoy ripping the piercings out.

As he grabs a handful of my cleavage, his hand around my throat slacks slightly and I know it's now or never. Using the dagger still in my hand I slam it into the side of his neck. The pain has him lifting his hands, but the shock has his reactions slowed, which gives me time to drag it out and slam it back in his throat from a different angle.

He falls sideways, finally able to grip his neck, but he's choking on his own blood, coughing and spluttering. I haven't got time to watch him die slowly, looking to the side of him I know what I need to do.

I lean in real close to his face making sure I have his attention in his last moments.

"What you weren't told is that when I'm triggered I turn reckless, lose all emotion, all control. I don't care what I do when in that state."

His eyes are wide trying to process my words.

"Unluckily for you, even though you couldn't fuck

with my mind, someone already had, now I'll see you in hell," I scream as my fingers wrap around his knuckle duster and I smash him in the face over and over again.

For attacking me.

For doubting me.

For touching me.

I've made the world a better place without this monster, but this place is filled with monsters.

I guess it's going to be my job to wipe them out.

They pushed me. It'll be their own doing.

Dropping my fists, I sit back from his lifeless body, trying to calm myself down, but I remember what I need to do now. Racing to grab both daggers, I try and wipe blood from my eyes to see what direction I even need to turn. It takes more time and effort than I'd like to climb up, but I make it nonetheless. I'm barely aware that my sports bra is hanging as a rag off my shoulders, showing my rack to everyone, my focus is to cut this rope.

I don't even look at what state both girls are in, and I don't question how reckless my next decision may be, but I stand on the block, raise both daggers, and slice both of the thin ropes at the same time. I hear their bodies drop to the ground, but I sink to my knees catching my breath and trying to gain as much energy as possible.

Wiping my eyes again I look around me. The crowd is screaming and clapping. It's not a fucking happy victory, why would you applaud this display of violence.

"Luna."

Barely a whisper reaches my ears and I search around. Red is lying flat on her back trying to take a full breath, I throw myself at her side checking her over.

"Breathe, Red, just breathe. You'll be okay," I assure her.

Tears fall freely down her cheeks.

"I'm so sorry, Red. So sorry that you were dragged into this. I'm going to make them pay, every last one of them." Determination laced in every word.

Feeling movement around me, I see Maverick.

Maverick Miller is my current favorite person in this place.

He has an oxygen mask which he places over Red's face and a towel which he hands to me. I try to wipe the blood from my face but it's a little difficult to get it under control, I think stitches are in order. Glancing down my chest, blood pours there too but not as bad as my face.

"I've got her from here Luna, they're waiting for you

to address the room," he murmurs and carries her away.

Address the room? For what? What do they want me to say? Thanks for watching my soul burn to ashes?

I climb down slowly trying to show as little pain as possible. Reaching the bottom, I see a top being held out for me. Looking up to see where it's come from, I find myself falling straight into Kai's eyes. The love and admiration I feel in the air from him has me wanting to break down and let him console me, but I refuse to let that happen.

I take the top with a nod, throwing it on without removing the sports bra.

"Ladies and gentlemen, I give you Miss Luna Steele, the winner of The Death Pyramid trial," Mrs. Dietrichson announces to the room.

She's trying to not sneer at me so openly but she's struggling.

"Miss Steele, how do you think you will fare in The Games in December after today's experience?"

I take a moment to look around me and process what she just said. So, The Games are in December, that's three months away. Everyone is staring at me waiting for an answer, while also taking in my current state.

I snatch the microphone out of her hand, done with her

fake shit.

Raising the microphone to my lips, I let the darkness continue to wash over me, needing it in this moment. I lift my other hand with my daggers gripped tightly and point them at Rico and my mother. They're behind all of this, I know it. They are part of the darkness and I'm sure there's a lot more of them, but they are the ones who came at me. My own fucking mother and that vile piece of shit.

I'm going to make them regret it. Make them all regret it, and I'll start by making sure the weakness of my past is no more. Even if that means I stay in this current state of mind forever.

My voice, void of any emotion, booms through the speakers.

"My father once told me, never tiptoe through life Luna, let them hear every motherfucking step you take, Meu Tesouro. With that said here's your warning, I'm fucking coming for you."

KC KEAN

EPILOGUE

Kai

I hand her my shirt, grateful she accepts, but my Sakura isn't in there right now.

What I just had to witness will never compare to what she endured.

The way she was able to gain allies in such extreme circumstances showed me the person she was, the life she could offer us.

I am in awe of her.

Not for her physical demonstrations, but for staying true to herself and offering a safer path.

Through the trial and through life.

Nothing could compare to Luna's presence. She was my sun and my moon. The darkness that engulfed me was blinded when she was near.

She made me feel hope.

She made me feel peace.

She made me feel passion.

All of which I lost to this world when they took my sister.

I was lost in the darkness, searching every nook for a sliver of information, barely coming up for air.

Now I was truly woken.

To a future with answers, and Luna by my side.

TO BE CONTINUED …

MY BLOODLINE

AFTERWORDS

Oh my gosh. As if you have read this far **happy crying face**

This was such a huge leap for me on a personal level, but I am beyond proud of myself.

I promise if I've left you itching for Book 2 I'm working as hard and as fast as I can while still striving for perfection.

I want to say a big thank you, to you, the readers! Making this possible and hopefully enjoying the crazy worlds inside my head.

This adventure started back in May and I haven't looked back since.

Here's to more adventures and you hopefully being a part of it.

Much love <3

THANK YOU

So, how much space do I have here to tell everyone how much I appreciate them? I feel like I'm winning an Oscar with a thirty second timeframe to spit everyone's names out.

The biggest thank you must go to my handsome! You have encouraged me, believed in me, and taken control of the house to ensure I can give this my all. There would be no book without your presence.

Next, my beautiful children, you have been amazing supporters. Cheering with me at every milestone, and joining in with the happy tears and dances. You are full of grace and mischief. I love you both to the max!

Then to my girls that I have claimed for all of eternity. Val, Emma, Hope, and Katy! Thank you for being such a strong support network. I couldn't have wished for such fabulous people to help me along this journey.

ABOUT THE AUTHOR

KC Kean is the sassy half of a match made in heaven. Mummy to two beautiful children, Pokemon Master and Apex Legend world saving gamer.

Starting her adventure in the RH romance world after falling in love with it as a reader, who knows where this crazy train is heading. As long as there is plenty of steam she'll be there.

ALSO BY KC KEAN

Featherstone Academy

(Contemporary Reverse Harem Academy Romance)

My Bloodline

Your Bloodline

Our Bloodline

Red

Freedom

The Allstars Series

(Contemporary Reverse Harem, Sports Romance)

Toxic Creek

Tainted Creek - July 9th

Twisted Creek - September 14th

Printed in Great Britain
by Amazon